"Brings to life the struggle of Montana's miners and settlers to bring civilization to the frontier. The reader feels the fear and frustration that finally drove the Vigilantes to take the matters into their own hands. . . . Thoroughly enjoyable."

—Conrad Burns, U.S. Senator, Montana

"Dempsey blends fact with strong dialogue and characterizations to bring history to life."

—*Publishers Weekly*

"Al Dempsey . . . brings early Bannack to life with fine attention to detail, and a sure knowledge of the type of person drawn to such 19th century gold camps. . . .

"Many of the events he portrays are controversial, and the historical record is loaded with conflict. But Dempsey works through the various versions of events with a fine reportorial skill, and gives us what is probably the most authentic version of events.

"This is a marvelous read."

—*Billings Gazette*

"Brings back to life a very colorful and intriguing period in Montana's early development as a State. Dempsey makes the remembering entertaining and extremely worthwhile."

—Montana Governor Stan Stephens

Tor books by Al Dempsey

Copper
Dog Kill
Miss Finney Kills Now and Then
The Six States Super Centennial Celebration Book
The Stendal Raid
What Law There Was

A TOM DOHERTY ASSOCIATES BOOK
NEW YORK

WHAT LAW THERE WAS

A Tor Book
Published by Tom Doherty Associates, Inc.
175 Fifth Avenue
New York, NY 10010

Tor® is a registered trademark of Tom Doherty Associates, Inc.

Cover art by Larry Selman

ISBN: 0-812-58184-9

First edition: January 1991
First mass market printing: June 1992

Printed in the United States of America

0 9 8 7 6 5 4 3 2 1

Dedicated to
Betty and Terry Nobles

With special thanks to:

Larry Lund, M.W. Grand Master 1989–1990
John Barrows, Grand Historian 1989–1990

Also, a special thanks to my friend, Bob Leete.

It was Bob who first said to me: "Hey, have you ever heard about the Vigilantes down in Bannack?"

PROLOGUE

On a promontory 350 feet above Mullan Pass, in the Garnet Range of the Rocky Mountains, an outcropping of granite rock had been worn flat and smooth by wind and rain. On the rock a small leather Bible lay open to a much-read passage. Standing in front of the Bible was Nathaniel Langford. On the other side of the rock stood David Charlton and George Gere; all three had doffed their hats, and all of them had placed their arms across their chests in the ritual manner.

It was early evening on September 23, 1862. The men had been busy since dawn with their duties as part of a wagon train of settlers on the long trek from Minnesota to that part of the frontier that was to become the state of Montana. The horses and oxen had been worked hard, and an early rest had been called once the party of fifty wagons and 159 settlers had cleared the six-thousand-foot pass. The party would camp in the flat, high meadow just west of the crest.

The sun had eased itself below the tops of the mountains to the west, and darkness was coming on quickly, but there was still light, still the residual brilliance that painted the trees a darker green and etched dramatic slices of color where canyons and gullies reached up into the next range of mountains ahead of the party.

It had been Langford's idea to leave the main party and find seclusion. That he had also found a naturally formed rock slab to serve as an appropriate altar was pure luck. Langford looked at his two brothers in fraternity, then he invoked:

> "Most Holy and Glorious Lord God,
> The great architect of the Universe,
> The giver of all goods and graces,
> Thou hast promised that,
> 'Where two or three are gathered
> together in Thy name.'
> Thou wilt be in their midst and bless them."

So was opened the first meeting of Master Masons in the mountains which were to be the foundation and backbone for the territory called Montana.

The three men had brought none of the tools of their Craft. They had with them no trowel or square or plumb; they bore none of the symbolic ornaments of their offices, and they wore no aprons. But as Ancient, Free and Accepted Masons, they were executing their right to open a meeting informally and come together as Brothers.

Langford, in later years, would write, "We exchanged fraternal greetings, spoke kind words to one another, and gave ourselves up to the enjoyment of that elevation of spirit which Masonry alone could evoke. When we left the summit of that glorious range of mountains, to descend to our camp, each felt that he had been better and happier for the confidential interchange of Masonic sentiment."

That incident expressing the spirit of Freemasonry was to be the precursor of events which would carve a niche in Montana history and lore. . . .

CHAPTER 1

(Saturday, November 8, 1862)

"Cora, that you in there?"

"Clay Barrow, you get away from here!"

"C'mon, Cora, I gotta go!"

"I just got here!"

"Hurry!"

There was no response from inside the privy. Clay Barrow twisted his body through two complete, impatient, panicky turns, then his voice dimmed to an urgent plea as he begged: "Ple-eze let me in, Cora."

Cora Harris snapped back, "Go do it someplace else!"

The evening was a full hour into dark, the temperature had fallen to just above freezing, and an uncomfortable drizzle made waiting for a turn in the outhouse nearly impossible.

A slight spill of light came from inside the saloon, music from a poorly played fiddle barely audible through the shouting and laughter. Clay squinted his eyes. Could he see well enough in the dark to find a spot where he could answer the necessary call of nature? The ground had turned to an oozy, slick texture which would make walking fearful. As cold as it was becoming, there was a good chance the ooze would freeze. Moving out into the pitch dark would be too dangerous. He demanded: "Dammit, Cora, you through yet?"

"I'm coming," Cora yelled back. "Damn, yer a rude one, Clay Barrow. Ain't you never got any manners?"

The door flew open and Cora Harris' face showed pursed lips and glaring eyes. She was as pretty as any girl in the camp, but Clay Barrow had no time for romance. He dove through the door as he dropped his trousers; he did not bother to close the door.

Cora cried, "You are a PIG!" and ran back along the pathway leading to the saloon.

She bounded up the three rough planks of the back-stairs and, once inside, began growling angrily to herself; no one in the packed room was paying any attention to her. She snorted, "Ya'll are a bunch of pigs, just like Clay Barrow!" She was still ignored.

Cyrus Skinner had named his grubby, seedy gathering place the Elk Horn simply because someone had come along with a modest rack of elk horns about halfway through construction. The building was eighteen feet wide and thirty-seven feet long with a roof just an inch over seven feet high. The walls, of dressed logs, would have been taller, except that logs had become scarce and costly in the gold camp while Skinner was building. He was satisfied. The final product provided just what he wanted; a place for prospectors to have some diversion from panning and digging for gold. The saloon also accommodated those who came to all mining camps to mine the miners. Gamblers, sporting ladies, and just plain crooks all wanted to ensure that a struggling prospector had an easy way to divest himself of his hard-earned gold dust and nuggets.

Cora looked through the smoky haze. Nothing had changed in the five minutes she had been gone; no fistfight or knifing or shooting had erupted to add to the evening's entertainment. There were about the same number of people swilling down the cheap, water-cut whiskey Skinner offered; a few more people than the night before and a few less than would probably be there the next night. Ever since the previous July 28, when prospector John White had uncovered a handful of worthy nuggets in Grasshopper Creek, the isolated patch of barren land had been attracting men. Nearly a month later, on August 23, Wash Stapleton, working in the muddy bank across the creek, extracted an extraordinary cluster of nuggets. By September, the word had flown through the Mountain West. All those coming to Bannack were finding rewards, because just about any man willing to pan a shovel load of gravel was washing out color, and the word had continued to spread. Now, in November, the gold camp was in a boom; four hundred gold-hungry prospectors were working the creek and bordering creek banks. Another hundred or so people were in the camp selling goods, wares, and services. Cora Harris was marketing her skills as a waitress, taxi dancer, and sporting lady.

Dern bunch of fools, she thought, *and that's the truth.*

Cora groused a lot, but her cruel comments seemed to endear her to the lonely men who sought her favors. While she was revolted by the men and their wiry beards, their bearlike breath, their polecat body odors, she still found working a gold camp a thrill. She could, easily, leave any time she wished. She had ferreted away ten ounces of top-grade nuggets which, at the prevailing $14.50 an ounce, would give her enough money to take her any place she chose. With the kind of money she had hidden in her innocuous rag doll, she could head out to Portland, in Oregon—she had been headed there two years previously when she had run away from home looking for some of the adventure she was denied by her parents. Or she could simply return home; surely her parents would forgive her transgressions. Maybe not her father, who was a tough, stern Methodist minister, but there was no question about her mother. Mothers could always find a way to forgive.

Still, because she had just turned nineteen, she retained her lust for excitement and she was satisfying that lust right here.

"Cora, get us some damned drinks!"

The loud command had come from the far end of the room, penetrating the din of voices that saturated the saloon. From behind the bar, Cyrus Skinner yelled at her: "Get yer ass moving; you ain't getting paid to stand around!"

Cyrus Skinner was the kind of man who looked the way he sounded: nasty, crude, and ugly. He had a bushy head of black hair that he seldom bothered to brush, his lumpy face generally wore a dark stubble of beard that accented small, dark eyes under a mat of tangled eyebrows, and his yellowed teeth complemented an oversized pair of lips. He was tall enough to swing a fist easily across a bar, but he carried extra pounds of belly overhanging his belt.

Cora ground her teeth together to keep from yelling back at Skinner. Some flip words from her would only earn a sound thrashing later in the night. "I'm going, Cy, don't you be worrying none."

He snarled, "Just you do your job."

Someday I'll be killin' you, you son of a bitch.

She headed quickly toward the man who had demanded service.

It was not easy to move through the saloon, because the place was jammed tight with tables and chairs and benches. Skinner had thought of adding a couple of billiard tables, but he could cram six card tables into the space needed by one for billiards, so that idea had been quickly dismissed. Having space for men to play cards was the main way that Cyrus Skinner drew people to, and kept them in, his saloon. He took a modest fee from each table, but Skinner also sold whiskey to those playing. That was his mother lode.

Cora moved as deftly as she could, but there was no way to avoid the customary patting of her bottom or rubbing of her legs as she squeezed her way through the room. When one young prospector, emboldened by seeing others take their liberties—and by a few drinks—tried to touch Cora's breast as she wiggled past him, she gave him a smack on the arm as she spit out, "You pay for that service, boyo. No free feels with this girl."

The youth's eyes widened and he looked around to see if he was going to be laughed at by his peers; he was, and he glared at Cora's slim back as she moved away. One of the young man's new friends said, "For a pinch she'll let you lift her skirt, Vic. Just dip your fingers into your pouch, pinch out some dust, and she's yours for ten or fifteen minutes."

Vic Voit did not want to believe that the girl who had just passed him was that kind of a girl. He was embarrassed that he had tried to touch her, and he knew his friends were simply teasing him. She was too damned pretty to be a loose woman.

Cora was just one table away from her destination when she was stopped politely next to a table occupied by seven men, none of whom was playing cards. The man who stopped her was Hank Crawford. He'd been in the camp for five weeks running a butcher shop; five weeks made him an old-timer. He asked, "Could you see if there's any bread and cheese, Cora? My friends just arrived and they'd appreciate a bit of food."

Cora snapped, "You want a restaurant, you go to Goodrich's, they sell food."

As soon as the words were out of her mouth, Cora regretted being rude. While the majority of saloon patrons were rough prospectors or gamblers trying to fleece the prospectors, there were many like Hank Crawford, hardworking tradespeople who came to Skinner's simply because there were few other places to go in the camp; most social life pivoted around the saloon.

She let a natural smile come to her mouth and a

softness to her voice as she said, "I'm sorry, Hank, things are dern frantic here." Then, looking at the new arrivals, she continued, "Y'all can guess that from the looks of things. Jest a minute and I'll check to see what they have to eat behind the bar."

One of the men nodded, then said, "No hurry; we're here for a while."

"I'll be back in a minute, don't you be worrying."

"Cora, move yer ass!" The order came from a voice to her left.

Cora pressed her lips together into a barely visible line; she hated to be embarrassed in front of proper folks and now, as she usually did, she was blushing with shame. She stormed up to the cardplayers at the next table and hissed: "Goddamn you, Dick Sapp, you'd better be watching your mouth."

Sapp burst out laughing.

Cora cried, "I'm telling you to be showing some respect!"

Sapp said, "There's only one place my mouth does your bidding, Cora, and that's when it's on yours. And the best respect I can show you is to let you dip a little deeper into my pouch after you and me have done a bit of jinking."

"There might not be any more *jinking* for you, Dick Sapp; I'm mad at the way you treat me."

Sapp smiled and looked around the table at the others, who were waiting for him to deal. He moaned, "Aw, ain't that just pitiful, poor little girl." And he moved his hand gently over her bottom.

She let her mouth come slowly back to a full smile and her eyes fluttered coyly. She did not want to push Sapp too far. He was one of her better customers. He had arrived in the camp just three weeks ago; she had been in the camp for only a month before him, and he had immediately staked out his claim to her services. Sapp was not cheap, unlike many of the men who relied on her for affection. On many of her visits to his room he allowed her to take an extra pinch or two from his bags of gold dust. With a pinch equaling about a tenth of an ounce, she could do as well from a session with Dick Sapp as many prospectors were doing after a whole day of panning. She had even begun to let her fingernails grow longer so she could pinch out a few more grams of the dust; Sapp noticed, but only warned her not to scratch him up, especially on the face.

Sapp moved his hand up to the small of Cora's back, then allowed it to slip down to give a gentle caress to her bottom. To the men at the table he said, "Now ain't she some special tall drink of water, boys?"

Cora was tall, five feet seven inches, and her body was startlingly slim. Her chest was approaching flatness and her hipbones jutted out even under the full cut skirt of her dress. Her hair was a soft, light brown, and she wore it neatly trimmed in a manner that framed her face—her full pair of lips, modest nose, and very large, blue eyes. Since reaching womanhood, Cora had felt cheated of some physical attributes needed for a happy life, but Dick Sapp had, she felt honestly, praised her features, even her tiny bosom. He had given her a feeling of pride that she had not felt before and, with some reluctance, she was fond of him. But she kept up her guard. She had been burned before in romance. Since leaving home two years previously, she had allowed herself to fall for men who spoke lovingly to her, and she had always ended up being abandoned after she had given herself, and generally most of her money, to the supposed suitor. She would not let her guard down with Sapp.

He rubbed his hand softly on the curve of her bottom as he said to the others, "You blokes don't have a chance at getting yer wick dipped with Cora here," then, looking up at her, he asked, "ain't that right?"

Cora giggled. "That's right." Batting her eyes again, she added, "That is, unless you got a bag of dust that I can dip into."

All of those at the table burst into a raucous laughter,

including Dick Sapp. He was merely gambling to make his score and would pull back to the States as soon as he had taken what he could from the prospectors.

Turning back to the cards in his hand, he said, "Hurry now, girl, get us a couple of rounds of drinks; we have card playing to do."

Cora twisted and turned through the mass of men at the tables. She hated the way the place was so cramped, but Skinner was no stranger to gold camps, and he knew that at any moment one of two things could, and historically would, happen: either the gold would run out, or a new, more attractive strike would be made someplace else. Skinner was going to milk as much as he could, as quickly as he could, out of the generous gold pouches of the prospectors. Cora had little time to worry about that, she was more concerned with wiggling between tables.

Skinner's rough-hewn bar took up eighteen feet of the thirty-seven feet available on one side of the room. His sole concession to the possibility that Bannack might turn out to be a long-lived camp was that he had ordered a proper oak bar from Salt Lake City, but it might be weeks or even months before the bar arrived. Wagon freight service was, at best, not at all predictable. Along the wall opposite the bar were plank benches two feet wide that could be, and were, used as bunks by men who had just arrived and had not yet erected tents or shacks or any kind of shelter on their claims. At the back, a door gave access out to the privy and at the front was a double door entrance that also provided the only ventilation available. There were two openings cut into the walls that Skinner swore were going to be used for windows, once the windows arrived. He had had the openings roughly boarded up to keep out the cold, but he did not mention that he had not placed the order because he wanted to see if there was a future worth the investment.

As Cora approached the bar for Dick Sapp's drinks, she sensed nervousness in the other two girls who worked as waitresses and dancers in the saloon. Cyrus

Skinner was at the far end of the bar, where two men were obviously in argument. Cora asked the girls, "What's going on?"

Lori Charles said, "Two yokels fixing to cause trouble. Skinner's gonna do something; I can feel it."

Beth Warren picked up her tray of drinks and said, "Skinner's gonna kill somebody someday; I don't want to be around when it happens." Beth moved quickly toward the far end of the saloon; Cora guessed that Beth would be slipping out the front door any minute. That made Cora angry, because it would mean waitress work split two ways rather than three.

Cora had seen her share of nasty fights in the two years she had been bouncing around saloons, but she had never seen anyone actually killed. She was also anxious to be out of the bar when that happened. But she could not leave, because Cyrus Skinner was providing the best way to earn money in the camp, at least for a pretty woman.

Cora looked down the bar. Skinner was obviously trying to mediate the argument between two strangers; he was also reaching under the bar for one of the four axe handles he kept handy out of sight. Cora called: "Cy, I'm taking six for Sapp's table." She started pouring measures of whiskey, but kept an eye on what was happening with Skinner.

Skinner was upset by Cora's call. He wanted to stop any fight from beginning but he was also angry at Dick Sapp. He was convinced that Sapp was not giving up Skinner's share of the poker pots. Besides, Sapp had already run a tab, with seven rounds of drinks not yet paid for.

Cora winced as she saw Skinner move, even though she knew what was coming. His left hand darted across the bar and grabbed one of the troublemakers, and his right hand suddenly, in a movement too quick to be seen, swung the axe handle to land with a sickening thump on the head of the other. The blow caused the man to sway but not to fall unconscious, because Cyrus

Skinner was experienced enough to apply just the right force; a tiny rivulet of blood trickled down the man's forehead. "Now," growled Skinner, "the two of you hold your peace and get out of here. Don't come back tonight!"

Skinner still held the first man's jacket, and the axe handle floated dangerously close; neither man argued. Slowly, deliberately, Skinner released his hold, and the two men hurried, nearly running, toward the back door. Skinner quickly tossed the axe handle into its hiding place and moved down to Cora's end of the bar, saying, "Now, what the hell are you doing?"

Cora Harris feared Cyrus Skinner, and with good cause. When Cora had been in the gold camp just two days, she had gone to Skinner for a job in his saloon. One of the requirements he imposed had been that she provide him with sexual favors. That provision had lasted for only three nights, until a new girl had shown up, but Cora had already found him to be a brutal, mean person. Occasionally, in the months she had been working for him, he had demanded her favors for a night, and she dreaded each incident. She did not want to provoke him into belting her right there in the saloon or into demanding that she spend the night with him. Besides, she was committed to providing an evening of companionship for Dick Sapp. "Damn, Cy, I wasn't doing nothin' wrong. Sapp seems to be having a good run of luck, I just figgered . . ."

"You don't get paid to figger nothing, girl. You deliver drinks, dance a bit, and spread your legs when you can; that's it!"

Cora bit her lip at Skinner's words. *I'll slit your throat some night, Cyrus Skinner, that's a promise.*

Skinner softened at the look on her face as he said, "Now don't go pouting on me, Cora Harris. You do your job and you ain't in no trouble."

She offered a demure smile and replied, "You're a nice man, Cy."

Skinner pushed the tray slightly toward Cora. "You take these over to Sapp and have him settle up; now!"

Cora picked up the tray, turned, then turned back as she said, "Oh, Hank Crawford is at a table and he's askin' for some cheese and bread. Ain't none of them drinkin'."

Skinner looked down the room and seemed to know exactly which group was not drinking; he made it his business to know such things. He lowered his voice as he growled, "If them's some more of Crawford's *upright* citizens, they never will be drinking." Then, after a pause, he said, "I'll see what I have. Tell Hank to come over and ask for himself; you got other work to do."

Cora picked up her tray and began to negotiate the intricate journey back to Dick Sapp's table. On her way, she stopped to relay Skinner's message to Hank Crawford. As she turned to continue to Sapp's table, she found her way blocked by the young man who had tried to fondle her before. She ordered, "Move!"

He stood there awkwardly for a moment, then sputtered out, "I'm sorry . . . sorry about what I did."

Cora was so used to being pawed that she had a difficult time remembering what he had done. When she finally did remember, she said, "Look, old man, don't worry about it. Just keep yer hands to yerself."

The use of "old" was not sarcastic. Vic Voit was—and looked to be—a full twenty years of age. A man who reached thirty was an elder, and one thirty-five was considered ancient. Cora paused for a second and saw the contrite look on Vic's face; it was a nice, friendly face. She was suddenly taken with his eyes, which were nearly gray, and by the curl of his lip that was forming not quite a smile. He was just slightly taller than she, and he looked as if he could not weigh more than 150 pounds. His innocent look triggered a confused feeling of anger in her.

He gave an innocent grin and said, "I'd like to talk to you."

"I'm busy!"

"Later?"

"I'll be busy then, too."

She eased her way around him, but he managed to wiggle between the tables and chairs and was beside her just as she arrived at Dick Sapp's table. She snapped at him: "Leave me alone!"

He pleaded, "I just want to talk."

Cora's eyes flared with anger and she had opened her mouth to speak when a rough hand grabbed her shoulder and yanked her around. She yelped as the tray tilted and she was spun around to face Clay Barrow, whose eyes were showing his own anger. Her tray of drinks went spilling, some onto Vic Voit, the remainder onto the back of Dick Sapp's head and neck. Sapp, who was holding a winning hand, merely shook his head so he could keep concentrating on the game, but Vic Voit yelled, "Let her go!"

Barrow growled, "Next time I need the privy, you get out!" and he slapped her face.

For a gal who had been raised in a Methodist minister's home, Cora had learned how to take a lot from life. She had seen Clay's hand coming and had avoided any harm by simply riding with the blow. There had been a slight sting, but no damage. But that was when the real trouble started.

At almost the same instant that Clay Barrow's palm contacted Cora's cheek, Vic Voit bellowed: "Don't you touch her!" and launched himself in a frenzy against Barrow.

Cora cried, "Stop! He didn't hurt me!" but the genie of violence had been let loose and it would take more than Cora's pleas to stop it.

Voit had an advantage; Clay Barrow did not expect anyone to cause a fracas simply because a sporting woman was slapped in the face. Voit pushed Barrow backward; they both landed in the middle of a table among the cards, poker chips, and whiskey glasses.

As the two fell onto the table, Vic rolled off onto the floor and received a bruised hand when it was stepped on by one of the poker players who was scrambling for safety. Barrow managed to break two fingers on his right hand when he threw a punch at an innocent bystander and hit the heavy wooden leg of a table. Cora Harris ended up in Sapp's lap, listening with disbelief to the incredibly rude things he was whispering in her ear. Cyrus Skinner vaulted over the bar wielding his trusty axe handle to restore peace and inflicted three broken noses, one black eye, and two gashed skulls on three customers.

In the aftermath, Cora was soundly scolded by Skinner: "I don't pay you to start fights in my place, bitch." Clay Barrow spent the rest of the evening trying to find out who had interceded on Cora's behalf: "I'm gonna bust some bastard's face."

Vic Voit found a quiet table and pretended to be interested in the card game: "No, sir, I didn't see who it was that grabbed you."

Within five minutes, a semblance of order had returned to the saloon. Dick Sapp promised to pay Skinner for the six broken glasses, so long as Cora did not have to accept responsibility for the fight. Skinner agreed. A glass that cost two cents in Salt Lake City went for twenty-five cents after making the four-hundred-mile freight wagon trip to Bannack.

Immediately after things had calmed down, Cora left Sapp's table and went to Old Brod Staley, the runaway slave from Alabama who picked up a few dollars a night playing the fiddle in the saloon. "Brod, now you listen up, no more fast music. Right?"

Old Brod, who was tall and thin and not yet thirty, nodded. "We've got to keep the blood calmed down; that what you mean?"

Cora grinned. "I mean we don't need no more fights, and there's only three of us girls on tonight. We ain't in no shape to dance with all of those drunks."

Brod said, "There's only two of you, Miss Cora. I saw Beth running out the front door as soon as the fight started."

"Damn! I suspected that. That's all the more reason to keep things calmed down. You'll do that, won't you?"

Brod agreed and moved back to his chair by one of the two cast-iron stoves that provided heat for the room. The fires in them were small, because there were enough bodies in the saloon to keep the place warm. He began fiddling.

The crowd was tense for a short while, but the easy sound of the fiddle and some nervous laughter began to lighten the mood. In about half an hour, the atmosphere returned to what could be considered normal: voices raised over the card games, boisterous laughter where jokes were being told, and the constant hum of talk about the most important matter of the camp: what color would the creek's dirt produce the next day?

It was seven minutes before eight o'clock when Bannack experienced its first killing.

Cora had been working the front of the room while Lori Charles worked the back. The fact was, they could have used Beth Warren and two or three more girls to do the job right. One of Cora's customers had asked if he could pay in greenbacks. Cyrus Skinner, like most Westerners, had an aversion to paper money from the States; with the Civil War going on and the federal government printing paper not backed by gold or silver, people were looking for hard currency. To get approval before accepting the greenbacks, she went looking for Skinner, but he was not behind the bar. At the far rear of the saloon was a small area partitioned off to function as a sort of office and storeroom for whiskey. In it, Cora found Lori Charles sitting limply on one of the short stacks of wooden cases. She asked, "Where the hell's Cy?"

Lori said, "Well, he sure ain't here. You can see that for yourself. I wouldn't be taking a break if he was."

"Is he out in the privy?"

"I didn't see him go anywhere. He was behind the bar the last time I looked."

"Well, he ain't now!"

"So what? Pour your own drinks; you ain't got no broken arm."

"Well, smarty, I don't need drinks. I got some tenderfoot trying to pass me some paper money."

"You might as well not ask; Cy will only chew off your head. You know that."

"It's all the guy has."

"Does he have any rebel dollars? Cy wants them more than greenbacks."

"It ain't right giving the guy only forty cents for a dollar."

"Cy's giving fifty cents for rebel money."

"It just ain't right!"

Lori Charles shrugged her shoulders and tilted her head in a way that spoke volumes; she was not going to talk further.

Cora went back into the main room and was halfway down the bar when the bangs came.

There were two shots outside almost at the same time, then a pause and another shot.

Everyone in the saloon froze for a moment, then there was general confusion as they tried to force their way out the front door to the street.

The drizzle had stopped, but the temperature had fallen, and a slight glaze had spread over the ground. The first men out of the door slipped on the icy surface, but the mud below the glaze was soft and, with just a little care, it was possible to stay erect.

People were pouring out of the other buildings and shacks that lined Main Street. A few men ran from the flimsy structure called the Goodrich Hotel, three men came out of Kustar's Bakery. Across the street was Stone's Washhouse, which always closed before sunset, but Mrs. Stone was standing in front of the building holding one of her children comfortably on her hip.

At first no one could figure out the source of the shooting. Finally, at the west side of the saloon, on the rutted section of mud named Second Street, someone spotted a body lying on the frozen earth.

The crowd massed around the body; voices were still until someone up at the front of the group said, "He's dead." There was a shocked flutter of whispers. Then the man doing the looking added, "He's been shot. Shot dead!"

The crowd's chatter fell to a murmur and the murmur became a silence that permeated the night; no killing had come to the camp before.

Cora and Lori Charles stood there listening, unable to see much of anything; all they could hope for was to hear who had been shot.

"Lemme through!" It was Cy Skinner, elbowing his way from the back of the crowd. He was carrying two lamps that he had brought from within the saloon. As he pushed past Cora, he demanded, "What the hell's going on?"

Cora had been struck dumb by the incident; she tried to speak but no words came. Cy said, "Dammit girl, get back inside and work," then, seeing Lori and Old Brod, he growled, "Both of you, too. Get back inside."

He pushed on toward the front of the crowd.

As soon as the announcement of death had penetrated, the crowd had begun to draw away from the body. Cy Skinner made his way easily past the final barrier of watchers. Hank Crawford and two of his newly arrived friends were bending over the lifeless form.

Skinner gruffly demanded, "What's up?"

Crawford looked up. "It's good you brought some light, Cy. Take a look."

Skinner handed one of the lamps to Crawford, then bent down to peer at the shooting victim. "Hmmm," Skinner said. "He's one of the ones that was fixing to fight a while back."

Crawford asked, "In the saloon?"

"Yep," Skinner said, "mean one, too. See that bump on his head? I had to put that there when he started to get out of hand."

The body was lying on its side and the men saw that the victim had been shot twice, once in the back of his left shoulder, once in his upper chest. He had an egg-sized bump on his forehead, the left pocket of his canvas work jacket was torn, and his boots were covered with mud well up over the ankle. No one had any guesses about the pocket tear, but they all agreed that the mud had probably gotten there when the man was spun around by the impact of the bullets; the thin skim of ice on the surface of the mud broke easily when walked on. A deep frost had not yet made the ground rock-hard, as it would be when a hard freeze came to the mountains.

No one seemed to know what to do. In the four months of life experienced by the Bannack gold camp, seven men had died in mining accidents, and three men and one woman had died from natural causes. But death by violence was not easy to handle. The young man on the ground would have to be buried, but what was to be done about finding the killer, and what was to be done with the killer, if and when he was found?

It was Hank Crawford who took charge.

"Okay, boys," Crawford said as he stood up from looking at the body. "Let's get this poor fella someplace where we can keep him till morning." There was an uncomfortable shuffle among the men in the front ranks; none seemed anxious to touch the murdered man.

From within the crowd came, "There's a cabin down near the footbridge; it ain't done yet."

Crawford asked, "Whose cabin?"

A man stepped forward and said, "I'm George Clayton. It's my cabin, and you can use it. It has no roof, though."

A voice offered, "We can cover him with a tarp."

Another voice said, "We can bury him in the morning."

Cyrus Skinner said, "I guess we'd better carry him down there. Not much else we can do."

Still none of the crowd seemed willing or able to make any move to help.

Hank Crawford looked at the men. "You four," he said, and he pointed to four men in the front rank, "take the body down to Mister Clayton's cabin. Do it now."

The four took hesitating steps forward.

Crawford announced, "I think we'd better try and find the other man."

Cyrus Skinner said, "Hell, the damned murderer is probably a mile down the gulch now. Ain't no sense looking."

"First off, we don't know if he is a murderer; second off, he might be wounded. There were three shots. I say we give a look for him."

A few of the men offered to help out. In a couple of minutes, Crawford had formed the volunteers into three search parties. One search would go down Grasshopper Creek, the second would head upstream, and the third, the largest party, would spread out around the camp.

Cy Skinner was grumbling. Just before Crawford dispatched the men on their tasks, Skinner asked, "What the hell you gonna do with him if you find him?"

That brought a halt for a moment. Finally, Crawford offered, "If he doesn't have a good story, we'll call a Miners' Court."

Each mining camp lived by rules and regulations set down by a forum-type government that dealt mainly with rights to claims. But most initial meetings of prospectors also established some basic standards of conduct as being within the jurisdiction of the camp. The laws of a Miners' Court generally satisfied the needs of a loose-knit community. The Bannack Miners' Court had not made any stipulation as to murder; but that could be rectified in a meeting.

Skinner growled, "Damned foolishness if you ask me. Just stupid!" And he pushed his way roughly through the crowd toward his saloon. He spotted Cora and Lori and snapped, "What the hell you two doing still out here? I told you to get back to work!"

Cora stammered, "We were just watching."

Skinner demanded, "Well, get the hell back inside and clean up. We're closing for the night."

Back in the saloon, Skinner slammed and bolted the front door as soon as Cora and Lori entered. His voice mean, he said, "Get this place cleaned up!"

He stormed off to the back where he disappeared into the small office. Lori and Cora were left just inside the door. Lori was trembling, her whole body quivering. Cora asked, "What's the matter, Lori?"

"Don't know! I can't stop shaking. That whole thing scared the devil out of me."

Cora put an arm around the other woman and said, "Take it easy. You've been around this sort of thing before."

"Not like this."

Cora admitted, "Well, I ain't never seen a dead one. But we've seen fights and cuts, that sort of thing. It's all the same."

Lori could not stop shaking. "Not a dead man. And there's one more thing . . ."

Cora prompted, "Come on. What's getting to you?"

Lori said, "You know, back in Colorado, in the gold camps, and out in California, things happened, but there was always some law around. We're out here at the end of ever, and there ain't no person to stop this sort of thing. I'm scared to death."

Cora had not been scared up to that moment. She realized Lori was right: there had been some authority in the other places she had lived. If not a proper police department, at least a legally appointed sheriff or marshal. Suddenly she was angry at Lori for having mentioned the subject. She snapped, "Well, ain't nothing we can do about it. Let's clean up this place and get out of here."

They moved quickly, collecting the dirty glasses and stacking up the mounds of scattered cards abandoned when the shooting had occurred. Cora, trying to lighten the mood, asked Lori, "You ever figger out how they can run out of here and not leave any of their money?"

Lori said nothing, just worked as quickly as she could.

Skinner had not come out of his tiny office. Cora was just as happy. He was angry, and when he was that way he frequently demanded she stay around and let him beat up on her. She wanted only to get out of the saloon.

With the work done, Cora and Lori went to the office. By the back door, Cora called, "We're leaving, Cy. See you tomorrow."

She took Lori's arm and urged her out.

Skinner called, "Hey, come back here!"

Cora gave Lori a slight push, and the two of them leaped down the backstairs and hit the ground running. They were, by that time, having to muffle their giggles. Cora ordered, "Behind the outhouse!"

They slid down the path and cornered the privy just as the rear door of the saloon flew open and Skinner boomed: "Get back here!" There was a pause, then: "Cora Harris! Git yer ass back here! Now!"

The two girls huddled in the shadow of the outhouse and nearly gave themselves away as they looked at each other and burst into silent laughter. After another pause, they heard Skinner snorting, "Dirty bitches! They got no consideration." He slammed the back door shut.

They stood in the cold for a full minute before they felt it was safe to move. When they were ready, Lori asked, "Where we going? I don't want to go back to the house."

They rented a room from a family named Stinson. The Stinson cabin was situated in a lonely spot, down by Grasshopper Creek. Cora and Lori shared the room with Beth Warren, the waitress who had run out of the saloon earlier, and Lucinda Simons. The Stinson family was accommodating to the girls, except that Carl Stinson drank too much. Lucinda would not be in the cabin because she was working in Kustar's Bakery and would be there until midnight. Cora asked, "Shall we go see Lucinda?" Lori agreed and they moved in the shadows between buildings to make their way along Main Street.

The Kustar Bakery did most of the bread baking for the camp. Mutta Kustar was a gaunt, thin woman who looked much older than her thirty-two years. The Kustars had had a rough time as immigrants until they found Bannack, but they were doing well financially with their bakery. By the time Cora and Lori arrived at Kustar's, Gustav and his son, Otto, had left to join the search for the missing man involved in the shooting. Mutta and Lucinda were working on the next day's bread supply. Lucinda Simons was an enigma to Cora Harris: there seemed to be no valid reason for her to be in the gold camp. Lucinda had arrived two weeks after Cora, and they had met when Lucinda rented sleeping space from the Stinsons. The first attribute that had impressed Cora was the way Lucinda declined the offer of a job at Skinner's. There had been no hint of reproach toward, or judgment against, Cora making a living by selling her body. Lucinda Simons had simply stated that there must be some kind of work she could do where she did not have to be around drinking and gambling.

Cora guessed that Lucinda had come from a very religious family, but Cora was wrong. Lucinda Simons had been married to a wealthy Alabama plantation owner who had sold out and left the South when the Civil War seemed inevitable. Beauregard Simons had made the mistake of using some of the proceeds from the sale to enjoy a few games of faro in St. Louis. Having some considerable luck, Lucinda's Beau began to play cards seriously—and to drink. He had ended up an impoverished drunk and been shot to death in a poker game. She had been left a widow. She was not inclined to return to her family in Alabama, because she felt the cause of the Confederacy was lost, so she sold her last pieces of jewelry and set out for Oregon City near the

Pacific Coast, where she had a cousin who might help her begin a new life. But the wagon train on which she had paid passage was attacked by Shoshone Indians between Soda Springs and Fort Hall in the Oregon Territory. Lucinda lost everything. At Fort Hall, she had been offered three options: wait four to six weeks for the next protected wagon train, ride free on a military supply train headed down to Salt Lake City or join the party of merchants, prospectors, and suppliers headed north for the new prospecting camp called Bannack. Lucinda dreaded the thought of a long wait in the primitive military fort with its gambling and drinking, and she had heard frightening things about the Mormons who had settled around the Great Salt Lake. After meeting some of the people headed for Bannack, and deciding they seemed to be honest, industrious individuals looking for a new beginning, she opted to go with them up into the mountains.

During the two-week trip to Bannack, Lucinda made friends with Mutta Kustar, and the friendship led to the offer of a job in Kustar's Bakery. Lucinda came to enjoy the hard labor required to produce the daily bread for the camp, and she was proud of making $1.50 a day, which was sometimes more than Cora and the other sporting ladies earned. The handsome wage was a special blessing, considering that she did not have to submit to the maulings of the dirty prospectors.

In the front of the bakery was a small counter and shelves that held the bread for sale; the middle, and largest section was where the mixing bowls, kneading tables, and ovens were located; in the rear was the cramped living space for the Kustar family.

Cora was past the sales counter and into the workroom before Lori had closed the front door. Cora's voice was high with excitement as she asked, "What do you think of our shooting?"

Mutta Kustar was dividing a watermelon-size mound of dough into loaves; Lucinda was punching down a batch for a second rising. Mutta, without looking up, snarled, "Damned fool men, going shooting and killing."

Lucinda stopped work and asked, "Did you see it?"

Cora went to a small table at the side of the room where substandard loaves of bread were set aside. She broke off a chunk and began chewing as she answered, "Ain't nobody saw it, leastwise, ain't nobody admitting. We saw the body, though."

Lori had finally entered. She said, "We did *not*!"

"Did too."

"Did not!"

"Well," Cora admitted, "We didn't get a real good look. But it was there, dead as you please."

Mutta looked up but kept her hands working as she said, "You girls stop this talk. It's no good. A man dead and you'd think it was a party."

Lucinda said, "Mister Kustar and Otto have gone out to help in the search. How long will they be?"

Cora offered, "I can't guess. Might be a long time."

Mutta Kustar growled, "This camp ain't fit for humans. It's cold, it's dirty, it's ugly. We got no right here; this is no place for human beings to be, no, by God."

Cora said, "Some people think Bannack will grow into a big town. There's them that say the gold and silver will not play out here."

Mutta came back, "Every camp there's the same thing. This one will not last; none do. You can count my words on that, Cora Harris, sometime soon, no more gold."

In all of the prospecting camps that produced well in the beginning, an almost desperate hope grew that the camp would turn into a permanent home. That was why the first men in, when the numbers were only in the tens or twenties, would plot out a townsite and give names to streets. Bannack had been a good find. In the first four months of production, there had been $325,000 panned from Grasshopper Creek and the adjacent stream banks. Little of the money had stayed in the camp. There were supplies, fetched all the way from Fort Benton or Salt

Lake City, to purchase and transport. A few prospectors, not more than a dozen, had taken their findings, sold off their claims, and gone back to the States as rich men. Most of the men continued to stay in the camp and found just enough color to keep them looking for more. John White, who made the first discovery in Grasshopper Creek, would eventually pan just over $90,000, but he would end up a town drunk and pauper. The people who really profited from the gold camps were those who made a quick find and got out, or those who sold goods and services to the hopeful prospectors. Mutta Kustar realized that she and her husband had better make quick money and leave, although her husband had visions of Bannack as the place where they would spend their lifetimes. Neither of them could possibly have guessed their future in Bannack.

Cora had heard Mutta Kustar's prediction before. She said, "I've had to move on before. I'll do it again. Ain't no skin off my nose if the gold runs out. I don't like the mountains anyway."

Lucinda, who had seen real mountains for the first time three months previously, said, "I like the mountains, but I don't like the people. Seems the worst types have come flocking to this place."

Lori walked over to the bread table and began eating; she stood there with a blank face, just chewing. Lucinda noticed, and asked, "What's wrong?"

Lori, without the customary brightness to her voice, replied, "I'm leaving this camp. I've had enough."

The others looked at Lori. Cora asked, "You itching about that boy gettin' shot?"

Lori shook her head. "Not so much the shooting; I'm scared to death because there ain't no law here . . . nothing!"

Cora laughed. "There's law here, don't you go worrying about that. You saw the law laying out there on the ground. These stupid prospectors are always ready to shoot somebody."

Mutta had finished loading the pans with dough and wiped the gluten from her hands. "You don't worry about that, Lori. This place will either disappear one day soon or them miners will elect a sheriff. Don't you worry about that."

Lori's eyes glistened with small tears, and her voice cracked as she said, "I'm leaving. First chance there is, I'm going."

Cora started to speak, but closed her mouth again. In the gold camps, she had never made any real friends, but knowing Lucinda, Lori, and Beth was a nice feeling, a feeling she wanted to hold on to. She was fearful of breaking down and crying herself.

Mutta Kustar said, "Let's go back to my parlor and I'll make us all some tea."

Lori snapped, "I don't want any tea; I want to go home, and I want to be out of this damned place."

Mutta smiled. She said, "Maybe tomorrow. We'll see then; things might be better."

Cora said, "Lucy, when you gonna be through?" She knew that Lucinda worked until midnight, but she was hoping that Mutta would let her off early. Cora felt she was going to need her help calming Lori down.

Lucinda said, "I can't leave, Cora; we've got too much to do here."

Mutta said, "I'd let Lucy off, but, with the men out until who knows when, I do need the help."

Abruptly, Lori said, "I'm going home." And she moved toward the front door. Cora took another chunk of bread from the surplus table, said, "Lucy will pay you for this, Mutta; see you later," and ran to follow Lori out into the night.

It was dark, but there was enough light from the buildings on Main Street so that Cora could see Lori only a few feet ahead. Lori was not hurrying. Cora caught up and the two walked quietly; Cora was becoming worried about Lori.

One rule for boarding at the Stinson cabin was that the

girls had to be quiet when at home. Carl Stinson was one of the few prospectors who had brought a family with him; his wife Kathy and their three children. Although a heavy drinker, Carl worked hard and needed his sleep. Kathy, in addition to raising three children and running the household, also picked up a few extra dollars doing laundry. So the four boarders were usually very careful not to make noise.

As they opened the door and stepped onto the dirt floor, they saw Kathy Stinson sitting by the roughly made plank table that served a multitude of purposes. It was not unusual for Kathy to be awake at late hours, mending or ironing, or sometimes even reading by the dim light available. But tonight, she was simply sitting, not doing anything; a most unusual sight.

Cora asked, "What is it; is something wrong?"

Kathy usually maintained a healthy, happy attitude. She enjoyed whatever life offered. But tonight the brightness was missing. Kathy replied, "I'm worried about Beth."

Cora said, "Beth left work early, but she was not sick; she didn't seem sick."

Kathy said, "Go into your room and take a look."

Lori and Cora found Beth sitting on her bunk, hands folded in her lap, staring at the floor. Cora sat down next to her. "What is it, Beth?"

"Nothing, I'm just tired. I'm gonna leave this damned place." Her voice was flat. Lori sat on Beth's other side and said, "We'll go together. I'm ready to leave, too."

Beth, still flatly, asked Lori, "Did you see it?"

Lori said, "I didn't see anything, but I'm scared to death of staying here. This place is crazy."

Beth said, "I saw it. I don't want to stay here anymore. I want to go home. I want to see my folks." Her voice was still without inflection. "My folks will have me back. I don't want to be here. . . ."

Kathy Stinson had entered the doorway. She said, "That's the way she's been since she came home. She just keeps saying she's leaving."

Cora put her arm around Beth's shoulders. "What is it, Beth, what happened?"

Beth snapped, "Nothing! Nothing happened; I didn't see anything."

Cora looked at Kathy, and the two women exchanged silent questions with their eyes. Cora rose from the bed and went back into the front room with Kathy. Cora said, "What the hell could it be?"

Kathy said, "Could it have anything to do with the shooting?"

"No, not a chance; Old Brod saw her leave way before it happened."

Kathy said, "Well, something happened to that poor child. She's in a bad state."

Cora offered, "Maybe a good night's sleep will help. She's been working hard; maybe she'll be better in the morning."

Kathy said, "I hope so. Let's try to get her to lie down."

It was hard work to convince Beth to rest. She kept insisting that she was going to catch the coach to Fort Benton and only slowly accepted the fact that there was no stagecoach at that time of night. Lori, who was not in much better shape, climbed into her own bunk, and the two were asleep in a few minutes.

Cora and Kathy resigned themselves to waiting for morning before anything could be done to change Beth's mind. They talked briefly about the killing, and then, when it was close to midnight, they also went to bed.

CHAPTER 2

(Sunday, November 9, 1862)

The next day dawned sunny and clear, and the camp came awake to begin its routine. The temperature had eased up to thirty-eight degrees.

Someone remembered that it was the Sabbath.

It was not easy to tell one day from another in a gold camp; the work was the same from one day to the next. There was always dirt to be panned and flumes to be built to bring the vital water to the workplace. Prospecting was a labor-intensive venture. When a man had time, he would pitch in on a community project, such as the ditch that would run water to the various claims on the north side of the settlement.

It was not surprising that only 28 out of about 450 people attended the religious service that took place at noontime.

The service was held in the nearly completed Roundhouse across the creek on the patch of land named Yankee Flat. The Roundhouse was planned as a protective fort to which the residents could flee in the event of an Indian attack. The few Indians in the area, from the Bannack and Crow tribes, showed no signs of hostility, but in the frontier West one had to be on guard. If the Roundhouse were to be needed, it would be just barely large enough for the people in the camp and only a few days crammed inside the log fort would probably be nearly as fatal as any Indian attack. Fortunately, it had not been needed, yet, and in fact it never was.

There were plenty of Bibles for the worshipers, but only two Presbyterian and three Methodist hymnals. Old Brod provided the music with his fiddle. Although there would be no formal religious services in the camp for a full two years, some organization came today from Hank Crawford, the butcher, and Nathaniel Langford, a man who had come to the camp to go into business but who had also staked out a paying claim far up Grasshopper Creek. Each of the two men read a passage from Scripture, and the rest of the service was taken up with vigorous singing. At the end, Langford asked if any in the patchwork congregation might want to say a few words. Kathy Stinson asked if it might be possible to start a Bible school program for the following Sunday. The general attitude was that Kathy Stinson was taking the whole thing a bit too seriously, but Langford supported her and said that he would try to come up with some sort of catechism that mothers could use as guidelines.

Someone asked if there was going to be any kind of a formal service for the young man who was killed the night before. Hank Crawford advised the gathering that the youth had been buried shortly after dawn without the benefit of a proper reading. The congregation opted for a minute of reverent silence in respect for the departed.

After a hearty rendition of "Rock of Ages," everyone left, feeling a bit better for the effort, a bit closer to civilization.

Most of the women with their children lingered outside the Roundhouse, visiting, gossiping, and pointedly avoiding any mention of killing thc night before.

The prospectors who had taken a couple of hours away from picks and shovels and pans to go to the service wasted no more time; they were off to their digs to take advantage of the good weather. When full winter came, there would be little chance for working their claims.

The businessmen also dispersed. Some went to their stores and shops; others took the long trek to Frank LeGrau's blacksmith shop at the east end of town. If the saloons were the nighttime social centers of gold camps, blacksmith shops, always warm in chilly weather, were the place to gather during the day. Just about everyone in a gold camp had need for a blacksmith at one time or another, and it was the best place for men to accomplish their version of gossip, which they called "serious discussion."

The subject of food was the first topic. The majority of men in the camp had no wives with them, and had to rely on their own cooking abilities or eat out. The Goodrich Hotel offered little in variety or quality, Skinner's saloon catered mainly to gamblers or heavy drinkers. The need for an honest-to-God, good-cooking café was something that would have to be addressed: soon!

The really serious discussion that afternoon centered on the killing the night before, and the search for the missing man they thought to be the killer. Some of the men had gone up Grasshopper Creek as far as two miles, but the night had been dark and there had been no snowfall to make tracking possible. There had been no sign of the man who had argued with the dead man in Skinner's saloon. One prospector said that he had seen two newcomers working an unclaimed patch of ground above his own claim, far down the creek. As the discussion evolved, the final consensus about the shooting incident was that the two men had made a strike, fallen out over their claim, and ended up with one of them dead and the other fleeing the camp.

Harry Phleger observed, "If we had caught him, what the hell would we have done with him?" A Miners' Court was only legal insofar as property claims and minor misbehavior was concerned.

Nathaniel Langford had finished tamping down his second pipe of tobacco. He gave a slight chuckle. "I had never thought of that problem, Harry." Langford continued his own thought, "Who is going to assume the responsibility? I heard some mention last night about calling a Miners' Court, and I just figured this sort of thing had evolved as part of each camp's rules and regulations."

"Not too likely," George Copley, an early prospector in the camp, offered. "Anyone who has been in three or four camps knows you've got to look at criminal punishment, but when a new strike is made, the majority of prospectors are new to the experience and the old-timers don't want to bring up the subject."

Frank LeGrau moved his body slightly for a more comfortable position as he sat on his anvil. He was a burly, serious-looking Frenchman with coal-black eyes and slicked-back hair. He had seen his share of new camps. "*Mon Dieu,* that's the last thing they talk about. New ones in camp find out 'bout greed. For sure."

Phleger nodded. "Two men can arrive at a gold strike and be friends from boyhood, but let a few good nuggets show up and there it is: greed."

Langford thought about that. "Is it really that bad? I mean, if the strike is good, then there should be nothing but joy and eagerness to get the gold and benefit from the work."

Copley scoffed, "You're a tenderfoot, Nat. Gold doesn't tarnish, but it sure will dirty up a man's soul."

Langford asked, "Suppose we had found that man?"

"Well," Copley said, "somebody was going to have to take him to the territorial capital in Lewiston."

"That's nearly three hundred miles!"

"Sure is, but that's what has to be done. No camp can get a sheriff or marshal until it proves out, until the gold runs for a while. Them damned territorial politicians don't like spending any money except on their own fat bellies."

Langford had not paid too much attention to talk about corruption of the territorial governments. Talk in Bannack had often been of getting a sheriff or marshal sent over from Lewiston, but no one had taken any real steps. "I guess the territorial people are just being careful with their money, what with the costs of the war, and all."

The other three men looked at each other with some amusement. Langford had become one of the leaders in the camp because they liked his ideas and his energy, but he was showing an innocence that would have to change.

It was Copley who took the duty. "Nat, there is something you will have to understand. Most all of us brought a belief in law and order with us, things we learned from our folks. It's almost as if we have a natural urge to see things organized and in their proper place. Out here in the wilderness there are some people who tend to forget about right and wrong. If there is no policeman, no judge to send them to jail, then they don't worry too much about breaking a law."

Langford gave a grim smile. "I guess there are some who feel there is no law to break."

Frank LeGrau eased off his anvil, went to the pot of coffee on the forge, and filled his cup. "Territorial, now. Just ain't no eff . . . enf . . ." He paused, groping for the word.

Harry Phleger helped him, ". . . enforcement."

"Help me on this," Langford asked. "How long do we have to be here in order for them to send a marshal?"

Copley replied, "Longer than we are at this time. The strike will have to run through next summer, at least."

LeGrau and Phleger nodded. Copley continued, "And there will have to be a lot more people. The territorial capital will react when there are enough people to make it worth their while."

Langford pulled himself up off the bench. "Hell, that's crazy. Now this thing last night, we had a man killed. It could be murder; we can't just let that sort of thing happen. We might not be a proper town or city but we are civilized people, citizens. That's a bunch of bullshit."

He walked over to the pot and served himself. The other men grinned at each other; Nat Langford was losing some of his innocence.

"When the time comes, we'll do something," Copley said.

Langford turned. His face looked stern. "Well, boys, I'm going to write to the territorial governor, and I am going to find out just how alone we are out here. We just can't go having people killed and nothing being done."

That was what the other men liked about Nat Langford; he was assertive in a logical way.

Langford added, "While I'm at it, I'm going to find out what the governor plans to do about some sort of medical help. There are people getting sick out here. We could use a hospital."

Frank LeGrau gave a laugh. "I been in some camps, Nat; no politicians be building us a hospital. We do it ourselves."

"Then let's do it."

Copley said, "It takes time and men and money. Where we going to get those things?"

"Dammit," Langford snapped, "we can make time. There are four hundred people in this camp. We can all kick in a few dollars."

"Not many of the four hundred have extra cash, Nat."

"Look, George, Chris Young has a sawmill and John Bozeman is cutting logs for cabins. I have made an investment with them and I'm sure they would supply the wood we might need."

Phleger offered, "We can probably talk a few men off of their claims for some labor."

"See?" Langford said. "If we think about it, then we can do it."

Copley observed, "You're going to have a lot of people laughing behind your back."

"I can live with that; we can't live without medical care. Maybe the governor can find us a doctor."

LeGrau laughed, good-naturedly. "Maybe you can get him to send us a sheriff or marshal, too."

"I'll try. Yes, I will, by God, give it a try."

Copley decided he could do more than just argue against things. "I'll sure do what I can, Nat. If we're going to get all of these good things, we sure ought to have a decent place to eat, too."

Langford asked, "Do any of you have an idea?"

LeGrau said, "I got one good idea."

Kathy Stinson returned home from church with her children to find the normally peaceful cabin in turmoil.

Beth Warren and Lori Charles were arguing with Cora Harris about leaving the camp; Cora was urging them to stay, but she was losing.

Kathy sent the children to play without changing their go-to-church clothes. Some of the girls' language was not fit for the youngsters. Kathy regretted not waking the girls for church; time spent in fear of the Lord might have tempered their behavior. Lucinda, at home because she did not work on Sundays, was not involving herself in the argument; she sat at the table drinking a cup of coffee from the pot Kathy had left on the stove.

Cora, still in her sleeping gown, paced the floor and waved her arms, shouting, "Dammit, you leave and I'll be stuck there alone! Ain't y'all got any feelings for me?"

Beth and Lori sat on the bench normally used by the Stinson children. Both held cups of coffee, and both were looking at the dirt floor. Lori raised her gaze and said, "Cora, it ain't no use. We talked most all night; we're leaving on the first coach."

Cora snapped, "You told me that and you told me that. You ain't said why! I gotta have a reason if I'm gonna face Cy Skinner or he'll kill me!"

Beth's dark eyes snapped up to Cora; they seemed to burn with a mysterious hate and a chilling fear. She did not speak.

Cora demanded, "Dammit, Beth, what's up?"

Beth went back to looking at the floor.

Cora grabbed Beth's shoulders and shook her. "What's wrong? Tell me!"

Beth avoided everyone's eyes. Cora released her shoulders and in frustration turned to Kathy Stinson. "Talk to them, please? They're gonna cause real trouble with Cy Skinner."

Kathy had poured herself a cup of coffee. She took a chair next to Lucinda, then asked Lori, "What's the trouble? Is it the shooting?"

Lori, eyeing Cora warily, replied, "Kathy, I'm scared; scared awful. That shooting last night just was horrible. I've heard that in camps one killing leads to another. But here there ain't no law, and I'm afraid what will happen. Cora won't listen."

Kathy nodded, then asked, "Beth, do you feel the same?"

Beth gave a faint nod of her lowered head.

Cora cut in, "She ain't spoke any sense to me since last night. The only thing she really said was: 'Did you see it?' That don't make no sense."

Kathy started to ask Beth to explain, but it was easy to see that Beth was too disturbed to talk. Kathy said, "I think you'd better give up, Cora. Lori and Beth have the right to leave; I can't really blame them."

Cora hissed, "Lotta good you been. Well, y'all can just stuff it. I'm through trying!"

She ran into the bedroom and quickly began to dress; the others could hear her cry. Lucinda rose and went into the room. Quietly, so quietly that the others could not hear, Lucinda said, "Cora, don't be angry with them. They're both scared to death; can't you see that?"

Cora had yanked off her sleeping gown and was pulling her shift down over her shoulders. "I'm scared, too, Lucy. But that ain't no reason to go running."

"You'd like to run, too, wouldn't you?"

Cora broke into fresh tears. "You bet your arse I want to run, but where can I run to? I ain't got no place to go."

Lucinda crossed the small room and gave a sisterly hug to Cora. As Cora's tears ran their course, Lucinda said, "They are silly to want to run from here, Cora. There's nothing bad going to happen to us. They're just being silly over a stupid fight last night."

Cora wiped at the tears on her cheek. "You ain't scared, Lucy?"

Lucinda smiled. "I ain't scared, Cora. There's no reason to be scared just because of one little incident."

"I've been around killings, down in Colorado; them's bad people in the Colorado camps. There ain't been no big trouble here. Am I being stupid?"

"Cora, the only *stupid* thing you ever did was to leave home in the first place; but that's in back of you. There are stupid people in this camp, but you're not one of them."

Cora smiled. "Them two is gonna git me in big trouble with Cy Skinner, you know that."

"Cy Skinner has no right to get angry with you. His business is his problem. It's not your fault that Beth and Lori want to leave. If he causes you any problems, I'll have Mister Kustar go talk to him."

"Would he do that?"

Lucinda laughed. "If he won't, then I'll ask Mutta Kustar; she'd put the fear of God into Skinner."

They both giggled at that, and Cora finished dressing. She told Lucinda, "I'm gonna make myself scarce until them two git out of here. Dick Sapp is staying in a cabin over on Yankee Flat; I'm gonna go there till it's time for work. Then Skinner can do what he wants." After a pause, she asked, "Y'all mean what ya said about getting Kustar to stand up for me?"

Lucinda said, "I promise."

Cora put on her wool coat and went out into the other room. She said, "I ain't having no lunch, Kathy. I'll see you tonight."

With that, Cora walked out of the cabin, not even looking at Beth and Lori. Cora couldn't try and say good-bye. She would, she knew, shed too many tears. She was going to miss her two friends.

After leaving the blacksmith shop, Nathaniel Langford walked west along Main Street and stopped in at Hank Crawford's butcher shop. Crawford did not have the luxury of taking the whole day off. After church he had gone directly back to his shop to begin preparing sausage. He had nearly finished when Langford walked in and decided to take a few minutes for a smoke. Langford lit up a cigar while Crawford filled his customary pipe. For visitors to Crawford's, cigar smoking was almost a necessity, because of the pungent odor from the abattoir.

The two friends smoked for a few moments, enjoying their tobacco. Then Crawford asked, "What was the word at LeGrau's? Much talk about the shooting?"

Langford said, "A little. I think the general idea is that it was a simple falling-out between friends."

"You think the shooting is a sign of trouble?"

"Hank, this is my first experience in a gold camp; I don't know what to expect. I know I don't like people going around shooting each other; that's damned bad, to my way of thinking."

"I've been in two camps before this one, and the only danger is if killings continue. I wish we could have caught that bastard. Having this thing just sitting here is not good."

Langford said, "Most of those I talked to are really pleased we didn't catch him. Feeling is that we'd be responsible for getting him back to Lewiston for a trial."

"That's garbage!" Crawford barked. "We could have tried him here in the Miners' Court."

"Then what?"

"If we found him guilty: banishment. That would warn the others who might get in the mood to do some shooting. People don't like the idea of finding a gold-bearing claim and having to leave it for someone else to make a fortune."

Langford smiled. "They really do think they're about to strike it rich, don't they?"

"That's what brings them into these godforsaken places, Nat; there's always that dream of the big strike."

Nathaniel Langford had been in the camp for only a month and a half, and he was still trying to digest all of the ingredients that went into such a community. He had come from a quiet, stable middle-western family of farmers; he had been fortunate enough to go to college, and had brought to the mountains a few dollars and an urge to create a life different from his father's. There had been no hard feelings when Nathaniel had left home, for he had gone out into the world with his father's blessings. But there were times when he missed his father's wisdom. There was much for a twenty-nine-year old farmer's son to learn, and so few sources of guidance. How much energy should he put into the place they were calling Bannack? Langford was full of enthusiasm for the community, eager to have it develop a form of government and build a school and a hospital.

Langford said, "I brought up the idea of a hospital to some of the others."

"And they were not all that big on the idea, right?"

Langford had discussed the notion with Crawford earlier, and Crawford had pointed out that a sense of civic pride was not likely to be present so early in a camp's development. Langford admitted, "It all seems so impossible trying to do something worthwhile. But I think they'll pitch in."

"Good."

"I'd hate to just give up."

"Nat, if this camp lives, people are going to be wanting men like you to get things done. Lord knows we've got enough kids to justify a school, and there are enough people getting sick, really sick, that we could use a doctor. Six or eight of the miners have the fever, some of them real bad. You know Will Bell?"

"Not very well. I've talked to him a few times. He's really sick?"

"Sick enough," Crawford said. "You can't spend eight or ten hours a day up to your hips in near-freezing water and not have something like the mountain fever get to you."

Langford shook his head. "Can we do anything for him?"

"Not much we can do. But you keep your good ideas and just be ready when the camp is, that's the best thing you can do for everybody."

Nathaniel Langford had inherited from his father a stubborn streak, and he was not going to turn loose of any of his ideas easily.

To change the subject, Langford asked, "Do you think we should be doing anything more about the shooting?"

"Not unless that other man shows up here. The whole thing is best left done with. There's no use keeping one small incident boiling in the pot."

Langford didn't want to leave it done with. To his mind, the shooting was a warning sign of dangerous lawlessness, a situation that he could not accept. When Langford had set out for the Rocky Mountains, he had never guessed that there would be places where there was no formal law. Where he came from, people caused trouble, but other people were also charged with maintaining law and order. The night before, he had seen his first example of what could happen when men were free to act as they pleased. Again, he fought down the urge to press the issue; he found himself looking more and more to Hank Crawford for guidance.

"I'd better be getting back to work, Nat. That meat is tomorrow's food for a lot of folks. They're depending on me."

Langford tossed his cigar out the open back door near the pile of offal from Crawford's last few slaughterings. Langford laughed. "It's good winter's coming; that could be a horror out there if it was hot."

"Don't worry about that. Every few days, some of them Indians down by the creek come up and clean the whole mess. I don't know what the hell they do with that stuff."

Langford shrugged his shoulders. "Now *that* is something I will keep my nose out of."

Langford left, saying he would see Crawford later that evening. Crawford went back to his sausage chores.

CHAPTER 3

(Sunday, November 9, 1862)

Two hundred and eighteen miles to the north northeast on that same Sunday afternoon, a man named Henry Plummer was sitting on a fallen tree trunk by the south bank of the Sun River.

Henry Plummer, who was five months past his thirtieth birthday, was a rogue who did not look the part. He was of average height, five feet ten inches tall, and slim at 162 pounds. He was handsome and he was dressed stylishly. He was not hesitant to use his strong graceful hands to help make a point in discussion, his smile was quick, and frequently his gray eyes flared with an intensity that could be frightening.

A three-inch scar on the left side of his head ran from his cheekbone to the edge of his brown hair. He generally wore his hat to avoid answering questions about the cause of the wound. At the moment, though, he was bare-headed.

Sitting beside him, wrapped in a warm wool cloak, was a woman named Electa Bryan.

It was not strange for Henry Plummer to be in the company of a woman; he was a womanizer of the first order. But it was surprising that his present companion was a gentle innocent product of a strict Protestant rearing. Henry Plummer would ordinarily be in the company of some harlot from a brothel.

Electa Bryan's soft blond hair was trimmed short in the name of practicality. She could not be called a striking beauty, but she was pretty. She had been blessed with bright hazel eyes, a petite nose, and a modestly full mouth. Her delicate chin, sharp cheekbones, and slender neck gave her a countenance that friends had described as angelic. She was a small woman, merely five feet two inches tall, and her weight only approached a hundred pounds. Her figure was proportioned to perfection, with hips and waist complementing the slight curve of her breasts. Electa was conversant in Scriptures, and she was trusting, which was to be her most costly virtue.

They sat in the chill of the November afternoon, watching the river flow, talking about the winter that was to come, thinking their private thoughts.

Henry was trying to find a way to be rid of his past, while Electa was trying to find a way to ensure her future.

"Oh, Henry, listen to them."

He had to refocus his thoughts to hear the shrill, bubbling voices of her niece and nephew playing on the riverbank a hundred yards upstream.

"Mary is such a sweet thing." Electa's love of her niece came easily to the ear.

Plummer chuckled. "Harvey is the one that will be causing trouble for your sister. He's going to be reaching into little girls' breeches as soon as he gets some iron in that tool of his."

Electa felt a shiver of excitement twirl around inside of her. Plummer was the only man who had ever spoken that way in front of her.

He knew he had shocked her; he took pleasure in grabbing roughly at the strict, firm Protestant ethic she had brought to the frontier.

"Oh, Henry, I do want children, soon."

"I'm doing all I can."

She punched him playfully on his shoulder. "You are awful!"

He looked back down and studied the lazy flow of the river. "Woman, we're lucky you ain't on your way right now."

"How do you know I'm not."

He turned and studied her. *Gawd, she is pretty. But what the hell have I gotten into? This was not what I was planning.* "That is not funny, Electa!"

"Well, I might be. You know that."

He looked back at the river. *I know you're pulling that cinch kind of tight, young lady. I have no plans to start raising a family. Three months ago I was sleeping with whores, and now I'm listening to the childish talk of the most innocent woman I've ever known.*

She had been studying him. "You are cute, Henry Plummer."

"Now that is just dumb, Electa. No woman has ever called me 'cute' and gotten away with it."

"What did all those other women call you?"

"Don't start that again."

"I have a right to know. Did they call you handsome? Manly? Splendid?"

The last one called me a coward because I was running out the back door when her husband arrived home. Should I tell her that? "Do you really want me to tell you?"

He hurt me the last time I pressed him like this. That awful story about the two girls who had slept with him at the same time. "That was a joke wasn't it, Henry? What you told me about those twins when you were the sheriff in Nevada City?"

It took him a moment to figure out what she was saying and his temper flared. When he had told her about the Johnson twins, she had started crying like a fool and made him feel guilty. "That was a joke," he lied, "I was just kidding you, girl. Can't you take a joke?"

A joke, he thought. *Some joke. I ended up killing a man*

and going to San Quentin. Do you want to hear about that, Electa?

It wasn't a joke, she thought. "I knew you were just teasing me, Henry."

He looked back toward the children playing. Martha Vail was concentrating on reading something. *Probably that damned Bible of hers.* He reached over and allowed his hand to come to rest on Electa's lap. She looked at him and smiled. He pressed down gently and she closed her eyes.

Now, isn't she something? Three weeks ago this twenty-year-old virgin cried for an hour after I dipped my wick in her. Now she's sitting there wanting it more than me.

"Don't stop, Henry."

He realized he had been stroking her skirt; he stopped immediately. "You're crazy, woman."

She opened her eyes and gave a flutter of her eyelashes. "I told you not to stop."

"There's some things I am not ready to accept; one of them is being shot by Jim."

"He wouldn't do that."

"He sure would."

Plummer did not believe that James Vail would shoot him, but he didn't want to press his own luck. When he had first met James Vail back at the end of August, he had found the man to be the personification of the dedicated Christian missionary. Vail had come to the Sun River Ranch in June to begin an experiment in farming for the Blackfoot Indians. He had brought along his sister-in-law Electa in hopes of having her set up a school for the Indians.

Plummer had come to Sun River after leaving Oro Fino, a silver-mining boom town 275 miles to the west. That was far enough away so that Vail would not suspect why Plummer had left Oro Fino.

Plummer had been traveling toward Fort Benton to take a boat back down the Missouri River to return to the States, but Electa had caught his eye. He had stayed overnight, thinking she might be easy to lure into his bed, but he quickly realized she was not a loose woman and that got his attention. Electa, a healthy, normal woman, was attracted to Plummer, who seemed to be an honest, sincere man. She had enjoyed his being at the ranch. Vail was grateful for an extra pair of male hands, and an overnight stay turned into what came to look like a permanent situation. Plummer moved into a small cabin near the horse barn and began handling chores that freed Vail to spend more time with the Indian farmers.

Plummer had played it very slowly in his attempt to bed Electa— a technique that had provided him with about seven weeks of celibacy.

"Why did you leave, Henry?"

"What do you mean?"

"Last month, when you left, I never did really understand."

Plummer tried to pull his thoughts together; his faulty memory made him a poor liar. He had ruined his original story of going to see his sick mother in Wisconsin when he had said he was going to see his sick sister in Baltimore. No one ever did find out much about his past. He liked it that way, but he did not like being caught out in a lie to Electa.

Three weeks earlier he had pulled out of the ranch because he had begun to feel he would never seduce Electa and he was getting tired of fixing fence posts and watering horses. He had been gone three days, making it to Fort Benton, but had been unable to clear her from his mind. He returned to the ranch on a Sunday, saying he had missed the last boat downriver. On Monday he had his way with Electa.

During his absence, she had convinced herself that she had lost him forever, lost him by protecting her virginity. With that hurdle behind her, she entered into her liaison with gusto but had been limited to only five encounters in three weeks. Plummer had imposed strict guidelines for their meetings to avoid any chance of being caught.

"I left because I could not get you out of my mind."

"You saw me every day."

"No. At night, when I was in that cabin by myself, you were always on my mind."

"Then why did you come back?"

"Same reason."

"Will you leave now that I have given myself to you?"

That's a tough one. I thought that all I wanted to do was to get in her breeches but there is something more to it than that . . . Hell, tell her.

He did. The words came with difficulty; he used every appropriate one, except "love." Still, in his way, he conveyed a deep admiration for her, and he made as much of a commitment as was possible for a man not used to romance.

Electa felt a welling in her chest. It was a pain she had been experiencing more and more. She was in love and wanted to marry this man who had come into her life.

He looked at her and was confused. She looked unhappy. *That's what I get for being honest.*

She reached out and took his hand. He looked up to where Martha Vail sat safely watching her children.

Softly, Electa said, "I miss you."

He turned back and smiled. Her soft, warm voice had an earthy quality when they were alone that was not there when they were with others. He said, "I miss you, too. Three or four days without ravishing you and I begin to break out in a cold sweat."

"It's been five days."

He teased, "You been counting?"

She came back, "I started counting about the first half day; I'm getting used to you."

"I'd like to *get used to you* right now!"

She giggled. "I think we could take a little ride on the buckboard; who would notice?"

Plummer burst out in a loud laugh. How this modest, demure woman had evolved into an honest and eager lover! Without yet knowing it, he was feeling something else for Electa, something he had never felt for a woman: he was feeling respect.

At Plummer's laugh Martha had looked downstream

to her sister and Plummer. Plummer asked Electa, "Do you think she knows about what we're doing?"

Electa blushed. "No, I'm sure she doesn't. She'd ship me off back home in a minute if she had the slightest idea."

Plummer reached over and put his hand back in the middle of her lap. Electa gasped. She was sure her sister was far enough away that she could not make out what Plummer was doing, but she hissed, "Stop it! You drive me crazy. Do you want me shipped home?"

Plummer, with no noticeable change of voice said, "I not only don't want you shipped home, I want you to marry me."

Electa had been praying to hear those words, but now she could not put words to her thoughts.

Plummer pressed his hand down gently, and she felt herself reacting. She put her hand on top of his and urged him to continue; she did not care about what her sister saw, soon it would all be very legal. Plummer asked, "No answer?"

She gave him a huge smile. "I would be the happiest woman in the world, Henry Plummer. I want to marry you, too."

He said, "We'll do it."

She stopped his hand, thrilling as it was, and said, "Let's go tell Martha."

Plummer's face changed slightly. The change was barely perceptible, but she caught it. He was frightened. He drew his hand away, smiled, and said, "I think we should wait; I don't think we should tell anyone right now."

Electa felt she was being cheated of a great moment in her life. Neither she nor her sister had ever dreamed that Electa would find a husband on the frontier. They had assumed that after a couple of years, she would return to Ohio, teach school, and then probably marry. With Plummer's proposal, all of that had changed and Electa wanted to share it, quickly, with her family—with the whole world. She could not hide her disappointment.

Plummer said, "We will tell Martha and James soon, I promise you that, my darling; just give me some time to plan our future."

"But why can't we tell them . . . now?"

He said, "I want to tell them what we're going to do after we're married. You can understand that."

Electa could not understand that at all. Her face made that clear.

"Just give me some time to think. I have three hundred dollars in dust and nuggets in my saddlebags, but that won't be enough to start out in the kind of style I want to provide for you. I want to take you traveling, to buy you nice clothes. I want to set myself up in some sort of respectable, profitable business. I might take us back and go into the hardware business with my father."

Electa did not reply. A week earlier, Plummer had told her that his father was a successful dairy farmer. She did not want to get into that question. There was enough confusion roiling about in her mind at that moment. All she wanted to do was to scream with joy, to tell everyone of her happiness, but her feelings were being smothered.

She sat staring blankly at the scenery that had been, just a few minutes before, so beautiful. The excitement of her betrothal gave way to fear that the whole thing might come crashing down. She could not speak.

Plummer spoke. He stumbled through sentences he hoped would placate her, he pleaded for understanding but offered her nothing to understand. He did not know what to do, past the moment of asking for her hand.

Electa tried to listen, tried to make sense out of his attitude, but she was disappointed. Plummer ceased talking. He joined her in silently looking at the river. Finally Electa said, "Henry, I know you will do what has to be done. I am sorry that I acted the way I did, it was silly." She let a smile come to her face. "I'm just a silly little girl, I know that. Whatever you want, however you want it, will be what I want for us. You just tell me what to do and I will do my best."

"My darling, just trust me. Let me do some thinking, then we can tell James and Martha. Please. Trust me for a few days."

She said shyly, "Will you be angry if Martha guesses?"

Touched, he had little doubt that Martha would guess. Electa was radiant, and there would have to be some explanation for that obvious development. He answered, "If she guesses, there is nothing we can do; but try not to look so lovely, and maybe she will not guess."

There was an excited yell from near Martha and the children. A lone man on a horse was crossing the ford upstream of Martha.

Plummer tensed as he always tensed when a rider came into the farm complex. He lived in fear of someone coming who might expose his past to Electa and the Vails. Plummer had continued to wear his pistol in a holster on his hip. Even James Vail had agreed that it was a good idea. Electa saw it in a romantic light, that her man was willing to fight for her life. He reached down, touched the familiar wood of his pistol's handgrip, then stood. He offered his hand and helped Electa up; they both began to walk upstream along the riverbank.

Suddenly Plummer came to a halt. He had recognized the incoming horseman. It was the rider's misshapen hat, the long dirty trail coat, and the way the man sat in the saddle, for Jack Cleveland knew how to sit a horse. He was one of the last people Henry Plummer wanted to see.

Electa asked, "What's wrong, Henry?"

Plummer, absently, replied, "Oh, nothing. I know that man, and I don't like him being here."

Electa took Plummer's arm. "Is he a friend?"

Plummer considered no man his friend. The people he had known for the past several years were not worthy of the title. He said, "I know him."

Electa was excited at the prospect of being able to talk to someone who could tell her of her man's past. She urged Plummer forward.

The man was pulling up near Martha and the children. He called, "Hey, Plummer, you old bastard, what you doing in these parts?"

Under his breath, barely loud enough for Electa to hear, Plummer said, "Filthy-mouthed no-good; what's he doing here?"

Roughly, Plummer removed Electa's hand from his arm and hurried ahead, his long steps forcing Electa to run to keep up with him. Plummer passed Martha, who looked bewildered by both the vulgar greeting and Plummer's obvious anger.

Cleveland had dismounted, pulled off his ankle-length riding coat, and tossed it up onto his saddle.

As Plummer came close, Cleveland said, "I'll be a son of a bitch if you ain't a sight. What you doing here with these Christian folks? I'd have bet . . ."

Plummer's glacial expression cut off anything more Cleveland might say. Plummer grabbed the halter of Cleveland's horse and, with the other hand, grabbed Cleveland's arm. He moved both back in the direction of the ford.

Cleveland blustered, but allowed himself to be manhandled until they reached the spot where Cleveland had crossed the river, well out of earshot of Electa, Martha, and the children. Plummer demanded, "What the hell you doing here? Tell me!"

Cleveland, replied, "I was just heading for Fort Benton. Only stopped to give the damned horse a breather. What's got into you, Henry?"

Plummer snapped, "What's got into me is that these are damned nice people here, and you come busting in with that filthy mouth of yours."

Cleveland burst out laughing: "Filthy mouth! Ain't that something? You ain't no saint."

Plummer's face twisted into an angry glare; his gray eyes seemed to take on a burning color, and his lips pulled back, baring his teeth. "Quit laughing or, by God, I'll drop you right here."

Cleveland did not lose his smile. He had seen

Plummer angry, he had even seen Plummer kill; but then, Cleveland was, himself, a seasoned gunslinger. "Tell me what you've got going here, Henry. How long you been camped out with this bunch of sodbusters?"

Plummer answered, "I came a while back and been helping them out a bit. They're nice folks. They're trying to help the Indians."

Cleveland scoffed, "Helping the *Indians*! Best way to help them savages is to kill 'em. Gawd, you know that!"

"I don't have anything to do with the damned savages. I just like the folks here. I'm moving on soon."

"Today?"

"Not that soon."

"Maybe I'll just hang here with you. Kind of see what's so nice about these folks."

Plummer demanded, "Where were you headed when you stopped here?"

"Like I said: Fort Benton. Heard that a slick dude stole some Wheelock sidehammer rifles from the Union Army and has them for sale up in Fort Benton; just what I need for a bit of work I'm fixing to do."

Plummer's interest was piqued. He relaxed slightly. "Where you fixing to do some work?"

Cleveland asked, "Ain't you heard about the strike down near the Beaverhead? Place called Bannack."

"Some people passing through said something about it."

"You interested?"

"I'm not interested. I'm through with that life, Jack. I've come too close to having my neck stretched; I'm out of the game."

Cleveland shrugged. "Suit yourself. You want to ride to Fort Benton with me?"

Plummer shook his head. Then, after a pause, he said, "I think you could move on right now. You don't want to be around these folks; they're simple people."

Cleveland eyed him curiously. "You scared I'm gonna tell 'em about what you used to do?"

Plummer snapped, "I'm not scared of nothing you

could say, but you'd better be. You talk too much and you might end up shot."

Cleveland laughed again. "Henry, you couldn't shoot me. Hell, we been down just about all the roads there is; you couldn't shoot me."

"Don't test me, Jack."

"Ain't planning to." Then, with an evil grin, he said, "Maybe I'll just go say good-bye to the ladies. I ain't been around *simple people* lately." Without waiting for Plummer's reaction, Cleveland walked back to where Electa stood with Martha.

Plummer caught up quickly and ordered, "You be leaving now, Jack."

The two men had come within hearing distance of the ladies. Anxiously, Plummer listened as Cleveland said, "Just wanted to say my howdies, ladies. Old Henry and I go way back. We had a couple of things to say before I could be proper and polite."

Plummer, caught in Cleveland's trap, was forced to say, "Martha, Electa, this is Jack Cleveland. We used to . . . well . . . we worked together."

Martha nodded. Electa smiled and said, "That is a nice surprise; to find friends out here in the wilderness."

Cleveland grinned. "It's likely Henry and I would find each other just about anyplace, ma'am. It sort of seems to just happen."

"Jack's leaving now," Plummer cut in. "He's got to get on the way to Fort Benton."

Martha said, "That's too bad, Mister Cleveland. I'm sure you'd like to stay."

Jack Cleveland had been looking at the two women. They were both attractive; Martha had filled out since bearing the children and her face showed a few wrinkles, but he especially savored looking at Electa Bryan, who carried a sensual innocence about her. Cleveland, like Plummer, knew only dance-hall girls and prostitutes. Electa, standing there in a simple, brown calico dress, aroused him. He began to fantasize about what she would look like minus the dress.

Martha repeated, "I said: it's too bad you have to leave."

Cleveland pulled his attention back to Martha but did not speak.

Electa had been looking at Jack Cleveland. He was a scruffy person compared to Henry Plummer. His clothing was filthy, with spots of food on the front of his shirt, and his trousers showed where he had wiped grease off his hands. He was carrying 180 pounds on his five-foot-six-inch frame. He had bushy eyebrows and a nose that had obviously been broken more than once. The lower half of his left ear was missing, and he had a crimson scar showing above the kerchief he wore around his neck. His hair was matted, his boots were worn through in two places. Electa was startled by the contrast between Cleveland and her lover. She said, "Could you think of staying over, Mister Cleveland?"

Plummer said gruffly, "He has to get going."

Cleveland looked down at the Vail children and said, "Now ain't these two fine-looking youngsters? I bet they are a real blessing to take away the loneliness out here in these parts."

Martha asked, "Do you like children, Mister Cleveland?"

Cleveland replied, "Oh, I sure do, ma'am. Children are just the nicest thing in the world."

Plummer repeated, "Jack's got to be on his way, Martha. He can see the children on his trip back."

Cleveland rubbed the three days' growth of whiskers on his chin. He said, "Now that you mention it, I could stay overnight. It's getting too late to make Fort Benton tonight."

"You're leaving," Plummer ordered.

Electa said, "Now, Henry, why make him go? The poor man is tired; you can see that."

Cleveland, enjoying baiting Plummer, said, "I am sure tired. Wouldn't mind staying over."

"We've plenty of food for dinner," Martha offered. Then, looking at Plummer, she said, "Henry, it would be so nice for you to have a chance to visit with an old friend."

Plummer wanted to take out his gun and force Cleveland to leave, but that could trigger a whole series of events that he did not want to start. Reluctantly, he said, "I guess it wouldn't hurt. He can bunk in with me in the cabin."

Cleveland, with a mocking tone to his voice, said, "Darn, Henry, you've got your own cabin. Now ain't that something else!"

Plummer opened his mouth, but Cleveland was too quick. "I'll just go get my nag over there. She's ready for a good rest, anyway."

Plummer's face was tinged red as he watched Cleveland walk to his horse. Electa said, "He seems such a nice man, Henry."

Plummer puffed out some air in disgust.

Martha said, "I'm going to take the children up to the house and start getting the evening meal ready. Will you come, Electa?" They left.

Alone, Plummer waited, fuming. As Cleveland led his horse to Plummer, it did not help that Cleveland was beaming like a naughty little boy who had just bested one of his parents. "Hey, Henry, don't look so ugly. I'm just hoping for some fun."

"You might be looking to get dead, Jack. You're pressing me pretty close."

Cleveland came up to Plummer, stopped, then said seriously, "You don't own this whole damned country, Henry Plummer. Now, you get a smile on your face, or maybe we will have to settle this thing nasty-like."

Plummer did not smile. "You'd be smart to pack out of here right now, Jack. I don't plan to take any of your guff."

"I won't be giving you any trouble. All I want is a chance to try and diddle that young gal; what's her name?"

Plummer seethed with rage; he could not let Cleveland know his feelings about Electa, not until he figured out when he was going to get married. He merely said, "They are two gentle women, Jack. Don't start anything."

Cleveland ignored him. "How about you take one and I'll take the other. Where's the husband?"

"Jim Vail will be home soon. There's going to be no taking of either of those ladies; this isn't Lewiston."

"Is it like Oro Fino? Remember the times we had in Oro Fino?" Cleveland smirked. "They still remember you in Oro Fino."

Plummer was not amused. Ten minutes before he was planning how to marry and to start a good new life with Electa Bryan. Now he was struggling with a living memory of the past he had hoped was dead. But Henry Plummer had spent his life calling more on his wit than on his gun. He would rid himself of Jack Cleveland, then get on with life.

Plummer forced a smile. "Bring your damned horse and let's get her some feed."

They left Cleveland's horse in the corral and took his gear to the visitors' cabin where Plummer was living.

The building was a log structure measuring twelve feet square with a shed roof. There were two sets of bunk beds, a table, four chairs, and even a bookcase moderately supplied with reading matter. Unlike most frontier cabins, this one had a plank floor and even two rugs. A comfortable place to rest, except for one thing. "Where's the stove?" was the first thing Jack Cleveland said as he entered.

Plummer laughed and said, "No stove."

Cleveland tossed his blanket roll and saddlebags onto a vacant bunk as he asked, "Don't these yokels know what winter can be out here?"

Plummer went to his own gear and lifted out a pint bottle of whiskey. "James Vail is interested in teaching the Indians how to be humans and how to keep those Indians from massacring the settlement." He went back to the table and pulled up a chair.

Cleveland sat and reached for the bottle. Plummer said, "Not too much, Jack. These are hard Christian folks, and the Methodists don't take too kindly to drink. Vail knows I take a nip now and then, but I don't want to get him in trouble." Then, seriously, "And I don't want you to get yourself into trouble with me."

Cleveland took a short swallow, smacked his lips, and said, "I'll be no trouble, really, Henry. But can't you just feel what it'd be like to have that pretty little piece out here in this cabin? Hell, maybe both of us could have her at the same time. Never tried that; what about it? I can just see her naked body on that bunk of mine. Gawd, that'd be nice."

Plummer took the bottle and drank to wash the words back down his throat. A fight with Jack Cleveland was not in his plans. With his temper under control, Plummer asked, "Now what's this about the new rifles? What in God's name do you need a fancy rifle for?"

Cleveland reached for the bottle but halted when Plummer raised a warning eyebrow. "Henry," he said, "that gold strike down near the Beaverhead is a healthy one; I've seen some of the sacks that's come out of there and I'm set on getting my share. Cyrus Skinner's already there."

Skinner! If he is there, then good money is there.

Back in August when Plummer had left Oro Fino, he thought he had said good-bye to Cyrus Skinner forever. Maybe Cleveland's arrival at the Sun River Ranch was a hidden blessing.

Plummer asked, "What's Cy doing there?"

"What do you think?"

Plummer's eyes demanded an answer.

"He's got a saloon, what else?"

Plummer smiled. He and Skinner had owned two saloons together in the past three years, and saloons were the best source of information in a gold camp. "Good pickings?" he asked.

Cleveland eyed the pint of whiskey. "The best. That's what I hear." Plummer nodded his okay.

While Cleveland was taking his drink, Plummer sat

there thinking. Plummer was carrying twenty-four ounces of dust and nuggets in his pack. The last he had heard, the assayers were paying $14.50 per ounce; he had close to $350 to his name, and although that was more than he had told Electa, it was not enough to begin the kind of life he wanted. If the new strike was really good, then Plummer might just be able to make one score so big that he would be able to do justice to his dreams.

Plummer asked, "What's so important about getting a new rifle, Jack? How come you've got to go all the way to Fort Benton before you go down to the Beaverhead?"

Cleveland held the bottle and replied, "Might have to do a lot of work alone, Henry. I don't know who will be there to help out. I know they're running a stage into the place, and those stage drivers are carrying rifles now. I need something with the range to stop them."

Plummer's mind was moving fast. If the stagecoaches were arming their drivers, then there was only one reason: gold shipments.

Henry Plummer had helped write the book on how to rob people carrying money out of gold camps. He reached over, took the bottle from Cleveland, and replaced the cork. "That's enough drinking for right now. We might want it later."

Plummer went to his bunk, where he put the bottle away. As he turned, he said, "What would you say if I told you I might go down to the Beaverhead with you?"

Cleveland jumped up and boomed, "Hot damn, Henry Plummer! Ever since I rode into this stupid place and saw your ugly face, I been hoping to hear that. When do we leave?"

Plummer did not pause. "What about tomorrow morning?"

Cleveland beamed. "I'm ready. First thing." Then, after a moment's thought, he added, "That'll give me time to give that pretty gal a treat she won't forget."

Plummer walked over to stand a bare three inches from Cleveland. "You keep your distance from Electa. And watch your mouth."

Cleveland asked, "You got that claim staked out or something?"

"Maybe I do and maybe I don't. Just keep away from her."

Cleveland broke into a grin. "I'll be a son of a bitch. You been messing with her, ain't you?"

"What I do is my business. If you want me to help you out, then you'll listen to what I say, and I say that you forget Electa."

Cleveland snarled, "When we get to the Beaverhead, I'll take your orders just like I've always done. But until we do, I'm my own man; you know that."

Plummer said angrily, "You heard what I said," and he turned and walked out of the cabin. Looking up at the farmhouse, he saw that James Vail had returned from the Blackfoot village. He called back to Cleveland, "Go get yourself washed down at the stream. They'll have us to dinner in a few minutes."

Cleveland came to the doorway and said, "Look, Henry, don't be mad. I ain't trying to cut in on your piece of cake. I'll watch myself." Then, in a wicked tone of voice, he added, "But if you don't want to take a tumble with that gal, let me know."

For the first time Plummer was clearly seeing the outlaws he had worked with. He knew he should have told Cleveland the truth about Electa right up front, but he had felt he would be staining her in some way by even discussing her with a man like Cleveland. He gave a slight nod and said, "No harm done. Just stay away from her."

Cleveland pressed, "You sweet on her?"

"Don't worry about her. Come on up to the main house when you've washed off the road dirt."

"Do I have to wash up, for God's sake? Can't a man be comfortable with these church people?"

Grudgingly, Plummer laughed, turned, and headed up to the house.

Sunday dinner in the Vail house was modest. The Indian village had sent over a joint of venison, Martha had cooked the last of her summer carrots, and Electa, with the help of the children, had made two large trays of biscuits. For dessert there was a rhubarb pie left over from the previous day, but there was enough for everyone to have an adequate slice. At the end of the meal, Martha apologized to her guests for the lack of potatoes, explaining that the shipment from Fort Benton was overdue.

Plummer said the meal had been luxurious. Cleveland was cramming his mouth with one last biscuit dabbed with butter and honey.

The meal had been taken early so that the kitchen could be cleaned before dark. While the women saw to the dishes, the children were sent off to begin getting ready for bed.

The Vail farmhouse was about as good as could be found on the frontier. It measured thirty feet on each side, with one corner partitioned off to provide a bedroom for James and Martha. Electa and the children slept in a finished loft above the kitchen and bedroom. The remainder of the downstairs functioned as a sitting room and office for James Vail. There were two wood stoves, one in the kitchen for cooking and one in the main room to provide heat for the rest of the house.

Plummer and Cleveland took seats on the sofa and Vail took his desk chair. As they settled, Jack Cleveland emitted a loud belch, followed by, "I guess I'll be farting next; rhubarb does that to me every time."

Plummer glanced with embarrassment at James Vail, who had, throughout the whole dinner, shown some dismay at Cleveland's behavior. Twice Plummer had kicked Cleveland under the table: once when he used cuss words as punctuation and then when he started telling a story about a brothel in Oro Fino. Plummer was relieved that Cleveland had not caused more disruption. He felt sure that Martha Vail regretted inviting them for dinner.

That afternoon, Vail had gotten a newspaper from a passing wagon train. The issue was only two and a half weeks old; it was a precious source of fresh news. Vail talked about what he had read: a stirring account of the Battle of Antietam in which General Burnside had given a good showing; a report on President Lincoln's visit to General McClellan, who was not doing at all well with the Army of the Potomac; the news that the Union Army had started using field ambulances to bring in the wounded.

Cleveland cut in, "Ain't there no damned news about the Confederacy? What kind of junk paper you got there? Anything in there about Jeb Stuart? He's a real hero!"

Vail bristled. "Mister Cleveland, you are a guest in our home and I do not want to insult you, but I would appreciate your watching the words you use."

Cleveland, confused, looked at Plummer, who said: "Quit cussing."

Vail then said, "Furthermore, we are loyal to the Union. I would appreciate your not exposing our children to the enemy point of view."

Cleveland reached up and picked out a sliver of meat from between his teeth. He stared at James Vail for a second, popped the piece of meat back into his mouth, and chewed. He said, "Well, shit, I guess I ain't welcome here no more."

With that, he stood and walked out the front door.

Henry Plummer felt his face go uncomfortably red. He knew Martha and Electa in the kitchen had heard the exchange. Plummer said, "Jim, I'm sorry about that."

Vail countered, "No reason for you to be held accountable for that sort of man, Henry."

"Well, you've got to understand; there are all types out here. They're about half for the Union and half for the

Confederacy. Jack Cleveland is just one of those who is willing to fight for a lost cause."

"Then he'd do well to go south and fight, rather than hiding out here."

Plummer smiled and said, "I'd bet the Confederate Army would not mind having him behind a gun; he's good." After a short pause, he added, "But there is no excuse for his conduct this evening."

"I'm just glad he is a former friend of yours."

"Well, he isn't all that *former,* Jim. As a matter of fact, I'm going to have to do some business with him shortly."

Electa came in from the kitchen and asked, "What does that mean, Henry?"

James Vail was taken aback by Electa's boldness. "Electa, remember your place."

Plummer stood up and put an arm around Electa's shoulders. "She's got a right, Jim. Being you and Martha are the only family Electa has here, I'd like to ask you for her hand in marriage."

Electa swung her head around at the announcement; she had resigned herself to secrecy. Martha had heard and she ran into the parlor from the kitchen. She said, "My dear Ellie, this is just wonderful!"

James Vail rose, carelessly dropping his newspaper on the floor, and shook Plummer's hand. "Well, this is surely splendid news, Henry!" Looking at Electa, he asked, "When did all of this happen, Ellie?"

Electa was so flustered she did not know what to say. She merely stood there with a broad, happy grin on her face.

Plummer rescued her. "Nothing really happened, Jim. It's just that I felt it was time to settle down, and you folks were kind enough to bring Electa out here to the frontier." Then, with a contrived look of admiration, he smiled at Electa. "I guess it was just good luck for me that you brought her."

Martha stepped forward and gently pulled her sister into her arms. "I couldn't be happier for both of you."

Plummer announced, "All I have to do now is finish up some business affairs and we'll tie the knot."

Electa was so elated that she did not mind what he had to do. James Vail, out of natural curiosity, asked, "What will that entail, Henry?"

"Well," Plummer said as he sat back down, "I own some property down in the Beaverhead Valley, and Jack Cleveland told me this afternoon that he has a buyer. As soon as I can settle that matter, I'll be back here and take Electa off to begin our life together."

Electa and Martha went to the kitchen, where they whispered happily about the new turn of events. In the front room, Plummer wove a convoluted tale of property investment which would provide him with the money to see that Electa did not want for earthly goods, improvising very well as he went along. Finally he said, "I'd better get out of here and pack up. I must leave first thing in the morning."

Electa flew in from the kitchen, protesting. Plummer smiled at James, saying, "Seems I've taken on a serious responsibility."

Electa pleaded, "Don't go now, Henry. Please stay for a little longer. We've so much to plan."

Her voice carried a tender, exciting lilt that Plummer found difficult to resist, but he did not want to spend the evening embroidering his story for the well-meaning Vails. James Vail was no fool, and Plummer might just slip up in his fiction. He said to Electa, tenderly, "I'll see you before I leave in the morning. We can talk then."

"I want to walk you to your cabin."

Plummer looked questioningly at the Vails; Martha said, "I see no problem with that, Henry. After all, you are now engaged."

Plummer smiled. "I guess that's the truth, Martha. The deed is done; all formal-like."

Plummer and Electa walked out into the twilight. The sun had set beyond the mountains but there was still light in the sky. In the pastel colors from orange to blue played out above them, even the dinginess of the farm compound looked tolerable. Plummer had his arm around Electa and began walking directly toward the cabin, while Electa tried to steer him in the other direction, toward the barn at the far end of the compound. "Hey," he said, "I've got to get back to the cabin."

Electa said, "I want us to have some privacy."

Plummer realized what she was suggesting and halted. "Listen, young lady, they'll all be watching us now; there's no way we can be alone. Not tonight!"

"I want to."

"I do, too. But it is not in the cards tonight."

She came against him and kissed him eagerly. He responded. They were almost out of sight of the farmhouse, and the lone tree in the compound partially obscured the view from the cabin. Plummer's hand slipped down her back and pulled her tight against him; she pressed her body close to his. She pulled her mouth free for an instant and said, "I want to be with you."

Plummer felt himself weakening; but he knew they would be suspect now. They would be watched. He was not going to be caught rolling in the hay. He pulled back, placed his hands on her shoulders, and said, "Not tonight. I want to, but not tonight."

Softly she said, "You can't send me to bed feeling like this."

"I feel the same way."

"Then let's do something about it."

"We can't."

"Why not?"

"Because your sister or Jim might catch us."

"I don't care. I want you."

He was touched by her tenderness and excited by her sexual aggressiveness. This was a new experience for Henry Plummer; Electa Bryan was a wholesome woman in love. But his reaction was not what Electa wanted. She said, "You're going away, Henry, and I need you to be with me."

He thought for a moment. He said, "You go back and

go to bed, and I'll meet you in the barn before sunup in the morning. How about that?"

She would have no part of that suggestion, and he needed several minutes of kiss-interrupted discussion to convince her. In the end, she agreed; her passion had not subsided, but his caution prevailed. Just before they parted, she asked, "How long will you be gone?"

He said, "I don't know." And, reacting to the pained look on her face, quickly added, "But not long, really, only as long as it takes to finish up my business affairs."

"Is it far?"

"Not too far. About three or four days' ride."

"Can I write to you? I'll write simply shameless things that will make you want to return."

He laughed. "You don't have to write shameless things to make me want to get back to you. I have memories of all the things we do together."

"Should I write?"

Plummer said, "You write; I'd like that."

She grinned, kissed him once more on the mouth, then pulled back and asked, "Where do I write? What's the name of the place?"

Plummer answered, "A place they're calling Bannack. Write to me there."

CHAPTER 4

(Monday, November 10, 1862)

Cora Harris was scared out of her wits. She had been living with fear since the moment when Beth Warren had admitted why she was leaving Bannack.

Beth and Lori Charles had left that Monday on the noon stage for Hellgate. Cora was wishing she had left with them.

On Sunday, Cora had had to go to work and tell Cy Skinner that Beth and Lori had quit; they would not be coming back to the saloon. Skinner, predictably, first slapped Cora in the face, then demanded to know what she had done to cause Beth and Lori to leave. Cora bore the abuse; she was used to being swatted around. She had handled Skinner by telling him that she was almost certain that Beth and Lori would be coming back to the saloon. It was easy for Cora to lie to men.

On Sunday night, she returned to the Stinson cabin exhausted after doing the work of three. She found Beth and Lori with their possessions packed; there was a stagecoach scheduled the following morning and they intended to leave with it. That news did not unnerve Cora. Her upset came later, when they were in their bedroom and Beth Warren said that on Saturday night, she had seen Skinner shoot the young prospector.

Beth had left work early, scared by the fight that had broken out. She had walked home, she said. Once at the Stinsons', however, she had felt guilty about leaving Cora and Lori to do all the work, so she had decided to go back to the saloon. She had not returned directly to Skinner's, but had wandered around, walking down to Grasshopper Creek, then back up to where John Manheim was building his huge new brewery. Manheim's workers were still at work and had a fire going, so she stopped and chatted with them for a few minutes, then took the path that ran east next to the Bannack Ditch on the north side of the camp. As she came along the path toward the saloon, she heard an argument, a nasty argument, going on between the two men she had seen squabbling earlier in Skinner's. Old Brod's violin and the usual noises from inside obscured the shouting, but she could hear that they were fighting about the gold they had found that day. There was not much light, but the two men were standing near the saloon, the side bordering Second Street. She saw Skinner coming around from the back of the saloon. She guessed he must have gone to the privy and heard the argument in progress. And Skinner had a gun.

Beth shivered at that point in telling the story; she seemed to want to talk, yet it was difficult for her to do so.

Skinner had the gun in his hand. He came around the corner. The two youths did not see him.

"I saw Cy standing there in the shadows. He was listening. I wanted to run, but I was afraid Cy would see me, so I stood there rigid, like ice. My daddy showed me how a deer can go near invisible just by not moving; I didn't move. Then it all happened in a flash. Cy raises the gun and shoots, two quick ones: bang . . . bang! The one boy was hit and fell, the other one ran like a bobcat with a poker up his arse. Cy let loose with another shot at the runner."

She was breathing heavily as she relived the horror. Lori, who was herself terrified, put an arm around Beth to comfort her.

Beth continued, "Quick as could be, Cy ran over to the boy laying on the ground and grabbed at the body; he was feeling for pouches of gold. Cy was like a wild man, clawing at the boy's jacket. I saw Cy rip a pocket and yank two pouches loose."

Beth's hands were shaking, moving almost as if to reenact the moves Skinner had made. Cora asked, "What'd you do?"

"I stood there! What the hell was I supposed to do?"

The three women were silent for a moment; from the other parts of the cabin, they could hear the Stinsons and their children breathing in their sleep.

Beth took two deep breaths herself before she went on, "Well, Cy jumps up and looks around; he looked mean. You know that mean look he gets on his face when he's mad at us; the look he had then was different than that. He looked like he'd kill anything that moved. I didn't move. He looked right at me; I swear he must have seen me; I wasn't more than fifty feet away. But he didn't say nothing. He jumped up, ran around in back of the saloon and down toward the outhouse. He was moving fast; faster than I ever saw Cy Skinner move. Then he tossed them two pouches of gold up onto the roof of the outhouse and ran along the ditch, past Goodrich's. Then I lost sight of him."

Cora asked, "What'd you do?"

Beth's eyes locked open and her jaw moved. Then she answered, "I ran over and grabbed the gold, then ran back the way I came."

Cora exploded: "Good Gawd! You took the gold!?"

Beth did not answer. She reached under the thin mattress on her bunk and pulled out the two sacks.

Cora whispered, "You're crazy!"

Lori whimpered, "We're all gonna be killed!"

Later, after they had calmed down, Beth told them she guessed there was better than a pound of dust and nuggets in the pouches; surely enough to pay all of their fares to Fort Benton or Hellgate with enough left over to give them a start someplace else. Beth offered to share her spoils with Cora, as she was doing with Lori, and said she would include Lucinda Simons, who was at work in Kustar's.

Cora did not sleep that night. She kept waiting for Cyrus Skinner to come charging in and kill all of them in their beds. It was while she lay there in the darkness that she realized she could not lie to herself. She doubted that Skinner would ever learn that Beth had witnessed the murder and theft. She doubted that he would follow them out of the camp to reclaim the gold. If she left the camp the following day with Beth and Lori, she would never know what Skinner might have done. That realization decided her to stay; she wanted to know.

So, as she opened the door of the saloon that Monday after Beth and Lori had boarded the stagecoach and left the camp, she was scared out of her wits.

She was startled when she closed the door. The saloon was empty, except for two strangers sitting at a corner table drinking coffee and three drunks sleeping on the primitive bunks along the west wall. Skinner was behind the bar, anger on his face, obviously in a foul mood.

She pulled off her cloak as she crossed the room to the bar. She asked, "Where's all the customers?"

Skinner growled, "Dammit, don't you know nothing? There's weather coming; maybe a snowstorm. Them stupid bastards are digging like fools to get ready for winter. You heard about LeGrau?"

"The blacksmith?"

"Yeah. Building a café. Ain't that something?"

"Might be good."

"I'll lose business. Probably a bunch of our customers up there helping him build it, too."

Cora realized she had an opening. "Well, I guess it won't be too bad about Beth and Lori."

Skinner poured a tot of whiskey into the tin cup of coffee sitting on the bar. He said, "What do you mean 'too bad' about them two bitches?"

Cora replied, "Beth and Lori left on the stage to Hellgate. They just up and pulled out."

Skinner's eyes flared with anger. "Where'd they get the money?"

Trouble. Quickly, Cora blurted out, "They been making out pretty good from diddling the new arrivals."

Skinner snapped, "That's a lie! They're supposed to share that with me and they ain't been giving me that much."

Impulsively Cora said, "I think they might have been cheating on your share, Cy."

"Why didn't you tell me?"

"I was afraid, Cy, afraid they'd kill me or something. They were bad girls, you know that."

In her youth, Cora Harris had picked up the trick of crossing her fingers so as to negate a lie; so she had kept her fingers crossed all the time she had spoken to Skinner. She was sure Beth and Lori would forgive her destroying their reputations to get out of a tight spot.

Skinner sipped his coffee. "You'd better be getting somebody to help you. I'm not going to lose business because of poor service; you understand that?"

Cora said, "I don't know any girls who can work, Cy."

Skinner demanded, "What about that Lucinda? She'd be good for this place."

"Aw, you know Lucy doesn't like to diddle for the customers."

"What's wrong with diddling? She too good for that?"

Cora knew she had made a mistake. Skinner felt that diddling customers was just about the same as wiping tables or sweeping the floor. She did not reply. She took her coat back to the storeroom and put on her apron. She was going to go through the day on tenterhooks, waiting for Skinner to ask more questions about Beth and Lori. She dreaded the moment.

The Sunday conversation at LeGrau's had triggered a later conversation between Frank and his wife, Renee.

If Frank LeGrau satisfied everyone's image of a blacksmith—strong arms, barrel chest, gruff-looking face—then Renee LeGrau surely satisfied the stereotype of a Frenchwoman: she was beautiful. She was slight enough to be called willowy, tall enough to be considered svelte. She had a face one would have expected in an elegant salon rather than the coarse setting of a gold camp. She also had a personality that allowed her to blend into any community. And, even though she wore the standard calico dress, she did something to it that made it look like a Paris gown. On top of all of that, she possessed tremendous energy.

The LeGraus had some space that could be converted into a café, the holding stable Frank used for horses waiting to be shoed. Those horses could be moved out into a pen; the stable would make a nice-sized place for people to get a proper meal. Renee was excited about the prospect; she was a gregarious person who loved being with people and she had a marvelous talent for creating tasty dishes.

"Now," Frank had said firmly, "you don't go getting zat food all fancy. Understood?"

She gave a winsome smile.

"Meat and potatoes, Renee. Remember zat!"

"What about pies and biscuits?"

Frank was grievously spoiled by Renee's baking; her fruit-filled breakfast rolls bordered on being sexual for her romantic Frenchman.

He chuckled. "Not too much of zat stuff." Then, warmly, he added, "Maybe a little . . . now and zen."

On Sunday night the pair of them had gone to the stable and figured out the basic plan. At dawn on Monday he was sawing wood and hammering nails. By midmorning, he was needing lumber. Planks were delivered from the sawmill before noon, and a floor was set in place. In the meantime, two carpenters had built a few simple tables and chairs; by sundown two wood stoves were in place and fires started.

Renee had spent Monday collecting provisions, and three hours of the afternoon produced dainty sets of window curtains. Frank teased her about the homey touch, but admitted that it did add a touch of style to the café.

They collapsed into bed at ten o'clock on Monday night, smiling at the prospect of opening their new business the next morning.

CHAPTER 5

(Tuesday, November 11, 1862)

A quartet of men sat at a table near the stove in LeGrau's brand new café.

Nathaniel Langford held the match to his pipe and puffed softly to light the new tobacco. Speaking between his teeth as he watched the embers glow, he said, "That's shocking. Are you sure of the facts?"

Smith Ball, who had arrived on an early stagecoach, replied, "As sure as you can be about facts that come out of people's mouths."

Langford asked, "Is there anything we should be doing about it?"

"There's not much to be done until the authorities issue a warrant or something. I'd think that he's worth keeping an eye on, though."

Smith Ball fit improbably into the camp. He was just slightly overweight, which seemed strange for a man with so much energy. His cheeks were puffed, and speculation was that they became that way from the mouthfuls of nails he used in his bootmaking business. He had been sitting with Langford, Harry Phleger, and John Bozeman for only a couple of minutes when he mentioned that Cyrus Skinner was suspected of murder in Oro Fino, a gold camp 210 miles to the northwest of Bannack. The facts that Ball had related were skimpy at best. According to Ball, the previous August, about the end of the month, a prospector had struck a rich claim, panned out eighteen hundred dollars of gold, and sold the claim for an additional thousand dollars. The prospector had been a frequent patron of Cyrus Skinner's saloon in Oro Fino, and was last seen there as Skinner had closed for the night. The following day, Skinner had sold his saloon and had left town. That night, the body of the prospector was found in a diversion ditch just four hundred feet from Skinner's saloon. Ball said that the authorities in that part of the territory were looking for Skinner.

Langford gave the news some thought. He did not admire Skinner, but there was not much evidence against him. True, the man had arrived in early September with enough cash and gold to build and stock his saloon; but that could have been money made from the sale of his previous establishment. The best thing to do would be to wait and keep a wary eye on Cyrus Skinner.

Gold camps were rife with rumors best forgotten, Langford had come to learn. But there had been many bad incidents at Skinner's, and it had become a gathering place for the more disreputable types in the camp.

Nathaniel Langford looked around the busy café. He was pleased with the development. Earlier today he had offered to invest in the café. LeGrau, who was always cash shy, had accepted the deal, and was now at his anvil calculating how he would use Langford's three hundred dollars to improve the café. The deal was the first of many that would create a fortune for Nathaniel Langford in the territory. Because he could see the potential for the future, even the distant hope of statehood, Langford was determined to make sure that men like Cyrus Skinner did not ruin a good thing for the hundreds of honest people who were already in the camp and those who were sure to follow so long as the gold held out.

Talk at the table switched to Smith Ball's stories about the recent progress of the Civil War. Langford already knew most of what was being said, and he let his mind wander back to the shooting the previous Saturday night. Was it possible, he wondered, that Cyrus Skinner had been involved in the killing? If he had, and if it could be proven, then some action would have to be taken by the residents.

Langford was just about to ask Smith Ball a bit more about what had happened in Oro Fino when George Dart walked into the café and called to Mrs. LeGrau, "Renee, I need a hot cup of coffee and something to eat."

Harry Phleger called, "Hey, George, she ain't Renee anymore; we're calling her the head camp cook."

Dart made his way through the crowded café and pulled up the last empty chair available. He asked, "Where'd she get a name like that?"

"Well," Phleger said, "she's running this place good, and we need someplace to get honest cooking, so we named her head cook."

In the laughter, Langford's purpose was lost. Renee brought a steaming cup of coffee and two hot bran muffins to the table. Dart said, "I need this. I'm frozen from that damned Dunlap cabin; they don't have any heat in the place. Poor old Willie Bell is sick as hell there."

Langford asked, "Is he still fighting the mountain fever?"

Dart answered, "He hasn't stopped fighting for three days now. It's a damned shame we don't have a doctor here."

Langford said, "I think we should get the camp together tonight and figure out some way to convince a doctor to come, and figure out how to build a hospital while we're waiting for a doctor to get here."

Dart said, "Won't do Willie much good, I'm afraid.

He's looking real bad." Dart bit hungrily into one of the muffins and washed the mouthful down with a long drink of coffee. He wiped his mouth, then said, "Willie's nearly out of it, for sure. He was laying there, sweating like a pig, and kept asking me if I was a traveling man. Damnedest fool things come out of a dying man . . . asking if I was a traveler."

Nat Langford glanced immediately at Harry Phleger; both men's eyes asked a silent question. Langford turned back to Dart and said, "You're right, George, sickness does make a man say strange things. What did he say exactly?"

Dart drank some more coffee. "Just what I said, about being a traveler. Just kept asking."

Phleger asked, "What were his exact words, George? Can you remember?"

"He asked: 'Are you a traveler?' That's the exact words."

Langford looked at Phleger, then said, "Well, boys, I've got to be going." He stood. "Maybe we can set a camp meeting for tonight to see about getting a doctor."

The other men at the table nodded. Harry Phleger stood and aid, "I think I'll be going along with you, Nat. I've some work to do."

The two men left and walked up toward Main Street. They had just reached the corner when George Dart came hurrying up to them. The men stood for a moment, then they all smiled warmly. Langford asked Dart: "Are you a traveler?"

Dart nodded. "That's why I did that. I needed to find out if anyone else was available; Willie Bell is near dead."

Langford said, "Let's go."

"We'd better hurry," Dart said.

The Dunlap cabin was as good as many shelters in the camp; but many of the camp structures were little more than canvas tents. The Dunlap cabin had log walls, but the roof was only a large canvas tarp stretched across the top with a ridgepole providing a slight incline for snow and water to run off. William Bell was alone in the cabin. He was a pitiful sight. His cheeks had little under them other than bone; his eyes were sunken into dark pockets. His hair was slick with perspiration. He was resting on a straw-filled mattress and he was covered with three thin cotton blankets. Langford squatted next to Bell and asked, "How you feeling, Willie?"

Bell replied, "I'm feeling like hell, Nat. Really not good at all."

Langford touched Bell's forehead; the fever burned. "George here tells us you were asking if he traveled. Is that right?"

Bell could barely move his lips. Weakly, he said, "I was hoping to find some travelers."

Langford asked, "Where you been traveling, Willie?"

Willie drew on his strength and said, "I travel to the East." Then, after another struggle, he asked, "Where do you travel, Nat?"

Langford gripped Bell's bony hand. It was hot with fever. "We travel to the East, too, Willie. We're here with you."

Dart and Phleger carried a bench over to the pallet and sat down. There was a full minute of silence, silence except for the labored breathing of Willie Bell. Then, with a great effort, Bell said, "I'd like to have the Rites of the Order, Nat. Can you see to that?"

Langford looked at the two other men; each of them shrugged. He leaned down and said, "Willie, tell me about your Craft." The other two men leaned close so they could listen.

Bell spoke in a whisper, but after only a few words, he began a fit of coughing. Langford, still holding Bell's hand, reached out his other hand and wiped the perspiration from Bell's brow. "Take it easy, Willie. Don't try to speak."

Langford turned to his friends. "We owe it to him, I think."

"There's no question about that," Harry Phleger said. "If he wants it, we owe it."

George Dart added, "That's why I came looking for help. I think we should do it."

Langford leaned down to Bell and said, "Willie, we'll see you have proper Rites . . . that is, if you need them. Now, the most important thing is for you to get well. Do you hear me?"

Bell hissed, "You have to promise. Do you promise?"

Langford said, "You have our promise, Brother. Don't worry about that. Just think about getting better."

He stood up and walked to the sheet of canvas that functioned as a front door. As the other two men joined him, he said, "We've got to get him out of this wretched place. We can take him to my cabin. He'll sure die if we leave him here."

Phleger offered, "My cabin is closer."

Dart said, "We'll need some kind of wagon to move him."

Langford said, "Yes, we will. One of you stay here with him."

Dart volunteered; Langford and Phleger stepped outside and were deciding where to get a wagon when George Dart came out: "I don't think we have to get a wagon. He's dead."

The men went back inside and looked at Willie Bell.

Langford said, "Well, we couldn't save him, but we made a promise. We'd better get to that."

Hank Crawford finished butchering the two oxen that the camp would be buying the next day and had walked down to the creek just behind his shop to clean his knives and wash the blood from his hands. At the end of each day, he tried—and always failed—to purge himself of the pungent, rusty odor of blood. The heavy, musky scent seemed to permeate his clothing and skin. He was washing at an abandoned wooden flume. It had been built at the end of August by John White, on the site of his first strike. White's claim had played out quickly—and richly—and he was working two other claims further upstream. There was enough water still running through the leaky flume for Crawford's purposes.

Crawford had been trying to find a way to begin working the two gold claims he had bought from a despondent prospector, but he was making more money selling meat than others were from panning gold. Most merchants in the camp shared the same problem. The men who were prospecting were willing to pay whatever was demanded for goods and services so that they could prove out their claims. Prospecting took little initial capital: a shovel, a pick, a pan, and a bit of food, and the prospector was in business. But if a vein was discovered, a developer was needed to bring in equipment and hire workers; it took big money to accomplish that. Hank Crawford could not see how he was going to be able to get into his claims. He was making out well, sending his profits out to his bank in Salt Lake City, but he was not so far ahead that he could afford to speculate on a big scale. So his claims up on the creek were lying fallow. According to the camp's rules and regulations, he was going to have to get someone working them soon or the claims would lapse. A claim had to be worked one or two days a week so as to prevent speculation by outsiders from completely closing down a possible bonanza.

Crawford finished washing his knives and began scrubbing his hands with a bar of lye soap. He was tempted to give up the butcher shop and go digging in the bank of the creek, but he was proud of his trade, and liked the feeling that he was a part of a community.

From behind him, Nathaniel Langford called, "Hey, Hank, you nearly through?"

Crawford looked over his shoulder and saw his friend standing in the back door of the butcher shop. He called back, "I'll be done in a few minutes."

Langford started down the back steps. Crawford smiled as he watched his friend gingerly negotiate his way around the waste pile a few feet from the back door. He went back to cleaning his hands.

As Langford came up, he was hurriedly filling his pipe, and striking a match to the tobacco. Sucking on the stem, Langford said, "Dammit, Hank, I really don't know how you do it. That mess stinks!"

Crawford replied, "You get used to it, Nat; you get used to just about anything out here."

"I'll not get used to men dying, young men dying for no reason."

Crawford dipped his hands into the chilling water for a final rinse. "You still fretting over a doctor and a hospital? Don't be so worried; we'll have those things."

"That's not worrying me, right now. Willie Bell just died."

"Oh, damn," Crawford said. "He seemed to be a fine young man. I heard he was sick."

"Mountain fever."

"It takes a lot of them."

Both men were silent for a moment, then Langford said, "Willie asked for the Rites of the Order."

Crawford looked down at his hands; they seemed clean. He began wiping them with a towel. He asked, "Was Willie qualified?"

"I spoke to him of the Craft. He was struggling because he was just about dead, but he gave enough responses to convince me."

Crawford finished wiping his hands and reached to pick up his knives. "Well, there is you and me and Harry Phleger; that ain't many to give a proper ritual."

"And there's George Dart. He identified himself to me just a while back. He's a Brother."

"Still, four men seem like too few, leastwise as far as I remember from my lodge back in Maryland."

Langford said, "All we need is three. I opened and closed an informal lodge with just three. Sure as I stand here, we can bury a Brother with four!"

Crawford was wrapping his knives, his cleaver, and his

sharpening stone. Then, with everything neatened up, he said, "I think we should see if there are any more Brothers in the camp."

"I'm not opposed, but we will have to get the word out quickly. We should bury him tomorrow."

"Well, what do we have to lose? We can just start mentioning that there will be a Masonic funeral tomorrow morning."

"We'll have to investigate any who want to take part."

"We can do that tonight. Suppose we put the word out and call for a meeting tonight at my cabin. That won't take too long."

"I think we can do it that way. We can also talk to the men about getting a doctor here and a hospital built."

"It'll be nice to see how many Brothers there are in the camp. What would you guess?"

Langford thought back over the three months he had been in Bannack. "I'll put it at ten, counting us four."

Crawford shook his head. "I say eight, maybe eight, including us."

Crawford picked up his bundle, Langford knocked out the tobacco from his pipe, and the two men walked back up toward the butcher shop.

Crawford asked, "Like to go to LeGrau's for some coffee?"

"I'd like that, Hank. That would be real nice."

Cora Harris was having an awful time keeping up with the demands of the drinkers. She carried a tray to the insistent new arrivals, who were rude because she had taken so long with the order. As she set the glasses on the table, she wondered what Cyrus Skinner had been worrying about: there was no visible lack of business at the Elk Horn Saloon. As night fell the faithful drinkers had made their way back to Skinner's.

Two of the first men into the bar that evening had been Clay Barrow and Vic Voit. The two men who had met on opposite sides of a barroom brawl had become drinking buddies. She had seen similar developments before, but she had never been able to understand the mentality of men in that regard.

But that was not the only thing that confused her. Clay Barrow had diddled her three or four times before, and he must have told Vic Voit about her availability as a sporting lady. Yet Voit had not approached her, even though he had offered to walk her home after the bar closed. All he wanted to do was talk. Talk! She would have been nasty to him if he had not seemed so innocent; she was not about to play the pure girl from a church picnic for Voit or any man; she wanted to earn money.

This evening she was having to do so much waitressing that she could not even be nice to customers who might be able to afford a dollar or two for a diddle. Even Dick Sapp had become brisk with her when she refused to stay at his side while he was making his living at poker. Sapp had once offered to take her in on a full-time basis, but now, because she was having to work the whole saloon by herself, Sapp barely had time to say anything to her other than a gruff demand for whiskey.

Cora was beginning to wonder if the extra work since the shooting was starting to have an effect on her looks, because the men in the saloon had nearly stopped trying to fondle her as she passed, and she had not had an offer for her services since Friday night. She began to wish that she had gone away with Beth and Lori. Maybe she should leave when the next stage came.

Skinner yelled: "Cora, get your ass over here!" He was standing at the poker table where Dick Sapp was running a game. As she approached, Skinner reached out and grabbed her arm roughly. He snarled, "Mister Sapp tells me you been neglecting your job."

Cora bristled. "Dick Sapp! You lousy bastard! I ain't been neglecting nobody; you know that!"

Sapp looked up, grinning. "Take it easy, darling. All I said to Cy was that he ought to be getting more help."

Skinner was still gripping Cora's left arm and his

fingernails were digging into her skin. But Dick Sapp made her more furious. She snapped, "You are a real bum, you know that, Dick? I'm doing the best I can. . . ."

She was fighting to hold back tears, and not just because of Dick Sapp or Skinner; she was dead tired from work. Before she realized what was happening, Skinner was yanking her away, almost dragging her to the back of the saloon and his office. As soon as they were inside, he flung her across the small room. She banged her leg against a stack of whiskey crates; her thigh ached from the impact. Skinner crossed the room and slapped Cora strongly on the side of her head. There was a loud ringing in her ears, and tiny flecks of bright lights bounced around in her eyes. Skinner snarled, "You learn to be good to my customers, bitch! I've had enough of your attitude."

Cora started to speak but her jaw hurt. She tried again, but the evil look in Skinner's eyes halted her. She had seen Skinner angry before, but the look was different this time; he had the look of a devil. Trying to keep her voice calm, she said, "Cy, take it easy. I didn't do nothing wrong."

Skinner hit her again. She fell back across the whiskey crates, and he grabbed her by the front of her dress and yanked her to him. She heard her bodice rip and, for the first time in her life, she was afraid that she might be killed. He said, "I'm going to teach you a lesson, smart bitch. Tonight you stay after work."

Her eyes betrayed her silent thought: *Not on your life, Cyrus Skinner!* and he used his free hand to slam her again. This time, she flew across the room and landed on her back on his small desk. She rolled on her side. The front of her dress had separated, exposing her breasts. She was fumbling at the cloth, trying to close the gap, when Vic Voit appeared in the doorway.

Voit demanded, "What's going on here?"

Skinner spun around, shouting, "Leave me alone!"

Voit tried to make his young voice carry some of the

mean authority that had just been thrown at him, but he still sounded like the young man he was as he said, "Don't hurt that lady."

"This whore? You call her a lady?" Skinner snatched Cora's hands away from her chest and snapped, "She's halfway undressed. You pay me a dollar, and I'll give you the rest of her. Bare naked!"

Voit stepped forward, and Cora saw Clay Barrow standing behind Voit. Barrow grabbed Voit by the shoulder, trying to pull him back out of the room.

Skinner demanded, "Clay, you with this little pup?"

Barrow answered, "He's had a couple of drinks, Cy, no harm done." And Barrow tugged on Voit again.

"Skinner," Voit said, "you got no right to beat up on a lady."

The tableau was frozen in front of Cora's eyes. Skinner had once boasted to her that he had punished a bad waitress by stripping her bare and then making her service every patron in his bar and Cora had a vision of such a thing happening to her. There was a split second where Skinner seemed to be deciding whether to slap Cora around or to go after Vic Voit. In that instant, she rolled off the desk, scrambled across the floor, and made it out of the office between the legs of Vic Voit. Before anyone realized what had happened, she was on her feet and running out the back door of the saloon. Behind her, she heard a roar from Skinner and then a yelp from Vic Voit as the battle began in Skinner's office.

Cora did not care; she was free.

She clutched the front of her dress. Night had taken a strong hold on the air and she was shaking from the cold, but she would not stop. She ran all the way to the Stinsons' cabin and burst through the front door breathing heavily.

Mrs. Stinson was at the table, sewing. Carl Stinson was asleep on the small sofa, and the children were obviously in bed. Mrs. Stinson looked up. "Child, what has happened to you?"

Cora nervously said, "Nothing, yet! I'm just glad to make it here."

Carl Stinson woke up and he asked, "What's wrong?"

His wife said, "Nothing, Carl, go back to sleep; I'm going to make tea for Cora and me."

Hank Crawford's cabin was the site of the meeting set for seven o'clock.

Crawford, Langford, Dart, and Phleger had spent the afternoon passing the word that there was to be a meeting of Master Masons that night in the Crawford cabin. They spoke to everyone they met; they also drew up half a dozen small handwritten notices which they posted around the camp. The posters stated: "Brother William Bell, AF&AM, passed from our camp this morning. Those qualified and wishing to honor his request for a proper burial are asked to meet tonight at seven o'clock in the cabin of Hank Crawford."

By six-thirty, a surprisingly large crowd had gathered in front of Crawford's cabin, many more than either Crawford or Langford had guessed. By seven o'clock, it was obvious that the modest cabin would not be large enough; over a hundred men had shown up. The crowd was told to go on over to the Roundhouse, where an investigation of those claiming to be Master Masons would take place. Langford and his three friends spent until midnight examining those who came. An amazing total of seventy-six residents were proven to be qualified.

A weary Nathaniel Langford smiled as he closed the small leather-bound ledger he had used to list the names of those men who had passed the examination. He looked across the table at George Dart and said, "That was quite a shock."

Dart grinned back. "A total of seventy-six; a surprise, as well as a shock. We have enough to start a lodge, by golly. How do you start a lodge, Nat?"

"I haven't the slightest idea how that is done." Then, in a more lively tone, he added, "But, I'm going to find out."

Hank Crawford came to the table and sat down. He said, "I could sure use a drink."

From across the room, Harry Phleger said, "I could, too."

Langford yawned. "To go to Skinner's would be an insult after the good experience we had here tonight. I'd still join you in a drink, though."

George Dart said, "I've got a bottle at my cabin. Shall I go get it?"

Langford pulled out his pocket watch. "It is quarter past twelve. Maybe we should just call it a night."

"We'll have a big day tomorrow," Phleger said. "It'd probably be wise to get to bed."

Langford said, "We'll need an apron."

"And we'll have to get evergreen boughs," Dart added.

Crawford stood and crossed the room to a chest sitting by the far wall. He opened the chest and took out a white leather apron. Holding it up, he said, "It's mine, but I'll gladly donate it to Willie. Is that okay, Nat?"

Langford nodded. "I'm sure it is right, Hank, and it is a fine gesture, too."

Phleger said, "I'll get the evergreens in the morning. It shouldn't be too much trouble."

Langford said, "I've asked a few of the newcomers to meet me up on the knoll north of the camp to dig the grave. We should be all ready by nine o'clock. That's when I told everyone to be there."

Dart stood and said, "I'm ready to leave."

Langford said, "It's a good thing we did tonight, Brothers. I feel it portends better things to come." Then, with a smile, he added, "Now, let's go get those drinks. We earned them."

CHAPTER 6

(Wednesday, November 12, 1862)

Dawn came slowly; fast-moving clouds kept hiding the light of the sun. Henry Plummer had been awake for over an hour, but Jack Cleveland slept heavily, mumbling unclear words as if he was still as drunk as he had been when he wrapped himself in his blanket.

Plummer had added a few small pieces of wood to the campfire but he had not started boiling coffee, because he did not want Cleveland to wake up; Plummer wanted some time alone. He had a lot to think about.

The time he had spent with the Vails at the Sun River Farm had been strange to him: the comfortable routine of family life, meeting Electa Bryan. The ordinary life of ordinary people was an enigma to Plummer. He had, for so long, lived in the netherworld of society that he had forgotten what it was like to live with something more than daily survival on his mind. He was used to plotting and scheming; he was not used to an atmosphere of family unity. When he had first stopped at the farm, he had been mildly attracted to Electa and had thought to seduce her, then pass on out of her life. But Electa had awakened an emotion that he could not define. He had heard people talking about a thing called love, but he knew that what he was feeling did not qualify for that serious term. Still, there was more to this than a casual carnal conquest. He was having to deal with an unknown. He was confused, thinking of getting away, running free of the mental turmoil, but he also felt strongly that he would return to Sun River and marry Electa.

Plummer did not like traveling with Jack Cleveland. The two of them had been acquaintances for nearly three years and in that time the two men had shared not only adventures but the bounty of illegal activities. They had had a type of camaraderie built on experiences that had caused their victims financial, physical, or mental injury; Plummer had not cared what happened to others. His attitude had been just fine for him back when he had been running with various bands of outlaws. There had been an excess of drinking and womanizing and Plummer considered himself somewhat of an expert in both of those matters. He counted whiskey drunk in barrels and women seduced in legions. Associating with men such as Jack Cleveland had been satisfactory in the recent past—but Plummer's life seemed in a process of transition.

Plummer looked over at Cleveland, whose arms and legs were twisted around a single blanket. He was annoyed. They were beginning their third day on the tiring, boring trail. With another companion—and in earlier days—it would have been tolerable, but Cleveland was a bore. He seldom spoke; when he did, it was to speak lewdly about Electa. Plummer still wanted to keep his marriage plans to Electa a secret from Cleveland, because Cleveland was such an unpredictable, wicked soul.

Despite this, Plummer knew he needed Cleveland. For Plummer to benefit from the new gold camp at Bannack, he would need men, men like Jack Cleveland. Plummer might face a well-organized, tightly structured camp, and then his criminal pickings would be slim. Or perhaps the camp would be a bawdy, rowdy place. That would be to Plummer's liking, but he would still need men of Cleveland's ilk, men who were able to go to work quickly.

Cleveland stirred, rubbed a dirty hand over his bearded face, then looked at the fire. He asked, "No coffee?"

Plummer picked up his water-filled battered blue-enamel coffeepot. He set the pot directly down on the coals of the fire and dropped in a handful of ground coffee. Still without speaking, he rose and went to a nearby bush where he snapped off a thin twig which he took back to the fire and set across the top of the pot to prevent the coffee from boiling over. Then he said, "Get up, Jack, I want to be riding soon."

Cleveland worked his way out of the tangle of blanket and walked over to urinate on the same bush where Plummer had plucked the twig. Plummer said, mildly, "I hope you didn't use that bush last night."

Cleveland came back as he buttoned his fly. "I don't rightly remember; maybe I pissed in your boot."

Plummer shook his head. There had been a time when that feeble joke might have seemed funny; now Plummer had less tolerance for such ribaldry.

Cleveland began fixing up his bedroll and added, "I do remember one thing about last night; I dreamed about that poontang up at Sun River."

Plummer bristled.

Cleveland went on, "She came to me and pulled up her skirt and spread her . . ."

Plummer jumped up. "Goddammit, Jack, get her off your mind!"

Cleveland grinned. "She sure seems on your mind, Henry. I got to tell you, you been a pain in the arse the past couple of days."

"I'm just wanting to concentrate on what we've got ahead of us. Let's quit talking about women."

"Hell, we ain't talked at all about women, Henry. What'd you do, take that woman and yer ashamed to tell yer old buddy?"

Plummer did not answer. He grabbed his tack and stalked off toward the tethered horses. "Let's saddle up. We've got miles to make today."

"Saddle up? Shit, we ain't even had coffee. I ain't going no place without coffee in my gut."

Plummer went on and saddled his horse, taking longer than necessary, simply to stay away from Cleveland. When the coffee had boiled, he went back to the fire and poured himself a cup of the bitter, thick liquid. Cleveland did not talk anymore while they broke camp. When they were in their saddles, he tried to taunt Plummer with another description of the dream, but Plummer merely spurred his horse forward, out of listening range.

Cleveland was also showing the strain of the trip; he was getting sick and tired of Plummer's attitude. He hoped that things would change once they arrived in Bannack. If pickings were good, it should bring Plummer back to being the man he used to be.

The day had dawned brightly in Bannack with a silvery frost decorating the ground and trees. On a good-sized knoll, northeast of the camp, the original prospectors had allocated two acres of land that held little hope for producing any gold. The knoll was known as Graveyard Hill. Here, William Bell was about to be put to rest in his coffin.

Many of those who climbed the knoll were interested only in seeing a Masonic service; few of them could afford time to do more than bury the dead quickly and get on with living. The others in the gathering were the seventy-six Master Masons who had discovered each other the previous night. People were dressed in their everyday clothes. The prospectors had slicked down their hair, and the housewives had doffed their aprons. Those in business and the trades came in their work attire; only a few of the Masons had put on their Sunday best.

Because he seemed to know what he was doing, Nathaniel Langford was appointed to act as Master, and Langford in turn directed Hank Crawford to act as Chaplain.

Six pallbearers had borne the coffin up the knoll, and it was resting next to the freshly dug grave on two sawhorses. Langford stood at the head of the coffin. He was pleased with the turnout, even though he realized many were there merely as sightseers. Nothing of this sort had happened in the camp before, and few in the crowd could remember a Masonic service being performed in any other mountain gold camp.

Langford said gently, "We thank you for coming this morning. We will not be long, because we know that all of you must be about the work of the living. But we have come here to bid our farewell to William Bell, and that is what we will do now."

He turned to Crawford, who handed Langford a sprig of evergreen. Then Langford intoned, "Brethren and friends: From time immemorial it has been the custom among the fraternity of Ancient Free and Accepted Masons, at the request of a Brother, to accompany his remains to the place of interment and reverently place him among the peaceful surroundings of his final resting place. In conformity with this usage, we have assembled in the character of Masons to offer up to his memory before the world this tribute of our affection, thereby demonstrating the esteem in which we hold him and our close adherence to the noble principles of our fraternity."

The mourners and spectators had formed in a semicircle near the crest of the knoll. Nearly everyone had a good view of the proceedings. At the east end of the arc, Cora Harris and Lucinda Simons had found a place toward the back of the crowd. At the far end of the gathering, Vic Voit and Clay Barrow were paying as much attention to Cora and Lucinda as they were to the ceremony. They could see the girls were enjoying the spectacle; Vic Voit wished he could get closer to Cora, but the service was too solemn to make such an obvious move.

Across the crowd, Cora whispered to Lucinda, "Ever seen so many folks?"

Lucinda whispered back, "Not in a long time. It's sort of nice." She was letting faint fragments of the burial of her husband drift into her mind.

Cora said, "I don't see Cy Skinner. I bet he'd like this crowd in his saloon."

Lucinda nudged Cora in the ribs and said, "Hush, people are looking."

People were not looking at Cora; they were merely doing what everyone else was doing, enjoying the peaceful moment by glancing around at their friends. The residents of the camp were essentially law-abiding. Some had come to the mountains to get away from the Civil War raging back east; some were there hoping to find their fortunes. Once in the mountains there was one common bond: survival. None of Cyrus Skinner's cohorts were in the gathering, and not many of Skinner's customers were there, either. When the word had spread around the camp that a special funeral was going to be offered for a man few people knew, Skinner and his ilk had made derisive comments and poked fun at the event. Most of those on the knoll were pleased that the rowdy crowd had stayed away. With the church service the previous Sunday and now a proper funeral, the residents were trying very hard to think of the camp as a home, even though they knew they were there only until the gold ran out. Hopefully, it might run a long time.

Cora whispered again, "Mister Langford sounds almost like a preacher, don't he?"

Lucinda replied, "He has a nice voice; now be quiet."

Langford had finished the prayer, and he turned to Crawford, who handed over something. Most people in the crowd could not see what it was. Holding the object up, Langford said, "The white leather apron is an emblem of innocence and the badge of a Mason, more ancient than the Golden Fleece or Roman Eagle, more honorable than the Star and Garter, or any other order. Its pure and spotless surface is to us an ever-present reminder of purity of life and rectitude of conduct, a never-ending argument for nobler deeds, for higher thoughts and greater achievements. This apron, a symbol of service, I now place over the body of William Bell, who has served faithfully and well."

While Langford was setting the apron on the top of the coffin, Cora said, "That's kind of nice, ain't it?"

Lucinda did not answer. She did not want to encourage Cora to talk.

Langford stood back, held up a sprig of evergreen, and said, "The evergreen, which once marked the temporary resting place of one illustrious in Masonic history, is an emblem of our enduring faith in the immortality of the soul."

Cora rose up onto her toes to see better. She asked Lucinda, "What's he doing?"

Lucinda smiled and said, "He's talking, Cora. I thought you were a preacher's daughter; didn't you ever go to a funeral?"

"Never. Momma wouldn't let me. I wish I knew what he was doing."

Lucinda had to stifle a giggle. Cora was twisting and stretching so hard that it almost looked as if she would fall.

Langford ended his ritual by placing the evergreen on the coffin under the apron. Then, as he spoke again, the pallbearers eased the coffin down into the grave. After saying the obituary and committal, Langford indicated for Crawford to speak as Chaplain.

Crawford said, "Grant unto our Brother eternal rest and refreshment, O Lord, and let the mystic light perpetually shine on him. The Lord bless us and keep us; the

Lord make His face to shine upon us and be gracious unto us; the Lord lift up the light of His countenance upon us and give us peace, both now and forever- more. Amen."

From the other Master Masons came, "So mote it be."

There was a long moment while those on the knoll thought their private thoughts. Some dwelled on the passing of a fellow being, some gave themselves over to wonder about their own future in the frontier, whether they would pass away and be the object of a similar ceremony. And there were a few, like Cora Harris, who respected the intentions of the others, but knew that none of it applied to her. She saw herself as one of the mountain hummingbirds that had been in the camp when she first arrived and then had disappeared. She had panicked, thinking the birds had all died; then someone had explained that the birds had migrated south. She liked that word: "migrated." That was how she looked upon death—when that time came, she would simply migrate to another place where death was not a threat; she would never be put into the ground like poor Willie Bell.

And there was Lucinda. Lucinda who had just two months previously seen her bridegroom buried in the ground outside Fort Hall. Lucinda knew the finality of death, and to her belief, the living had a duty to go forward, no matter how great the pain of loss. At that moment, she felt as if it was time to let her mourning drift away from her thoughts. She had done her duty to her Beau. Now it was time to reenter life. She looked at Cora and said, "We'd better go."

Cora asked, "Is it over?"

"It's over."

Cora spotted Vic Voit and Clay Barrow at the far edge of the crowd, beginning to walk toward her. She elbowed Lucinda. "That's the one I told you about; the young one who fought Cy so that I could get away."

Lucinda looked in the same direction. For the first

time since they had known each other, Cora had taken notice of a man in any way other than as a customer. It was almost as if Cora was letting some romance come into her life. Cora urged, "Let's move! I don't want to talk to him." The two women hurried down the path leading back to the camp.

Voit saw Cora and Lucinda drawing away and he came to a halt, grabbing Barrow's arm. "Hold it, Clay. They're gone."

Barrow argued, "We can catch 'em."

"I don't want to look a fool."

"Forget looking a fool, I want to get next to that Lucinda. You ever smell that gal?"

Voit laughed. "What do you mean, did I ever smell her?"

"Vic, that gal smells great. She smells like bread and jam all at the same time. Shit, I like that smell."

Voit said, "Well, I got my eye on that Cora Harris. Danged if she would just say thanks for last night; I'd sure like that."

"Cora ain't gonna say thanks. You'll be lucky if she tells you to go to hell; she's that kind."

"She ain't."

Barrow gave a chuckle. "You'll find out."

"We'd better get to work."

The Sunday after the fight in the Elk Horn Saloon, Barrow had run into Voit, who still played innocent about hitting Clay. Barrow had told Voit there was an opening on the Kohrs' claim. Like about half of the men in the camp, Clay and Vic hired out to work for someone else. Con Kohrs, who owned the claim, had given them the first part of the morning off to attend the funeral. Voit said, "Con is up talking with Mister Langford. Maybe he'll give us another hour to get some coffee at LeGrau's."

Barrow watched Lucinda and Cora disappear down the path. He scratched his chin and said, "You think Lucinda will be there?"

Voit answered, "How do I know? What do we have to lose?" Vic's hope was that Cora Harris would be at LeGrau's Café.

Barrow agreed; there was nothing to lose, and the two men walked up the slight incline to where a group of Masons had stopped to talk. Barrow figured that Con Kohrs was a member because he seemed to be in the thick of the conversation. Barrow approached Kohrs and said, "That was real nice, Con. I think I'd like to be joining up with your bunch."

Clay Barrow had no idea what he was talking about; he was merely trying to ingratiate himself with his boss. Kohrs was a broad-shouldered man who was starting to go bald even though he was only twenty-nine years old. He wore a beard that was more of a muttonchop trimmed close.

Con Kohrs smiled. "Funny you should say that, Clay, we were just talking about that sort of thing."

Nat Langford interjected, "We can't let you in right now, Clay, because we don't have a lodge here yet. But we're thinking about applying for a dispensation to open a lodge. When we do, we'll be talking to you."

All Clay Barrow was after was a bit of time to go and see Lucinda Simons. He smiled sheepishly and tried to speak, but all he could get out was a stammer. Seeing his friend's problem, Vic Voit took up the cause and said, "We'd both like to know more about that, Con. You let us know, okay?"

Kohrs smiled. His smile quickly turned to a frown when Voit added, "We're going to go and talk about that beautiful service . . . down at LeGrau's. Is that okay?"

Kohrs' frown stayed on his face, but he was feeling very good about the funeral and he himself was wanting to stay and talk some more with Langford. He said, "You boys take a half hour or so; I'll see you at the claim then."

As Vic and Clay hightailed it down the hill, Langford said to Kohrs, "They seem to be a good pair of boys."

Kohrs shook his head. "Those two make one good boy.

That Barrow fellow is the worst man I've ever hired. But Voit—even though he's only been with me one day, I know that Voit does double duty covering Barrow."

"Why don't you fire Barrow?"

Kohrs grinned. "If I fire Barrow, then Voit will walk out. I'm getting the work done because Voit is such a hard worker."

"They are loyal to each other."

"Seems that way, but they've only known each other for a few days."

"I've learned that friendships firm up pretty quickly out here."

"I guess you're right, Nat."

"They seem like a sturdy pair."

"They are that."

"That is a good thing for us to look for. If we form a lodge, we'll need men with loyalty." Then he added, with a soft smile, "And men who are strong enough to help build a lodge."

Kohrs nodded. "I'd go for the Voit boy, but I might be tempted to blackball Clay Barrow. I'm not sure Barrow is all that reputable."

"Well, all of that is moot until we are able to gain a charter, and we'd better be getting to that. A great thing happened here today."

Hank Crawford said, "I think we all agree with you, Nat. It was a remarkable turnout."

Langford said, "You know, there were seventy-six good men and true who dropped the evergreen into the grave of Willie Bell. As we stood around the grave with uncovered heads and listened to the impressive language of our beautiful ritual, I felt more than on any former occasion how excellent a thing it is for a man to be a Mason. It is quite fitting that we use this moment to begin the work needed to form our lodge; the time is right."

Moving down the hill, Voit kept having to remind Barrow not to run. All of the other people returning from the funeral were acting with a modest decorum out of respect for the occasion.

But Barrow was barely able to hold back. "Hurry, dammit, Vic! We ain't got that much time."

Lucinda Simons had stopped in at LeGrau's on opening day and Cora had tagged along, looking for a job. The fear of going back to Skinner's was so strong that she was willing to do almost anything to make a living, anything other than returning to the Elk Horn. Cora had been dismayed when Renee LeGrau had tried to hire Lucinda away from her job at Kustar's Bakery, yet Renee had politely turned away Cora's request for employment. Cora knew that she carried the stigma of being a sporting lady and saloon waitress. Her hope was that Renee would think about lowering her standards. There were not that many women in the camp to fill jobs. Lucinda had privately decided to intercede for Cora on the grounds that the only way Cora would become respectable was if someone gave her a chance.

That day LeGrau's was packed with funeral-goers socializing before returning to work. Lucinda and Cora were forced to share a table with several prospectors. One of them, a craggy-looking man named Drury Underwood who had been in the camp since the early days, made a joke of Cora being out of work and kiddingly suggested she come and dig on his claim. The remark had been made lightly, but Cora, seemingly affected by the solemn funeral, burst out crying.

For the first couple of moments, Lucinda and the men at the table thought Cora was overreacting, or, at worst, just not taking a joke. But the tears, once turned on, did not stop quickly. After a few seconds, the crying was accompanied by a moaning wail; everyone in the place began looking to see what could be causing such turmoil.

Lucinda was embarrassed, the prospectors were confused, and Cora was bleating like a sheep caught in a ditch.

Those customers who did not know Cora Harris

assumed the bawling female was a sister, wife, or daughter of the man who was just buried. Their general reaction to the loud display of mourning was to taste their chocolate sour or their coffee bitter; they left quickly. Those who knew Cora were just as confused. Some thought—for no good reason—that she was a former lover of Willie Bell; some thought—with very good reason—that the men at the table had insulted her and that a fight was sure to ensue. Many opted to get out quickly, and within a couple of minutes LeGrau's Café was half-empty. Drury Underwood and his two companions made feeble excuses to Lucinda and the men were out the front door just behind the first who departed.

Renee LeGrau stormed over to the table where Lucinda sat bewildered and Cora sat weeping. Renee demanded, "What is going on here? Are you trying to turn my place into another one of Cy Skinner's bawdy houses?"

Lucinda was still speechless; the tirade triggered more wailing from Cora.

Renee demanded, "What the devil is going on?"

Lucinda found her voice and said that Cora had just started crying; there was no apparent explanation.

Renee was tired. The day before she had done well, but she had noticed some weak spots in food preparation that needed strengthening if she was going to be successful. Because she was not completely herself, she took a firm hold on Cora's shoulder and gave a slight shake. She ordered, "Stop this crying right now! It is no good for you!"

Cora slowed down slightly, but could not stop sobbing. Lucinda said, "Cora, what's the matter?"

Cora moaned, "I'm so sorry to be in this dumb camp . . . I hate the mountains! Everything is rotten here."

Renee and Lucinda looked at each other in confusion, because Cora Harris had a reputation for being one of the tough ladies in the camp. She had been working in a saloon, cavorting with drunks, and living a fast life. Now, Cora was talking like a reformed young lady, and the words did not fit the reputation.

Renee sat down at the table and eased up her grip on Cora's shoulder. "What's hit you so hard, Cora?"

For the next couple of minutes Cora babbled on, making little sense. Lucinda and Renee were able to gather only that Cora was fed up with the life she had been leading, that the ceremony up on Graveyard Hill had sobered her up, that there was no way she could get out of the life she had been leading. Finally, Cora ran out of steam. Renee looked at Lucinda and asked, "Do you think she's serious?"

Lucinda did not know what to say. This . . . this act; yes, Lucinda thought, it had to be an act. But what was the goal? What was Cora trying to accomplish? "I guess all that has been going on has gotten to her. I don't really know."

The three women sat there for another full minute. Renee took their cups and went to get refills. She brought back a cup for herself as well and, as she sat down, asked Cora, "Are you really done with working in Skinner's and all of the other things that I've heard about you?"

For the funeral, Cora had put on a modest, high-necked white blouse that was buttoned all the way to the throat. She wore a black wool full-length skirt, and her hair was demurely piled up onto the top of her head in the manner of a schoolmarm. She was not wearing any of the makeup that she normally used; she looked quite innocent. The tears streaming down her cheeks did not distract from the image; Cora looked for all the world like a redeemed woman. Weakly, as if all her strength had just been flushed out of her with the tears, she said, "Renee, you don't know how bad that life was. I hated it . . . every minute of it."

Lucinda Simons studied Cora intently. In the few weeks she had known Cora, there had never been any such attitude. In fact, Cora had unsuccessfully tried to involve Lucinda in the sordid life of a saloon girl. Lucinda had never wanted to make a transition from widow to wanton, and Cora's attitude had resolved itself into a good-natured sort of kidding. Hearing Cora profess remorse made Lucinda suspicious, but she did not speak.

Renee LeGrau, despite being tired and physically taxed by the demands of the new café, could not avoid her one blind spot in dealing with others; she collapsed at the sight of anyone gripped by remorse. Frank LeGrau had found his wife's failing a drawback in doing business, but he accepted what he considered a flaw because she worked extra hard when her judgment proved to be in error. Renee asked, "Why don't you just leave, Cora? If it was me, I'd leave right now."

Cora nodded. She lifted her hand and wiped a tear away as she said, "I know what you mean, Renee. But I don't have that kind of money."

Lucinda knew that Cora had three full leather pouches of gold hidden back in their room. Lucinda still did not speak; she was trying to analyze just what was going on.

"Cora," Renee demanded, "are you being honest with me about wanting to leave Bannack?"

Cora nodded, then added, sniffling, "Renee, I ain't been more honest about anything in my whole life."

"Swear to God?"

Cora's slight hesitation was a tip for Lucinda, but Renee did not sense the moment. Cora said, "You bet I do, Renee. I swear I want out."

Renee pursed her lips as if she did not want to taste the words that were in her mouth. She rubbed her eyes, scratched her neck, then finally said, "If I gave you a job, would you save your money and go back home?"

More tears from Cora. With a sniffle, she answered, "I'd do anything to make some honest money, Renee, anything." A gulp, a hard swallow, and she added, "I'd even scrub these floors for you if you'd let me."

Lucinda sat back, looked at the ceiling as if she had

become a student of cobwebs, then stared at the blank wall across the room. She could not look at Cora.

Renee waited a long time before she said, "Well, Cora, if you promise to behave yourself I'll give you a job; I could use some help here."

Cora gave a pathetic smile, then whimpered, "I sure do thank you, Renee. I'll do a good job."

Renee stood and said, "Well, you go get into some working clothes—" She cut herself off, gave a warm grin, and said, "Not any of those saloon frillies, Cora. Get into some honest working clothes and come right back here; we'll be having a busy lunch today, I suspect."

Cora offered, "I can start right now."

"No, those things are too nice. There's grease splattering in the kitchen and there's splashing from washing the dishes. That blouse and skirt look good enough to wear to church. You do plan to go to church this Sunday, don't you?"

Cora wiped off the tears from her face and said, "I'll be at church, you bet."

Lucinda stood, spoke a quick good-bye, and headed quickly out the door, leaving Cora standing with Renee.

Renee, confused, asked, "What's wrong with Lucy?"

Sweetly, too sweetly, like sugar flowers on a wedding cake, Cora said, "She's probably touched at your kindness, Renee."

That added bit of syrup nearly lost Cora her job before she even went to work. Renee LeGrau might have a weak spot for people in trouble, but she was also perceptive enough to sense when someone might be taking advantage; she bristled for a moment. Cora realized she had overplayed her act, but she recovered with "I mean that Lucy is probably pleased to see me doing some honest work . . . for a change."

Renee's instincts generally provided her with good counsel, but the fact was that she needed help in the café, and besides, that wailing performance had been so dramatic that she was convinced it could not have been false. "Well, hurry, then. I want you back here quickly; there's work to be done."

Cora batted her eyes and smiled, but kept quiet. Cora had also developed her own instincts, and she knew when to quit. She went out the door to find Lucinda standing a few feet up Fourth Street, her arms folded and her eyes flaming with indignation. Cora approached her friend with caution.

Up the street, at the corner of Fourth and Main, Vic Voit and Clay Barrow stood watching the two women.

When Vic and Clay had arrived outside LeGrau's Café, they had been met by the outpouring of customers escaping Cora's dramatic crying jag. Vic had asked one of the exiting patrons what was going on—he could hear the wailing inside the café—and when he was told it was Cora, he decided he would stay away until he knew what had happened to her. He and Clay had been waiting up Fourth Street.

Barrow said, "Let's get down there."

Vic was reluctant to put himself in the position of being unable to help the woman who had taken his fancy. He hesitated, then said, "Let's wait and see."

Barrow snapped, "Vic, you've had me waiting long enough. I want to see if that Lucinda will give me a sniff."

Vic agreed to move, but slowly; he also agreed to try to talk to the girls. Even as they started down the street, Vic grabbed Clay, halting their walk. He could see Cora leaning against LeGrau's building with one hand over her stomach, the other hand up at her mouth. She looked for all the world as if she were about to be ill. Lucinda was waving her hands in the air. Vic could not hear what was being said, but Lucinda seemed to be angry. Vic said, "We ain't going down there . . . not yet."

Clay also felt reluctant to become involved with a woman in the midst of vomiting. He halted; the two men waited.

In front of the café, Cora was giggling so hard that she

ached. Lucinda was so angry that she could not muster the words she wanted to throw at her friend.

It was good for Cora that Renee LeGrau could not see out the front of the building; Cora's job would have gone down the ditch.

Cora, bubbling out words between giggles, said, "I swear, that was the smoothest thing I have ever done, and y'all had better believe me."

Lucinda hissed, "You should be ashamed of yourself, Cora Harris. I never saw such a disgusting performance."

Cora, still snickering, said, "But I got myself a job."

"At the price of lying. No good will come of that. What's happened to you?"

"I'll do my job; I always have worked hard, even for Cy Skinner."

Lucinda weakened. Ever since they had met, Lucinda had found Cora's impish ways irresistible. She said, "Renee has put her trust in you; you can't fail her."

Cora became serious for a moment. "I will, Lucy, I'll do right by her." Then, coyly, she added, "I might even stop messing around with the damned prospectors."

Lucinda did not reply. She had never chosen to pass judgment on Cora's way of life; that was Cora's business.

Cora said, "I'd better be getting back to the cabin and put on a work dress; might as well start out right."

The two women began walking down Fourth Street to Creek Lane. Up near the corner of Main and Fourth, Clay Barrow groused at Vic Voit, "See! They're going to get away from us." He yanked the hat off his head and slapped his thigh angrily. "Gol-dern it, Vic, you went and screwed us up again."

Vic Voit studied the girls before he said, "It looks like Cora's okay. Let's go catch them."

Barrow came to life and grabbed his friend's arm. "We'll go this way."

Clay led Vic running west along Main Street; people shook their heads at the two young prospectors playing games when they should be working. The two reached the corner of Third Street, then went full tilt until they reached the corner with Creek Lane. Vic Voit had a hard time keeping up, because he was wearing gum rubber boots, but he slid to a halt beside Clay just as Cora and Lucinda came to the corner.

Trying desperately to cover his shortness of breath, Clay said, "Howdy, ladies, fine day, ain't it?"

Vic Voit yanked his hat off and tried to mouth a greeting, but no words came. Cora gave an insulting "Hrrumph" and Lucinda looked straight ahead as they walked on. Clay Barrow reached out and grabbed Cora's arm. There was no way he would have been so abrupt with Lucinda.

Cora snapped, "Clay Barrow, get your hands off me!"

Clay pulled harder, trying to stop Cora. Vic Voit snatched at Clay's arm and demanded, "Leave the lady alone."

Clay laughed. "All I want her to do is stop. Hell, she knows to do what I say. Right, Cora?"

Cora swung a roundhouse punch at Clay's head. He ducked, and she was only able to land a glancing blow. Vic Voit jumped in and yanked at Clay's arm, and that gave the two women a chance to be clear of the two men, who were redirected from romance to arguing about what had just happened.

Creek Lane ran parallel to Grasshopper Creek and was pockmarked with holes dug early in the development of the camp, but it was possible to walk easily around the diggings. As they hurried away from Vic and Clay, Cora said, "That young one is kind of cute."

"You said you were through with that life."

Cora came back, "I'm not thinking about him like that; I think he's kind of cute, that's all."

Back at the Stinson cabin, Lucinda helped Cora pick out a dress that would not offend Renee LeGrau. Lucinda said, "Now, you behave yourself, and things are going to be better for you. I think it is shameful the way you tricked Renee but maybe some good will come of this."

"Don't worry. I'll show you I can handle working at that café; just don't worry."

So Cora Harris began a respectable job at LeGrau's Café.

That was how she came to be the first person to meet Henry Plummer when he rode into town.

Henry Plummer was fed up with Jack Cleveland and Cleveland had had enough of Plummer's attitude by the time they approached Bannack. The tensions were not lessened when Plummer insisted they move slowly before entering the camp.

The day that had dawned brightly had turned sour by two in the afternoon when Plummer and Cleveland first caught sight of smoke rising from Bannack. Mother Nature had been kind that year. September weather had lasted all the way into November. Those who had spent any winters in the Rocky Mountains knew it was too much to expect clear days and mild temperatures to last much longer. Looking at the clouds roiling in from the west, Plummer knew the reprieve was over. He still would not risk riding brazenly into any camp; there were too many people on the frontier who knew him, too many people who knew his reputation.

If it had been up to Cleveland, they would have ridden right into town, right down Main Street, and right into the biggest saloon. That was the way Jack Cleveland handled life; he barged in, not caring what the result was to himself or anyone else. Henry Plummer liked to plan, and he was good at planning.

Cleveland growled, "Dammit, Henry, look at them clouds! We're headed into one hell of a storm."

"Look at that rope on your saddle, Jack, and think about that hemp tight around your neck. We don't know what the hell we'll run into in that camp. We'll give it a quick scout, then head in."

Not trying to hide his anger, Cleveland agreed.

The normal route into Bannack was a nearly level wagon road that approached from the northwest.

Plummer decided that it would be best to ride due south, up over some hillocks west of the camp, then go due east so that they would actually approach from opposite the wagon road. Cleveland, despite his foul mood, saw the logic of Plummer's suggestion. The trip would add a full hour to their ride in, and they would arrive as darkness was falling, but it was, Cleveland finally admitted, "The best way. Dammit, though, I'm in need of a bit of poontang; it's been a long time. You think Cy Skinner has any sporting ladies available?"

Plummer spurred his horse. "If there's a prospector buying whiskey, Cy Skinner will have his share of ladies available."

"I wouldn't be in such bad shape if you'd have let me diddle that woman back at Sun River."

Plummer spurred his horse again, taking his anger out on the animal. He would get into that camp and rid himself of Jack Cleveland, one way or another.

Within half an hour, the skies above them had begun to cloud over and a light smattering of wispy flakes had started falling. By the time the two men had made the loop south of the camp, a substantial snowfall was coming down. As Plummer and Cleveland turned in toward the camp, they met up with prospectors coming down the road that led beside Grasshopper Creek to the main workings at Discovery and Geary's Bar and Jimmie's Bar. The diggers returning to Bannack took little notice of the two strangers. They were only interested in getting inside out of the snow; they wanted food and drink. The weather had gone cold.

Plummer and Cleveland rode close together, bonded by the fear of the unknown reception awaiting them. They walked their horses carefully over the timber bridge across the ditch at the east end of the camp and drew to a halt at the end of Main Street. Both men studied the layout. The campsite was similar to dozens of other camps they had seen in the prospecting regions of the mountains. Main Street was a rutted dirt lane about fifty feet wide. Log buildings, frame shacks, canvas tents, and various kinds of improvised shelters bordered it. There were four intersections with side streets.

Cleveland said, "Why the hell do they do that, Henry?"

Plummer, not taking his eyes away from the camp, snapped, "What do you mean?"

"Why do they build things up like this? Every damned time, they gotta build."

Plummer did not respond. If it was not that he might be needing Cleveland's brawn and gun, he would not even be riding with the man. Cleveland snarled, "Hell, all they need in a camp is a good saloon and a good whorehouse."

Plummer nudged his horse forward down Main Street. About half the prospectors were going down Fourth Street, and the rest were moving west toward a cluster of buildings three blocks away on Main. He opted to follow the people who were going down the nearer Fourth Street and they led him to LeGrau's Café. Cleveland followed along, grousing about not heading directly for the center of the camp, but Plummer had his reasons. Just as when he played poker, he wanted to take his time evaluating what the draw was going to be.

Inside the café, Renee LeGrau and Cora Harris were working hard to keep ahead of their customers' demands; the bad weather was bringing in large numbers of people earlier than normal. Renee was pleased with herself for hiring Cora; there was nothing Cora balked at doing.

When Cora had returned to the café to begin work, she had arrived dressed primly and properly in a modest cotton dress with a long skirt. Cora had pulled her hair back and wore a blue ribbon holding the hair neatly in place; she looked the part of a respectable working girl.

Not much attention was paid to Henry Plummer or Jack Cleveland as they came in through the front door. The customers were trying to get warm; Cora and Renee were busy serving cups of coffee and bowls of soup and stew. Plummer took off his hat, slapped the snow off it against his thigh, and scanned the room as he made a quick inventory of the people. He smiled to himself; there were no familiar faces in the place. Cleveland came up behind Plummer and said, "This ain't no place to get a drink. I told you we should move into the camp. I'm leaving."

Plummer ignored Cleveland's departure. He shucked off his knee-length riding coat and hung it on one of the wooden pegs driven into the log wall. As usual, he replaced his hat to hide the scar at his hairline. He crossed the room to a table near the warm stove and sat. He did not have to wait long. Cora Harris had spotted Plummer as soon as he came in the door: a well-dressed man, handsome, and with a mysteriously attractive glance. Cora moved quickly to Plummer and asked for his order.

Plummer, interested in food and warmth, but more interested in feeling his way into Bannack, replied, "I'm new in camp. What's good?"

Cora liked the soft, gentle tone of the man's voice, but she had dealt with men on the frontier, and she knew this one was no country boy. She said, "Mister, we've got soup and biscuits and stew and biscuits. You name your choice."

Plummer smiled. He had developed a sense for women, and he knew that this one was more than simply a café waitress. He said, "I'll take a bowl of stew, and I've got in my pocket a quarter eagle if there was some bright young lady who'd serve up some information along with the food."

Cora was instantly on guard. Strangers coming into camps wanting information were either lawmen or jealous husbands, and she had developed a dislike for both of those types.

Plummer sensed her reaction and said, in a low voice, "I'm just looking for some friends."

"Friends like who?"

"Well, like Cyrus Skinner. He's a good friend and I was told he'd headed this way."

Cora was now convinced Plummer was a lawman. Cyrus Skinner was not the kind of man to have friends. She snapped, "I'll get you your food, mister. I ain't selling information."

In the kitchen, Renee had paused for a moment and had seen Cora talking with the stranger. As Cora came to the stew pot, Renee asked, "That man giving you trouble? I've never seen him before."

As Cora filled the bowl, she answered, "He's new and looking for people; I think he's a bounty hunter."

Renee looked out at Plummer and guessed Cora was probably right; the man was not dressed like a prospector. She said, "Don't waste time talking with him; we're busy and I'm going to have to make another batch of stew."

Cora felt an urge to snap at her, but stifled the urge. After only a few hours of working in the café, she was coming to like it. She picked up three fat biscuits, put them on the bowl of stew, and went back to Plummer's table. As she set the food down, Plummer dropped the gold $2.50 coin on the table and said, "You keep what's left after the price of the food, pretty girl. I guess you're thinking I'm a lawman after old Cy, but you're wrong. I'd like to know where to find him, though."

Cora tilted her head like a little girl. She could not figure this man out; few people ever were able to read Henry Plummer. She asked, "You a gambler?"

Plummer picked up his spoon to begin eating his stew. "I've played a few games in my life."

"You know Dick Sapp?"

Plummer grinned. "I've known Dick Sapp about two or three years. He in the camp?"

Cora frowned down at Plummer and said, "Mister, I don't know if that's any of your business." She walked away, leaving the gold coin on the table.

Customers kept coming into the café and so it was a full ten minutes before she was able to get back to Plummer. In the meantime, three prospectors had taken empty seats at Plummer's table; sharing tables was the only way to accommodate all of those who wanted food.

As Cora took the orders of the three men, out of the corner of her eye she saw Plummer watching her, grinning to himself; she started to get angry. She did not like smug men, and this stranger carried enough smugness for a whole saloon of men.

Plummer said, "Miss Cora, these men tell me Cy Skinner is running a place just up the road."

Cora snapped, "That's them talking, not me." She glared at the other men at the table, because they had told Plummer her name and probably a lot more about the life she had been leading in the camp.

CHAPTER 7

(Winter, 1862–1863)

The cold that came in November settled in like an unfriendly and unwanted guest. It brought along its usual cruel, dangerous companion: snow. There was no record keeping of temperatures or snowfall, for there were few thermometers in the region. But old-timers had memories, and that winter was remembered as one of the meanest in the northern Rocky Mountains.

The daytime temperatures were measured in single digits; clear, stark nights, when the stars seemed to come down to inflict a penetrating chill on the earth, were in the minus numbers, as low as thirty-five degrees below zero. There were stories of hammers shattering nails as men worked to build shelters against the frigid air; there were stories of gum-rubber boots frozen so hard they crumbled into pieces when prospectors tried to put them on in the morning. Going to work was no simple effort with snow drifted three to four feet deep across roads and paths. Men desperate to continue finding gold tricked themselves into thinking they could work in the thirty-four degree water of Grasshopper Creek. They even built bonfires to soften the frozen mud of the creek banks in a futile attempt to find some glimmer of gold dust. The hardy few who ventured out into the cold to seek fortune did poorly; the many who accepted the winter-imposed idleness did not fare much better, because there was nothing to do other than sit around a café or drink whiskey and play poker in a saloon. The camp had grown enough to justify three new cafés and two new saloons but LeGrau's and Skinner's were, by virtue of longevity, still the places of the old-timers. To compound the problems of boredom, Bannack was isolated; those in the camp were stuck there, and the rugged mountains between the camp and civilization seemed like prison walls. The freight-wagon and stagecoach roads were open only to those who risked death in the unmerciful elements. Supplies were getting skimpy.

The pioneer settlers in Bannack did not see themselves as extraordinary beings; they were simply hoping to make their lives a bit better than they would have been in the towns and villages from whence they came. What they experienced was an extraordinary battle for survival.

They all lived with cold. There seemed to be no sure way to get warm, especially after a day working a claim along the creek. Frostbite was common, and no one was exempted from the jabbing pain of chilblains. Simple cuts and minor broken limbs became serious threats to life. The women of the camp were not out of harm's way: a walk to a store for supplies could produce frozen cheeks and numb feet, and hanging out laundry produced cracked skin that could quickly fester into a dangerous infection. The children simply cried.

Those who had come to Bannack not to find gold but to provide goods and services to the prospectors were applying their energies to preparing for the spring, when the mining would resume and a new influx of prospectors would be arriving. Buildings were being erected for residences, stores, and shops. Timbers were being harvested from the sparsely forested slopes near the camp. Plans were being made, dreams were being brought to fruition. There was a prevailing hope that the camp would prosper.

Even with the horrid weather, there were new arrivals: lucky individuals who had braved the weather over the mountains. Some of the new arrivals were prospectors who had ignorantly started toward Bannack too late in the season to avoid being caught by the weather; some were criminals, who had had to leave their former locales to escape the law. By midwinter, the population had grown to 820 souls. The place was getting crowded.

From the Meeting Minutes Book of the Bannack Provisional Lodge AF&AM.

DATED: *Wednesday, December 17, 1862*

The Lodge was opened in due form with Brother Nathaniel P. Langford sitting as Worshipful Master; Brother Harry Phleger as Senior Warden; Brother George Dart as Junior Warden; Smith Ball as Chaplain; and Drury Underwood as Secretary.

. . . Brother Kohrs announced that he was willing to donate a full half acre of his land for the erection of a proper Lodge building . . .

. . . several opinions and suggestions were offered as to ways to raise money for the building of a schoolhouse . . .

. . . a vote was taken and passed in regards to the ordering of lodge paraphernalia in anticipation of the petition for dispensation being granted from the Grand Lodge of Nebraska. A collection was taken up to finance the purchase. . . .

. . . a long discussion took place regarding the possibility of asking the local saloons to curb their hours of business so as to improve the quality of life for our town, but there was no final resolution to the matter . . .

DATED: *Thursday, January 22, 1863*

. . . with Brother Neil Howie taking the chair of Brother Phleger who was ill with a cold . . .

. . . Brother Langford complained that there has still been no word from the Grand Lodge in Nebraska . . .

. . . the Lodge provided its thanks to Brother Kohrs for his sketch of the possible new Lodge building and N. P. Langford suggested each member take time to study the drawing during the time of refreshment . . .

. . . Brother Underwood read a letter of response he received from his cousin in Denver who has searched for a physician as directed in the request from the Lodge. Brother Underwood's cousin has found a doctor named John S. Glick, formerly of Ohio but practicing in Denver after studying medicine in St. Louis. The named Dr. Glick carries a sound reputation in private practice and in service at military posts. His surgical skills are reported to be of the highest caliber, and he has a reputation for donating his services to the needy. The discussion following the letter reading was slightly frivolous regarding the need for a surgeon considering the shootings and knifings taking place in our town, and the matter of Dr. Glick's charitable attitude was also received with some degree of levity considering there is little money being made in the town at this present time. The final resolution was that a collection was to be taken to raise $125.00 to send to Denver as an inducement to bring Dr. Glick to our town; said monies to be used to pay for transportation and resettlement costs of the good doctor. The collection produced $137.50 and the Secretary was instructed to send the monies to Brother Underwood's cousin in Denver . . .

. . . it was agreed that Brother Langford send still

another letter to the Grand Lodge of Nebraska to hurry along the petition for dispensation . . .

DATED: *Wednesday, February 18, 1863*

The meeting was opened and closed in the Third Degree in due form but abbreviated in time because the general public of the town had been invited to hear a talk regarding the Emancipation Proclamation that went into effect on January 1 previously. . . .

. . . reported there still was no word from the Grand Lodge of Nebraska . . .

. . . that Dr. Glick was scheduled to arrive in our town by the first of March . . .

. . . the report of the investigating committee regarding the petition of Mr. William Henry Plummer for admission to the Apprentice Degree was noted as unfavorable and the petition was denied . . .

. . . the call to refreshment was to be held in the Roundhouse considering the large crowd expected for the public meeting to be held by the Union Club.

Food was scarce. During the winter only three short wagon trains had made it from Fort Benton, and only five wagons had made it from Salt Lake City, so prices of some foodstuffs were exorbitant. Eggs were selling for twelve dollars a dozen. The offerings at kitchen tables were heavy on gruel and potatoes. Hank Crawford, the camp butcher, was unable to get cattle delivered to him from Cottonwood, or over in the Big Hole, where ranches had good supplies of beef. He resorted to hiring idle prospectors and some of the local Indians as hunters of wild game, and on many days the only meat available was deer or elk shot in the nearby woods.

From a diary of Cora Harris (undated)
Located in the Harris-Voit Family Archives—
Pasco, Washington

Some Christmas! Renee made me come to work at six o'clock and that's not all!!! I had to work until eight o'clock and I missed all the fun of the party at Goodrich's Hotel *and* I never did see Dick Sapp all day *and* it was after nine o'clock before Lucy gave me my present!!! Why did I ever go to work for that [sic] ~~b i t c h~~ —better not call her that . . . she might read this someday. I don't know how she found all of the turkey and chicken . . . she said she had it shipped in from Fort Benton but there was no wagon for the past two weeks so how did she do that??? Who cares!!! She is a [sic] ~~b i t~~ —I gotta watch that. Turkeys!! I worked like a pig!!! that's what I did and I'm tired of missing out on all the fun . . . Dick hardly speaks to me and he hasn't let me stay with him for the past month. . . . Did Lucy say something to him??? Will I ever know???

Entry noted only as Black Thursday
(probably in mid-January)

. . . I should have known! I guess I always knew it, but finding out was a real stab in my aching heart: Dick Sapp is a married man!!! I should have known he was too good to be true. And I had to hear it from some rotten customers in the café. . . . Mrs. Sapp is coming in on a wagon train from Colorado!!! I should have known that he would never really marry me like he said all those times in his cabin. Maybe I should just meet this wife of his when she gets in and we could talk about some things that we both know . . . we do know . . . don't we!! . . . !

A supply wagon arrived this morning from Salt Lake City and for dinner Renee made the best-tasting stew with the vegetables she bought from George Dart who had hired the wagon . . . even if the meat was venison—Ugh!!! I hate that wild game . . . but what else can we eat? . . .

Lucy has made friends with Penny Caven. . . . Buz Caven plays the fiddle with Old Brod up in Skinner's. . . . Penny seems like a nice girl but Lucy makes too much of it all. If Lucy keeps talking about Penny *this* and Penny *that* I think I'll scream!!! I have half a mind to go back and work for Cy Skinner . . . should I do that??? . . .

Washington's Birthday

Went to see Cy Skinner after work today . . . He said I could come back to work if I would move in with him in his SHACK!! Can you IMAGINE!!! I'm so mad at Lucy that I had half a mind to do it, but there are three other men living in that dump and I can just imagine what it would be like living with that bunch.

There are too many bad ones coming into the camp. I don't know how they get here through all of the storms and everything, but they do, and things are getting bad. . . . I'm glad I did not go back to work in the Elk Horn . . . lots of fights and all of that. Just about every night there is some fool either cut or shot. I hear that Clay Barrow got himself shot in the foot. . . . Maybe he can go and let snooty Miss Lucy take care of him . . . Lucy sure has gotten uppity . . . just because I work for the LeGraus but *she* works for the fancy Kustar's Bakery . . . WHO CARES???

The population of Bannack grew to 1,783 souls during the winter months, and the mix of good and bad was about equal. There were those eager—even greedy—individuals who were in the camp to dig for gold and try to make a fortune. That some of the good men were greedy was not to be criticized, because it was quite human to carry dreams of instant fortune after the plethora of myths and legends arising out of the California Gold Rush of 1849. There was a reasonable assumption that the mountains of the West were impregnated with gold just waiting to be uncovered and to make the finder a rich man.

The grizzly, bewhiskered, gnarled old prospector trekking around the mountains with his mule did not exist in the era; the demands were too much for any but the young and healthy. It was hard work to search and dig and pan for the nuggets and dust. There were legions of eager young men to satisfy the demand, and they responded to each rumor of a gold strike.

There were also masses of disreputable rogues for whom gold acted as a magnet—men who had fled the states of the Union to avoid conscription, and those from the Confederacy who either saw the futility of the Civil War or simply did not want to fight. There were also men who seemed to thrive on danger and had no reservations about killing or robbing. For Henry Plummer to prosper, he needed rogues: they were his strength.

From the letters of Henry Plummer
Private Archives—
Friends of Western History
Des Moines, Iowa

DATED: *27 December 1862*

Dearest Electa

Just as I guessed it would be, Christmas was absolutely awful without you. I wanted so much to leave this place and be with you and your family but there was just too much business here for me to leave. As I mentioned in my last letter, a businessman here named Mr. Cyrus Skinner has been

> helping me get started in some ventures and he felt it was important for me to stay. . . .

Plummer lifted his pen from the paper and gently removed some of the fibers that had been caught in the tip of his pen. He wiped his ink-stained fingers on the desktop blotter and smiled. It was not an evil smile, but a smile of irony. He was thinking about the party Cy Skinner had thrown on Christmas Eve. The Masonic group had held a reception at the Roundhouse, and there had been feasting at LeGrau's Café and an open house held by the Union Club at Goodrich's Hotel, but Cy Skinner's party in the Elk Horn Saloon had been the smallest and the best. It had been just as Skinner had promised—worth not going to Sun River. Somewhere Skinner had obtained a forty-pound beef roast and a fresh supply of beer. There had been jovial singing to the fiddles of Old Brod and Buz Caven. Before the dead of winter had set in, there had been an influx of unattached women to the camp, and Skinner had provided two sporting ladies for each man. To Plummer, it was a Christmas to remember but nothing really to bother Electa with.

> While I was forced to stay here, I managed to make the sadness a bit less by purchasing a lot, and I have arranged for a cabin to be built for us. It will not be fancy, my love, but I have ordered proper doors and windows so it will be a nice home, and I am sure you will be pleased. . . .
>
> [A]nd Mr. Skinner has suggested he and I purchase a couple of mining claims, which are quite cheap right now because there is no gold being produced and many of the men here are becoming discouraged. I do not share that feeling because this camp, of all the camps I have seen, holds great promise for the future. I know you will enjoy the life here in Bannack as soon as we are married. . . .

DATED: *17 January 1863*

[S]o I know you will be pleased with the mining claims we now own. I will not be working the claims myself but there will be enough hired hands available as soon as spring comes. Oh, my Electa, how I am waiting for spring to come when you and I will be married. Life is such a bore here; you cannot imagine. . . .

Dolly Grogan moved the tips of her fingernails up the back of Plummer's neck in the way that she had found excited him. He reached back and flicked her hand away, saying that he had to finish the letter. Dolly hated it when Plummer sat at the desk to write those damned letters to that damned woman up at Sun River. For a brothel madam, Dolly Grogan had a weak spot when it came to sharing Henry Plummer. He used to drive her crazy when he would consort with one of her sporting ladies; two weeks previously she had come close to jabbing him with a knife, but she had seen a look of instant hate explode into his eyes and she had known she could only cross him at her own peril.

As far as business associates are concerned, we have been very lucky. Several men have arrived in camp who have worked for me before, and they will ensure that things go our way.

Believe me, my Electa, we will have a wonderful life as soon as work starts again here in Bannack and you are my wife.

DATED: *21 February 1863*

[A]nd your letter was probably the nicest bit of news that I have ever received in my whole life. Electa, the way you say things is beautiful and I only wish I could put words to paper the way you can. Yes! I can remember the times we spent alone by the river and Yes! I can remember what you said when I touched you and Yes! I can remember the feeling I had when you xxx. I have to stop this, Electa, I miss you too much to even think about the things that happened. . . .

Plummer stood at the bar in the Elk Horn and grimaced as Cyrus Skinner made fun of the ink stains on his fingers. The letter writing to Electa had become a frequent cause of joshing between the two men; Plummer had soundly smacked Dolly Grogan for letting out the secret to Skinner, who fancied himself a skilled needler. Plummer had always been able to enjoy Skinner's sense of humor, even back in the days when the two men were in prison together, so there were no hard feelings. Plummer merely wished Skinner would cease teasing about Electa. Skinner, still teasing, asked if Plummer had written to Electa about how Jack Cleveland had been stewing for a fight with Plummer; Plummer snapped back that Cleveland was a filthy word and he did not write filthy words to his intended bride. Plummer had spent little time worrying about why Jack Cleveland was so intent on having a fight. Maybe Jack was crazy; maybe Jack had nothing better to do; maybe Jack wanted to get himself killed. Maybe it was all of those, and maybe there were more reasons. The point was that Cleveland was really pressing his luck, and Plummer's patience was wearing thin; the festering boil of hostility was going to come to a head soon, and Plummer was anxious for it to be over.

The saloon was quiet at that time of the morning. Skinner poured them two more drinks and advised Plummer that Ned Ray and Charley Moore had arrived in the camp during the night. Plummer grinned like a poker player who has just drawn to fill an inside straight. Over the previous few weeks, nearly a dozen desperadoes who had formerly worked with Skinner and Plummer had drifted into Bannack, and the ranks of dependable road agents had swelled to a substantial number. It would eventually grow to 120. The criminals had not come out of any loyalty to Plummer or Skinner, they had come as a normal consequence of activities in other gold camps. As a camp grew and prospered, the residents quickly sought to organize a government, and usually the first officer elected was a sheriff. Sheriffs made little money, but they did receive bonus payments that amounted to bounty fees, and a criminal was quick to make for new territories soon after a sheriff was elected. Henry Plummer was quietly, but quickly, assembling a cadre of experienced holdup men. Plummer sipped his whiskey as he looked at Cyrus Skinner. Both men knew the potential for illicit profit, and both were savoring the prospects. When Skinner said that the two new arrivals were bunked in at Dolly Grogan's whorehouse, Plummer said he would stop by and visit them. Skinner suggested Plummer might also avail himself of one of Madam Grogan's young employees to help him shake the need to be constantly writing letters to Electa Bryan. Plummer laughed, then said he might just do that.

Continuing the letter of 21 February

> [S]o I hope you will excuse me because I just had to take a short break and go to the café for some coffee and food to stop thinking those thoughts I had been thinking of you. . . .
>
> I met some old friends this morning and they are going to go to work for me as soon as things get moving again in the camp. It will not be long, my dearest Electa. I will be arriving at Sun River soon and then you and I will be married.
>
> As ever,
> /S/ Henry

CHAPTER 8

(Sunday, March 1, 1863)

Cora Harris was frustrated.

At the table occupied by Nathaniel Langford, Hank Crawford, and Harry Phleger, there was talk of a shooting. Cora never liked to hear talk about shootings but she had a healthy appetite for gossip. Unfortunately, the men were talking in low voices, and she was having to serve other tables as well as wash dirty dishes when there was a break from serving.

The three men had come in for an early breakfast. They had joked with her about going with them out to where Langford and Phleger were operating a very busy sawmill with John Bozeman. She felt it was really stupid to be going out when the temperature was pushing down toward zero again, and she told the three of them as much. Hank Crawford said he was not going, as if that made any difference to Cora; these men, all of them, were really not very bright. She wanted to hear about the shooting the night before.

Cora tried to stay by the Langford table and pick up

what was being said. She hoped Renee would take her turn at washing the dishes, but Renee was busy.

Cora had made an amazing transition over the winter months. She had completely abandoned going to Skinner's saloon and Goodrich's Hotel; she had primly changed her style of dress; she had blossomed into a healthy-looking young woman. Part of the reason for the change was that Frank and Renee LeGrau had taken an honest interest in her life. Frank had even built Cora a tiny cabin down near the creek on the same block as the café and his blacksmith shop. The cabin was not fancy, but it had a wooden floor and an adequate heat stove. Over the past months she had sewn curtains for the two windows, and then had shelves and a clothes closet built by Vic Voit. That was another reason for the change; Cora had started to let Voit pay court. The relationship was enhanced by Cora's insistence that there be nothing more between them than minor sparking. She had met with a fierce argument from him at the beginning. He had pointed out, as delicately as possible, that she had formerly been a loose woman in the camp and had even taken money for her services. Cora explained that her earlier existence as a sporting lady was not to come into their life, and so Voit resigned himself to merely having her as a girlfriend. She was tickled when he used the term, because she had never experienced the pleasure of a boyfriend; she had gone directly from being a chaste young woman to being a woman of the world.

The other major factor in her change was that she had discovered she could earn money in an honest manner and still have fun out of life. Another aspect of change had come from her relationship with Lucinda Simons. That was a trauma for Cora. Lucinda had let the environment of the camp affect her personality. She still worked responsibly for Mutta Kustar, and she still took magnificent care of herself, but she had actually begun spending time with Clay Barrow. Cora was not sure whether there was much to it, but she had her suspicions. Cora found Lucinda's situation unattractive.

That one thing aside, Cora was quite pleased with her new life. Over the winter the crowds hanging around the saloons had become rowdy and even dangerous; there had been several shootings, and three men had been killed, but it had been impossible to find out who was responsible for the killings.

Renee's voice pulled Cora out of her thoughts. "Cora! Take this food. Darn, girl, you're sluggish today!"

There had been a time when such a statement from Renee would have caused a spark between the two women, but Cora had come to love Renee like a sister, and the two were able to handle the tensions of a hectic day in the café. Cora looked up from the dish tub and smiled. "I ain't got my mind all here this morning. I was trying to listen about the shooting."

Renee scowled. "Learning about who got shot won't get them vittles down our customers. Get moving. We've a lot of work to be done."

Cora nodded, dried her hands, and picked up the tray Renee had loaded with four bowls of gruel and eight slices of buttered bread. Eggs and bacon had been off the menu for two weeks awaiting the next shipment from suppliers. Cora had to pass the Langford table on her way to the prospectors waiting for their breakfasts, and slowed as she tried to pick up a few words. All she heard was the name of Evans.

Cora served the prospectors; the Evans mystery was an old one and hardly worth the time for gossip. She asked one of the diggers, "Who got shot last night?"

None of the four could give her an answer; they were not the kind who would have been hanging around Skinner's saloon late enough to be privy to the shooting. In a fit of near pique, she walked over to the Langford table and stood there. Nat Langford looked up and smiled as he asked, "What is it, Cora?"

"You need more coffee or something?"

The men all shook their heads; she still stood there.

Hank Crawford, who spent most of the day delivering meat from his butcher shop, and thus was pretty well up on everyone, grinned and said, "Dick Sapp did not get shot last night, Cora."

All three of the men gave friendly smiles, but Cora's face turned as crimson as the wide ribbon she was using to keep her hair back. She pursed her lips into a thin line and snapped, "Hank Crawford, you are a rude man. I don't care about Dick Sapp or any of his kind."

She spun on her heels and stalked away.

Crawford, still grinning, said, "She's a good kid."

Harry Phleger agreed. "She's turned out well since she cut loose from Skinner's."

"If we could get more people to stay away from that place," Langford said, "the whole town would be better off. Cora Harris shows it can be done."

Crawford said, "She's tied up with that Vic Voit and he still hangs around Skinner's, every now and then."

"Just every now and then," Phleger countered. "Voit's still working for Con Kohrs, who speaks highly of him. Ever since Con got rid of that Clay Barrow, Voit's been behaving himself."

Langford said, "That Barrow is a bad one. He could have been in on the Evans disappearance."

"Barrow is clean on that one," Crawford said, "There's no doubt about it being Cleveland; I'd bet my shop on that."

In mid-January, George Evans had been hired to ride out to Buffalo Creek after some steers that had strayed away from a local ranch. Evans was a young fellow, a hard worker whose friends said that he carried all of his earnings on his person. His nest egg was reported to have been as high as seventy dollars. Evans left Bannack and was never seen again. A few days after he was reported missing, a rancher in the area found Evans' clothing partially buried in a ditch. A body was never found, and there had never been any evidence of who had committed the crime, but Jack Cleveland suddenly had money to spend. Many were convinced that Cleveland was responsible for the crime—but there was no proof.

Langford said, "But there is no way we could convince a jury."

"What we need is a proper sheriff," Harry Phleger said.

Langford nodded. "What would be best would be a U.S. marshal. Then there would be some law and order."

Crawford took a swig of coffee, then said, "Things will settle down as soon as the weather breaks and more people come in. Right now, it seems as though the bad eggs have the honest people outnumbered, and that always is rough."

Langford said, "The problem I am having, Hank, is that I've never been exposed to any situation like the one here in Bannack."

"I've been through this a couple of times; it works out."

Langford continued, "Good heavens, we don't even live in a *state;* and the territorial capital is out there hundreds of miles away over nearly impassable mountains. I come from a place where there are streets and homes and churches and schools. We had policemen to take care of troublemakers. Hell, we even had a dog-catcher."

Phleger laughed. "We have dogcatchers, too, Nat. Them Bannack Indians at the end of the camp are pretty good at catching dogs . . . and eating them!"

All three men laughed. Few people in the camp had much use for the Indian families who lived just outside of town. Only Hank Crawford held a tolerance for the Indians. Not only because they were dependable about removing the offal by-products of his butchering business, but because he had found that some of them had an ironic sense of humor that he liked. His main source of knowledge was Pipe Carrier, a Bannack brave who helped Crawford with butchering chores. Pipe Carrier was a man who could confuse Crawford with quips that would lighten a moment, and then come back later as a serious challenge. Pipe Carrier had planted a provocative thought in Crawford's mind just the day before when he said, "Hank, claim jumping is going to finish this camp; the land belongs to everyone." Crawford had mulled that concept over for hours, and still had not come up with an argument against it. After all, this land was "God's country."

Crawford said, "Take it easy on my friends, fellows. My friend Pipe Carrier might have something to say about our diet."

"No question about that, Hank. There's no telling what is in the mind of those savages," Langford said. He then added, "Well, gentlemen, I will be pleased when we bring some order to this community; God knows we need it."

Phleger replied, "We've done pretty well so far. There's money raised for the school building, and the doctor will be here as soon as he can get his house sold in Denver. Someday soon we will be hearing about the charter for our Lodge. Not bad at all."

Langford said, "I'm not all that happy about taking a twenty-five-dollar donation from Cy Skinner for the school fund."

"Hell, Nat," Crawford said, "We took ten dollars from Henry Plummer, and that was after we told him we didn't want him in the Lodge."

"I don't like money coming from either one of them."

Crawford smiled. "That twenty-five dollars from Skinner is about his profit for a couple of hours in that saloon."

Langford came back, "I guess I just don't like doing business with a saloon owner. They are a shoddy sort."

"Skinner's no good," Phleger agreed, "but neither is Henry Plummer. The man is smarmy."

"I don't think we'll be worrying about Henry Plummer for too long," Crawford said. "He's bound to pull out soon."

Langford asked, "You mean his trouble with Jack Cleveland?"

"Exactly."

Phleger said, "Cleveland keeps hinting that he knows something about Plummer. I overheard him saying that again last night, right here at dinner time."

Langford said, "I've had a bad feeling about Plummer ever since he came into the camp."

Crawford countered, "He's kept his nose clean, and I don't know how he has avoided a showdown with Cleveland. I was in Skinner's after dinner last night when Cleveland came in drunk and challenged Plummer again. Plummer simply left and went next door to Goodrich's; Cleveland followed him there and Plummer left that place. Plummer has more patience than I do; Cleveland is a nasty one when he gets drunk."

"Well, there's not much we can do about it until something happens." Langford pulled out his pocket watch and added, "We'd better be going; it's getting late."

Harry Phleger doused out his smoke in the empty coffee cup. "If I know John Bozeman, he's already there and has cleared out the site and probably will have felled four or five trees by the time we get there."

Langford looked at Crawford. "Sure you don't want to come along, Hank? Not a bad morning for a ride."

Crawford stood, drank the remainder of his coffee, then replied, "It's about ten miles out there, Nat, and you know it. I'd really like to have a piece of that sawmill but there's no way I can neglect my shop today; I'm expecting some cattle to come in from Cottonwood, and if I'm not here to claim them, then the damned Indians will have them all chopped by the time I get back."

Langford said, "We'll be up at the site for two or three days, at least. If you need anything, just send someone up for us."

Crawford reached into his pocket and extracted a silver dollar that would pay for all of the food that had been eaten at the table and still give Cora a gratuity. He said, "I know the site, and I know where to get you. We'll not need you, Nat. The camp will be just fine for a few days."

Crawford dropped the dollar on the table, Nat Langford called to Cora that they were leaving, and the three men headed out the door.

In the kitchen area, Cora's hands kept washing bowls and cups but she was watching the three men. She had picked up the mention of Cleveland and Plummer, but she had not been able to identify what the subject had been. Everyone knew about the feud between Jack Cleveland and Henry Plummer; ever since the two had arrived, Cleveland had been baiting Plummer, trying to start a fight. Plummer had not taken the bait.

Cora looked over at Renee, who was rolling out dough to make another batch of biscuits. Cora asked, "You think Jack Cleveland is crazy?"

Renee reached her hand into the barrel of flour, expertly tossed a proper amount onto the worktable as she answered, "I don't have time to go worrying about people being crazy or not, Cora. I hope you get too busy to worry, too." Then, with a sisterly laugh, Renee added, "Besides, if there was real trouble, then Nat Langford would not be leaving town for a few days, you know that."

Later that morning, just about half an hour before lunch time, Henry Plummer was sitting in the back of Goodrich's Hotel, chatting with two friends.

Goodrich's Hotel sat on Main Street, just east of Skinner's Elk Horn Saloon. Bill Goodrich had been successful the previous August panning gold and had used his capital to build a two-story structure that provided more profit for him than any effort he might have invested in working the creek bed. The top floor had been left open with bunks built out of rough lumber to provide sleeping space. Latecomers had to make do with blankets on the floor. The downstairs provided a bar too small to compete with Skinner's next door, a billiard table, and a barber chair near the front door. The main thing Goodrich provided for his patrons was a place to keep warm by one of the four wood stoves he kept blazing twenty-four hours a day, providing places for the prospectors to gather and talk. Talking was big in Bannack during the frozen winter months.

Today Plummer had an idea. Henry Plummer frequently had bright ideas about ways to make money. His legitimate ventures had never been highly successful, but a few of them had turned a profit and, most important to him, his activities as a businessman gave him credibility. His current scheme was the reprocessing of the tailings and residue left from the hundreds of claims along Grasshopper Creek. Plummer had lived for various lengths of time in fourteen different gold camps in California, Nevada, Oregon, and Idaho. He knew that the first work done by the prospectors was to skim off the surface gold that rested in creek beds or was embedded in the mud of the creek banks. It was that work that produced quick wealth for the prospectors. But the underlying objective was to find the source of the gold that had washed down the rivers, streams, and creeks; the goal was the mother lode.

Even while panning was producing income for the men in search of their dreams, there were those men who used dynamite to blast into the rock formations adjacent to the creeks in hopes of exposing a gold-bearing vein. What Plummer knew from other camps was that the rock left from blasting would probably contain some traces of gold. Extracting gold from the rock required time and equipment, so most early diggers opted to forget about that and to concentrate on what was available on the surface. Plummer was going to build a stamp mill to crush the rock, then process out the freed-up gold.

Plummer needed hired hands to work the equipment and handle the processing, so he was talking with Bill "Gad" Moore and Jeff Perkins. Moore was a hoodlum whom Plummer had known earlier and Jeff Perkins was a drifter who had taken to hanging around Skinner's saloon since his arrival five weeks previously. Moore and Perkins were seriously listening to Plummer, who was intently describing what was to be expected of the pair. The only thing they did not realize was that Plummer was merely using the business as a cover for what he and Cyrus Skinner planned as soon as the camp began producing gold again, come the thaw. Whether the idea originated with Cy Skinner or Henry Plummer is not recorded, but what is known is that the gold camp at Bannack was destined to find an ignoble place in history because of it.

Jeff Perkins was a quiet, innocent sort of youth, similar to many young men who traveled to the gold camps of the West. He was a month shy of his eighteenth birthday. He stayed in the camp because he felt he had no place else to go, since his father had run him off their Missouri family farm. He had made little money working for claim owners up along Grasshopper Creek, but he had been befriended by Cyrus Skinner, who doled out enough money to keep Jeff fed and able to play a few hands of poker—Jeff Perkins was a good poker player. Plummer had met the youth in a game at Skinner's.

Gad Moore was another case. Having turned twenty-one in January, he was looked on as an old hand, a dependable fist or gun when needed. Plummer had bumped into Moore in Carson City, Lewiston, and Oro Fino. Each time Moore had been of help to Plummer, and Plummer had responded by seeing that Moore always had enough pocket cash to buy a few drinks and visit the occasional sporting lady. Although Moore had not yet been brought into the Skinner/Plummer loose circle of promising brigands, he was confident that there were good things ahead, because Bannack seemed to be sitting on top of a really fine gold strike.

Plummer took his tin of cheroots from the table and offered the other two a smoke. Moore accepted; Perkins chose to slice off a chew from the plug he carried tucked in a small pocket in the crown of his hat. While Plummer and Moore were lighting up, Perkins worked the chew until it was soft enough for him to say, "Last night at Skinner's, Jack Cleveland was saying that he'd smash up any stamp mill you build, Henry."

Plummer blew out a fine stream of smoke. When Plummer had first headed toward Bannack, he had felt Cleveland's talents and experience might be useful, but Cleveland had proved himself to be only annoying. Plummer had never had any fondness for Cleveland, but since they had arrived in the camp, the relationship had degenerated into hostility. "Jack Cleveland is full of shit; same as he has always been."

Perkins wanted to ask why Jack Cleveland was so often badmouthing Plummer, but Perkins had learned early not to ask anything more than the time of day: questions were not well received.

Plummer said, in a quiet, convincing voice, "Jeff, we all have things in our past that we'd just as soon have forgotten. Maybe Jack feels he knows something about me that I don't want bantered about. That does not mean I've anything to be ashamed of, Jeff, it only means that I don't want a foulmouth like Jack Cleveland talking about me."

Gad Moore cut in. "Don't worry about Jack, my boy, I'll do him if he comes bothering you and me."

Perkins moved the chew around to his cheek and said, "I'll help. I'm getting pretty good with that gun."

Plummer and Moore both nodded; Moore had given Jeff an old revolver to practice his shooting and he had become, they both knew, a pretty good shot.

Plummer had little doubt that his conflict with Jack Cleveland was going to end up in a skirmish. He had hoped that Cleveland might leave the camp, because Cy Skinner had tried a couple of times to convince him to move on, but that effort had been for naught, and Cleveland was getting more and more brazen in his taunting of Plummer.

Plummer wanted to avoid having Cleveland mouthing off about the shooting of a saloon keeper in Oro Fino. Cleveland had been in Oro Fino when Plummer had shot Patrick Ford to death, and there was an outstanding warrant in the investigation of the shooting. Cleveland, like only a few others, knew for a fact that Plummer had murdered Ford; Plummer did not want that matter discussed. He would see Cleveland gone from the camp or buried in the ground. Either way, Plummer would allow no chatter about Patrick Ford and Oro Fino.

The three men sat quiet for a moment. A man was nearly asleep in the barber chair while he was being shaved. Old Brod was making some extra cash filling in for the barber, Buck Stinson, who had gone out of camp the day before to help John Bozeman build the new sawmill. Old Brod hummed an easy, gentle tune as he worked the lather onto the customer's face. There was that comfortable clack of billiard balls rolling around the green felt table. Every now and then one of the pool players grunted as he missed an easy shot. Over near the small bar, at a rickety table, two men played checkers on a wooden board. The board was so worn that arguments frequently developed over where the black and red squares began and ended.

Jeff Perkins expertly spat a goodly quantity of tobacco juice at the side of the stove, and the hssss lasted longer than anyone guessed it should. The whole moment was worth enjoying.

Plummer was feeling splendid. His future seemed secure, and he was even giving some thought to breaking his ties to his nefarious friends like Cyrus Skinner. In devising his plan for processing out the tailings, Plummer had discovered that his ideal was economically feasible. It would be possible for him to make a profit, a handsome profit, by running the operation. He let his imagination place a cloak of respectability on his shoulders and he liked the feeling. He saw himself being invited to join the Union Club, and he thought those

Freemasons who had rejected him might reconsider. Nat Langford and Hank Crawford were big voices in both the Union Club and the Masons; he would have to cultivate their confidence. The Masons would be the first effort, because there were only ten men fool enough to have meetings promoting the saving of the Union; there were over a hundred now in camp who held those silly, secret meetings of the Masons; numbers, those were important. He felt that Bannack had the potential of lasting past the initial boom of panning for gold; the place might become a proper town, a place to which he could bring Electa, a place where they could raise a family and have a future. He had confidence in himself, confidence that he could succeed in a business venture. He had proved that to himself half a dozen times before in other frontier towns.

If Henry Plummer had not been a man who savored the occasional sip of the quiet life; if he had followed Gad Moore's suggestion that they go to Skinner's for a beer; or if he had followed his stomach's plea and gone to LeGrau's for a bite of lunch, his future and the future of Bannack might have been painted with a different brush.

But Plummer sat there in Goodrich's Hotel lobby taking a little enjoyment in life.

And Jack Cleveland walked in.

There are several recorded testimonies of what happened that day in Goodrich's Hotel. All state that Jack Cleveland was drunk; all agree that he wore a pistol stuffed in his belt.

The downstairs of Goodrich's Hotel was one long open room. Windows provided enough light to see the length of the room and Cleveland immediately spotted Plummer sitting with Jeff Perkins and Gad Moore. In a loud voice, he slurred, "Now ain't that a bunch of lousy bastards!" He staggered ten feet inside and leaned against the pool table.

Bill Goodrich was up on the second floor, but he heard Cleveland's voice and he knew Plummer was downstairs; Goodrich began moving toward the stairs.

The barber chair was right by the front door, next to one of the two front windows. Old Brod Staley grabbed a towel and began furiously wiping off his customer's shaving cream. The man protested that Old Brod was not done shaving him; Old Brod, in his mellow baritone, said quietly, "Mister, this shave is *done;* I'm going to lunch." Old Brod was followed out the front door by his customer.

The pair that had been playing pool placed their cues on the table and moved out of the way.

Cleveland shouted, "There's that goddamned Jeff Perkins. I been looking for you, Perkins!"

Henry Plummer placed a hand on Perkins' arm as he said, "Take it easy, Jeff. Cleveland's just got a lot of mouth."

Perkins could not take his eyes off the drunken Cleveland. "Henry, I don't have my gun. It's upstairs with my tack."

Plummer advised, "Just take it easy."

Moore said, "I'd like to take that son of a bitch! He's asking for real trouble."

"You take it easy, too, Gad. We've seen Jack drunker than this."

Cleveland moved forward, bumping into the billiard table, nearly falling down. He kept moving. He lurched up to the bar just as Bill Goodrich came down the stairs. Cleveland demanded, "Gimme a drink, Bill."

Goodrich moved behind the bar. "I'll not be giving you a drink in your condition, Jack. You go upstairs and sleep it off, then I'll stand a round or two on my own. How about that?"

Cleveland weaved for a moment, then snapped, "Shit, I got a right to a drink if I want it." He looked through his watery eyes back toward Plummer. Cleveland growled, "Look at them bastards. I want a drink."

Goodrich did not reply, but Cleveland saw that Goodrich had reached his hand under the bar; everyone knew that Bill Goodrich kept a broken table leg under there for unruly customers. Cleveland began walking toward the rear where Plummer waited. As he moved, he snarled, "There's that asshole Jeff Perkins who owes me money. Pay up your debts, Perkins." He halted seven feet from the table and repeated, "Pay mc my money, Perkins!"

Jeff started to rise, but Plummer held him back. Jeff's voice cracked with anger as he said, "I paid you! You're drunk and you still know I paid you that money."

In February, Jack Cleveland had loaned Jeff Perkins three dollars. Gad Moore, and others, had seen Jeff repay the loan. But ever since Jeff had started working for Henry Plummer, Cleveland had been insisting that Jeff had not repaid the loan.

"Drunk!" Cleveland shouted. "You dumb pup, what do you know about being drunk?"

Plummer's eyes showed only contempt. His voice was calm as he charged, "Jack, I know what drunk is, and you're drunk. Now get the hell out of here and leave us."

Cleveland had difficulty moving his line of sight to Plummer. When he finally was able to focus, he hissed out, "What you getting into this for, Henry? You his nursemaid or something? You taking care of this little snot-nosed Johnny Reb?"

Jeff bounded up out of his chair, shouting, "I ain't no Johnny Reb!"

Plummer stood and put a restraining hand on Jeff's shoulder, but his eyes never left Jack Cleveland. "Jeff, you go up to your bunk and get that thing we were talking about."

Jeff paused, not really hearing Plummer's words. Plummer repeated himself. For a moment Jeff Perkins was still confused, because he knew Plummer was wearing his own revolver. Plummer, still glaring at Cleveland, ordered: "Move, Jeff!"

Perkins was shaking with anger, but he moved cautiously around Cleveland. Once Perkins was heading up the stairs to the second floor, Plummer sat down. Not once did he look away from Cleveland.

"You taking care of your little boy, Henry?"

Plummer came back with, "That's no business of yours."

"Well, just maybe it is my business," Cleveland snarled. "I was the one who brought you here; if you're giving work to Perkins when I'm needing work, I think that is my business."

Plummer countered, "I came here by myself, Jack, and I owe nothing to you."

Cleveland sneered. "Maybe you do owe me, Henry Plummer, maybe you owe me for keeping my mouth shut."

Plummer's teeth were just visible through the thin slit of his lips. He leaned forward with his elbows on the table. "Nobody ever accused you of keeping your mouth shut, Jack. That's one trick you never learned."

Cleveland wobbled to the edge of the table and with some effort put the palms of his hands on the tabletop for support. In a hushed voice, he said, "I've kept my mouth shut about Oro Fino and Pat Ford, right?"

Plummer said nothing. Gad Moore knew all there was to know about the Oro Fino killing, and Cleveland was talking so low that none of the others in the room could hear what was being said.

Cleveland whined, "Come on, Henry, tell Perkins to give me some money, I'm dead broke."

Plummer thought about giving Cleveland a couple of dollars, but he had done that before on several occasions and Cleveland still did not behave himself. Plummer was trying to keep his own temper under control but he was not having much success. He snapped, "Go find some work and get paid. Then you'll not be needing to bother honest people."

Cleveland leaned forward. Across the table, Plummer lifted his elbows off the table and lowered his hands out of sight. Cleveland's smell was awful. Plummer was fastidious about his person. He wore clean clothing and he bathed whenever possible; Cleveland's clothing was filthy and he was washed only when he happened to be caught out in a downpour. Tiny flecks of spittle dripped out of his mouth onto his four-day growth of beard. He leaned even closer and, in a foul whisper, said, "I can tell you something about Jeff Perkins if you want to know."

"There's nothing I need to know about Jeff. Just get the hell away from me, Jack."

Cleveland pushed himself erect, still weaving. He said, in a louder voice, "Yeh, I'll get the hell away, Henry. You know that Perkins is turning to squaws. You know that, don't you?"

Unnoticed by anyone, Jeff Perkins had come back down the stairs and was standing with his pistol in his hand, just ten feet away from Cleveland. Perkins raged, "You're a goddamned liar, Jack Cleveland, I ain't after no squaws."

Cleveland turned his head, grinning. He reached up and wiped his grubby hand across his mouth. He gave a snicker. "Maybe you ain't chasing squaws, Perkins, maybe you ain't. But you'd better put that gun someplace other than in your hand or you're dead."

Jeff did not move.

Plummer spoke in a quiet, even tone. "Jeff, come over here behind me."

Jeff paused, then took the advice.

Cleveland watched the move, then gave a raspy laugh. "Yeh, Perkins, you listen to Henry Plummer. He can tell you all about squaws."

Behind the bar, Bill Goodrich called, "That's enough, Jack. Come on over here and I'll give you that drink."

Cleveland did not move. He glared across the table and said, "Tell them, Henry, tell them about that squaw gal you got up at Sun River." Then, taking his gaze away from Plummer and looking around the hotel lobby, he announced, "You didn't know that, did you, none of you. Old Henry here had himself a pretty Indian poontang on a farm up at Sun River."

Henry Plummer jumped up, knocking the table hard

enough to spill glasses. His chair crashed to the floor behind him. His voice hard, he growled, "You son of a bitch, I'm tired of this! Draw your gun!"

Cleveland spun his head back to see Plummer standing there, revolver in hand. He staggered back five steps, speechless.

Plummer demanded, "Draw your gun, dammit. NOW!"

Cleveland went for the gun tucked into his belt. When his fingers wrapped around the butt, Plummer fired.

Plummer's first shot went wild; the second slammed into Cleveland's right hip. The impact lifted Cleveland off his feet, and he fell to the floor. He lay on his side for a moment, then turned and came up to his knees.

Plummer stood there, eyes locked on Cleveland, hate showing; Henry Plummer had been pushed too far.

When Cleveland was hit, his pistol had fallen right beside him. Weakly, he took the gun and made a move to get up. He saw that Plummer was still aiming at him. Sounding sobered up, but still with a pitiful whine, he pleaded, "You wouldn't shoot a man when he's down?"

Plummer snapped, "No, you son of a bitch! Get to your feet."

Cleveland had barely raised one knee off the floor when Plummer fired again. One shot banged into Cleveland's chest, went past the heart, and lodged against his spine. One shot hit Cleveland's right cheek, just below the eye, and lodged in the brain. The third shot missed and cut a gouge in the floor beside where Cleveland fell.

Still pointing the gun at the fallen body, Plummer spat out, "There, you son of a bitch; don't call my woman a squaw!"

Before the last shot had been fired, Gad Moore had also drawn his gun and was at Plummer's side while the smoke was still rising out of the barrel of Plummer's six-shooter. Moore said, "We'd better get out of here!"

Plummer said, "I've got one shot left; I'd like to put it in his mouth."

"Forget it, Henry. The bastard's dead!"

Looking down at the pool of blood beginning to spread on the floor around Jack Cleveland, young Jeff Perkins felt as if he was going to be sick to his stomach.

Plummer, responding to the pressure of Gad Moore's hand on his arm, began to walk to the front of the room. He paused for a moment at the bar. "You saw him go for his gun, Bill?"

Bill Goodrich nodded before he glanced back at the fallen victim.

Plummer said, "You remember that, Bill, you remember that."

And Plummer walked out onto Main Street.

Bill Goodrich had experienced his share of shootings, and he had seen blood spilled on the floor of his hotel lobby before, but he had never seen a pool of blood grow quite so rapidly. He moved from behind the bar to where Cleveland lay dying.

When the confrontation had started and Old Brod had left the hotel with his customer right behind, the word had begun to spread along Main Street. As soon as the participants were known, people began making for Goodrich's Hotel; a fight between Jack Cleveland and Henry Plummer had long been expected. Old Brod had gone directly to Hank Crawford's butcher shop. Crawford was penning up two steers in back of his shop; with Old Brod's help, he finished quickly and hurried to Goodrich's in hopes of averting any shooting. Crawford had been only fifty feet from the front door of Goodrich's when the shots rang out. He had begun to run and had nearly banged into Plummer, Moore, and Perkins as they hurried out onto Main Street. Plummer stopped for a moment, looked at Crawford, and said, "Hank, I shot that bastard. He was drunk and he pulled his gun on me."

Crawford said nothing.

Plummer's voice was tense, the pitch higher than normal as he added, "I'm telling the truth, Hank. The lousy bastard drew on me."

Gad Moore's voice was steadier than Plummer's as he declared, "That's right, Hank, I saw it."

Plummer added, "You ask Bill, he'll tell you."

Crawford found his voice. "This has been coming for a long time, Henry."

"He's been pressing me and I had to shoot him."

Crawford nodded. Plummer, Moore, and Perkins went around the corner and headed north on Second Street to Plummer's cabin.

Inside Goodrich's, Hank Crawford was met by a deathly silence. At the far end of the room a crowd of a dozen men stood around Jack Cleveland on the floor.

Crawford joined them quickly and found Bill Goodrich kneeling down, holding Cleveland's head up out of the pool of blood. Goodrich looked up at Crawford and shook his head in that ominous way people use to convey resignation to the inevitable. Crawford stooped and asked, "Is he alive?"

Goodrich nodded. "But I don't know how. The poor bastard is shot up bad, Hank."

An awful, sickening gurgle came from Jack Cleveland's throat, and he coughed out a clot of blood and mucus. Both Goodrich and Crawford were startled when Cleveland whispered, "He shot me, Bill. The bastard shot me."

Goodrich and Crawford looked at each other, then down at Cleveland. Blood was still oozing from the hole below his eye, but the bleeding from his chest seemed to have stopped. Crawford looked up at Old Brod and said, "Get me something to put over these wounds."

Goodrich said, "There's bar towels by the cash drawer, Brod; bring them over."

Old Brod returned with the bundle of cloths in seconds and handed it to Crawford, who placed one towel over the chest wound, one on the cheek. It seemed better not to be able to see the holes in the man's body. In a slightly stronger voice, Cleveland said, "Bill, that bastard shot me. I never thought he'd do that."

Crawford looked at Goodrich. "We've got to do something for him."

Goodrich chewed at his bottom lip. "I can't put him upstairs, Hank; I've got twenty men sleeping there tonight."

Crawford nodded, then looked up at the crowd. "I need some help carrying him. I'll take him to my place."

The men did not move; they seemed to be mesmerized by the presence of imminent death. But the look on Crawford's face finally jogged a couple of them into action; they began gingerly turning Cleveland onto his back in order to lift him. Others pitched in, and two men began carrying Cleveland out of the hotel. Their task was not made easier by the groans of pain from the victim.

Bill Goodrich said to Crawford, "It's good he was drunk; those wounds have to hurt like hell."

"Was he drunk enough to draw on Plummer?"

"I don't know who drew first. It all happened too fast. I can tell you that Jack was being pretty foulmouthed and was really challenging Plummer. I don't know if I could have taken the abuse as long as Henry took it."

Crawford said, "You know, I'm damned near convinced that Jack killed the Evans boy, so maybe it is all for the best."

"I don't think Jack will make it, do you?"

"No way, Bill. That one hole in his face should have killed him. We'll see what we can do for him at my cabin."

"If there's anything I can do, let me know."

"About all any of us can do is to pray for his soul right now; the time for doing something was weeks ago. We should have banished him from the camp."

Goodrich, with a grim look on his face, replied, "Now it looks like he's going to pay with his life. We have to get this camp under control."

Crawford nodded. All of the honest residents of Bannack had felt the building tensions through the winter, and there had been hundreds of discussions, but nothing had been done. Crawford headed toward his cabin.

The men who had carried Cleveland the two blocks from the hotel had let themselves into Crawford's one-room cabin and set the wounded man on the single bunk against the east wall. When Crawford walked in, he saw that someone had lighted the two kerosene lanterns even though it was midday. There were no windows in the cabin, and it seemed right to try to push the darkness out of the place. One man was at the wood stove stoking up some warmth, two men stood by watching the fire, two other men leaned against the back wall. It was as if they all needed to distance themselves from the imminence of death. Crawford went to the bunk and bent down. In a solemn, hushed voice, he asked, "How you doing, Jack?"

Cleveland's eyes were full of pain and confusion. He asked, "Hank, am I gonna die?"

Crawford forced a slight laugh. "Hell, Jack, ain't no reason to think about that. You just get better fast. How's that?"

Cleveland stared blankly for a moment. "I'm cold, dammit. I'm cold."

Cleveland was covered with a thin, woven blanket. Crawford said, "I'll get you more covers."

Cleveland reached up a hand and weakly stopped Crawford from rising. "I want my blankets, Hank. Plummer has my blankets."

Crawford hesitated. "I've got blankets, Jack." With another forced smile, he added, "Hell, an ugly mule like you could even use one of my horse blankets."

Cleveland looked blank for a moment, realized it had been a joke, smiled, and said, "That's funny, Hank, real funny. But," he began to try and lift himself up on his elbow, "I want my own damned blankets. They're mine!"

Crawford did not want to get involved with Henry Plummer and some stupid blankets. Just as he was about to say he would not leave, Cleveland added, "Please,

Hank, you gotta get my blankets; they're about all I've got left."

Crawford realized that he had to try. He turned to the other men in the cabin. "Would one of you go to Plummer's and ask for Jack's blankets?"

There was no response.

Crawford turned back to Cleveland and said, "I'll go get them. I'll be right back."

As Crawford walked the three blocks to Plummer's cabin, he realized that he knew practically nothing about Jack Cleveland, just that he was easy to dislike, a man who was about as antisocial as anyone in the camp, and a man who very possibly had murdered the Evans youth for a few dollars. Not many had friendly feelings for Jack Cleveland. But the man was about to die in a place where few would call him friend. No one knew a family that could be written to or of a wife or children who should be told. Hank Crawford was frustrated.

When he arrived at Plummer's cabin, he climbed the two steps to the tiny porch and knocked on the front door. From inside, immediately and briskly, came a challenge: "Who the hell is it?"

As soon as Crawford identified himself, the latch was lifted and the door yanked open. Plummer stood there with his revolver in his hand. Before Plummer said anything, he looked around to see if Crawford was alone. Satisfied with that, he snapped, "Is he dead?"

"No."

"What did he say?"

Crawford moved uncomfortably with a slight fidgeting of his feet and a shrug of his shoulders. "He said he wanted his blankets."

"His *blankets*!"

"That's what he said. He claims you have his blankets, Henry."

Plummer's eyes showed anger—or fear. Hank Crawford could never be sure later of what he saw in Plummer's eyes that day. At that moment, he could never have imagined how the shooting of Jack Cleveland was going to lead to trouble between Plummer and himself.

Plummer growled, "That's the damnedest lie I've ever heard, Hank Crawford. That man's laying shot on Bill Goodrich's floor and all he's talking about is blankets! That's bullshit!"

Crawford took the insult; he wanted to get back to the dying man. He said, "He's not at Goodrich's; we moved him to my cabin. Look, Henry, do you have Jack's blankets or not? I don't care one way or the other."

Plummer backed out of the doorway and motioned for Crawford to come inside.

The cabin Plummer had built for his intended bride was well appointed. There was a back door and three windows—extravagant in a community where windows and proper doors were shipped from Salt Lake City at considerable expense. There was a wooden floor and adequate furniture. There was no sign of Jeff Perkins or Gad Moore, but sitting at the pinewood table were George Ives and Charley Reeves, who were two other bad eggs in the community. Ives and Reeves looked up sullenly as Crawford entered the cabin.

Plummer walked to a built-in closet at the back of the cabin. As he reached into it, he said, "I've got a bedroll that bastard has left here for months. I guess that's what he means about blankets."

Crawford remained just inside the door and waited for Plummer to bring the bedroll to him. Plummer stopped a half-dozen feet away and demanded, "What else has that son of a bitch said to you, Hank?"

Crawford held his temper and said, "I swear, Henry, all he asked for was the blankets. I know it sounds crazy, but maybe he is in such pain that he doesn't know what he's talking about."

From the table, George Ives asked, "Is he gonna die, Crawford?"

Crawford nodded his head, then said, "At least he

looks pretty bad." Turning to Plummer, he added, "You really hit him, Henry."

Plummer's face was grim. "He drew on me; no man draws on me and lives."

Crawford gave a shrug and reached out to take the bundle. "Seems a damned shame that a man dies and that's all he has to his name."

"He's got more than this; he's got a bad reputation. That's for sure." Plummer handed the bundle to Crawford, who nodded a curt thanks and started to leave. As he stepped through the doorway, Plummer asked, "You sure he hasn't said anything else?"

Over his shoulder, Crawford answered, "Nothing, Henry, he's barely whispering."

"You think he's out of his mind with pain?"

"I'm no doctor; he looks like he's hurting pretty bad."

George Ives had risen and came to stand beside Plummer. Ives said, "I understand he was pretty drunk when the shooting happened."

Crawford said, "I wouldn't know; I wasn't there."

Plummer snarled, "If he's blabbing bad things about me, Hank Crawford, I'll come shoot him right where he lays. You understand that?"

Crawford answered, "There's no reason to talk that way, Henry. The man is just about dead; let it lie. I don't think anyone will hold it against you."

Plummer did not answer that, so Crawford nodded a good-bye and left. As soon as he was out of earshot, Plummer ordered, "You two get out of here and leave me alone. George, I want you to go to Crawford's cabin and keep your ears open; I want to know what that bastard is saying. Charley, you go to Goodrich's and Skinner's; see what's being said around there. Get back to me if you hear anything bad. Move."

Charley Reeves and George Ives were used to taking Plummer's orders. They left wordlessly.

Alone in the cabin, Plummer flopped down into a chair at the table. The shooting was bad enough; it would hurt his respectability in the camp. But there were witnesses to verify that Jack Cleveland had been very drunk and that he had been taunting Plummer into a fight. So he could ride out any bad results of the shooting. It was what Jack Cleveland was saying to those who would listen in Crawford's cabin—if he started talking about the murder of Patrick Ford back in Oro Fino, then there could really be trouble.

More and more, over the past few weeks, Henry Plummer had been giving serious thought to abandoning his life of crime. His thoughts of marrying Electa Bryan had begun to make him want a stable, honest way of living. If he had to defend himself in the shooting of Patrick Ford, then all that could be lost.

Plummer slammed his fist down onto the table and two coffee cups, only half-empty, bounced in the air. "Hell!" he shouted. "Why this; why now!"

CHAPTER 9

(Monday, March 2, 1863)

The three men who were paid fifty cents each to dig a grave for Jack Cleveland groused about the labor; breaking through two inches of frost was not an easy task, surely worth more than fifty cents on a cold Monday morning. But the grave had been dug, Cleveland had been buried, and the dirt had been set back in place. All that remained of Jack Cleveland were a few meager possessions and a memory.

The law-abiding residents of the camp faced Cleveland's death with mixed emotions. None of them approved of gunfights and killings, but the prevailing conviction was that Cleveland had killed the Evans boy and that Cleveland had deserved to die. That his death came not at the end of a proper hangman's noose was unfortunate, but the result was the same. So the honest people of the camp tried to go on about the routine of winter survival.

But something happened to the personality of

Bannack after the shooting of Jack Cleveland; something bad.

It was as if the shooting had been a license issued for the rowdy element to come to the fore, to accelerate their dangerous behavior. Within hours of Cleveland's death in Hank Crawford's cabin, the drinking became more active, the mood in the saloons more boisterous. In Cyrus Skinner's Elk Horn, during the hour after the death was announced, there were four fights resulting in two nasty knifing incidents. The men who called themselves friends of Henry Plummer accepted the shooting as a sign that their hero had finally stopped the foolish talk of starting an ore-processing mill and of going straight; they felt it was a sign for them to resume their old ways, the ways of easy money.

Even though Plummer had dispatched George Ives to Crawford's cabin, and even though Ives had reported back that Cleveland had died without revealing the story of Oro Fino, Plummer could not, would not, accept the fact that Cleveland had not told.

Henry Plummer had convinced himself that Cleveland had not taken the secret of the Patrick Ford killing in Oro Fino to the grave. He was sure Cleveland had, instead, left the information on the doorstep of hell for anyone to pick up; and he firmly believed that Hank Crawford had been the one to do so. Plummer remained holed up in his cabin, sulking over his imagined misfortune, and refused pleas from his cronies to come to Skinner's and join in the drinking. His cronies were like criminals just released from prison; they were intent on debauchery.

The most flagrant abuse came from Plummer's close friend from Oro Fino, Charley Reeves.

A month previously, back in early February, Reeves had bought a young Indian girl from the tribe of Bannacks living at the edge of the camp. The girl had put up with Reeves' violent beatings for as long as she could stand them, then, finally, had fled to the safety of her father's tipi. Reeves had given little thought to the girl until the camp's badmen began letting loose. Now Reeves decided he'd like to have his woman back with him.

Charley Reeves, like many of those around Henry Plummer, was a seedy man in both appearance and personality. In his twenty-five years of life, he had learned to dress in a shoddy, unkempt manner. The left side of his head looked as if someone had used it as a chopping block, which was not far from what had actually happened. Two years before, Reeves had taunted a Chinese cook in a small café in Lewiston, Idaho Territory. The cook had finally lost his temper and had attacked Reeves with a meat cleaver, delivering three glancing chops around Reeves' head before he was subdued. The cook escaped with his life only by hiding in Lewiston's sizable Chinatown; Reeves avoided losing his left ear only by some quick stitching performed by Henry Plummer's mistress. Reeves' dirty and ugly appearance was reflected in his attitude toward others; he had no respect for honest workers and little respect for anyone at all other than Henry Plummer.

The day after the shooting of Jack Cleveland, when Charley Reeves decided to reclaim his Indian girl, he recruited another Charley, Charley Moore, to join in the adventure. Both men were well into being drunk even though it was just past midday.

The name Bannack translates into "Sheepeater," which the white men took to be a derogatory term. In fact, it attested to the bravery of the tribe's hunters, who tracked and killed the elusive and resourceful Rocky Mountain sheep. The area of the gold discovery by Grasshopper Creek had been a traditional summering ground for the tribe. When the white man came and started to dig into the ground, four families had opted to remain in the area through the winter. The Indian leaders had been fascinated by the foolishness of the prospectors who dug dirt and wallowed in mud, and who were willing to pay outlandish fees for freshly killed elk and deer. The four families of the village had traded for unheard-of treasures, such as heavy iron cooking pots, soft warm blankets, and even a box of bullets for the two Sharps carbines owned by the tribe. The eldest family leader had pulled off the most extravagant coup when he had sold his fifteen-year-old daughter to the silly, ugly white man for a handsome buck knife, three cotton blankets, and a nearly new mackinaw jacket with a matching hat replete with three wild turkey feathers.

When the elder's daughter had returned to the tipi, there was some worry that the goods would have to be returned, but when the ugly white man did not show up with any demands, the daughter reentered the family's graces. There was some resentment that the daughter had suffered cuts and bruises, but those injuries were dismissed as the strange custom of the white man.

The white population of the camp was ambivalent about the presence of the Indian village. On the frontier, it was widely agreed that the Indians were uncivilized savages, but it was known that the Bannacks were not warlike, and were not especially territorial, so the prevailing mood was to let them stay on the land that had been their hunting grounds for a millennium. Sometimes a few drunken prospectors would go to the village and try to rouse some conflict, but for the most part, the situation was peaceful.

After Reeves and Moore had finished off most of another bottle of whiskey, the two men staggered their way along Main Street, crossed the plank bridge to the Indian village, and began calling out for Daisy, the name Reeves had tagged onto the Indian girl, whose real name was Flying Dove.

It was bitterly cold that day, and the members of the village knew from the wind and the sky that a snowstorm was coming to the area. Experience told the elder that the storm would probably be the last one of the winter, so there was no sense in going out to try to hunt; the day would be spent in the comfort of the tipis and in conversation about the future. It was agreed that they would not winter near the white man again; some burdens were simply not worth the suffering.

Reeves and Moore blundered into the main tipi. Even in the dim firelight, it was easy to see Reeves' "Daisy" cowering in the corner.

The men of the village had tried to ignore the yelling outside, but when the white men intruded into the privacy of the tipi, some of the Indians took umbrage. The Bannacks did not speak English, and the two white men did not speak Bannack, so there was much gesturing with hands. Reeves was demanding that he be given back the woman he had paid for; the Indians were demanding that the pair get their asses out of the tipi. There was a scuffle, some pushing and shoving, and, before they realized what had happened, Reeves and Moore found themselves out in the cold afternoon air.

Reeves yanked out his pistol and barged back into the tipi just as the elder was coming out. Reeves used the butt of the pistol to knock a welt on the man's head and scurried away, followed by Moore. They yelled back that the Indians had better deliver the woman to Skinner's, or else there would be big trouble. The Indians yelled back that Reeves and Moore probably ate some awful-sounding things in their diet and one of the Indians gave an astounding account of the genealogy of Charley Reeves. That might have been all there was to the incident if the girl had returned to the white man, but none of the village residents saw any sense in her going back where she would probably be mauled again. The incident might also have died a natural death if whiskey had not been so available, and if the two Charleys had not been able to expand their account of the encounter into what seemed tantamount to a major war. By the time a third round of drinks had been swallowed in Skinner's saloon, the number of belligerents had grown to five men, armed with four pistols, a banged-up Lefever

Arms 10-gauge shotgun, and an Allen and Thurber double-barrel shotgun. With their Dutch courage well tended, the five men set off for the Indian village to reclaim Reeves' woman.

There are conflicting stories as to whether an argument preceded the violence or whether the quintet of men simply began shooting—but when the smoke had cleared after the three minutes, the Indian elder was dead along with two squaws, one young boy, and an infant. In addition, a French-Canadian trapper turned woodcutter named Pierre "Frenchy" Cazette had been shot dead, with a single bullet hole in his head. Cazette, a friend of the Bannack Indians, had gone to the elder's tipi when he heard that the old man had been injured with a blow to the head; he had paid for his kindness with his life.

LeGrau's Café was nearly empty at the time the shots were heard. Only two men sat at a corner table drinking coffee. Renee and Cora were getting ready for the customers who would be coming in for dinner. At the sound of the shots, the two women paused, looked at each other. Renee went back to her work but Cora seemed frozen. She was unable to accept the sound of gunfire as a normal part of daily life. Before the shooting had finished, Frank LeGrau came hurrying in from his blacksmith shop and ordered: "You girls stay here. There's shooting in the Injun village."

Cora was glad to know what was going on; she was beginning more and more to fear the possibility of Vic Voit being shot. But knowing the trouble was at the Indian village gave rise to another fear she harbored: an Indian uprising.

As LeGrau ran out the back door followed by the two customers, Cora went to stand by Renee at the breadboard. Cora asked, "You think them Indians could cause trouble?"

Renee kept kneading the mound of dough in front of her. "First off, those Bannacks are not a bad bunch.

Second off, Frank and the others can handle any problem that might come up. Third off, you better be getting those potatoes peeled and into the kettle, or we're going to have some hungry, angry customers tonight."

Cora started to move, then paused. "You sure?"

Renee snapped, "I'm sure we need those potatoes peeled and cooked."

"I mean, are you sure that Mister LeGrau and the others can handle the Indians if something starts? I hear Indians can be damned mean. I hear they killed a lot of people coming west."

Renee stopped for a moment, looked up at Cora, and answered gently, "Cora, you don't have to worry. Frank and I will look after you, you know that."

Cora gave a polite smile, but she was not reassured. Despite their kindness to her, she felt that the LeGraus would pull out of the camp fast if things went really wrong, and there was no reason they would see to her safety.

Cora had been giving a lot of thought to her own well-being recently, and to the future. There was not much in the camp to encourage bright prospects, because most of the men were so intent on digging for gold and raising hell that they seemed to think little of their own futures. Vic Voit fell into that category in some respects. She could depend on him to come around and spend time with her; that was nice. But every now and then, he had to take off to Skinner's or to the new saloon over by the ditch, "to be with the boys," was the way he put it. She fumed silently every time he used that expression. Alone in her cabin, she admitted to herself that she was getting sweet on Vic and she was satisfied he was developing feelings about her. She sure wasn't ready for marriage, absolutely not to some crazy galoot who was spending his life hoping to make a fortune out of the muddy banks of Grasshopper Creek. As she worked out some of her frustrations by peeling the potatoes for dinner, it dawned on her that Vic Voit might be just the type of man to give her the security that Renee LeGrau found in her husband.

As she worked her way through the pail of potatoes, Cora began daydreaming about what her life would be like if she did settle down with a husband. Vic Voit had been seeing her through the whole winter. Granted, she had lost her temper several times because of his "going off with the boys," but there had been a couple of incidents when he had done things that had made him attractive, such as the time when he had given her wood carvings of a squirrel and a rabbit. She had pooh-poohed his gifts but, in fact, she had the carvings sitting on a shelf in her cabin. They were her only really nice bits of decoration. She looked on Voit's thoughtfulness in a new light. Maybe it would be possible for her to be nice to him; maybe he could give her the feeling of security that was missing in her life. She was snapped back to reality when Renee called across the kitchen, "What could be keeping them?"

Cora, confused, asked, "What'd you mean? I didn't hear you." For a couple of minutes, Renee had been speculating aloud as to why her husband had not returned from the shooting. The tone of Renee's voice brought a response: "Hey, Renee, there's nothing wrong. There ain't been any shots since the first ones. He's probably up having a drink at Goodrich's."

Renee gave a weak smile; Frank LeGrau did not hang around any bars.

It was another twenty minutes before Frank showed up, and when he did he was with Hank Crawford, Drury Underwood, Jerry Rockwell, Quentin Lear, and, to Cora's surprise, Vic Voit. Cora had never seen Voit in the company of the camp's leaders. The men looked serious.

Frank LeGrau went directly to Renee, took her by the arm, and led her out the back door, talking to her in a tone so low that Cora could not hear a word he was saying. Hank Crawford asked in a flat voice if the party could have some coffee and Cora said she'd get some right away. Vic Voit came up beside Cora and asked if he could help her, seeing as she was alone. Cora said, "That'd be nice, Vic." As he began to load the filled cups onto a tray, Cora asked, "What was all the shooting about?"

"Some drunks shot up the Indian village."

"That ain't nothing new."

"It's new this time; there's five or six of them dead. One of them was only a baby!"

Cora felt a sobering chill through her whole body, as if someone had opened the door of a warm cabin on a subzero night. She had almost been able to accept shootings and even killings, but this . . . a whole group of people, innocent people, had been killed. She spilled a little coffee on the counter top. Voit touched her shoulder. "You okay, Cora?"

She felt weak, as if she might faint. The touch of his hand on her shoulder was comforting. She pulled herself together and smiled. "Don't worry about me; I just felt funny for a minute." Then, as she looked at him, she asked, "You sure it was a baby killed?"

His face was solemn. He nodded. Briskly, so as not to dwell on the whole thing, she grabbed the tray and said, "Thanks for the help."

He walked back to the table beside her and sat down as she served the coffee to the others.

Crawford asked, "Is there anything to eat?"

"It's too early for dinner, but there's some soup and biscuits left over from lunch time." She took orders for three servings and went to the kitchen area.

Hank Crawford had been in his butcher shop when he heard the shots. He would not have gone out to see, except for the number of shots and the direction from which they had come. Crawford had some tolerance for shootings and violence in the saloons, because he felt that if people wanted to put themselves in harm's way, then that was their business. This time he was incensed at the cruel and wanton shooting by men who were obviously criminals. He was silently grateful that Pipe Carrier and his hunting party had stayed out longer than planned. The incident could have been worse, if such a horror could be worse.

"Damned rotten bunch," he said.

Quentin Lear, an early Bannack settler, scratched at the whiskers on his chin. "We gotta hang them; no question. This time we get out the rope and do some neck stretching."

Drury Underwood, a skinny young prospector, sipped his hot coffee and offered, "If there was ever a reason to hang a killer, this is it."

Jerry Rockwell, who had come into the camp during the hard part of winter and was making a start by building cabins, asked, "Do you think that talk at Skinner's was right? I mean about Reeves getting even with the Indians for killing his family and all of that?"

Underwood snapped, "That's bullshit! If some Indians did kill Reeves' family, that don't mean he can go shooting up *these* Indians. Hell, the Bannacks have never been known to go raiding white settlements."

Crawford agreed. "There's no reason for anyone to go killing people like that." There was a pause; Crawford took the lull to light his pipe. "I sure wish Nat Langford was here; we could use his advice. I wonder if we should send for him?"

"I agree with you," Underwood said. "Nat said he was thinking about going to the capital in Lewiston to try and get us a proper sheriff."

"Yeah," Rockwell said. "We could use a sheriff a hell of a lot more than we could use that sawmill Nat is working on. We won't be needing any lumber if everybody packs out of town because of Reeves and his kind."

Cora arrived with the food, and the men fell silent as the bowls were placed. She lingered to hear what the men were going to say, but they merely began eating. Finally, resigned, she said, "If you need anything, just yell."

Jerry Rockwell asked if there was any butter and

honey for the biscuits. Cora said she'd get them, and Vic Voit put down his coffee cup, saying, "I'll come with you."

Cora accepted the offer gratefully; in the kitchen she pressed Voit, and he told her what he knew.

A number of people had made it to the Indian village before the gunsmoke had begun to dissipate into the air. Hank Crawford had taken charge of things. Three of the Bannacks who had not been killed had suffered nasty wounds. Once the wounded were being looked after, Crawford set out to discover what had happened. The lack of a common language caused some delay, but it was finally clear who had done the shooting and the probable cause of the conflict. Crawford had never approved of prospectors buying Indian squaws, and he had even had words with Charley Reeves about it. Ironically, Pipe Carrier had not seemed to be disturbed by Reeves' purchase; he had told Crawford that Flying Dove was not worth the price. Crawford did not look forward to speaking with Pipe Carrier when he returned from the hunting trip.

As soon as the turmoil at the village had been subdued as well as possible, Crawford enlisted a handful of men to go looking for Reeves and Moore. They went first to Goodrich's Hotel. No sign of the wanted men there. The group then went into Skinner's saloon. When they let it be known what they were after, they were greeted with derisive comments from the patrons and absolutely no help from Cy Skinner. In fact, Skinner demanded that the search party leave his establishment. The next logical place to search was the cabin of Henry Plummer—but Plummer's cabin was empty.

Frustrated, angry, and determined, Crawford sent two men to guard the west road leading out of town and two men up the gully to guard the eastern way out, although darkness was already falling. Crawford's next step was to take a break at LeGrau's Café in order to put together some kind of proper search of the camp.

"They've got to be here," Crawford said as he finished off the last of his biscuits by wiping the soup bowl clean.

Rockwell said, "We'll find them; don't worry."

Quentin Lear left the table for another serving of soup, but before he moved away he said, "I'll be betting they're out of the camp by now."

"With Henry Plummer helping them, they're sure to get away clean," Underwood offered. "That Plummer knows the mountains damned good."

Crawford said, "We don't *know* for sure that Plummer is helping them."

"If he ain't," Underwood came back, "then I'll be more wrong than I've ever been in my life."

Others began drifting into the café, and a large-sized crowd collected around Crawford's table. Cora, getting overwhelmed by the demand for service, ducked out the back door to find Renee.

Renee and her husband were standing inside his blacksmith shop, near the warmth of the forge, talking seriously. Frank LeGrau was arguing that they should leave Bannack; Renee was arguing that they were building a future in the camp and they should stay. The discussion was cut off when Cora walked up and explained that she needed help in the café; Frank said he would be talking to Renee later but that she'd better think about pulling out.

Cora Harris was getting a sinking feeling that she was about to be abandoned.

CHAPTER 10

(Wednesday, March 4, 1863)

Henry Plummer had panicked. In his panic, he had made some errors in judgment, and he was trying to recover.

After the shooting in the Indian village, two of the shooters and one of the bystanders had fled to Plummer's cabin, seeking help and advice. Their action had been understandable; Plummer had been cultivating their loyalty for the previous two months.

When Plummer had found Cyrus Skinner operating his saloon in Bannack, he had renewed their association, which extended back over five years to when the two had met in San Quentin Prison in California. None in the camp knew that the two had been convicted of murder; few knew the two had cooperated in illegal activities in other gold camps; and only one or two people found the friendship a warning sign of trouble. Plummer and Skinner did well in hiding their association: Skinner operated the Elk Horn; Plummer posed as a man in camp ready to make investments and build a future.

Slowly, attracting no attention, the pair began to build a collection of scoundrels ready to do their bidding. Skinner let the motley group hang around the saloon; Plummer doled out dribbles of money to keep the band loosely tied together under the guise of potential employment in legitimate business ventures.

Plummer had heard the shooting, but had stayed in his cabin, still brooding over what Jack Cleveland had said before he had died. When the attackers had burst into his cabin and told him what they had done, he was furious with them and frightened for his own safety. That was the moment when he panicked.

The trio that had come to him were Bill Mitchell, who had gone along as a sightseer, but who felt guilty now; and the shooters, the two Charleys: Reeves and Moore.

Even gripped by panic, Plummer was able to organize well. He sent Mitchell to advise Cy Skinner of the situation, and sent Moore to find enough food for the escape. Plummer and Reeves ran the block to Goodrich's stable, where they saddled up four horses.

Skinner showed up as the men were mounting up and Moore arrived with supplies so skimpy they would last little more than a day. Plummer retained the appearance of calm while trying to make proper decisions. Skinner, arrogantly confident that nothing would be done to the shooters, tried to talk Plummer out of leaving. Plummer could not resist the urge to bolt, because of his fear of Jack Cleveland's dying words.

The quartet pulled out of camp just ten minutes after the last shot had been fired into the Bannack tipis.

Darkness came within a half hour, and that aided in the escape. Around midnight, one of those famous spring snowstorms began dumping two feet of powdery flakes on their route. Plummer's scheme was to head north past Deer Lodge, then on to the Mullan Road, which was the main east–west trail. At Mullan Road, the others could head west to Hell Gate, or could go east with him; he was going to collect Electa Bryan at the Sun River Ranch, then head back to begin a new life in the States.

His plan fell to pieces when the snow became so heavy that they lost their way. They had to stop about four in the morning and wait for daylight to continue.

The snow backed off just as the first glimmer of dawn arrived, but it was still heavily overcast. Plummer told his companions to stay put; he would scout around for some sign of a familiar landmark. During the winter months, Plummer had ridden all around the region neighboring Bannack. His purpose had not been to be ready for an escape, but to gather expert knowledge of the routes in and out of the camp. That information was critical for his future plans. The investment in exploration was paying off; in twenty minutes he came to Rattlesnake Creek and knew they were just twenty-five miles out of camp, much too little distance for twelve hours of travel.

When he rode back to where he had left Mitchell and the two Charleys, he was greeted with another wrinkle: Charley Moore had disappeared.

Plummer stood there trying to subdue a new surge of panic. Charley Reeves was getting ready to mount up as he said, "Damn, Henry, I don't know where he is. Let's get moving."

Plummer's panic was turning to anger.

"What do you say, Henry?"

Bill Mitchell joined in, "If we're only at the Rattlesnake, we'd better haul ass."

Plummer was tempted to ask Reeves why he had let Moore walk off but he knew that each of the Charleys was about a brick short of a full load.

"We'll give him a few minutes."

Reeves moved away from his horse. "I'm gonna make a fire."

Plummer's temper snapped. "Dammit, Charley! Why don't you just ride back and tell them where we are? You know they're coming after us!"

Reeves stopped. He did not like being yelled at by anyone.

Plummer saw the look on Reeves' face, and made

ready to defend himself.

The sound of a rifle shot exploded. It was close by.

Plummer dove behind a tree, Bill Mitchell ran toward his horse, and Charley Reeves grabbed for his gun, snarling, "What the hell was that?"

Plummer lowered himself into a crouch behind the tree, so angry at Reeves that he did not care if the man was shot.

From not too far off, Charley Moore's gravelly voice hooted, "Hot damn! I got him!"

Reeves called, "Charley! What the hell you up to?"

"I got me a goddamned rabbit!"

Henry Plummer approached a decision: should he leave this trio of lunatics, or should he go on and lead them to safety? He decided to wait a few minutes before taking any drastic action. He rose, reholstered his gun, and walked a few feet away from Reeves to lean against a tree. It was not long before Charley Moore came stalking out of the dense woods proudly holding up a medium-sized cottontail by the ears. He seemed elated with his trophy. He announced, "Now we got something to eat. I got us a meal, you can see that."

Charley Reeves snarled, "Shit, Charley, look at the damned thing! You shot half of him away."

Reeves was quite right; there was barely enough meat left to feed a bunkhouse dog. An argument ensued about what they could do to salvage a meal from the rabbit, and the argument progressed into an academic discussion about how best to shoot small game.

Plummer decided he would pull out and leave them.

He pushed himself away from the tree and began walking to his horse. He was frozen in his tracks by a strange voice that boomed out: "Just stay where you are!"

The voice sounded far enough away to be out of pistol range but easily within reach of a rifle. Plummer lunged forward, grabbed the reins of his horse, and shouted: "Head into the woods!"

Moore and Reeves might not have been too smart, but they trusted Plummer. All three of the men ran deeper into the woods.

Two shots roared in the crisp, dry air, but the shots were high. That gave heart to Plummer, because he figured the shooters were not intent on killing. The fugitives tripped, stumbled, and banged their way about fifty yards through the deep undergrowth. Reeves had had enough sense to grab his horse, which gave him access to his rifle; Moore and Mitchell had left their mounts behind, so they only had sidearms. Plummer had followed them, leading his horse; they all stopped in a dense cluster of trees.

He assigned each man an area to cover, tied his horse to a tree, and then began to backtrack, hoping to see who was out there shooting at them.

It was Quentin Lear, leading a four-man posse dispatched by Hank Crawford. From LeGrau's, Crawford had sent three search parties out, one to cover the Grasshopper Creek drainage, one west toward the Big Hole, and Lear's group to head north. With Lear were Bob Higgins and Jerry Rockwell, both prospectors in their early twenties, and Larry Davenport, near thirty and a saw operator at Bozeman's mill. They had been using lanterns during the night's snowstorm; they had picked up the trail of the escapees before dawn. The rabbit-shooting blast of Charley Moore had been the final aid.

As Plummer had made his way back to the edge of the woods, he had been careful to stay hidden. He was crouched behind a fat aspen tree when he spotted the breath rising from Quentin Lear. Plummer needed another vantage point. He started to move and Larry Davenport shouted: "Hold it, mister!"

Plummer froze.

Lear eased up from the protection of a fallen tree. He called: "Is that you, Henry?"

Plummer was trying to get his bearings. There were at least two men out there; he needed to know if there were more. He called back, "Hell yes, it's me, Quentin. What's up?"

Plummer flicked his eyes back and forth, trying to evaluate his opposition.

Lear called back, "You traveling with Reeves and Moore?"

"Who wants to know?"

Lear snapped, "I want to know, Henry. We're taking them in."

"In where?"

"To Bannack; they're escaped criminals."

Plummer kept himself covered by the tree. "Don't try to read me the law, Quentin; I've been there. Reeves and Moore ain't escaped, because they've never been captured, and they ain't criminals, because they ain't never been convicted. Now, don't pull my leg, Quentin."

Lear had not planned on having to reason with anyone. He said, "We're taking them in for shooting the Indians and Frenchy Cazette."

"By whose orders? You become a judge or something, Quent?"

Lear was becoming more and more frustrated. Tracking the killers through the night had been a tense business, and now he was having to play like a lawyer. He snapped back, "Listen, Henry, we all decided that Reeves and Moore should answer for their crime and—"

"Crime! Shooting some savage Indians is a crime?"

Lear shouted angrily, "Frenchy was no savage; they killed him, too."

Plummer did not reply. Lear called, "What's your stake in this, Henry? We've got no problem with you. We want Reeves and Moore."

"Suppose they don't want to come with you?"

"You didn't answer. What's your stake?"

"They're friends. They asked me to help them find their way to Hell Gate."

There was another pause. Then Lear said, "Henry, I want to talk to you. Come on out."

"I don't talk until I know what the odds are; who's with you."

"There's some of us here. Don't worry about that. Just come on out."

Plummer moved just clear of the tree. "I'm showing myself, Quent. Now you show yourself."

Lear stood up. As he was brushing the snow from his pants, he ordered, "You others, stay under cover. I'm doing the talking with Henry."

Plummer did not move. Off to Lear's left he saw breath steam rising. Another man. Back, far behind Lear, Plummer heard a horse whinny. He guessed there were at least four, probably more. Things were looking serious.

Plummer waded through a deep drift of snow to where Quentin Lear waited. As he came near, he said, "Let's get this over with fast, Quent: it's cold and I've got traveling to do."

Lear smiled. "You can leave right now, Henry; we have no call on you."

Plummer said, "If I go, my friends go."

Lear moved his rifle up under his left arm and rubbed his hands together. "Your *friends* are in trouble, Henry. We're taking them back to the camp." He noticed Plummer glancing around. "There's no way out, Henry. There are six of us here, and four on the other side of where Reeves and Moore are. We're serious about this."

Plummer could not tell whether Lear was bluffing or not. The two had never played cards—Lear did not play cards—so Plummer had no way to judge.

"Okay," Plummer said with resignation in his voice. "What's the deal?"

Lear was nonplussed. He had been given no power to negotiate a deal. He had been told to bring back the men who had shot up the Indian village. "You got to help me on this one, Henry. All Hank Crawford said was to bring 'em back."

Plummer's whole outlook changed in that instant. A

few minutes before he had been running like a fugitive, leading other fugitives to freedom. His hopes for the future now had some chance of survival. He still harbored a fear of being exposed by what Hank Crawford might know about the Oro Fino killing, but Quentin Lear had given Plummer a chance to present himself as a reasonable, community-minded individual.

Plummer gave Lear a two-sentence history of his own experience with law enforcement, then said, "These men have rights, Quent. You know that."

Lear agreed.

"So they have to know what they are facing. I called it a deal, but it is really just a guarantee of their rights. Right?"

"I guess so."

"Fine." Plummer relaxed. "Let me go talk to them."

"We don't have all day, Henry."

"It won't take long."

It took two and a half hours for a deal to be struck. Bill Mitchell and the two Charleys stayed hidden in the protection of the dense woods, and Plummer did all of the thinking and talking. His first two sessions with Lear involved allowing the trio to go free; that wore down Lear's resolve quite a bit. The next two sessions were for an absolute understanding that the trio, if they returned to Bannack, were doing so of their own free will. Lear finally gave in, because he felt the point was moot, so long as they returned. The last session centered entirely on what Mitchell, Moore, and Reeves would face. In desperation, Lear made a promise that there would be a proper jury selected. Plummer had made it sound so reasonable: "Twelve good men and true, Quent. That's all any man can ask."

Lear had originally supposed that the three would face a trial in front of the Miners' Court. That was an accepted form of judicial proceedings in gold camps. When a prospecting district began attracting people, those working claims signed up as members of the district and agreed to abide by the rules and regulations. Frequently, the miners would call a court to settle criminal actions, where the worst penalty was banishment and forfeiture of property and claims. What confused Lear was that a trial by jury sounded awfully official and, "Damn, Henry. Those friends of yours could be hung!"

Plummer smiled. "They'll take their chances."

Plummer had evolved his own plan of how the whole thing would be settled, and the plan demanded the promise of a trial by jury.

Quentin agreed.

"I'm asking for a guarantee, Quent. I need your absolute guarantee!"

Lear was tired. He had ridden all night; he was as cold as he had ever been in his life, and he was having to argue an issue about which he knew nothing. "You got it, Henry."

Plummer breathed a deep sigh of relief. He extended his hand. As they sealed the deal, Plummer called: "Come on out. We're heading back to Bannack."

They arrived in the camp a half hour before sunset.

Few people were on the streets. The snow and cold and mood of the camp kept most people indoors by their fires.

Plummer and Lear rode ahead of the posse and its charges; they were told to go to Hank Crawford's butcher shop.

Three hours earlier, when he had had time to think, Crawford had realized the camp was sitting on a tinderbox that could ignite at any moment. He had sent Vic Voit out to Bozeman's sawmill with the message: Get back here—quick!

Crawford saw Plummer, Lear, and the others arrive outside his shop and prayed that Langford and Henry Phleger would get there soon.

As the party stomped into the shop and began the

ritual of shaking off snow and trying to get warm, Crawford asked, "Any problems, Quent?"

Lear shook his head and extended his hands to the warmth of the stove.

Crawford looked at Plummer, who had dropped his coat and gloves to the floor and was beating the snow from his hat. "Henry, what's your stake in this?"

"No stake." Then, with a smug look on his face, he added, "I was just traveling with some of my friends."

Crawford felt his stomach knot; something was afoot, but he couldn't grasp it. Hoping to gain some time for Langford to come back, he said, "I guess we'd better get you men something to eat."

Plummer said, "Look, Hank, Quent here tells me that you have some authority to go arresting my friends. Was he right?"

Crawford hesitated; he had no authority. "Henry, there was a horrible incident yesterday and the members of the camp want something done."

"I can't argue with that."

"Then, what's your point?"

"The point is: have you arrested my friends?"

Crawford paused, could find no denial in his mind, and replied, "I have."

Plummer gave a curt laugh. "Then you'll have to stand for dinner."

"What do you mean, Henry?"

"I mean, if you have these men under arrest, then you have to pay for their meals. You understand that, don't you?"

Crawford was relieved. "I'll stand dinner, Henry. That's the least I can do."

From near the stove, Charley Moore announced: "I got a rabbit out in my saddlebag."

Reeves groaned, "Ugh! Charley, did you bring that danged thing all the way back here?"

"It's mine, ain't it?"

Plummer laughed loudly. Then, after a lull, he asked, "Where we going to eat?"

Crawford stated, "Not LeGrau's; Renee is pretty upset."

Plummer said, "We could get Cy Skinner to hustle us something up."

Crawford shook his head. "I've got some bread and cheese in my cabin. How about that?"

Charley Moore complained, "Aw, hell! I want something hot! What about me cooking my rabbit?"

Reeves reached over and smacked his cohort. "Will you quit with that stupid rabbit!"

Crawford asked, "Suppose we get Renee to fix up some plates. We can feed them right here."

Quentin Lear offered to do the duty, and Larry Davenport offered to help.

The meal was a quiet event, except for the noises Moore and Reeves made slurping the bowls of soup Renee LeGrau provided. The food was nearly all consumed when Nathaniel Langford, Harry Phleger, and Vic Voit entered Crawford's shop.

Plummer put aside his bowl and was on his feet before the door closed. "Nat, glad you made it back here." Langford's face showed the strain of the hard ride back to camp and worry over what was going on; Vic Voit's report had been extensive and, if true, the situation was volatile at best and deadly at worst.

"What's going on, Hank?"

Plummer bristled. He did not like being ignored. Before Crawford could speak, Plummer said, "There was a bit of trouble, Nat."

Langford turned and looked at Plummer. Plummer felt he was at an ideal moment to get close to Langford. Over the past three weeks, Langford had organized ten of his friends into a Bannack chapter of the Union Club, a fraternity of leading citizens supporting the Union and in opposition to the Confederacy. Plummer had no particular political inclination one way or the other, but he did have a driving desire to be accepted by the leaders in the camp. This was another ingredient he needed to advance his scheme with Cy Skinner.

Langford said, "Henry, I understand from Vic that you shot Jack Cleveland yesterday. Is that correct?"

Plummer had been moving so successfully in gaining an advantage for Mitchell, Moore, and Reeves that he had not allowed his own predicament to worry his thoughts. "In self-defense, Nat. The man tried to kill me."

Langford turned to Crawford and asked a silent question. Crawford said, "It looks that way, Nat. From what I can find out, it was self-defense."

Langford looked at the three accused shooters. "What about them?"

Crawford answered, "A lot of people saw the whole thing."

"Am I hearing the beginnings of a kangaroo court here, gentlemen?" Plummer asked. "I think we all know the law."

Langford had started taking off his coat. He looked at Plummer. "Just what is the law, Henry?"

Plummer smiled, confident that he was being accepted by Langford. "Well, Nat, the law is that these men may or may not have killed anyone; they are due a trial by jury."

Crawford jumped up from his chair. "Hold it right there, Henry! We're out here at the end of nowhere. We don't have a judge, we don't have a courthouse, we don't have a way to pick a jury. We do have a Miners' Court. That's who is going to try these three."

Langford raised a hand. "Hold it a second, Hank. I think Henry is right. If murder has been committed, then we have to take them to the proper authorities."

Crawford threw his head back in frustration. "Nat, you're talking about transporting them three hundred miles to Lewiston."

"If that's what it takes, then that's what we will do."

Crawford's shop fell silent.

Langford took an empty chair and sat by the stove, next to Charley Reeves, who was licking the bottom of

his bowl. Plummer rolled a cigarette and passed the fixings to Moore; everyone seemed to be waiting for someone else to speak. Crawford went back to his chopping block and stood there staring at nothing. He was the one to break the silence.

"Nat," he said, "let's you and me take a walk."

Langford had barely worked the chill out of his body, but he sensed the serious tone to Crawford's voice. He stood, picked up his coat, and followed Crawford out the back door.

They walked in silence down to the edge of Grasshopper Creek. Crawford said, "Nat, what has gone on here is dangerous, real dangerous."

"I only know what Vic told me."

"Well, it was pretty awful."

He spent the next couple of minutes giving the details of Plummer shooting Jack Cleveland, and of the senseless killings in the Indian village. When he finished that, he then said, "And there is something more coming up, just like a bubble of swamp gas in a pool of slime."

"You aren't letting this get ahead of you, are you, Hank?"

"No, Nat, I'm not. After Plummer shot Cleveland yesterday, some black mood was let loose in this camp. I started looking around at what was going on."

"I admit that it is not a nice sight."

"It's worse than that. I've been so damned busy trying to keep food moving to my customers that I hadn't noticed, but there is a hell of a bunch of bad ones collected here."

"I've noticed some influx of drifters. I assumed that was standard for gold camps. This is my first one, you know that."

"I know that. It is my sixth, and I've never seen so many toughs congregating together."

"We'll have to keep our eye on them."

"More than that, Nat—I think they have a leader."

The night was dark, the sky was clear, and the star

glow was helped by light shining from inside the buildings. Langford studied his friend; Crawford looked more serious than Langford had ever seen him.

"Give me your thoughts, Hank."

"I think that Cy Skinner has something to do with it, and I think that Henry Plummer has something to do with it."

"That's a serious charge."

"I don't have anything to prove my point; I only have a feeling."

"If they are involved in something, what can it be?"

"Nat, I just don't know."

"How large is this? Do you have an idea on that?"

Crawford hesitated. He was reluctant to speak his thoughts, as if he might make his fears become fact by giving voice to them. "From what I saw last night with the bunch at Skinner's, then at the Indian village, and around the camp today, I'd guess there are a hundred and fifty, maybe two hundred drifters who are not here to earn a living honestly."

Langford could not accept the vision of a huge concentration of no-goods, and of what that collection of evil souls could do to an isolated, remote community devoid of any semblance of law enforcement. He said, "We've got to do something emphatic, right now."

Crawford turned to look at his friend. "There is one thing we should *not* do."

"What is that?"

"We should *not* have a jury trial."

"That doesn't make sense, Hank."

Crawford gave a wry smile. "If we have a jury of twelve men, then I promise you those killers back in my shop will get off scot-free. Scot-free!"

"I do not believe that!"

"Believe it. There are a hundred and fifty gunmen wandering around our camp. They will intimidate a jury so quickly that you will not believe it. Who in his right mind would vote for conviction if there was the threat of walking out of the trial and being shot dead? *I* would vote for acquittal. I know it sounds cowardly, but I mean what I say. Think about it."

Could it be that Hank Crawford was right? If he was, then there was only one option. "We will have to take them to Lewiston. That is the only answer."

The chuckle from Crawford was laced with irony. "Nat, if I am right and Skinner or Plummer or . . . or somebody, has a control over this mob of ruffians, they will stop us. If we send ten men to take Reeves, Moore, and Mitchell to Lewiston, they will send twenty to stop us. If we send twenty, they'll send forty."

Another thought came to Langford's mind: where would they find ten or twenty men willing to leave their mining claims or businesses for two or three weeks to make the trip? He said, "Dammit, man, there has to be an answer."

"There is: a Miners' Court."

"Hank, I'm a newcomer; how could that be the answer?"

Crawford made a motion toward the east, along the ditch. "A walk might warm us up." They began walking. "Nat, a Miners' Court is made up of the whole camp population. The worst sentence they can impose is banishment, and that might be enough to quell the rowdy element. Besides, it is a vote of all the members. There is no way any individual can be singled out for retribution."

It would be a compromise, Langford acknowledged in his own mind, but at what a price. The tragedy visited on the Bannack Indians, the death of Frenchy Cazette, all of that would be punished with virtually a slap on the wrist for the guilty. Langford stopped walking. "Hank, I cannot subscribe to that concept. If justice is to be done, then we must have the strength of our own convictions. I'll serve on that jury; and I will find eleven others to share the duty."

"Nat, I like you. I have been honored that you let me

count you as a friend, but I will fight you on this. I will fight you for your own good. I do not want to see you killed."

Langford was touched, but he was not weakened in his resolve. Politely ignoring Crawford's declaration, he said, "How soon can we get a camp meeting together? We have to put this problem before all of the people; we cannot make decisions for them."

Crawford nodded. "People want to see something done. It won't take an hour to get them to the Roundhouse."

"Let's do it, Hank. It is our duty."

The meeting in the Roundhouse began a few minutes before nine o'clock.

Reeves, Moore and Mitchell had been taken to bed down in Hank Crawford's cabin and were under guard by six volunteers. There were a few men who did not get the word, and there were a few who stayed in Skinner's and the other saloons, but virtually every man—and a few adventurous women—crammed into the building.

Nathaniel Langford was privately critical of himself, because it seemed that just about everyone else in the camp realized the dilemma they were facing. The debate raged for an hour and a half. Finally, when Langford said he would assume the responsibility for drafting a panel of jurors, everyone voted for a jury trial. There were knowing smirks among the disreputable men present. They would be ready to go to work as soon as twelve fools were ready to put their lives on the line.

Nominations were made, and votes taken, electing Jeremiah H. Hoyt as judge for the trial, William Rheem as defense attorney, and George Copley as prosecutor. Hank Crawford was appointed as sheriff, a post that served as bailiff and court reporter. As sheriff, Crawford would also be required to impose any sentence handed down by the court.

With that business out of the way, Judge Hoyt named

the entire camp membership as a Coroner's Jury, in order to dispose of the shooting of Jack Cleveland by Henry Plummer.

Testimony was taken from witnesses who actually saw the incident, and from those who had heard Jack Cleveland's frequent rants about his feud with Plummer. Underlying the whole procedure was the prevailing belief that Cleveland had killed young George Evans, and that Plummer had done the camp a service by ridding them of a blight like Cleveland.

It was found that Plummer had killed in self-defense, and he was absolved of any further charges in the case.

The trial for Moore, Reeves, and Mitchell was set for ten o'clock the next morning.

CHAPTER 11

(Thursday, March 5, 1863)

Justice came into the camp not knowing what was expected of her. Law and Order waited outside, patiently. They were due for some new experiences.

At seven in the morning there was a de facto meeting in LeGrau's Café. Nathaniel Langford met with Hank Crawford, Harry Phleger, and Con Kohrs. At seven-thirty, Judge Hoyt, prosecutor Copley, and defense lawyer Rheem arrived. Talk was centered on just how the trial was supposed to be conducted. The closest they came to having any real knowledge was that Con Kohrs and George Copley had each served on juries prior to coming to the wilderness. Jeremiah Hoyt was beginning to enjoy his role as presiding judge; however, that bloom faded when he was reminded that he faced the real possibility, as Harry Phleger put it, "of getting your ass shot." Judge Hoyt settled back to listen.

Cora Harris and Renee LeGrau had been working since five o'clock; they had figured that there would be a flood of business because of the trial.

Cora had been surprisingly proud that Vic Voit had been considered important enough to be the one selected to recall Langford to Bannack. She was beginning to find herself more and more pleased at the attention he had been showing to her. She had been really impressed when he had shown up at her cabin just after midnight to tell her what had happened at the miners' meeting, and had been amused when she invited him in and he refused, saying that it would not look right. She had not especially liked his advice to stay in her cabin the next day, because the bunch down at Skinner's saloon were becoming ugly. She knew how to handle those no-good drunks! Still, all in all, she had liked his visit.

Cora had not taken Voit's opinion about trouble seriously; but now she remembered the killing in November which Beth Warren claimed she had witnessed, and which had led to Beth and Lori Charles leaving the camp. Maybe, she thought, she should have gone with her two friends. She shook off the thought.

A few minutes after the other men had settled down at their table, Vic Voit came hurrying into the café; Cora felt a slight tingle of excitement as he waved to her before joining Langford's party.

Hank Crawford signed to Cora for her to bring Voit a cup of coffee. Voit, as he was doffing his hat and coat, said, "Mister Lear was sleeping; that's why he's not here."

Langford asked, "Is he coming?" He stirred his coffee.

Voit replied, "He'll be here in a few minutes." Cora set down his cup. "Thanks, Cora."

Langford turned to the others. "We need Quentin badly, men. He will be our main witness that our culprits were, in fact, escaping."

Bill Rheem, who had drawn the dubious task of defending Moore, Reeves, and Mitchell, sipped his coffee, then said, "Maybe I will try to prove they were only out hunting. Didn't Hank say that Charley Moore brought back a dead rabbit?"

Crawford admitted, "I did say that, Bill," then added, "and you try any foolishness like that and *you* might end up on trial."

There was laughter.

Cora looked from the kitchen, saw Vic laughing along with the other leading residents of the camp, and felt a glow of pride. She said to Renee: "Isn't he cute?"

Renee, her hands covered with a batter for chicken that was to be fried, snapped, "Forget your cute Vic. Get that bread out of the oven."

Cora looked wounded; Renee gave an honest, but patient smile, and Cora was back to being happy.

At the table, Langford urged a stop to the laughter. "We have to get serious with this, gentlemen. We could be looking at sentencing men to the gallows."

Bill Rheem shook his head. "Nat, I want this to be as fair as possible, and I do not intend to treat it lightly. There is one thing you might as well face: those boys are not going to get the rope."

Langford looked around the table. Excepting Vic Voit, who would not have presumed to present an opinion on such a serious matter, all at the table had tried to convince him that his hope for a fair trial was wishful thinking. They were willing to go through the procedure, but only to get the matter behind them. They all hoped the situation would calm down. Langford was convinced of the guilt of Reeves and Moore, and he honestly wanted to see justice served.

George Copley asked, "Have you found any others to serve with you on the jury?"

Langford had not. He had spent an hour trying to convince some residents to serve with him; none were willing. His last hope was that the judge could enlist a panel once the court was assembled and he said so. Judge Hoyt was skeptical about his chances.

Copley asked Crawford, "Has Pipe Carrier come back from his hunt? I will need him to act as a translator."

Hank Crawford looked away for a moment, took a full breath, then answered, "He won't be available, George."

"Dammit, Hank, you promised you'd get him."

"I went to the village this morning. He was packing out. His papoose and squaw were killed by Reeves and Moore."

From around the table came: "Oh, no," "That's awful," and "Poor guy!"

Crawford said, "Yeah," then took a few seconds to compose himself. "I didn't know, either. In the confusion, I never stopped to ask. The poor bastard is taking them down to the Yellowstone to bury them. Shit!"

He stood and walked to the window, and spent a couple of minutes looking out at the snow on the ground.

Quentin Lear came in the front door and joined the group at the table. Both the prosecutor and defender wanted to hear the details of Lear's capture of the outlaws.

As that topic ended its course, Langford told his friends, "Henry Plummer came to my cabin last night. About one in the morning."

They all looked at him, waiting.

"He is a cool character," Langford said.

Lear shook his head. "I know what you mean. I spent most of yesterday with him, five and a half hours on the ride back to the camp. He is one smooth talker." Lear accepted a cup of coffee from Cora. "And those two shooters, they're more dangerous than a gut-shot cougar."

Langford called to Crawford, "Hank, you'd better come hear what Quent has to say."

Crawford returned; he looked as if his mood had passed.

Lear said, "Reeves and Moore are just plain crazy. Mitchell seems like a nice enough kid, just tied up with a bad bunch. But the other two—make sure there are no guns close to them today; we could be in serious trouble."

Langford looked at his friend. "Hank?"

"I know what Quent means. I had those two in my cabin all night. We are going to have to have guards in the courtroom, or who knows what will happen. I still think there is a group working out of Skinner's."

The talk focused on what could be done to prevent an ugly disruption in the Roundhouse during the trial. The suggestions were feeble; if a free and fair trial was to be offered, then there could be no major encumbrance to the proceedings.

Langford brought the meeting to a close. "Hank, you have the prisoners there on time. Use as many men as you can get."

"I'll do my job, Nat."

"George, you had better be lining up what witnesses you can induce to testify."

Copley gave a weak smile of agreement.

"Jeremiah, best lay low until right before the time of the trial. I think Hank can find a couple of men to stay with you. Men with guns."

Judge Hoyt gave a manly shrug but looked to Crawford for confirmation.

Langford seemed to take a bit too much time putting away his pipe and tobacco. At last he looked at Voit. "We have a tough job for you; can you handle a tough job?"

Before Vic could answer, Con Kohrs stated: "Vic Voit is a dependable man. You can count on him."

Hank Crawford cut in, "Hell, Con, how can Vic say no to anything after that?"

Langford cut off the crossplay: "We'd like you to wander down to the Elk Horn and keep your ears open for any trouble."

Innocently, Voit asked, "Trouble at Skinner's, Mister Langford?"

"No, trouble coming out of Skinner's. We should know if they are planning to disrupt things this morning."

Vic smiled. "I'll guarantee you they are planning to disrupt things." He saw his attempt at a joke fall short of the mark. "What I mean is, I'll be glad to go take a look."

Langford patted Vic's shoulder. "You're a good man."

Cora started out from the kitchen as she saw them begin standing; she wanted to talk to Vic. But he bolted out the door immediately.

Hank Crawford spotted the disappointed look on her face and said, "I'll tell him to come back in a little while and have a cup of coffee with you, Cora. We just sent him on an important mission."

Her hurt was lessened by the boost in her pride.

Plummer and Cyrus Skinner held a predawn meeting in Plummer's cabin, trying to decide how to best help Reeves and Moore. Bill Mitchell was asleep on a quilt Plummer had lent him to cushion the floor; Plummer had wanted him close at hand in case the decision was made to flee the camp again. Also at the meeting were George Carrhart and Ned Ray, two former road agents who had worked for Skinner and Plummer in Oro Fino, and who had arrived in the camp two days previously. Plummer had asked how they had missed the shoot-up at the Indian village. He accepted their explanation that they had been bunked down at Madam Grogan's bawdy house, and had not even heard the shots. Skinner was skeptical, and wondered if the pair was going soft. From their talk now, there was no fear of softness; they were promoting a plan to go to Hank Crawford's cabin and rescue Reeves and Moore. Plummer and Skinner did not like the scheme, because of the threat of Reeves or Moore being killed in the attempt. All those in Plummer's cabin agreed, however, that something had to be done to save the two Charleys from the rope.

Skinner had brought a bottle of whiskey to the meeting, which did not help provide clear heads for planning. Plummer, however, was not drinking; he was determined to find a way out of the problem.

There was a good deal of talk but very little accomplished during the session. As the time to leave drew close, Plummer said, "I think we have to put enough people in there to scare the bejezus out of any fool who is dumb enough to serve. That'll do the job."

Skinner growled, "That won't do a damned thing! What we do is raise so much hell that Langford and his bunch are not able to do anything."

George Carrhart slurred his words as he added, "Then . . . we can vote to have Henry take our Charleys to Lewiston—"

Ned Ray cut in, laughing, ". . . and they never make it anyplace. Great idea!"

Skinner nodded. "It ain't a bad idea."

Plummer said, "The flaw is that Langford might choose to send Hank Crawford and a whole bunch of those goodie-goodies to Lewiston. Then our Charleys are dead men."

Skinner lifted the bottle from the table and took a long swig before handing it on to Ned Ray. A dribble of saliva ran down Skinner's chin and hung on his two-day growth of beard. He said, "Okay, we'll go along with your plan, Henry, but I'm not going to the meeting. I'll keep a half dozen of our men handy at my place, and we'll be ready if anything goes wrong." Skinner looked at Plummer. "I don't want anything to happen to my boys; that's all. I've got a lot of money invested in them, and I want to see a return."

"We'll do it, Cy, don't worry." Plummer added, "Ned, you go round up our boys and have them at the Roundhouse in time for the trial. Be there about nine-thirty. Okay?"

Ned stood, swayed a bit, then plopped back down into his chair. "Hell, Henry, them that ain't over hanging around Crawford's cabin is already up at the Roundhouse. You don't worry, we'll be raising enough hell to get this settled the right way."

Plummer laughed. "You're right about one thing, Ned, this damned mess will be settled the right way . . . *our* way!"

There were those in the camp who made an honest-to-God effort to make that trial day come off well.

The majority of prospectors and businessmen realized they had to take a stand, to bring a halt to the lawlessness that had brought tragedy to the Bannack tipi village.

A segment of the camp that day brought with them a position of moral righteousness. To them, the Judeo-Christian ethic of adherence to the laws set down in the Ten Commandments was ingrained; the principles prescribed in Magna Carta were tantamount to gospel; and the rights defined in the U.S. Constitution were to be held inviolate.

There was another segment at the trial that day, a segment that said: Bullshit.

The Roundhouse had been made as ready as resources would allow. No chairs were provided for spectators, because chairs took up space, and chairs were easy to toss across the room. There was the traditional courtroom bar that looked more like a ranch's post-and-rail fence, because it was the contribution of two unemployed cowboys. The jury was expected to sit on three heavy benches made of resawed timbers; splinters were easily come by. The defense and prosecution had tables and chairs; no one thought it strange that they had come from the Elk Horn Saloon. On a raised platform constructed overnight, sat a large, polished oak pedestal desk for use by Judge Hoyt. No record exists of where such a splendid piece of judicial furniture was obtained.

The stage was set for the players to arrive.

The Roundhouse was made of logs as an octagon forty-six feet in diameter. The first to arrive in the building were greeted with the aroma of newly cut pine, that unique perfume of one of God's gifts to man. As the building filled up with spectators, however, the pungent odor of frontiersmen took hold, and would not release its grip for weeks.

No less than sixty ruffians arrived early, assigned by Cy Skinner and Henry Plummer to disrupt the proceedings. The place was packed to overflowing a full thirty minutes before the scheduled time to begin. The disruptive element made a point of randomly moving back and forth through the crowd, bumping needlessly into prospectors, orally abusing businessmen and tradesmen. Very few vulgar expressions were left unused that morning. There were claims that some new words had been invented just for the occasion, but none who recorded their impressions were bold enough to set the words to paper. It was not long before tensions hung in the air like week-old beef—rank and ugly. It was a given that the ruffians were getting drunk, but even some of the more stalwart members of the gathering had fortified themselves with a few drinks before arriving.

Intimidation was not limited to rude bumps or crude language; the agitators demonstrated their contempt by firing off their handguns into the ceiling. As a matter of common sense, several prospectors trekked back to their quarters and returned with their own weapons.

At two minutes before ten o'clock, Nat Langford and Hank Crawford arrived as an escort for Judge Hoyt. Those sent to disrupt the trial dug deeply into their supply of demeaning vitriol. Judge Hoyt began feeling the proud obligation of his new undertaking, and he cast stern glances at those who insulted him. Langford and Crawford had to use some muscle to make way to the far end of the building, where the judge climbed up onto the platform and took his seat. He wore a black cutaway coat and silk string tie, a commendable effort to appear up to the task before him.

Nat Langford had put on a brown suit with a brocade vest; the attire elicited obscene comments. Hank Crawford wore work pants, but had on a clean white shirt covered by a leather vest. Because he had been named sheriff for purposes of the trial, snide comments were offered about the absence of a badge. When lewd observations were made as to where Hank could properly place a badge, he nearly lost his temper.

Exactly at ten o'clock, a squad of ten men arrived escorting Reeves and Moore, and William Rheem, functioning for the defense, was ushered to the defense table. During the stir caused by the appearance of the accused, George Copley managed to sneak through the crowd unnoticed. This coup was enough of an insult that a half-dozen agitators pushed their way to the prosecution table and delivered curses at him while he tried to look busy studying his sheaf of notes.

"Let the court come to order."

Judge Hoyt's pronouncement was truly a cry in the wilderness, except the wilderness was no place of silent beauty. His words were lost in a din of noise so encompassing that he wondered, himself, if he had actually spoken.

He tried to give the order again. It was swallowed up as if it had been a leaf falling to mossy ground. The judge looked at Hank Crawford.

Hank yelled: "Let's quiet down, now. We have a job to get done here."

He had yelled at a volume he felt excessive, but there was no reaction. He doubled his effort, and there was a slight drop in the intensity of the din. A third yell brought the sounds down to a manageable level; manageable until the agitators realized who was speaking. Crawford stood there accepting the hoots and catcalls, until the abuse ran its course. Then, speaking over a constant rumble, he announced: "The Bannack Mining District has called for this criminal trial in the matter of murder."

From the front of the spectators came a challenge: "Who says? You and Langford?"

Crawford held back an urge to look at Nat Langford or Judge Hoyt. Crawford recognized the challenger; it was Ned Ray, obviously drunk, obviously coached in what to do and say. Crawford knew he was facing the influence of Henry Plummer and Cyrus Skinner. Well, those two were not going to have their way in this matter.

Ignoring Ned Ray, he said: "Court is in session."

The cheers from the law-abiding people barely overcame the heckling of the troublemakers.

Crawford huddled with Judge Hoyt and Langford at the judge's desk.

Crawford said, "This is going to be tough."

Langford gave a grim smile. "We did not think it would be easy."

Judge Hoyt reached for the hammer he was using for a gavel. "Do I have the power to clear the courtroom?"

It was a light moment for Langford and Crawford; Jeremiah Hoyt was trying to do his best.

Langford looked at Crawford. "Do you think you could use some of the prisoners' guards to go out into the spectators and keep things calm?"

"There are a lot of guns in this room, Nat."

Hoyt offered, "What about asking Reeves and Moore to help quiet their friends? They might do that."

Crawford shook his head. "All that pair wants is to stop this trial. We'll get no help from them."

Langford looked out toward the mass of faces jammed into the room. "By damn, we are going to have justice here, Hank."

"We all want that."

"Then let's get something done. Send your men into the crowd. If shooting starts . . . well . . . so be it!"

The success of trying to discipline the rowdy ones was nominal. A pocket of calm would appear, but then it would disappear when an eruption developed across the room.

In two hours, all that was accomplished was that the judge had managed, in a short lull, to declare the court in session, and, in another lull, Hank Crawford was able to issue a call for jury volunteers. Nat Langford was the first to step forward.

With a stroke of improbable genius, George Carrhart, a crony of Cy Skinner's, offered to serve as a member of the jury.

Some quick thinking by Nat Langford stemmed a possible rush of brigands to the jury. The tradition of having prospectors sign rosters as members of a mining district was something new to Langford's ideas of broad-based suffrage, but he had filed a claim and signed up as a district member. Just about every businessman in the camp had filed claims on some section of Grasshopper Creek. There were no known claims filed on by Skinner's or Plummer's chums. Another legal huddle, this time with the defense and prosecution lawyers, led to an announcement by Judge Hoyt: "Only properly signed up members can serve on this jury."

Crawford felt a glimmer of hope; maybe this was going to work. Boldly, he called to Carrhart, "Thanks for your civic-mindedness, George. We'll have to get along without you."

There was a burst of applause that actually overrode the angry yells of Carrhart's chums.

In the next few minutes, a mild display of duty showed itself in the Roundhouse. Barney Hughes, who worked Claim Number 6 below Geary's Bar, volunteered. He was followed by Charlie Reville, the man who had panned the first pinch of gold out of Grasshopper Creek; by Ase Stanley, Claim Number 62 above Discovery; and by Augustus Graeter, Claim Number 9 below Geary's Bar.

No one else volunteered. Judge Hoyt called for a lunch break. "One hour, folks. Let's be back here no later than one o'clock."

The first really good thing of the day happened: the Roundhouse emptied out, quickly.

Renee LeGrau, Cora Harris, and Vic Voit were standing by the café's cookstove. Renee was enjoying watching Cora listening to Vic report on the morning's events.

The transition of Cora back to a modest, demure young woman gave Renee a sense of joy, as she knew she was partly responsible for the change.

The two women were taking advantage of the lull created now that all of their lunch customers were eating; Renee had organized quick meals in anticipation of the rush. Vic was relishing his role as a reporter to the women.

"Then what happened, Vic?"

"Cora, you wouldn't ever believe it; four of them volunteered."

Renee asked, "Will they get the twelve they need?"

"That's a hard one. I don't know if I'd have the guts to sit on that jury."

"Sure you would, Vic. You're tough."

Renee smiled at Cora's pride; the next item on Renee's agenda was to angle these two nice young people into marriage.

Renee asked, "Vic, will you volunteer?"

"I ain't signed up, Renee. I don't have a claim."

Cora insisted, "You don't even think about it, Vic Voit. You are doing enough already."

Cora's attitude was typical of many residents of the camp. Everyone wanted to see the violence stemmed, but there was the real threat of retribution from the outlaws. Cora did not want to see Voit placed in that kind of jeopardy; she had seen her share of gunshot wounds.

From the front of the café came the call: "Cora! We need some coffee!"

That was the signal for the end of their break; serving of Renee's custard pie would take the rest of the lunch period.

"I'd better get back to the table," Vic told them.

Cora demanded, "You let us know what happens, Vic Voit. You miss on that, and you are in trouble with me."

Vic did not miss the message: Come to the cabin tonight. He thought that was pretty nice, and he went back to Langford's table to await the delivery of the pie.

Langford had not taken one bite of the stew that sat in front of him; he had smoked three pipes of tobacco.

With him were the four men who had volunteered for jury duty and Hank Crawford. Judge Hoyt was at a different table with prosecutor George Copley. Defense attorney Bill Rheem had the unattractive obligation of eating with the two Charleys in Crawford's cabin. The rest of the tables in the café were jammed to capacity; the prevailing mood was somber. Langford and the other volunteers had canvassed the lunch patrons, and managed to convince only five more men to accept the duty of serving. They were still two short of the needed twelve good men.

"I never guessed it would come to this," was the comment from Charlie Reville. "When I saw that first color in my pan, I figgered there'd be a whole bunch of good come from it. I think I'll sell out and move on."

None at the table took Reville seriously. His first claim was just about played out, but he had three others, all very promising. Langford knew the three claims would be valuable; he might even buy them himself. But he also knew the compulsion that drove men to limitless hardship in their search for gold.

Langford had not been able to eat because his stomach was churning. The job of finding jurors had been more difficult than he had ever imagined, and he had serious doubts about being able to muster the remaining two.

Vic suggested, "You'd better eat, Mister Langford. It could be a long day."

"Just not hungry, Vic."

"You need your energy."

"We need two more jurors."

"We'll find 'em." Charlie Reville talked with the degree of optimism found in a true prospector.

Langford chuckled. Then, "I hope you are right, Charlie."

Hank Crawford had not felt much like eating, either, but he was wise enough to know the afternoon session might run for a long time, so he had finished off his own meal and eaten Langford's biscuits. After he used his handkerchief to wipe his mouth, he said, "I had an idea this was going to be tough, but not as bad as it is. Skinner is determined to win this battle."

"We need to be stronger."

"No question, Nat. But, looking at it realistically, he is winning, so far."

Langford stared down at his uneaten food. "That kind does win, sometimes. But, dammit, they just can't be allowed to turn this place into a den of thieves. There are too many good people involved. The men and women who made their way to this place deserve better."

"We're trying to give it to them."

"And we will. By God, we will!"

Crawford pulled out his watch; it was ten minutes to one o'clock. He yelled, "Cora, you getting us some dessert?"

Cora was scooting from table to table, serving portions of pie as quickly as possible. "Hold your horses, Hank Crawford."

Crawford looked at Vic. "That is some young lady."

Vic beamed. "Ain't she something?"

Langford could not resist Renee's pie. Vic went to the kitchen and told Renee, who personally delivered two large slices. "You eat these, Nat Langford. I don't want people saying my food ain't good enough for you."

Langford and Crawford were five minutes late getting back to court, because he did eat the second piece of pie.

Jeremiah Hoyt is credited with filling out the full panel of jurors. From somewhere he found the right words, and put them in the right order, to deliver a message of civic duty. At three o'clock, the full panel was sworn in by Hank Crawford.

The harassment by Skinner's gang had not lessened, but it seemed as if it was not having the desired effect. The crowd of honestly interested spectators began issuing some of their own growls.

Judge Hoyt spent half an hour explaining what was expected of the jury. Then he instructed Hank Crawford to present Bill Mitchell for trial.

Mitchell was not in the Roundhouse; Crawford and three other men left to find him.

During the delay, Skinner's bunch of scoundrels spent considerable energy harassing the twelve men of the jury. With Hank Crawford out of the building, they brazenly went right up to the jury box, arrogantly announcing what could be in store for anyone bold enough to find any of their friends guilty of anything.

Carrhart and Ned Ray took turns in being abusive; Langford received the brunt of the abuse. Jeremiah Hoyt wrote later that he had not believed there were twelve men who could keep their composure in the face of such threats.

A couple of times, Judge Hoyt ordered the display to stop; that merely diverted the hostility from the jury to the judge.

Outside the Roundhouse, Crawford had had a hunch, and he was playing it. He took his three men across Grasshopper Creek, down Main Street, to Goodrich's Hotel. Instructing his men to wait outside, he went into the hotel.

Old Brod was sitting in the barber chair, reading a month-old newspaper, Bill Goodrich was standing behind the bar polishing a whiskey glass, and as Crawford had guessed, Henry Plummer sat by the potbellied stove.

"'Afternoon, Mister Hank."

"How you doing, Brod?"

"Fine, sir. I am simply fine, thank you."

Crawford walked back toward Plummer.

"You want a drink, Hank?"

Crawford smiled at Goodrich. "No thanks, Bill. I won't be long."

Crawford reached the stove, turned around one of the wooden chairs, and sat. "How are things, Henry?"

Plummer looked at Crawford for the first time. "Well, Hank Crawford. What brings you in here? Is your big, official, mighty illegal trial over? That was short."

Plummer, as usual, looked as if he had just arrived in town. He was wearing light brown wool trousers, a dark brown suit coat, and a dark green silk vest. His face was shaved clean, his boots were polished, and his hat looked brand new. The black leather tip of a holster showed below the bottom of his coat.

"The trial has just started, Henry."

"Don't say. What's taken so long?"

"Some problems, just small things. We are going now."

"Seems like it took you a long time, Hank. I guess I should have done my public duty, and come over there to help you out." Plummer leaned forward, his face was only two feet from Crawford's. "But, then," Plummer's voice was almost a whisper, "maybe you don't want anybody around who knows the law. Not with you running an illegal court."

"It is all legal, Henry. You know that."

Plummer showed a thin smile, his eyes fixed on Crawford's. "I know shit, Hank Crawford. Where I come from things such as 'duly elected' and 'full protection' are talked about before anybody starts running a trial. What you people are running is a kangaroo court. Nothing more."

"What would you have us do, Henry? Take them to Lewiston?"

"That's what I would have done."

"Their friends would have made sure we never got them to Lewiston, you know that."

"I know nothing of the kind, Hank. If they killed them Injuns, they should have a trial in a territorial court. You know that. Dammit, man, why won't you listen to reason?"

"Henry, all I'm looking for is some peace and quiet in this camp. There are a lot of good people trying to make a go of it here; I plan to help them."

"Even if you break the law?"

"I'm not breaking any law. You've been around the frontier enough to know that we are doing what has to be done. We don't have the time or the manpower to go hauling them to Lewiston." Crawford's face flushed red. "Dammit, Henry, you are no tenderfoot. We are doing what has to be done!"

Plummer leaned back in his chair. He moved his hand to an inside coat pocket and extracted a silver case. He took out a cheroot and offered one to Crawford, who accepted. After the ritual of lighting the cigars, Plummer inhaled a long drag, slowly blew out a blue-gray stream of smoke. He looked at Crawford. "Hank, you're absolutely right."

Crawford waited for the twist he knew would come. Plummer fooled him. "I know you are right, Hank. I agree with you."

Crawford doubted if he was hearing right, but he knew he had. After collecting his composure, he asked, "Then why, why in God's name, are you causing so much trouble for the camp?"

"Hank, I am not causing any trouble. What the hell do you mean?"

Crawford paused to think. There was no way to tie Plummer to the obscene behavior of the camp rowdies over in the Roundhouse. Sure, Plummer knew Cy Skinner, but there was no evidence that the two were anything more than friends, possibly even only acquaintances.

"You were helping Reeves and Moore escape."

"I have known those men for years, Hank. They were in trouble, and they came to me for help. What would you do if, let's see . . . if Nat Langford came to you asking urgently for help? I didn't know what happened with the damned Indians; I still don't know!"

"What about Bill Mitchell? He is supposed to be appearing in court right now. You tried to help him escape, too."

Plummer took another puff. "Bill? You want Bill? Why he's over waiting in my cabin. I let him stay there so none of the damned hotheads in this camp could try to lynch him. This camp is in an ugly mood, Hank."

"It's not an *ugly* mood, Henry. They want to stop the violence."

"Then tell them to quit stirring it up with trials and things like that. This camp will do just fine if it is let alone."

"Bill Mitchell will appear as ordered?"

"I'll bring him. He ain't hiding . . . except to save his skin."

"Let's go get him. The judge ordered me to bring him in."

"I'll go along with you."

Plummer then leaned forward again, was close to Crawford's face. "I'll tell you this, Hank Crawford: one person tries to lynch Bill Mitchell, or anybody else, and the shooting will start."

Crawford felt a surge of anger at the threat. His feeling did not subside when Plummer added: "And I'll start it."

Crawford had a dozen things he would have liked to throw at Plummer; he did not like, or trust, the man. But the job at hand was to get Mitchell to the court. He stood. "Let's go take him to court."

Plummer rose, opened up the door to the stove, and tossed in his cigar. He neatened his coat as he said, "Just make sure that phony court of yours is dealing from the top of the deck, Hank. You make damned sure of that. Right?"

Crawford did not reply.

The arrival of William Mitchell in the Roundhouse caused an immediate rise in the level of heckling by the ruffians; they quieted just as quickly when they saw Henry Plummer coming in the door, too. The catcalls turned to cheers; Judge Hoyt banged his hammer for order.

Things finally quieted, and the charge of accessory to murder was read against Mitchell.

Five witnesses were called by the defense. Not one of them could swear they saw Mitchell do anything other than stand around as Reeves and Moore shot up the Indian tipis. Then William Rheem called his client to the witness stand, where Mitchell admitted being in the village, watching the shooting, and doing nothing to stop the carnage. He swore he had gone there "to see the Injuns get shot up."

The jury went into a huddle at their benches. In five minutes they gave their verdict: guilty as an accomplice.

A slight ripple of comment, pro and con, flowed through the spectator section. Judge Hoyt imposed sentence in a loud, stern voice. "Bill Mitchell, you are found guilty by a jury of your peers. The sentence is that you are banished from this camp; that you forfeit any mining claim you might have; and that you turn in your gun to the sheriff. Case closed."

Cheers came quickly from the rowdy element. Bill Mitchell turned, and held his hands clasped over his head.

Through the noise, the judge announced: "We will adjourn until six-thirty. Hank, you have Reeves and Moore here right on time. I want this all over tonight!"

The building emptied slowly; some of the tensions seemed to have lifted, but the rowdy element was only taking a rest.

Madam Grogan's Dance Hall was a large, two-story building, located on the northeast corner of Main and Third streets. The madam had arrived early in the camp, bringing a corps of attractive young ladies who were skilled in accommodating the special needs of prospectors far removed from city life. Since her arrival, she had invested in decorations that enhanced her establishment: red velvet drapes, tasseled window curtains, plush sofas and chairs, and mirrors, lots of mirrors. The ground floor offered room to dance, to play cards, and to have a few drinks. The front two-thirds of the upstairs was divided into small rooms that served a double purpose, one of which was for her employees' living quarters. The back one-third of the upstairs was Madam Grogan's private area: a parlor, a large bedroom, and a smaller room reserved for serious, high-stakes poker games.

The poker table had been covered with a linen cloth, on which sat plates ready for a steak and potato dinner. Cyrus Skinner was seated on one silk-brocaded armchair; it was five o'clock. The trial of William Mitchell had been over for half an hour.

Dolly Grogan was pouring coffee from a silver pot into a china cup, and Skinner was indelicately resting his hand on the bulge of her bustle. "I hope this is okay, Cy."

"Just fine, Dolly. Anything you do is just fine."

She returned the pot to the serving table. "You're happy, Cy?"

"I'm always happy."

"I mean about the Mitchell thing. Him getting off."

Skinner slurped some coffee. "Good goddamned thing for this camp that he did. Shooting savages ain't no crime."

Dolly looked at Skinner and laughed. She had come to Bannack from Denver. She had been run out, which meant she had done something awful, considering the corrupt state of that city. Her adult life had been a rough one and she counted men like Cyrus Skinner as friends, tough, mean, violent friends. The everyday worker or businessman supplied the large bulk of her income, but men like Skinner provided the power to stay in business.

The knock on the door was so light that it even sounded polite. She grinned. "That'll be Henry; he's the only man I know who'd knock like that."

She was right. Plummer walked in, gave Dolly a peck on her cheek, and said, "Thanks for the loan of the room, love. Best for Cy and me not to be seen together; not tonight."

As Plummer was taking his chair, Skinner growled with a sarcastic laugh, "You simple bastard! They tell me you went right into the Roundhouse!"

Plummer nodded.

"I ought to kick your ass."

"Save your ass-kicking for later. They might decide to swing our Charleys from a rope."

Skinner looked at Dolly. "Get out."

She gave him a polite smile. "I have the steaks and things right here, ready to serve."

"We'll find them. Get out."

Plummer gave Dolly an understanding smile; he knew she wanted to stay and listen. He said, "We won't be long, Dolly. Don't worry about the food."

Dolly Grogan had not succeeded in her trade by being ornery to men; she left the pair alone.

As the door closed, Skinner said, "We'd better get our Charleys out of this mess, Henry."

There was a crystal decanter of whiskey on the table; Plummer poured a modest measure into his water goblet. "Cy, you should have been there. The boys did well. I mean, there was nothing they left undone. If you had seen it, you would feel the same way I do: the verdict will be not guilty."

"Bullshit! They found Mitchell guilty."

"They had to do *something.* All that came of it was a banishment. That's about all our boys are looking at; believe me."

Skinner was not comfortable with Plummer's certainty. Cy Skinner was never confident when dealing with do-gooders, and Bannack seemed to have more than its share for a brand-new gold camp.

He stood and went to get a plate of food.

Plummer finished his drink. He left the table while Skinner ate; Plummer could barely tolerate the way Skinner ate steak by holding it in his hand. Once Plummer had tried to suggest that a knife and fork would be more socially acceptable, and that comment had brought the two men to the edge of a gunfight. Plummer had given up on that kind of reform.

He distracted himself by looking out the window,

studying the buildings in the fading light. There was a lack of normal activity; no prospectors walking back into camp; no fires burning in cookstoves; only a few of the camp's kids playing by the ditch. The town had shut down for the trial; it was a big moment for Bannack.

He had developed a liking for this isolated place. He had been able to divorce himself from his past, and he might be able to make a go of it after he married Electa. There was the real possibility that Hank Crawford was carrying around the words of that damned Jack Cleveland, but when he had met Crawford in Goodrich's earlier, he saw that he might just be able to win him over by pretending to be a friend. It might just work. Of course, he'd have to soften Crawford up, first.

"You gonna eat, Henry?"

"I'm not hungry."

Plummer regretted saying that, because Skinner went and took his steak.

Once Skinner had finished indulging his gluttony, Plummer returned to the table and poured himself another drink.

Skinner worked his fingers in his mouth to dislodge some meat that had stuck in his teeth. During the task, he was saying, "If anything goes wrong there tonight, our boys are going to do some hot shooting—real quick. You understand that?"

"I couldn't agree with you more. We have to be ready for banishment; we might have to accept that."

"We can live with banishment. We'll make sure they never have to leave camp; that's easy. I just don't want to lose their shooting hands. Moore and Reeves are two of our best."

"We won't lose them."

"How're you so damned sure?"

"Only a feeling, Cy. I have this feeling that Langford, and Crawford, and the others realize they bit off more than they can chew."

"I ain't taking no chances, Henry. I'm having our

bunch back in there tonight, raising as much hell as possible."

"That will not hurt, Cy. That won't hurt at all."

Judge Hoyt called for order right at six-thirty.

Cyrus Skinner was true to his word: his contingent of hooligans were back in force; surely, evil comments were abundant.

The two Charleys were greeted by their compatriots as heroes, with cheers of support.

Nat Langford sat with his fellow jurymen, ignoring the spectacle of the arrival, watching the jury's reaction. There was no outward show of fear on their faces, but tensions were evident. For a moment, he regretted ever getting involved, then he remembered his feelings when he heard about the senseless deaths of the innocent Bannacks and Frenchy Cazette.

George Copley began stating the case for the prosecution. Langford was impressed with Copley's efforts; considering that the man had no legal background, he stated the facts in a sound manner. Copley was unable to provide any testimony from the Indians because of the language problem. Still, Langford felt that might be for the best, because the appearance of the Indians in the Roundhouse could have triggered more violence from the troublemakers.

Copley was, however, able to provide seven witnesses who all swore they saw either Moore or Reeves actually shooting into the tipis.

William Rheem, the reluctant defense spokesman, shocked the gathering when he put Charley Reeves on the witness stand and opened with the question: "Mister Reeves, did you do any of the shooting the other day in the Indian village?"

"You bet your ass!"

There were gasps from the spectators; the ruffians were jolted into silence.

"You do not deny this?"

"Nope."

"Did your friend, Charley Moore, do any shooting?"

"Yep."

George Copley was stunned by the line being presented by the defense.

"Now, Mister Reeves, how can you ask this gathering to sit here and not think you guilty of murder?"

Reeves licked his lips, scratched his itchy beard, and looked at the jury. "I guess you folks is just new to this place out here, and I guess you ain't yet learned what is going on. But, after a while, you'll get to know what is right."

Rheem urged, "Get to the point, Charley."

"Right." Reeves turned to look at the crowd of spectators. "Back in forty-nine, back when people were hauling ass to Californee, three good friends of mine—one of them my cousin—was killed and scalped by them heathen Indians. All I was doing was squaring the score."

Five minutes of chatter, yelling, and hoots erupted in the Roundhouse.

Langford sat stunned, unable to accept the outburst. The man had blatantly, even proudly, admitted to murder; murder with forethought! What was causing Reeves' friends to be so jubilant? Langford looked at his fellow jurors; they were impassive, as if they had not enjoyed hearing the confession.

When a degree of calm returned, Rheem directed Reeves back to that line of testimony. The accused described, in lurid detail, the deaths of his friends; he told of seeing scalps displayed in Indian villages around the West—although he did not mention the fact that no scalps were ever displayed in the Bannack village. Reeves' testimony was inarticulate, and it was decorated heavily with profanity, but it was an impassioned rendering of personal hate.

Before Charley Moore was brought to the witness chair, the troublemakers burst into a noisy demonstration of support for Reeves' testimony, advancing menacingly toward where the jury sat, threats and curses pouring out at the twelve.

Judge Hoyt motioned for Bill Rheem to come to the bench. He told Rheem to cut short anything Moore had to say. The judge feared, at the least, another demonstration, and at the worst, that the unruly loudmouths would take it on themselves to go out and finish off the Bannack village.

Charley Moore's testimony required less than fifteen minutes. His story was, improbably, identical to that of Reeves, including the detail of a cousin having been killed by Indians while traveling to the California Gold Rush.

The jury was given the case at midnight; they retired to Hank Crawford's cabin to deliberate.

It was two o'clock in the morning before the jury came back with a verdict. It is recorded that the decision of the twelve was for not guilty; the vote was eleven to one. That count had been the same from the first of eight votes; Nat Langford, from beginning to end, had voted for guilty.

The completion of the trial, the final statement of the judge, was set for eight in the morning.

The Elk Horn Saloon was jammed through the night; the criminal element celebrated right up until they had to go back to the Roundhouse.

Judge Hoyt announced that after a lengthy discussion with the jury, the accused were to be set free. However, there was the consideration of manslaughter, careless firing of weapons, and escaping to avoid justice. Those admitted factors were worthy of banishment from the camp.

Rowdy cheers rose in the Roundhouse. Everyone knew that there was no way the two Charleys were going to be sent packing: who would take on that job?

Nat Langford had learned a new lesson, and he did not readily accept it. This place, he thought, was right at the edge of civilization, and dangerous. That men could, with impunity, take the lives of others, would keep his new home from crossing over into the society of man. There would be no hope if Bannack could not take the first step toward normalcy; there had to be the establishment of law.

CHAPTER 12

(Tuesday, March 10, 1863)

After the trial, Mother Nature pulled one of her unpredictable tricks on Bannack. The skies cleared and the temperature rose. The old saw about waiting a few minutes if you did not like the present weather was especially appropriate that March in the mountains. The nights stayed cold, but the days were magnificent. The snows began to melt, and frost heaved up and released its hold on the land. In only a few days, new people began arriving in the camp.

From the Meeting Minutes Book of the Bannack Provisional Lodge AF&AM.

DATED: *Saturday, March 7, 1863.*

The Lodge was opened in due form . . .
. . . the communication from the Grand Lodge of Nebraska was read and a general vote of appreciation was taken regarding the intended visitation of Brother John Pearcy, Grand Secretary of the Ne-

braska Grand Lodge.

Dr. John S. Glick was welcomed as a Brother into the lodge and Brother Glick spoke in good terms of the accommodations the Lodge had secured for him in the town . . .

Brother Langford invested the membership with the facts of the events of the previous few days and there was a general discussion concerning the need to dispatch a delegation to the Territorial Capital in Lewiston so as to obtain some authorization for a properly constituted government . . .

Brother Pearcy read into the record the names of Brother Wilbur Sanders and Brother Sidney Edgerton who have just arrived in our town. Both Brothers passed their examinations, and each has provided information by which his membership in good standing will be verified with his former Lodge. . . . Brother Hank Crawford put forward the name of Victor Voit as a candidate to be accepted into the Entered Apprentice degree, and an investigation committee was appointed to look into the background of the candidate . . .

There were still unsavory types gravitating to the gold camp. That was to be expected, considering the history of earlier camps—but newspaper accounts about the gold strike at Bannack had appeared in virtually every newspaper back in the States during the winter, and decent farmers from the Midwest, factory workers from the East, and immigrants from both coasts found ways to travel toward the strong attraction that was gold. So did young men deserting or refusing to submit to conscription into the armies of the Union and the Confederacy.

By the time the snows had begun to melt and runoff water was roaring down Grasshopper Creek, the camp had grown to 2,760 souls.

Each new day saw the arrival of wagon trains and stagecoaches loaded with supplies and eager prospectors, and with a few business and professional people intent on setting up their trades or services for the mass of miners. Buildings were being erected to house the workers and the few families who came along; Bannack was quickly taking on the look of a real town.

The school was finally built, a one-room affair that was run by the Widow Bennett. An impressive newspaper was started by Henry Tilden, and there was talk that Jeremiah Hoyt was planning to erect a structure in which to provide theatrical and operatic entertainment for the camp. Harry Phleger and George Copley completed the Bannack ditch, and water management, so vital to the efficient panning of gold dust and nuggets, was becoming well enough organized that feuds and fights over water rights were much diminished. When a conflict did occur, people in the saloons now took the time to talk about it.

While the future of the camp seemed ensured, some residents were less sanguine about what lay ahead for them, but they kept hoping for the best.

The influx of new arrivals had been expected and, all through the winter, businessmen had placed orders for goods and materials accordingly. The privation of the deep cold months was relieved. Frank LeGrau was planning to expand both his blacksmith facility and the café, and he added two lots to his property. Dozens of others also saw that Bannack was about to bloom into a proper town. Along Main Street, fully half of the business owners had placed orders for planks to install wooden sidewalks, and off of Main Street, work was in progress on buildings, barns and houses.

From the diary of Cora Harris (undated)

I was shocked . . . shocked . . . shocked when Vic brought me a bouquet of flowers!!! No one has ever brought me flowers before . . .

Yesterday Renee surprised me. Lucy is going to come to work at the café as a bake cook because Renee is going to begin baking to sell to the new people coming to the camp . . . and Lucy has agreed to come and live in my cabin with me. Vic does not like the idea because Lucy is seeing that stupid Clay Barrow who is a PIG but Lucy promised me that she will not let him in our cabin and that is good for me but Vic still does not like the idea . . .

Vic is funny in that he talks all the time about marriage but he also talks all the time about how it is not right to get married so young . . . I'm old enough to know what I want and I wish he'd let me make that kind of a decision about my own life . . . MEN!!! They are really dumb!!

The law-abiding residents outnumbered the lawless faction, but guns being shot into the night air were more noticeable than the soft words of men intent on peace in the community. Some of the residents felt a cloak of fear descend on them like a fog on a wintery night, chilling and penetrating to the bone. The hooligans had only moderately tempered their behavior after the trial and banishments of Reeves, Moore, and Mitchell. It seemed to them the criminals had received only a minor punishment, sort of like getting their knuckles rapped by an irate schoolmaster.

For Henry Plummer, the incident had been chilling, because he was astute enough to know how close the whole thing had been. The people of the camp could easily have banded together and lynched Moore and Reeves. He had seen that happen in other gold camps. The jury trial was enough to make him decide to forget about dealing with Cyrus Skinner and his ilk, and to opt for a life within the less dangerous confines of a lawful society.

Excerpts from a letter to Electa Bryan

DATED: *10 March 1863*

[S]o, as you now know, my plan to set up an ore-processing mill is what is going to be the solid foundation for our life together here in Bannack. As I mentioned in my last letter, you should be talking to Jim [Vail] about moving here with your sister and his children. The school is operating with a fine teacher and the community is growing. This would be a really profitable place for Jim to settle down. Trying to run that stupid farm for Indians who don't want to farm—that is not for your brother-in-law. . . .

Before I close, I just thought I should tell you that Jack Cleveland is no longer in the camp and no longer bothering me and I am pleased with that. I will tell you all about that when I see you soon.

There was one main impediment to a pacific future for Henry Plummer: his conviction that Cleveland had passed on to Crawford the damning truth about the killing in Oro Fino. Before Plummer could move forward with his new life, he had to eliminate the menace that was possessing him. For that, if his scheme of making "friends" with Crawford failed, he would turn to the rowdy element he had helped to create. By then he could get on with his plans for Electa Bryan.

CHAPTER 13

(Wednesday, March 11, 1863)

Wilbur Sanders had just arrived in the camp. He did not plan to pan in the creek; he was a lawyer. He had come because he was sure there were going to be legal battles over rights and claims. After all, lawyers had been making handsome livings off prospectors' quarrels ever since the 1849 strike at Sutter's Mill in California. He was a relatively young man, not yet jaded about the lawlessness of the frontier, and he was shocked by the circumstances of the Reeves/Moore murder trials.

Sanders said to Langford, "If I'd been in camp, we would have shipped them off to Lewiston. That is the only proper way to settle that sort of thing."

Langford did not argue. He was simply happy to see a lawyer in the camp. Harry Phleger, who was sitting in the café with them, nodded.

"Just a few days," Sanders said, "I missed it all by just a few days."

Harry Phleger sipped his coffee. "You didn't miss anything, Wilbur. The whole damned thing was a nightmare."

Nat Langford bit off the end of a cigar, touched a match to the end, and then said, "Well, let's hope it's all in back of us now." He puffed comfortably on the cigar. "I'd like to take you up to the sawmill someday soon, Wilbur. I think you'll be interested in what we've done."

Sanders had expressed an interest in investing in the sawmill. The camp was demanding cut timbers and lumber at an amazing pace. Sanders was about to reply when Hank Crawford came bursting into the café. He called, "Cora, get me some coffee," then, as he dropped into a chair at the table, he added, "If you would, please, Cora."

Cora Harris' hands were all greased up from dicing chunks of beef for the evening's stew pot. Lucinda Simons had finished her last batch of bread and said, "I'll get it, Cora."

Cora smiled. "Thanks, Lucy." Cora was enjoying sharing her cabin with Lucinda. The two got along well except in the matter of Clay Barrow. It was awful to see Lucinda falling for him, what with Lucinda being a young widow and pretty as could be. But there had been only one direct discussion about Lucinda's behavior, and that had ended quickly when Lucinda told Cora that the whole thing was none of Cora's business. Cora had smarted over the incident, but living in the cabin together had eased the tensions. It still annoyed Cora that Lucinda was keeping company with a man like that. Vic Voit had told Cora to quit being so righteous. Without being cruel, he reminded her that she had only been away from working the saloons—and cavorting with Dick Sapp—for a few months. Cora liked the way that her Vic—she had assumed that proprietary title—could make her see she was being uppity. Everything was well in Cora's life; Vic, Lucy, Renee, and even men like Hank Crawford remembering to say "please" when they wanted something. She watched as Lucy took the coffee to Crawford. When Lucinda came back to the kitchen, she whispered, "Boy, is Hank mad. He's fit to be tied. Don't know what about."

Back at the table, Hank Crawford took a swallow of his coffee. "He keeps trying, damn him, he keeps it up."

Langford said, "Plummer, again?"

"Plummer." Crawford nodded. "This time he had Clay Barrow and George Hunter come into my shop. They said they wanted to buy some cut beef. Each piece I offered them was not right. They kept annoying me. When I told them to get out, they started yelling and cursing. In a few minutes I couldn't take it, so I picked up my rifle and told them to get out again."

"Did they?" Phleger asked.

Crawford's face was crimson. "Just as soon as I ordered them out, in comes Plummer—wearing his gun, just like always, with his hand sitting on the holster. Plummer said, 'You threatening my boys, Crawford?' and I said, 'You get your boys out of my shop before one of them gets shot.'"

"Who's this Hunter fellow?" Langford asked. "I don't recall the name."

"Hell, Nat, there's new ones each day; if we don't do something, there is going to be trouble, mark my word."

Sanders, who had met Crawford and liked him, said, "Hank, there's a provision under the law that can stop harassment."

Crawford gave a weak smile. "I'm supposed to be the sheriff of this town, Wilbur. How would it look if I took to hiding?"

Sanders said, "I'm waiting for a copy of the new Territorial Code. That will be taking a while, I'm afraid. But I'll look in the old code. It is out of date, but there has to be something we can do. This is not right."

Langford said, "No, it's not. Plummer has been hounding Hank since the trial. It has to stop."

Each day Plummer or one of his henchmen had challenged Crawford in some way or another. There was, it seemed, no real reason. All that Crawford could make of it was that Plummer thought Jack Cleveland had revealed some important information on his deathbed. Plummer had come alone to Crawford's butcher shop the day before and demanded to know—for the dozenth time—what Cleveland had told Crawford. Plummer was convinced that Crawford was lying.

The harassment was affecting Crawford's life and business. He had been planning to make trips to Cottonwood for beef, but he gave up the idea because he feared being bushwhacked out on the lonely road. He felt it necessary to hire someone to do the job, and that would add costs to his business. And it was only because Hank Crawford was well liked in the camp that there had not been serious gunplay. Several times there would have been shooting had not Harry Phleger and Con Kohrs stood beside Crawford when the threat of drawn guns was moments away.

Sanders said, "This is crazy. We can't have an upstanding citizen going through his day looking over his shoulder."

Crawford gave a good-natured smile and said, "You think of something, Wilbur, and I'll see that it's done." Then, seriously, he added, "I just hope you come up with an answer before I get myself planted up on Graveyard Hill." Crawford gulped down the last of his coffee and stood up. "Well, Plummer or not, I've got to be making a living."

Sanders smiled. "Don't worry, Hank, I'll work this out." Then, turning to Langford, he said, "Why don't we take a ride up to the sawmill? I've got a good buckboard rig stabled right here with LeGrau."

Langford pulled out his pocket watch. "We could be there and back before nightfall. That sounds good to me."

Crawford laughed. "Well, you men take care of your high finances; I've got a side of beef to butcher."

Langford signaled to Cora for more coffee as he said, "It's a nice day, but we might as well take some of this good coffee up in our bellies; it might still get cold out there."

Outside, the day was mild. The crisp air was heated by a bright sun and there was the smell of freshness in the camp. Crawford walked up Fourth to Main and then turned west; his butcher shop was a half block down on the north side of the street. As he turned the corner onto Main, Henry Plummer was leaning against a hitching rail, waiting.

Plummer's voice was mild and easy as he said, "I was wondering if you were going to be drinking coffee all day."

Crawford snapped, "It's none of your damned business, Henry." He began to cross the street but Plummer blocked his way.

Plummer said, "Listen, Hank, can't we just stop all of this and be friends?"

Crawford made no attempt to pass; he stopped and glared as he said, "I've no use for you or your kind, Henry. I don't want to be associated with you."

Plummer felt his own mood begin to swing toward anger. His shoulders tensed, and he felt the saliva in his mouth begin to dry. He said, "I can be a good friend."

"I've got all the friends I need."

Plummer took a deep breath. "I don't want this to keep going on, Hank; let's bury the hatchet."

Crawford was now the one trying to hold back his temper. "Henry, you and your hoodlums have called me a liar and a cheat and a whoremonger and anything else you think will raise my ire. You've threatened me, you've vandalized my shop, and you've made my life just one damned uncomfortable mess. I don't want your friendship; I don't want to associate with anyone who could do such things."

Plummer took a step closer and leaned forward. His voice was barely a whisper as he demanded, "Tell me what Jack Cleveland told you!"

Crawford let out a hiss of exasperation. "I've told you a dozen times: nothing!"

With that, Crawford stepped around Plummer and

began to cross the street. In a taut voice, Plummer said, "Hank Crawford, draw your gun or I'll shoot you down like the dog you are."

Crawford stopped and turned around. Plummer's right hand was resting on the butt of his revolver. Crawford growled, "You've made those threats before, Henry, so that's nothing new. If that's your game, I'll give you a good target; a target a man like you would be used to."

With that, Crawford turned his back and began walking toward his shop. Plummer stood there, infuriated and terrified. Crawford did not know it, but Patrick Ford, when he had been shot in Oro Fino, had been shot in the back.

An hour and a half later, Hank Crawford was in his shop, finishing up his work on a slab of beef that would be sold to housewives and cafés that evening. Helping Crawford was a young man named Frank Ray, who had not had any luck prospecting and decided he'd like to learn the butchering trade. A pair of children—they were the children of Carl Stinson—came into the shop and told Crawford that the Widow Bennett needed to meet with Crawford at her cabin.

Crawford thanked the children, doffed his bloodied apron, and told Frank Ray, "You wait on the bench out in front of the shop."

The youth argued, "I can finish up, Mister Crawford."

Crawford said, "You're doing real well, Frank, but I don't want to come back and find you missing two or three fingers. You just wait outside. I'll be back in a few minutes."

The Widow Bennett's cabin was north of Main Street on Fourth, just a long half block from Crawford's shop. He walked the distance without haste, enjoying the day. The Widow Bennett was a bright, attractive woman and, more importantly, she was doing a really fine job as the camp schoolmarm. At her cabin Crawford accepted a cup of coffee and they discussed how money was going to be raised to purchase the new textbooks that were needed for the school.

Unknown to Crawford, "Old Tex" Crowel, one of Plummer's henchmen, had been watching the butcher shop from Guerney's Boot and Shoe Store down the block, across Main Street. Within five minutes of Crawford's leaving the shop, Henry Plummer was heading east on Main Street, walking directly toward the cabin of the Widow Bennett. Plummer was carrying a rifle.

Frank Ray, sitting on the bench whittling on a chunk of wood, saw Plummer coming. The youth was aware of the feud between Plummer and Crawford. He also knew that Crawford had left the butcher shop unarmed. Ray eased off the bench, and succeeded in looking casual as he moved inside the shop, then ran behind the counter for Hank Crawford's rifle, burst out the back door of the building, and cut across the lot in back of the neighboring cabins. He ran full out to the back door of the Widow Bennett's cabin. His pounding on the door was answered in seconds by the widow. "Oh, my!" the modest woman said when Frank Ray told them Plummer was coming.

Hank Crawford told young Ray to stay in the back room of the cabin with the widow, then he went to the front room and peered out through the white muslin curtains. Henry Plummer was coming up Fourth Street; it was obvious he knew just where to find Hank Crawford.

Plummer was across the street, on the east side of Fourth. He came to a halt by a parked wagon, calmly put a foot up on a wagon-wheel hub, and cradled the rifle across his knee. Plummer could not see through the curtains, but he called out, "Okay, Hank, you come on out! I know you've no gun; I just want to talk."

Crawford studied the problem. Plummer was about sixty feet away, and the light was good. A small crowd was beginning to collect down at the intersection of Fourth and Main. Crawford left the window, picked up the cup and saucer he had left on the small end table by the sofa, and went into the back room. The widow and Frank Ray waited in tense silence.

Crawford lifted the cup to his lips and emptied it. He said, "Well, Bess, that's one fine cup of coffee," then said, "Let me have that rifle, son. It's time to put an end to this."

Ray handed over the rifle. "I'm coming with you, Mister Crawford."

Crawford opened his mouth to protest but the widow said, "Let him go with you, Hank; you might need help."

Crawford smiled. "Okay, Frank."

Ray grinned bravely.

Crawford looked at the widow. "Thanks for the coffee, Bess. I guess we'll have to finish our conversation later."

The Widow Bennett felt a lump come to her throat. All she said was another, "Oh, my!"

Crawford led the way out the back door. The afternoon sun was lighting the west side of the cabin. Crawford realized that Plummer was going to be partially blinded looking across the street. He motioned for Ray to keep well back. He eased his way to the corner of the cabin and slowly looked around.

Plummer was still there, one foot on the hub, gun cradled across his raised knee. As with many cabins, the ends of the logs used in building the widow's extended out about a foot from the corner, so Crawford had a perfect gun rest and also some protection. He brought the rifle up to his shoulder. He took a steady, measured aim, drew a deep breath, then squeezed gently on the trigger.

The echo from the first shot had not gone before Crawford had pumped a second round into the chamber and fired again.

Plummer lurched forward, crying out: "Some son of a bitch has shot me!"

The second shot went high, but the first shot had slammed into Plummer's right arm just below the elbow.

The bullet had traveled down along the bone and smashed into Plummer's wrist. Plummer groaned with pain, then screamed with fury as he saw Crawford come from behind the widow's cabin: "You lousy bastard! I'll kill you for this."

Some who witnessed the incident claimed that they saw Hank Crawford raise his rifle to finish off Plummer for good, but Frank Ray said that Crawford simply turned, handed the rifle back to him, and walked slowly back to his butcher shop.

The crowd at the corner of Fourth and Main were mostly friends of Plummer, and they flooded up the street to him. Frank Ray said later that he heard Plummer admonish his men not to go after Crawford, that Crawford was going to get his just deserts from Plummer.

Plummer was taken to his own cabin on Second Street, and three of his men went to fetch Dr. Glick.

Dr. John S. Glick had been born in Ohio and had taught himself medicine by reading books. He had finally made enough money to go to McDowell Medical College in St. Louis, Missouri, where he had earned his degree in surgery. He had experience with the U.S. Cavalry in Colorado, and knew a thing or two about gunshot wounds. The portly doctor made the gross error of announcing that Plummer's arm would have to be amputated. At that point, George Carrhart, one of Plummer's staunchest lieutenants, escorted Dr. Glick out to the front porch and delivered an ultimatum: "You cut off Henry's arm, or you let him die, and you are a dead man."

Dr. Glick made up his mind to save Plummer's arm.

That evening Crawford went to Wilbur Sanders' newly built cabin. He'd asked Langford and Harry Phleger to be there, too. He felt awful about shooting a fellow human being, even if the wounded man was Henry Plummer. Harriet Sanders did all she could to help the men alleviate Hank Crawford's concern, but pie and tea and soft words did not erase the guilt he felt.

Crawford was convinced that he should leave the camp as punishment to himself and to halt the conflict with Plummer. No argument, no persuasion could force him to change his mind. He formally deeded his property and butcher shop over to Frank Ray. Two nights later, on March 13, 1863, shortly after midnight, Harry Phleger, Nat Langford, and Frank Ray rode out of the camp and saw Hank Crawford safely on the trail to Fort Benton. From there Crawford would head on to St. Louis.

During the night following the shooting, Plummer's arm swelled to an obscene size and he slipped into a coma. For three days it was touch and go. The doctor was not allowed to leave the cabin, other than to go home and change clothes or to pick up a new supply of medicine. Amazingly, the arm was saved by the doctor's skills, but it would never again be as quick on the draw or as accurate at shooting.

Despite having the arm limited in use, and sometimes giving him slight twinges of pain, Plummer accepted the wound as a small price to pay to have the threat of Hank Crawford purged from his life.

CHAPTER 14

(Sunday, May 24, 1863)

On May 24th, Henry Plummer was elected sheriff of Bannack by a vote of 307 to 247. Few of the miners in the camp really cared much about who was to serve in the position. The job carried no salary, although the sheriff could collect fees for serving legal papers, arresting camp-rule violators, and housing and feeding any prisoners until the Miners' Court could meet to judge the accused.

Plummer had become reasonably popular in Bannack after he was shot by Hank Crawford, and not just among the criminal element, which had leveled off at about 120 scruffy, indolent no-goods. Plummer had expanded his claim holdings and had hired men working three separate patents along Grasshopper Creek. His stamp mill was providing an income for himself and was helping out other prospectors who had rich ore to crush before panning. He had even begun attending church with some regularity. Plummer did not react badly when his reapplication was rejected by the Masons. That slight was assuaged when he was permitted to join the Union Club. Plummer knew that Nathaniel Langford was not pleased that he had gained membership in one of the camp's two most powerful organizations, but he still tried to present a proud face. Langford had a deep and continuing mistrust of Plummer.

Many of Plummer's generous acts were noted by the miners. Just a week before, for instance, George Carrhart had died in one of the fairly common shoot-outs in Skinner's Elk Horn Saloon. Carrhart, who was asleep at the time, was shot when two poker players began a fight over cheating. Carrhart had died penniless. Plummer, out of his own pocket, saw that his friend had a proper burial up on Graveyard Hill. Many in the camp thought that was a noble thing to do. And there had been other visible acts of charity over the past two months.

So Henry Plummer became Bannack's second sheriff.

Langford was able to be civil toward Plummer, but trust was not there. He had hoped the new sheriff would begin to clean up the town, which had been sinking deeper into a morass of lawlessness since Hank Crawford left. But the more stable element had not been able to muster enough votes, and he could not find any other to be sheriff. Most people tried to find a way to live with the situation.

An event that would profoundly affect the future of Bannack occurred two days after Plummer's election.

Some weeks earlier, a party of prospectors had set out on an exploratory trip through the mountains and valley east of Bannack. They had split up into two groups, and both were harassed by unfriendly Indians and inclement weather. One group, led by Bill Fairweather, gave up and headed back to Bannack, tired and disappointed. On May 26, the Fairweather party was fifty-five miles east of Bannack up a long gully bisected by a small stream of water.

The place did not seem to hold much promise, but the party was tired, and found a safe, comfortable place to bed down. After a meal of fresh venison, four of the men broke out their picks, shovels, and pans as a matter of habit. Bill Fairweather and Henry Edgar drew the duty of washing the eating utensils and feeding the horses. Fairweather had taken the plates down to the stream when he saw a promising formation right above the bank. Curious, he pried out a sample and used a plate to wash it in the creek. There was more than a mere glint of color in the heavy residue of black iron flakes; there was a nugget. A good-sized nugget.

The next two hours were what every prospector dreamed about. They all dug and washed dirt, and when nightfall forced them to halt, they had panned out $27 from the creek. Two ounces of gold in the first try was more than enough to excite any prospector. The next morning there was more panning and more gold and the party found their bonanza—$168 collected by noon.

The Fairweather group had proved out their discovery; it held great promise. They were short of food, they were tired from their long expedition, and they would need supplies to begin the real work on their claims, so they packed up and headed to Bannack. They traveled with light hearts and happy thoughts. They arrived back in Bannack on May 30, two days after Henry Plummer's election and his departure for Sun River Farm to marry Electa Bryan.

CHAPTER 15

(Tuesday, June 2, 1863)

The Sun River Farm had been doused with ten steady hours of rain; everything was damp, and everyone was getting a bit feisty. Plummer's arrival that morning had been greeted by mixed reactions.

Electa had been thrilled when she saw Plummer riding up to the farmhouse in the drizzle that preceded the downpour; she had shrieked with excitement, and had run out with no cloak. She was in his arms the instant his feet left stirrups and touched the ground.

The long wait had been demanding on Electa's emotions. She had never been confident he would come back. The winter's bitter cold, freezing winds, and deluge of snow had been new and challenging for Electa, but she had also suffered rigors of doubt. After all, men had been known to toy with women's affections. Plummer's loving letters had done something to allay her fear that he had merely used her the previous fall. She read and reread them, and the paper showed much wear.

Then there was James Vail.

He had not made Electa's long, hard winter any easier. He had frequently tried to discourage the girl from pinning her hopes on Henry Plummer.

Since the farm was barely off the route west from Fort Benton, a few travelers would pause there for a meal or to stay overnight. Through the course of the winter, James Vail had heard several tales about Henry Plummer's previous life, and Vail had not liked what he heard. He did not want his sister-in-law to marry a disreputable, possibly criminal, person. He had tried to be subtle in his first admonishments to Electa, but his words seemed merely to make Plummer more attractive. When Vail had become more direct and emphatic, Electa's normally placid demeanor had turned contrary and even hostile: Did James want her to remain a spinster? Did James want to deny her a life with a husband and children?

James Vail had retreated.

He was not pleased to see Plummer. He had actually prayed that Plummer would not return to the Sun River Farm.

But now that he was here, James Vail wanted to have a private talk with him, a talk in which some matters of import would have to be resolved.

However, after dinner with the family in the main house, Plummer and Electa went out through the driving rain to the visitors' cabin. They were able to be together in all of the ways Electa had dreamed about and imagined during their long separation. James Vail was furious that Electa stayed with Plummer until ten o'clock that night, but he kept silent. Electa was so obviously happy.

After the noontime meal the next day, Vail asked Plummer to help him with a chore in the barn. Once they got there, James Vail accused Plummer of wrongdoing. Plummer was a glib talker with a convincing manner when he wanted to be, and he used all his skills with James Vail. He admitted to some shady dealings in his past and confessed to his share of brushes with the law, but he also said he'd seen the error of his ways and told convincingly of his personal reformation. James Vail was a missionary, and a gentle, honest person. He accepted Plummer's impassioned confession of sin and salvation. Plummer did not pose as a man who had gotten religion, but he presented himself as an ordinary, reasonable man who had made a few mistakes, and had learned from them.

By the time they left the barn, James Vail had become a supporter and friend of Henry Plummer. The trust and faith he put in Plummer would eventually be devastating for the well-meaning missionary.

Henry Plummer had weathered the meeting with Vail, but then he ran into an obstacle. There was no preacher available to perform a marriage ceremony. Many early settlers on the frontier, with honorable and sincere intentions, simply gathered friends together, announced their wedding, and read something appropriate from the Good Book. After the public announcement, a notation would be made in the family Bible, and then they would live together until a preacher showed up and made the arrangement valid. The Vails would not agree to such an unholy custom, especially since the children, Mary and Harvey, were involved. James and Martha insisted the wedding be postponed. After all, a proper minister of the gospel was due to arrive at the Sun River Farm in a few days.

The few days grew into three weeks, however, and the minister never did arrive. Plummer was, by that time, anxious to get back to his business interests, back to his job as sheriff, and back to the cabin he had build for his bride. Finally, James and Martha, after much soul-searching—to say nothing of fervent praying—agreed that they would allow the pair to be joined in matrimony by a Catholic priest, a Jesuit at Saint Peter's Mission, twenty miles away from the farm.

Much of what Plummer had told James Vail seemed sincere, that hc meant to distance himself from any illicit activities, and to be a good husband to Electa.

When the six men of the Fairweather party arrived back in Bannack from their prospecting expedition, the atmosphere in the camp quickly changed to that of a comic opera.

Six men known to all the old-timers, six men known to have been on a seven-week trek in search of gold, six men who were bursting with the excitement of a big discovery, six men who were trying to keep a secret—these six men failed.

Bill Fairweather had implored his partners to keep their mouths shut. His plan was to slip back into Bannack, take a couple of days to rest, then collect their supplies and sneak back out to the new gold find.

But each man, including Fairweather, had friends in the camp. And each man used some of the gold dust and nuggets to buy drinks in the saloons and supplies in the stores. In just one day, Fairweather and his group were being hounded by throngs of prospectors hoping to cut themselves in on the find.

Stealth was as elusive as quicksilver, however, and when Fairweather and his chums tried to sneak out of Bannack in the middle of the night of June 2, three hundred of their closest friends followed in the darkness. The farce went on for most of the two days needed for the trip to the gold-bearing gulch, and as Fairweather neared the goal he finally gave in: he and his friends were not going to be able to shake their stalkers. At midday on June 4, when they had come within three miles of Alder Gulch, as they had named it, he called a meeting. The eager, anxious trackers were grateful to drop the game, so in the meeting they began to set out rules for the new area. Following custom, it was settled that each claimant would be allowed one hundred feet along one side of the creek and the claim would go to the middle of the creek. It was agreed that the whole army of prospectors would depart first thing the next morning and that they would proceed in an orderly manner to the site, where Fairweather and the other five original discoverers would be allowed to mark off their claims first. Everything seemed amiable—but there was still larceny traveling with the flock.

As soon as darkness fell, three of Fairweather's original party took ten of their friends and left for the gulch. In the morning, when the remaining mob realized what had happened, there was near mayhem, which required a full three hours to calm down before Fairweather finally agreed to lead the way in.

Just about everyone involved later agreed that they had all been foolish in their greed, because Alder Gulch turned out to be a twelve-mile-long discovery that made hundreds richer than they had ever dreamed. In the first week, the realization came to them that they had, in fact, come on that elusive mother lode. They also formed a Miners' Court, elected officers, and set up the Fairweather Mining District. The first documents drawn up by the new camp dwellers showed the site name Varina City, in honor of the wife of Jefferson Davis, then president of the Confederacy. That moniker lasted just a few days. The man who was appointed camp judge, Dr. George Granville Bissell, a Unionist, said he'd be damned if he'd put up with that sort of nonsense, and he scratched in the easiest correction to the name: Virginia City.

The news of the discovery moved slowly, but when those wagon loads and stage loads of anxious new prospectors arrived in Bannack, they merely kept moving, following the steady flow that was pouring out of the camp. The feeling was that here, finally, in Virginia City was the real bonanza, the true Golden Fleece. The weather was good, transportation was available, and thousands came to the lonely patch of land in the mountains.

There was no keeping miners when the lust for gold grabbed them by the hand; Bannack's population dwindled dramatically. Still, some gold remained untapped along Grasshopper Creek, and the camp was a known destination for food and equipment shipments. So

Bannack became the base town for Virginia City. Goods arriving from Salt Lake City or Fort Benton came through Bannack, and those willing to stay on were able to profit from that fact.

But compared to what he had left, Henry Plummer returned with his new wife to what was already a ghost town.

CHAPTER 16

(Thursday, June 24, 1863)

Electa Plummer did not know what to make of her bridegroom's uncontrolled rage. She had never seen Henry Plummer like this. He pulled her around the camp as he looked for his friends, he gruffly pushed aside strangers who innocently asked him questions, and his eyes burned with anger. She was used to seeing gentle warmth in those eyes; now violent sparks leaped everywhere he looked. And then there was his language!

"Some bastard broke into the goddamned cabin! I'm the *sheriff*!" There were other random expletives striking her ears.

Electa knew the words—she had heard them from other girls tee-hee-ing about the naughty things boys said in the school yard—but she had never heard those words used by grown men in front of proper ladies.

They had returned to the cabin after the hectic tour through the camp. The cabin was in some disarray but, Electa felt, there was no valid reason to carry on so.

Henry stormed around, furiously trying to put things

back in place. As he set a chair back by the small kitchen table, he growled, "How the hell could they break into the cabin of the damned sheriff!?"

Electa turned and looked out the door; her dream of arrival in their new home was quickly decaying into a nightmare. She was seeing a side of her husband that had been hidden from her, and her eyes were beginning to tear up; there was no reason for his violent temper, no reason she could comprehend.

Her Henry was dealing with a sudden deluge of reasons for anger. Nearly all of the miners had pulled out of Bannack. The fact would make his ore-processing stamp mill virtually worthless. Who would need it? He would also be without men to work the claims he owned. Was he to dig and pan the dirt? And Cyrus Skinner had pulled out, leaving the Elk Horn Saloon in the charge of two newcomers who were strangers to Plummer.

Upstanding residents had also left. Langford, Phleger, and Sanders had moved to the new gold area to set up businesses. The word Plummer had heard was that most of the honest men were in Virginia City for a short time, that they would be back soon. But he needed more information so that he could plan his future. He had spent quite a bit on the cabin for Electa, and he had paid out most of his cash for equipment and salaries. Things were not at all what they had been when he left to get married.

He came to Electa, took hold of her shoulders, and turned her around. She was crying. He blurted out, "Now dammit, woman, don't add to my troubles. I'll get this all organized."

"Henry, I've never seen you like this."

"Well, get used to it because I've got big troubles."

"What troubles? I can help. Just tell me what to do."

Plummer felt a compelling urge to slap her, to stop her weeping and whining, to just stop her from distracting him from his problems. *Women out here have no place in men's problems!* But he checked the impulse; what had gone wrong was no fault of Electa's.

He held her shoulders firmly and looked at her. He was a lucky man to find such a beautiful woman and one so devoted. Not many men in a hard frontier town were blessed with a wife who had style and grace and vitality. His said softly, "Please, Electa, bear with me."

"I want to help."

"You can't."

"Why not?"

"I've got to sort this out by myself."

"But I can help; the way my sister helps Jim, the way my mother helped my father."

"This is different."

"How?"

Plummer did not reply. He did not know how his problems were different from other people's; all he knew was that his recent dreams and plans had all been dashed. He did not know how to handle the adversity he was facing. He needed some time alone to think, but before that, he needed facts. He brought in Electa's baggage from the buckboard they had brought from Sun River, then told her, somewhat briskly, to get unpacked, that he would be back in a short time.

He left abruptly. Electa felt a premonition of bad things to come. She began to have her first doubts about marrying Henry Plummer.

The one place Plummer had not been was LeGrau's Café, so he headed there. He walked four blocks through the town and saw not one individual he knew. The mud of the streets was drying out and the air was warm; beautiful weather for a rotten homecoming.

At LeGrau's, he found that Frank and Renee had gone to Virginia City and had left Cora Harris and Lucinda Simons in charge of the café. Voit had been enlisted to keep an eye on the blacksmith shop. Cora was quite happy with the arrangement, except that Clay Barrow loafed around the café mooning after Lucinda. Vic and Cora were now seriously talking about marriage.

Plummer was surprised at the change in the place. While he had been away, Frank LeGrau had set in four honest-to-God, six-paned, glazed windows that filled the room with a bright, friendly light. There were tablecloths and flowers in jars and cups on each table. The tablecloths had been the effort of Lucinda Simons, who had a knack for sewing; the flowers had been Cora Harris' idea. She had started going out each morning to pick the wild daises and lupine that had blossomed as soon as the weather had begun to warm. To Plummer, the place had the look of a modestly good café in San Francisco, and it seemed to him another sign that the town was going to settle down from a frontier town to a proper community, another reason for him to run a business, but another reason for him to be frustrated. What the hell was going to happen?

There were three unfamiliar customers bent over their bowls of stew. The only faces he recognized were Cora, Lucinda, and Clay Barrow. Cora was washing dishes, and Lucinda was drinking coffee with Barrow at a table in the far corner. Plummer crossed the room and joined them. Gruffly, he said to Lucy, "I need a cup of coffee."

Lucinda Simons meekly rose and left the table. Plummer said to Barrow: "What the hell's going on in this camp? You're the first friendly face I've seen since I got back."

Clay Barrow had always been on the fringe of the ruffians clustered around Cyrus Skinner, and he was elated to be asked an opinion by a man of Henry Plummer's stature. Self-importantly, he puffed himself up and said, "Ain't it awful, jest awful."

Plummer waited.

Barrow asked, "What'd ya need to be knowing, Mister Plummer?"

Plummer quietly said, "I need to know, how big is the strike?"

Barrow replied, "It's a hell of a strike there."

Lucinda arrived with a cup of coffee. After she set it in place, she began to sit down again, but Plummer said, "We're talking business."

Lucinda glared at Plummer. Barrow said quickly, "Hey, Lucy, jest let us do a bit of business, okay. You go on back to the kitchen."

Lucinda's lips drew into a thin, angry line. She turned abruptly and stalked off to vent her pique on Cora Harris.

Plummer sipped his coffee, then asked, "How big?"

Barrow grinned. "They've taken out sacks and sacks of nuggets already . . . really."

"If it's so good there, what are you doing here?"

Barrow smiled proudly. "Cy asked me to keep an eye on the Elk Horn."

Plummer snapped, "You keep an eye on the Elk Horn by drinking coffee here?"

"Well . . . I sort of been keeping company with that woman." He pointed toward where Lucinda stood pouting, then added shyly, "She's real classy, and I don't want none of these ones passing through to take a shine to her." He nodded toward the three men eating at another table.

"Is there any quartz showing up yet at the new place?"

Barrow scratched his chin. He did not know what quartz was. Plummer recognized the problem and said, "Any rock with gold in it?"

"Nope, just plain old dust and nuggets."

That news did not speak well for Plummer's stamp mill.

"Damn the luck."

Barrow did not speak, because he did not know what was disturbing Plummer.

Vic Voit came in through the front door and headed back toward the kitchen. Barrow called Voit over to the table. Plummer had seen Voit around the camp, but he did not know the youth. Barrow said, "Vic, you tell Mister Plummer what's going on over at the new diggings."

Voit knew Plummer and had even voted for him for sheriff, but that was before he had found out that Nat

Langford had little use for Plummer and the other friends of Cyrus Skinner, including Clay Barrow.

Still, Henry Plummer was the duly elected sheriff of the camp. Voit said, "It looks pretty big, Sheriff. The LeGraus are opening up a café there, and Mister LeGrau is planning to move his blacksmith shop."

The news that the camp's blacksmith was leaving was a real sign that Bannack's days might be numbered. Plummer asked a few more general questions and was rewarded with reasonable answers. After a few minutes, he announced, "I'd better be taking a ride over there, I guess."

Voit said, "I'm leaving in the morning; we could ride together if you like, Sheriff."

"You planning to move fast? I don't want to be slowed down by a wagon or something."

"Nope, I'm riding fast. A letter just came in for Mister Langford; looks like important Masonic business."

Voit winced as soon as he said the words; he knew that Plummer had been refused admission to the Masons, and everyone in the camp figured Plummer could not feel too good about that. Awkwardly, Voit said, "I'm sorry, Mister Plummer."

Plummer gave a good-natured smile. "Don't let that worry you. I'll take the letter if you don't want to make the trip."

Voit was flustered. He finally said, "Naw, I'll still need to be going . . . I've got to see Mister LeGrau, anyway."

The two agreed to meet at the east end of town at dawn, and shortly thereafter Plummer left.

Cora chided Vic for talking "to the likes of Henry Plummer." Vic grinned at her good-naturedly.

Back in the Plummer cabin, Electa did not take the announcement well. "But I don't want to stay here all alone. I don't know a soul."

Plummer was not in a conciliatory mood. He refused her proposal that they make the trip together, but he pointed out that he could be there and back much faster if he was not encumbered by worry about her.

Electa Plummer spent the first night in her new home crying herself to sleep. Plummer left before dawn the next morning to see what promise lay for him over the mountains to the east.

CHAPTER 17

(Saturday, June 26, 1863)

The gold camp called Virginia City was a mess, an absolute mess. The area up Alder Gulch, for a full twelve miles, had been a mass of heavy undergrowth and bothersome bushes, so several resourceful prospectors had decided to burn off their problems. The result had been a conflagration that wiped out nearly every tree and clump of brush in sight. The fire had been bad, but it had finally burned itself out, leaving mile after mile of black soot and gray ash. People in the camp were thankful that there was no rain to turn the streets and roads into mud, but they wished dearly that *something* would take away the residue of the fire.

Nathaniel Langford was living in a lean-to attached to a large wagon in which he had carted in lumber for the building of stores and homes from the sawmill that had become one of his major investments. He was living in miserable conditions but beginning to build his fortune. Wilbur Sanders was living in a twelve-foot-square army tent in which he slept at night and practiced law by day, building a reputation as a fair, honest lawyer.

When Langford and Sanders had arrived in the new gold camp, one of the first men they had met was Xavier Beidler, a fellow Freemason. Beidler had come to the mountains to dig for gold but found that he could do better buying and selling goods needed by the prospectors. Beidler was a stocky, short, powerfully built man who insisted on being called simply "X." He was a tough, aggressive type who was not reluctant to enter a fistfight or barroom brawl. Beidler quickly became friends with Langford and Sanders. Langford was the one to observe that Beidler's presence in Bannack would have been welcomed in the cause of electing a sheriff other than Henry Plummer. Sanders came up with the idea that they should attempt to have Beidler appointed U.S. marshal for the area, a move that would effectively reduce Plummer's power. Beidler was flattered by the suggestion and said he would be proud to serve the community if they wanted him. Sanders said that he was going to travel to the territorial capital in Lewiston as soon as possible.

In the meantime, they would do what they could to make the new camp into a proper town. Within the first three weeks, they had formed a Masonic Lodge and dispatched another petition to the Grand Lodge in Nebraska. Langford had believed that Bannack would grow into a substantial community, and Sanders had concurred after he arrived. Both men were now equally sure about the future of Virginia City, because more and more gold was coming down the hill as each day passed. In the first four weeks of digging, prospectors had torn from the earth $375,000 worth of dust and nuggets. Virginia City was about to make its mark in the West.

As was the custom, the city had been platted, with a master plan sketched out, including town offices and churches and schools. A plan was drawn up to dam the creek to provide a supply of water for the miners and the town.

Langford, Sanders, and Beidler were having coffee in the Gem Saloon on Wallace Street in the late afternoon when Henry Plummer arrived in Virginia City. The Gem was not really a saloon. It was simply a roof held up by large peeled logs under which Harry Sizeland had positioned some tables and a bar made of planks. He sold a limited amount of liquor, but he concentrated on coffee and tasty, quick meals, catering to the element in the camp that did not like Cyrus Skinner's Alder Creek Saloon. Between serving customers, Sizeland was nailing up walls to the logs. He planned to have the place complete with a wooden floor prior to the arrival of winter.

Langford was the first to spot Plummer riding into town, and he saw that Vic Voit was riding with him. Langford excused himself and went out into the street. Plummer gave him a broad grin and a warm greeting, but Langford made no bones about his feelings. He asked, "Vic, you started riding with the likes of Plummer here?"

Voit looked embarrassed.

Plummer helped out: "Now, Nat, you know none of your good Masons would be caught dead near the likes of me. I just tagged along with Vic here for the ride over." Then, looking around the burgeoning camp, he asked, "Where's Cy Skinner's place? I got some law business to discuss with him."

Langford, less harshly, answered, "Skinner's running his joint down on Cover Street. It runs along the creek. Turn downhill at the next corner and you won't be able to miss it. Just look for all of the dregs of society; they'll be there."

Plummer grinned at Langford. The grin was painted with contempt, because Plummer had accepted the hostile attitude of Nat Langford. He tipped a finger to his hat and spurred his horse along. Langford looked at Vic Voit, who quickly pulled out the envelope he had carried from Bannack and said, "I got something from the Nebraska Lodge."

"Well, Vic, jump down and come on in for some coffee. I want to read that. And there's a lot you need to know."

Voit dismounted. "I'd better get to finding Mister LeGrau."

Langford said, "Don't worry about Frank. He'll probably be here for coffee in a few minutes."

As Henry Plummer walked into the Alder Creek Saloon, Cyrus Skinner boomed out: "They gotta quit parking them oxen in front of my saloon . . . look at the pile of dung that just came in the front door!"

The place was crowded; hoots and cheers followed Plummer as he walked to the bar. Many in Skinner's did not know who Plummer was, but those who knew him were glad to see the man. Plummer and Skinner spent a few minutes catching up with each other: Plummer told about his marriage, and the shock of finding Bannack virtually deserted. Skinner gave a quick summary of opening his second saloon, including the hectic move of the mahogany bar on an overloaded wagon. A cluster of curious friends surrounded the pair. Skinner could see that Plummer had something he wanted to talk about, so he said, "Come out back and I'll show you my cabin."

Twenty feet from the rear of the saloon stood Skinner's cabin. It looked like a shack when seen from the outside, but inside, the place, although small, was comfortable, almost plush. There were two windows to let in light. Somewhere Skinner had found proper curtains and, more impressive, a large rug to cover the wooden floor. Plummer saw that a lot of hard cash had gone into the decoration and Dolly Grogan's tastes were in evidence. The two men sat at an oak table on cushioned chairs and began to talk.

Neither man left any record of what was said on that Saturday afternoon, but the outcome has been well documented.

The first move in the plot they hatched was to have Plummer announce himself as sheriff of the new camp.

Virginia City did, in fact, sit within the boundaries of the county as surveyed by the territorial government. Plummer would also appoint deputies to act in his absence, deputies who would be close friends of Skinner's. Several of Skinner's most dependable henchmen were assigned the tasks of spying on the camp to determine who was packing out, and how much gold was going with them. "Clubfoot" George Lane, a cobbler by trade and a thief by avocation, was to set up his boot repair bench in the general store. His job was to keep his ears open for news of departures. George Ives was charged with getting a job as a stable hand at Bob Dempsey's ranch, which sat midway between Virginia City and Bannack. The trip between the two camps was just about all a man could handle in a day, and hard on the horse besides, so Dempsey's ranch had become a place to exchange mounts or to spend the night. Dan McFadden was told to make himself available for work in the assay office. There he would be privy to a man's worth, down to the last dollar.

No one knows if two other aspects of the plot were hatched that day, but it is probable that they were. Each of their band was to wear a kerchief tied at the neck with a sailor's knot. If caught, they were to state loudly and clearly that they were innocent of any wrongdoing; "innocent" because that was what the Plummer gang would call themselves: the Innocents.

Plummer spent the rest of that Saturday appointing deputies and making it known that he was now the sheriff of Virginia City, in that order. Most of the 2,600 people in the camp gave little thought to the news; they were too intent on digging. Among the reputable men in the camp who did care, the universal feeling was that the development was not going to be good for anyone. There were still those who thought Plummer was not to be liked or trusted. Plummer did not really give a damn about what men like Langford, Phleger, and Sanders thought. He was going to see to his own fortunes in the way he knew best.

Gone were Plummer's grand plans for becoming a law-abiding, respectable businessman in the gold camp; in one more foray outside the law, he would make enough money to live comfortably for the rest of his life, and he and Electa would have a splendid future if all went his way. He departed for Bannack the next morning.

The effects of Plummer's plan took only four days to begin to show themselves.

CHAPTER 18

(Tuesday, June 30, 1863)

Among the four deputies appointed to oversee Virginia City, one was, for some unknown reason, an honest young man named Don Dillingham. The other three were Buck Stinson, Ned Ray, and Jack Gallagher—all dependable no-goods who had gravitated toward Skinner's saloon and Plummer's personality. The organized Plummer gang first manifested itself on a balmy afternoon when Dillingham overheard the other three plotting to ambush a miner who had struck it rich and was planning to leave with his wealth. Dillingham confronted the trio, and an argument ensued. Dillingham would not be drawn into the plot and threatened his fellow deputies with arrest. The three of them scoffed at his boyish innocence. He headed to the middle of town, where a Miners' Court was already in session, trying to solve a claim dispute. Dillingham was shot dead in plain view of nearly a hundred miners.

The shooting was such a shock to the startled witnesses that they were hard-pressed to believe what they had seen. Jack Gallagher, who had not actually fired a shot with his drawn gun, handed his own weapon to Buck Stinson. Then he arrested his two fellow deputies. A furious argument ensued about who actually did the shooting and, through charges and preposterous countercharges, there developed a real question as to what had actually happened. The Miners' Court turned from considering a serious case of claim jumping to trying to sort out how Don Dillingham had ended up dead.

Wilbur Sanders, who had been representing one of the litigants in the claim-jumping case, agreed to prosecute the deputies. Dillingham's body was still warm when the trial began. There was a fairly quick finding of guilty in the case of all three deputies. After an impassioned plea from Sanders, a sentence of death by hanging was pronounced. The prospectors who had taken part in the trial began to disperse, some to use the remaining daylight to work their claims, some just to get away from the sordid events. The rowdy element of the camp stayed.

Drunks, prostitutes, and ruffians in the employ of Cyrus Skinner began to clamor against the hanging sentence, taking the position that banishment was sufficient, since murder could not really be proven against any one individual. The atmosphere turned ugly as the ropes were prepared. Amidst the protests, a voice—some say it was Gallagher—demanded a second vote, a vote for banishment as the sentence. While all of this was going on, Sanders, Langford, and Beidler were trying to maintain order. The man who had served as judge left the scene, and the three witnesses who had testified also left. What had become a mob now shouted for the release of the trio. Sanders and his two friends left the scene in disgust. The mob quickly provided horses for the convicted men to ride out of town.

The three men who accepted banishment did not really leave the area. Buck Stinson went back to Bannack, where Plummer put him to work again as a deputy.

CHAPTER 19

(Summer, 1863)

Bannack began to recover from the exodus to Virginia City.

Each day dozens, sometimes hundreds, of eager people passed hopefully through Bannack on their way to the new strike. Some of those who passed through soon returned to Bannack because, by August, an incredible ten thousand people had packed into the area of Alder Gulch. It was reasonable that Bannack absorb some of the backwash from the tide of those thirsting for quick riches.

It was difficult to discern which was the satellite and which was the center. Virginia City had the mass, but Bannack had the structure of an organized community. The people at Alder Gulch had no time to worry over niceties; gold was there to be plucked from the ground.

Bannack was doing well supplying services and goods to those newly arriving; fortunes in gold dust and nuggets changed hands daily. It was amazing, considering the wealth, that the federal and territorial governments paid scant attention to what was going on in those mountains. But the federal government was fighting to preserve the Union, and suffered the carnage of Gettysburg in July. Washington did very little about the area. One example of bureaucratic attention to detail had been the appointment of Sidney Edgerton to be a territorial judge. Edgerton, a former congressman from Ohio, did not even know where the territorial capital was located, but he made his way to Bannack and there awaited instructions. The territorial government in Lewiston showed little more concern for the humanity flocking to the gold camps. In response to repeated appeals from Nat Langford and Wilbur Sanders, U.S. Marshal D. S. Payne was dispatched to the area to see if there was valid cause to establish a Marshal's office and appoint someone to man it. Payne's idea of diligently examining the problem was to approach the Union Club and Nathaniel Langford for their advice and opinion. The only logical candidate for the U.S. marshal's post was Henry Plummer, because he was serving as area sheriff. Nat Langford in a private meeting with Payne vetoed that idea, even though a secret vote of the Union Club members was in favor of the appointment. After three days in Bannack, Payne headed back to Lewiston to make his own recommendations. What he proposed would not be known for another nine months. As far as anyone could tell, from the attitude of the territorial government, they were on their own. The leaders of Bannack went back to running their own lives and planning their own futures.

The town—and most residents were now thinking of it as a town—began to take on a patina of permanence. Some of the slapdash log buildings were disassembled, the timbers squared off and the buildings rebuilt in a stronger, warmer, and more attractive fashion. More two-story buildings were erected. Bricks were imported and used. And many a home and business owner put wooden floors in their structures. Bannack was like a prize bull primped up for a county fair—shining, clean, horns polished, but still mean, tough, and unpredictable.

By midsummer, Main Street had seven restaurants, three bakeries, three hotels, a hardware store, and a grocery. On the side streets there were other places of business catering to nearly every need of those coming in to prospect for gold. And there were the inevitable saloons and bawdy houses to provide for the needs of men far removed from church and home. According to a map reportedly drawn by Nathaniel Langford, there were ninety-two structures in Bannack.

The Bannack Indians who had been living in proximity to the white men had left. There was, for the Indians, no understanding the brutality that had been shown.

Frank LeGrau had opened his new smithy in Virginia City. Within two months it had grown to be a minor foundry that produced customized tools and equipment for the prospectors. Renee LeGrau began another small restaurant which she was able to sell at a profit by mid-July, and the LeGraus used the money to build still another café on the first floor of a two-story brick building in Virginia City. The second floor was a modest, comfortable home for them. Frank LeGrau tried to persuade Vic Voit to turn blacksmith and run the less busy smithy in Bannack, but that did not work, so LeGrau talked Voit into being a teamster. With LeGrau's backing, Voit was soon running a freight service between Fort Benton and the gold camps. While Voit did not prosper on a grand scale, he did begin to have an income dependable enough to take some personal steps that had long been part of his hopes. The steps all had to do with Cora Harris.

Cora had become a working partner with Renee LeGrau in the Bannack café. Renee was fully occupied with her home, husband, and business in Virginia City, so she had turned over the operation in Bannack to Cora on a profit-sharing basis.

* * *

(From the Family Records *page in the Harris-Voit Family Bible)*

Married: Vic Voit of Pasco,
Territory of Washington to
Cora Harris of Bethlehem,
Commonwealth of Pennsylvania
On: July 10, 1863

(Inserted in the Bible in the same archives source, a yellowed page of paper that seems to have been a page cut out of Cora Harris Voit's diary)

To those who come after us in our family, please read this.

We hope to have children and we hope those children do likewise and we want you all, each and every one of our descendants, to know that we started our married life with little more than a grand and warm love for each other.

If we are able to leave you any worldly possessions when we go to meet our Maker, then we will be pleased, but if there is nothing like a house or money, then we want you to know that we are leaving you something more important: a history of respecting the Lord and loving each other. Take our hopes for you through your life. God bless you all.

[The document is unsigned]

Vic Voit was initiated into the Bannack Masonic Lodge as an Entered Apprentice two weeks after he was married.

Nathaniel Langford was prospering. The sawmill he had helped start was producing income as fast as the logs could be cut, and Langford's other small business ventures were all doing well. He had accepted the mantle of Postmaster for Bannack, and he used Voit's freight service to send mail out. Incoming mail from Fort Benton was also consigned to Voit's wagons.

Soon the wagons were also carrying out raw gold that had been bought by George Chrisman, a friend and business associate of Langford's, who was doing well with his gold exchange on the corner of Third and Main. Chrisman paid a fair price of $14 per ounce and assumed the problems associated with shipping the gold out to where he could receive the market price of $18 per ounce. He also acted as consignment broker for shipping gold to Fort Benton, Lewiston, and Salt Lake City. The main problem Chrisman had was paying off in greenbacks. Those were still not a welcome currency in the West, because the government back in the States had been simply printing money in an effort to pay for the Civil War. As a result, Vic Voit frequently hauled in sacks of heavy silver dollars to Bannack. In a move designed to add protection and security to the gold exchange business, Chrisman provided a small office in the back of his building for the camp's sheriff. Henry Plummer was grateful and pleased by the offer.

Plummer played his chameleon role with ease. He walked tall down the streets of Bannack and Virginia City by day, and met with his Innocents in the shadows of the saloons by night. As he had done earlier in his life of crime, Plummer, in his trusted position as sheriff, would listen to prospectors talking about their plans to pull out and head back to civilization. He would pass on the intelligence to the Innocents and, if the prospector followed the plans he had revealed in good faith to the sheriff, the prospector would be relieved of his gold and possibly his life.

It is not taking away from the story to say here that from June of 1863 until January of 1864, 107 departed prospectors were either discovered dead or were known never to have reached their announced destinations. Those 107 cases are documented. Others undoubtedly fell prey to the Innocents in that period of time.

Had the Fairweather party not made their discovery in Alder Gulch when they did, had the gold lain quietly for another year or two, the Innocents would never have come into being. Henry Plummer would have probably gone forward with his plans to become an honest, respected member of the Bannack community. He would have had an ordinary life with the love of Electa, and they would probably have started a family to grow up in the haven of a quiet mining town. But fate draws its own plan, and Henry Plummer was on a collision course with infamy.

CHAPTER 20

(Wednesday, September 2, 1863)

Electa Plummer was empty of hope.

She sat on what had become her chair in the front part of the cabin that Henry and she called their parlor. The game of making the cabin out to be more than it really was had begun back in her early days in Bannack, when there had still been some romance in her life, the kind of romance she had anticipated.

When Plummer had returned to Bannack, after abruptly leaving her alone on her first day in the strange camp he called a town, he had changed from the hostile, angry man who had exploded at the changes in the mining camp. He had returned to her the man she had fallen in love with, the man who could laugh, the man who was tender and considerate. She began to think that his poor behavior might have been an insignificant aberration. Plummer, once again gentle and thoughtful, tried his best to entertain her and to introduce her to the people in the camp. She tried to make a success of their life, tried as hard as she knew how.

It was not Electa's fault that she could not make a go of it as Henry Plummer's wife.

Plummer had brought back from the Alder Gulch camp a vitality born in confidence. Prior to his wedding, he had been trying to fight his way into the world of business, to become respected like Langford, Kohrs, Phleger, and the others. He had told himself that he would make a success of his legitimate ventures. He knew now that he had been kidding himself all along. He was afraid of trying to go straight, frightened to death of the ridicule that would come his way if—when—he failed. But he knew with the confidence of experience that he could run a gang of road agents without error. There would be no failure in doing what he knew how to do down to the last detail. He triumphed as the leader of his gang of road agents; he failed as a husband.

The simple fact was that the two endeavors were not compatible, as long as he was unwilling to bring Electa into the secret of how he was collecting the money that was letting him appear a dedicated sheriff and a successful businessman. He could not, would not, reveal to that innocent woman that he was merely a common scoundrel.

Overseeing the Innocents required him to be away from Electa, sometimes for days at a time. When he was not out of Bannack, he was frequently at Skinner's saloon, meeting with his henchmen. It was natural that he would also, not infrequently, consort with the sporting ladies who were in Skinner's employ. Though she had no actual proof, Electa was convinced that Henry was unfaithful to her.

She could probably have handled that if infidelity had been the only problem, but her loneliness was worse. At first she had busied herself around the cabin, sewing pillowcases and curtains. She prepared elaborate meals, but many of them went uneaten when Henry did not come home for dinner. She labored in the tiny patch of dirt behind the cabin to grow flowers and vegetables, but her efforts went mostly unnoticed. She tried to make friends with some of the women of the camp, but she was a shy woman, and the others were busy with their own lives.

So, she was leaving.

Her tears had dried on her cheeks, and the emptiness in the pit of her stomach was a physical pain. She had tried to tell herself that she would merely make a short visit back with her family in Ohio, but she knew in her heart she would probably never return to Bannack. At nine o'clock that morning, she had gone to George Dart's Hardware Store on Main Street and had purchased a seat on the stagecoach that was leaving at two o'clock for Salt Lake City. It was noontime now, and Plummer had not been home since yesterday morning, although he promised he would return for supper that night. Electa Plummer was resigned to leaving him a letter of explanation. That was written. She decided to take her bags to Dart's and wait there, rather than sit in the lonely cabin.

She propped the letter on the table, against a jar that held some flowers from her garden; she was about as sad as she had ever been in her entire life.

She was picking up the small leather valise that held all of her worldly possessions when Plummer arrived.

It took him a moment to realize what he was seeing. Gruffly, he demanded, "What the hell's going on?"

Emotionally drained, Electa blurted out, "I'm leaving. I've had enough of this place and you. I'm through!"

She felt an immediate pang of guilt because what she had said did not really express her feelings. She had said it all much better in the note left on the table; she had said it all much better to herself as she had rehearsed her declaration. But she was too exhausted to try and soften the news.

Plummer felt as if he had been struck in the stomach. He knew that he had not been an attentive husband lately, but all his efforts had been directed toward gathering wealth to provide a substantial future for Electa and himself.

Yesterday he had met with George Ives at the Dempsey ranch. Ives had heard of a really big shipment heading out of Virginia City with a man named Magruder, and he had told Plummer all he knew. Plummer had ridden through the night, nearly killing his horse to arrive in Bannack before Magruder. There was going to be a substantial gain for the Innocents if all went well.

But Electa was standing there holding a valise, and he was too tired to think.

He snarled, "Now stop this foolishness. Put that damned bag down!"

Electa placed the bag on the floor, but she did not speak. He sat down heavily on one of the chairs and demanded: "What's all this about?"

Electa found her voice and said, quietly, "Henry, I have to get away for a short while. I am most unhappy, and there is nothing here to make me happy."

"You've got one of the best cabins in the camp. You have all of the money you need to buy anything you want."

"I don't have a husband."

The statement chilled Plummer. He knew that he had been absent too much over the past couple of months, but he had been working: couldn't this woman see that?

Plummer snatched off his hat and rubbed the scar on his forehead; Electa knew that was a thing he did whenever he was about to explode. They had not had many arguments, because she seldom fought back, but she did not want her leave-taking to be marked by a nasty scene. She steeled herself for a verbal assault.

The assault never came. Plummer was too tired to fight and all he said was: "I guess it's best."

A long moment passed before she said, "You don't mind?"

"I do mind, yes, but I feel you have your mind made up; I think it might be good for you to take a vacation."

She looked at him, startled.

"Are you going to see your sister at Sun River?"

She shook her head. "I'm going to go back to Ohio. I'm tired of the frontier."

"That's a long trip."

"I'll not be gone long."

"Your sister and Jim are coming here next month. Electa, I put a hell of a lot of energy into talking Jim into coming down here—just so you could have your sister with you."

"I'll be back by then."

Plummer heard her words, but he doubted she would come back to the gold camp. He stood and crossed to where she had remained standing since he had come into the cabin. He took her into his arms and said, "I have just a few more weeks of work to do here, my darling. If you could just wait, then we could go together."

"I'm tired, Henry."

"I know." He stroked the hair that flowed down onto her shoulders as he added, "You have a good break away from here. I'll come to you just as soon as I can."

She turned her face up and kissed his lips tenderly. "You promise?"

"I promise."

They spent the next hour discussing the details of their separation. He took from his strongbox three of the two dozen leather pouches of gold nuggets that he had collected as his share in the operations of the Innocents. He gave her the addresses of several friends in California and Nevada and Minnesota, friends who might know where he was if he was not in Bannack or Virginia City. He made her write down the name of every person she might visit in Ohio and he made her promise that she would write to him. And finally, he gave her a promise that he would be with her before the winter set in.

Plummer was impatient; three times in two minutes he pulled out his pocket watch to check the time. He seemed so fidgety that Electa wished he would simply leave her alone to wait for the stage to load. She was not pleased at the prospect of the three- or four-day trip to Salt Lake City. The ride would be uncomfortable as the stage banged around in the ruts of the roads they would travel, billows of dust blowing up into the passenger section.

Plummer had taken her to LeGrau's Café, where he had Cora Harris fill up a good-sized wicker basket with food for Electa during the trip, as the stagecoach company had no proper rest stops until it reached Utah Territory. The gesture was nice, but Electa did not like going into cafés; she always felt people were staring at her because she was the sheriff's wife.

Now they were waiting outside George Dart's Hardware Store. Plummer pulled out his watch again.

Electa said, "Henry, do go on and do your business, whatever it is; I'll be fine."

Plummer was just about to accept her offer when the driver announced: "We're leaving. Load up!"

There was a flurry of good-byes as passengers began to climb on board. Plummer gave Electa a peck on the cheek, and she mumbled that she would write as promised.

In two minutes, the stage was moving west along Main Street, taking Electa out of his life.

Plummer turned quickly and headed to George Chrisman's Gold Exchange. Lloyd Magruder was due at Chrisman's shortly after two o'clock and he intended to be there. There was work to be done; Plummer had had enough of domestic dramas.

Henry Plummer was there, chatting casually with George, as Magruder and his men began carrying sacks of gold dust and nuggets inside.

Lloyd Magruder was a slightly built man of thirty-one years. He was prematurely balding and seemed to want to make up for that flaw by growing a bushy mustache. He had a reasonable sense of humor and a wily business sense. Early on, in midsummer, he had arrived in Bannack with a wagonload of merchandise that he had purchased in Lewiston. On the advice of the locals, he had immediately gone on to Virginia City, where he rented a cabin on Wallace Street. He had brought diverse stock, from rubber boots to picks and shovels, as well as personal items such as frying pans and cast-iron pots. In any unoccupied space, he had packed items like long underwear and bolts of yard goods, filling the nooks and crannies with packets of sewing needles, cutlery, and can after can of pipe tobacco. He had invested close to $3,000 in the goods and the massive wagon and team of oxen. When he had finally sold off the last of his items—including the wagon and oxen—he had in hand just over $14,000 in gold dust and nuggets. Magruder had struck it rich without ever lifting a pan of dirt.

Magruder's gold shipment was to be secured in Chrisman's strongbox overnight, while Magruder and his men rested before carrying it out. Plummer experienced another thrill when he heard Chrisman ask if Magruder would be willing to take along another $8,600 in gold sacks consigned to Chrisman for shipment to Lewiston.

Magruder felt comfortable in agreeing; he was traveling with a competent crew of guards. Robert and Horace Chalmer, two brothers, were to ride with him, along with Crawford Allen and Ronald Phillip.

Plummer suggested that there should be more men to ensure protection and offered to see if he could round up some others to go along, just for more security. Magruder agreed, so long as the new men were willing to work for $3.50 a day. Plummer felt confident those conditions could be met.

On his way from George Dart's to Chrisman's, Plummer had ducked into the Elk Horn Saloon, where he had told Cy Skinner to line up some Innocents, just in case they might be needed. Plummer went outside now and spotted a quartet of his men waiting a block away: Bob Lowery, Ken Howard, William Page, and Jim Romaine. Plummer led the men to Chrisman's.

Inside, Lloyd Magruder was impressed when Sheriff Plummer displayed so much concern that he actually deputized the quartet right on the spot. Magruder said, "I wish all of the towns in the territory were run like this."

At dawn the next morning, the Magruder party left Bannack, traveling down the same road as the stagecoach on which Electa Plummer had fled.

Plummer and Chrisman went to Bill Goodrich's Hotel and had a couple of drinks to celebrate a successful enterprise. The two had divergent reasons for feeling pleased.

The Lloyd Magruder party made good time traveling west over the mountain passes. They cut just south of the Pioneer Mountains, up through the Big Hole Pass, and out along the high plain of the Big Hole cattle-grazing country. They crested the Sapphire Mountains and headed north up the Bitterroot Valley along the precise route taken by Meriwether Lewis and William Clark fifty-eight years earlier to the day. At the Nez Percé Fork of the Bitterroot River, they turned west and made camp prior to the push over the final range of mountains between them and Lewiston.

They killed a buck deer and were roasting the venison as a snowstorm began. Dinner was delayed while lean-tos were erected. As soon as everyone had his fill of meat and the last of the bread they had brought from Bannack, the men organized their blankets and retired. There would be enough venison to eat with their breakfast coffee, and all seemed right with their world.

Shortly after nine o'clock, sleep came to most, and the red embers of the fire began to soften.

What happened just after ten o'clock was related by William Page, who, after the deed, seemed to regret his part.

Magruder was awakened when he heard Bob Lowery whispering to Ken Howard. Not a nosy sort, he rose from his sleeping place, gave a quiet greeting to the other two men, and went to the fire to light his pipe, saying, "Just thought I'd have a smoke."

As he stuck a twig into the coals, Lowery sprang to his feet, grabbed the firewood axe, and swung it viciously down onto Magruder's head; the skull split open and Magruder fell into the fire. In the next four seconds, the Chalmer brothers, as well as Allen and Phillip, were shot where they lay sleeping. Only Horace Chalmer let out a stifled cry; a second shot to his chest silenced him. Jim Romaine had pulled the trigger for that shot.

The killers tossed the bodies of the five victims into a ravine just to the south of the campsite. The next morning, with the snow falling more heavily, Plummer's men shot Magruder's horses and headed out for Lewiston.

The quartet of killers made the customary mistake of spending freely, and Lewiston's town marshal, Hill Beechy, began to question them about their wealth. Now, Plummer had found men he could depend on to carry out wicked deeds, but they were not the brightest souls on earth. The four evaded the questions, and then, when Beechy felt he had to turn them loose, headed out of town on the stage for San Francisco. But Beechy was tenacious about his feelings of foul play. He followed the four to San Francisco. There, with the help of local police, he got William Page to break down and confess.

No great portion of the money was ever recovered, and it was suspected later, when the story of the Magruder party could be reconstructed, that the sacks of gold had been passed on to a Plummer cohort in Lewiston.

Three of the killers were hung in Lewiston and went to their deaths silently. William Page died in the Idaho Territorial Prison, but he never revealed what he knew about the missing Magruder gold.

CHAPTER 21

(Thursday, December 17, 1863)

Cora smacked Vic on the side of his head so hard that his ear rang.

"Dammit, Cora, don't hit me like that!"

"You just make me so darned mad that I don't know what to do!"

"Well, that ain't no reason to hit me!"

Vic turned away from Cora and nearly fell when his left leg buckled; the burning sensation from the gunshot wound had not lessened in the two days since he had been shot in his thigh.

Cora could almost feel her husband's pain and she was as quickly remorseful as she had been angry; in a moment she had her arms around his shoulders, supporting him. She ordered, "Sit down. I'll get you some coffee."

Vic had arrived home five minutes previously. He had been shot two days before while crossing Spotted Dog Creek on the trip back from Fort Benton. That trip had been unprofitable and frustrating, and had ended up with him getting shot. He had been scheduled to haul some small orders, but the big cargo was three crates of silver dollars being delivered to George Dart, who was starting up a small private bank. The problem was that the crates had not arrived in Fort Benton, and except for a shipment of steel rods for Frank LeGrau and a bundle of law books for Wilbur Sanders, Vic had returned empty. But the road agents had known he was supposed to bring back $3,000 in silver Liberty coins.

At Spotted Dog Creek, half a day's ride west of the Continental Divide on the route south to Bannack, three road agents were waiting for Vic. He sensed they knew him, but he could not tell who they were. Their voices were distorted by the bandannas they wore over their faces. As soon as he saw them, Vic had announced that he was poor pickings, that he had nothing of value on his wagon. His comments were good-natured, almost friendly; he had no cargo to lose. He was ordered down, and he readily complied. Two of the bandits searched the wagon and found that he had told the truth, but the other bandit, the one who was aiming a gun at Vic, became angry. He demanded: "What d'ya got in your pockets?"

Vic, feeling the whole thing would end peacefully, gave an embarrassed grin. "I got about four bits. I ain't carrying nothing else, not even a watch."

"Empty your pockets, you bastard."

Vic pulled out his pockets and onto the ground fell four nickels, one quarter, and a dozen Indianhead pennies. A dirty handkerchief and a small folding carving knife came from his hip pocket. He announced, "That's it."

The two other men were climbing down from the wagon when the man with the gun growled, "You ain't supposed to come on this road with nothing, dammit!"

Vic explained that the shipment of silver dollars had not arrived in Fort Benton.

Vic's easy manner did not assuage the holdup man. He shouted, "You come on this road with nothing one more time, and I'll shoot you."

Vic did not like the tone of voice. He forced a smile. He had begun to say something when the man snarled, "I think I'll shoot you, anyway." And he did.

The bullet ripped through the fleshy part of Vic's left thigh and the wound started bleeding. The three men laughed, mounted up, and rode off; one of them took another shot, but aimed at the ground near Vic's boots.

The horses in Vic's team shied and reared at the sound of the shots, and he had to get them under control before worrying about himself. He was surprised that he felt no real pain, but the sensation of warm blood oozing down his leg was frightening. As cold as it was, he dropped his trousers and studied his wound. He saw that there were two holes, front and back on the thigh, so he guessed he was not going to have to worry about lead poisoning. He was able to stanch the flow of blood by tying some fairly clean rags around his leg with the two leather straps that he used on his bedroll. Riding on the wagon had not been difficult, but during the long drive the leg had tightened up. When he arrived back in Bannack, he had driven the wagon directly to LeGrau's stables and limped home. It was early afternoon and Cora had left Lucinda Simons in charge of the café. At home he said to Cora: "I've been shot." That was when she hit him.

Ever since Cora learned that she was pregnant, her personality had changed. She was as protective of her husband as it was possible for any wife to be, and she had begged him to stop driving the wagon, especially when he might be carrying anything that could be of value to the road agents. Cora was not alone in her attitude. Fear had spread into many minds in the camp; the effect had been chilling.

Cora had hit Vic out of frustration, a frustration similar to that being felt by a majority of the honest, hardworking residents of Bannack and Virginia City. There were too many killings, too many unexplained deaths. It seemed that nothing could be done to halt the lawlessness.

Cora brought Vic a cup of coffee from the pot on the cookstove and said, "I'm sorry."

He smiled. Vic Voit had nothing but love for his wife, and a little bop on the head was not going to test his feelings. He said, "No harm done."

She placed her hands on her hips and conjured up the most serious look she had. "You're gonna quit now. You know that."

He worked for time by sipping the hot coffee.

"You heard what I said?"

That question required an answer. He gulped before he said, "I've got to run the wagon to Frank over at the Gulch."

Just about everyone in Bannack called Virginia City "the Gulch."

Cora shook her head. "You're not going anywhere in that damned wagon."

"I've got steel that Frank needs in the foundry and a load of books for Wil Sanders."

"That's something! You're worried about some stupid steel and books and you don't give a damn about your baby!"

He grinned as he looked at the bulge pushing out her skirt. At five months she was beginning to show fairly well, and he wondered if they might just have twins. She snapped, "You quit grinning, Vic Voit! You ain't going to the Gulch."

Vic took a second sip of coffee. "I've got to go. Doctor Glick is there. I want him to look at my leg."

Cora looked down at his trouser leg, caked with a brownish-black stain. She softened, bent down, and wrapped her arms around his head; she was nearly in tears. "God, Vic, I don't want nothing to happen to you."

He enjoyed the way she grabbed hold of him like that; she had done it frequently since they had married. He said, "I've got to see the doctor."

She pulled herself erect. "I'm going with you."

Vic tried to stand but the pain in his leg halted him. He

countered, "You ain't going. I won't have it."

"I don't want you alone on that road, Vic. Suppose them holdup men try again."

Vic thought for a moment, then offered, "I'll take some help with me; I'll ask Clay Barrow to ride over. He's good with a gun."

"Clay Barrow! Ain't that the dumbest thing you ever said!" She threw her head back in a mock laugh. "Clay Barrow's as bad as any of them. He'd probably shoot you just for the fun of it."

Vic did not want to argue. He said, "I'll get some other help. Somebody will ride over with me."

"You get all the help you want, but I'm going. I know how to shoot, and I'll shoot those bastards if they come at you again."

"Aw, Cora."

"Don't 'Aw, Cora' me! I want our baby to have a father. I don't want to take that baby up to the graveyard and show him a slab of wood with your name carved on it like: 'He was a good man, shot dead' or something just as dumb. I'm going."

Cora did go along when Vic pulled out of Bannack an hour later. With Lucinda in charge of the café, she had gone to George Dart and borrowed a rifle. She rode beside Vic and did not even feel the cold as night settled. The moon was bright, and they made it all the way to Dempsey's ranch before they decided to call it a night.

Sometime before, Bob Dempsey had rented the ranch to George Ives, who was second in command to Henry Plummer in the group calling themselves the Innocents. With some of the holdup loot, Ives had built a proper bunkhouse, begun to operate a small kitchen, and erected a bar in the main house. George Brown acted as the main cashier and bartender. Brown had learned his skills from Cyrus Skinner, and he was a journeyman when it came to getting a traveler drunk enough to say more than he should about the gold he might be carrying.

Vic Voit hitched his team to a rail in front of the main house and led Cora inside. Inside, an ugly temper seemed as tangible as the warmth coming from the stove. Those who were talking spoke only in low, hushed voices. Vic did not like the mood. He had Cora sit on a bench by the front door and went to the bar to speak to Brown.

Voit had traveled the route between Bannack and Virginia City enough so that he was known. He quickly made arrangements for bunks and blankets as well as for the stabling of his team. Brown was unusually curt, and Vic finally asked: "What the hell's wrong, George?"

Gruffly, Brown said, "Damned fools from the Gulch are hunting Ives."

Vic was confused and he asked, "Why?"

"They say they found Tbalt dead."

"Who?"

Brown's eyes narrowed. "You paid for your bunk; don't ask so many questions."

Vic Voit raised his hands in a gesture of understanding and he went back to Cora. Because Cora was pregnant, Brown had assigned Vic two bunks in the main house, in a room at the back. There were six bunks in the room, but all were empty. Brown brought in a kerosene lantern and said, "I didn't mean to snap at you, Vic. I'm not feeling too good."

Vic nodded and told Brown to forget the incident. When Brown had left, Cora demanded, "What's all that about?"

Vic told her about Ives and added, "It has something to do with a dead man named Tbalt."

Cora gasped, "Oh, dear God!"

"What's wrong?"

"Nick Tbalt, he comes into the café."

"Is he tied up with Ives and that bunch?"

Cora sat down on the bunk and stared at the floor.

Vic sat beside her. After a couple of moments, he asked, "What is it, Cora?"

Cora looked at her husband, sad resignation on her face. She said, "Nick Tbalt is a nice young fellow."

"I never met him."

"He mostly works for ranchers, delivering cattle and things like that. He's just a kid, sixteen or seventeen, a nice, polite boy."

Vic nodded.

Cora went on, "Well, he's been missing eight or ten days. All the talk started while you were in Fort Benton; he went to get some cattle and he turned up missing."

"I guess he's dead now."

Cora paused, her face showing fright. "I hear a lot in the café, Vic. People are getting fed up. Each day, while you were away, the men coming into the café were getting more and more angry about Nick Tbalt. He was a nice kid and never bothered anyone. This place is getting nasty, Vic. I'm scared."

Vic had, himself, heard such conversations in both Bannack and Virginia City; there was a growing sense of anger at the foul deeds of the road agents. Thinking about what Cora had said, he guessed things might be coming to a head.

But his job was to run wagons and move goods. He'd let others worry about the road agents. Sure, road agents had shot him, but that must have been a mistake. Vic had always gotten along reasonably well with the men who hung out at Skinner's saloon.

He said, "Now look, lady, you don't go fretting over every stray pup that comes to the door. We've got our own life to live and we're doing just fine." He patted Cora's tummy. "The three of us are doing just fine."

"And you got yourself shot by them rotten road agents." Cora's voice was brittle. "You . . . Nick Tbalt . . . who's going to be next?"

Vic wanted to calm her. He said, "You just wait here. I'm gonna go stable the team. You get under the covers."

While Vic was out seeing to the horses, Cora lay down and pulled up the wool blanket. The chill she felt was not from the cold; she was scared. What kind of a future could she and Vic—and their baby—have in a place where youngsters like Nicholas Tbalt could end up dead?

It was cold and boring in the saddle, plodding along in bright moonlight, but the dozen men who made up the posse were warmed by the fact that they had done their job; they had captured the man they thought had killed Nicholas Tbalt.

The men of the posse did not have any legal mandate to render justice; they were merely a group of Virginia City men who were revolted by the news that young Tbalt had been brutally murdered for no apparent reason. Tbalt had no substantial cache of money; he had been merely moving a small herd of cattle to a winter range. His death seemed so senseless.

The body of Tbalt had been discovered by a man named William Palmer, who had been out hunting with his son. When they made their discovery, they went to a nearby, isolated camp, but the camp was occupied by a gang of ruffians who were, according to Palmer, so cavalier in their attitude that they came under his suspicion. Palmer recovered the body and transported it to Virginia City, where it was identified. The body had a bullet hole in the head and rope burns around the neck. Scratches and torn clothing indicated the body had been dragged through the brush after the shooting. Outrage spread through Virginia City. The posse had followed Palmer's directions and had found eight men gathered at the camp. The posse had been given the name of a ruffian named Long John Franck as the possible murderer, but when they found George Ives—the operator of Dempsey's ranch—and six of his henchmen at the campsite, as well as Franck, they began to wonder if the whole bunch had committed the foul deed.

After the initial challenge, Long John Franck was taken into custody. The posse moved a few yards away from the camp and advised Franck that he was very close to having his neck stretched from a handy tree. Franck resisted, until one of the posse took his lariat from the pommel of his saddle. Franck then protested his innocence, and finally said that he had protected the killer because he was afraid for his own life. In a whisper, Franck confessed that George Ives had done the actual shooting of Nicholas Tbalt.

With that, three men were left to guard Long John and the rest of the posse went back to the camp. There they told George Ives he would be taken back to Virginia City. Ives tried to joke with his accusers. When they showed no signs of weakening, Ives said, "Hey, boys, I'm innocent. You know what I mean: I'm innocent."

The men of the posse gave no reaction. Ives asked, "You men are working for Sheriff Plummer, right?"

The posse member standing closest to Ives said, "We're not working for anyone but Lady Justice, Ives. You're coming in with us."

As the posse and its prisoners rode through the night, Ives again treated the whole incident as some silly mistake. Ives was convinced that his friend the sheriff would come riding in soon and correct the error.

CHAPTER 22

(Friday, December 18, 1863)

Renee LeGrau fussed over Cora Voit as if Cora were a cherished, fragile arrangement of flowers. Any pregnant woman out on the frontier was special, and Renee was especially proud because she felt she had been instrumental in leading Cora toward the joyful life she was having with Vic Voit.

Renee and Cora were alone in the LeGraus' Virginia City apartment. Frank LeGrau and Vic were at Dr. Glick's surgery having Vic's wound tended to; the men had been gone for over an hour. Cora was mildly embarrassed by Renee's attentions, but more important, she was worried about Vic's leg.

There was no real reason for concern. The wound seemed to be clean, and Dr. Glick had an excellent reputation as far as gunshot wounds were concerned; many still remembered how the doctor had saved Henry Plummer's arm the previous spring. But Cora worried. She tried to broach the matter three times with Renee, but Renee was determined to avoid any such discussion;

she did not feel it was a proper topic considering Cora's condition.

Renee was just about to fix another pot of tea when the men came in, both smiling broadly. The women took that as an indication that all would be well with Vic's leg. Still, he was sporting a cane.

Vic said, "Look at the present Doctor Glick gave me. I told you, Cora, it wasn't any more than a bug bite."

Cora scoffed, "Some bug bite! You could have been killed. And look at you, hobbling around like some cripple."

They all laughed, even if Cora's laugh was not much more than a croak.

Renee asked if the men wanted tea; her husband said he'd pour small drinks of whiskey for Vic and himself. After everyone sat down, Frank LeGrau said, "There's big doings."

Renee asked, "What big doings?"

Vic said, "They arrested George Ives for shooting that German kid."

Cora demanded, "George Ives . . . Cy Skinner's friend?"

"The same one," Frank LeGrau said. "Apparently they have him cold. There's a trial set to start tomorrow."

Renee cut in, "I don't like all of this. There could be trouble in this town."

Vic said, "Everybody seems pretty pleased that there's a trial set. People are pretty mad."

"Everybody except you," Cora snapped, "and you get yourself shot in the leg."

Vic frowned at Cora, but Renee said, "She's right, Vic. You should have some protection out on the roads the way they've been lately."

Frank said, "Maybe we ought to hire some shooters to ride with you."

Vic shook his head. "If there'd been one with me the

other day, then I'd probably be dead. I'm better off the way I am."

There was a pause. Then, suddenly, Cora announced, "Well, we're leaving."

Renee looked startled. "Cora, you're staying to eat with us; you know that."

Cora stood up. "I don't mean leaving right now; I mean: we're leaving Bannack."

Vic looked at her, openmouthed.

Frank asked, "You want to come live here in the Gulch? We can set something up for you both here."

Cora folded her arms and pursed her lips; Vic Voit knew his wife was now very serious. "I've had enough. I just decided that this life ain't the kind of life any family should try to fight. There's shooting and killing and it just ain't right." She turned and looked at her husband. "Vic, I love you too darned much to let you get yourself killed without ever even seeing our child."

Vic looked at Frank LeGrau for support. LeGrau said, "Don't look at me; she's your wife."

Renee stood up. "I think she's right. Cora and Vic have worked hard, and it would be a horror to see something bad happen now."

"Vic, I'd hate to lose you," Frank LeGrau said. "I don't know how we'd run things without you handling your end."

Vic took a deep breath. "You've not lost me yet, Frank." Then he looked sternly at Cora. "You can't decide something like this just on the spur of the moment."

"It ain't on any spur of anything, Vic Voit. I've worried about you every time you go out on that damned wagon."

"We shouldn't be bothering Frank and Renee about this."

Renee put a hand on Cora's shoulder. "Vic, we'd be hurt if you couldn't talk about differences in front of us; we're all like a family." She looked at Cora. "And Cora's carrying a child for all of us."

Vic Voit had done a lot of growing up in the year and three months since he came to the mountains. He suddenly realized that he was causing Cora a lot of anxiety and, in that moment, he accepted her position. His decision showed on his face.

Frank LeGrau was the first to recognize it. He said, "If we're going to get you two out of here before winter sets in, we'd better get to planning."

There was a pause while everyone in the apartment absorbed the decision. Vic said, "Well, if we're leaving, I'd better get that load of books over to Wil Sanders."

"Don't be silly, Vic; I'll see to that," Frank said.

Vic stood, steadying himself with his cane. "If I'm leaving, then I don't plan to leave with any black marks in my book. I promised Wil that I'd bring him the books, and I'll do it."

"I'll go with you," Frank said.

"Fair enough, I could use the help."

Cora touched Renee's hand, which was still resting on her shoulder. "Renee, I hope you don't hate me for this."

"Don't talk foolishness. Lucinda can run the café, and if she doesn't work out, then we can just sell it off. Don't you worry about anything more than that baby you're carrying."

Vic said to Cora, "You sure do get tough when you make up your mind."

Cora smiled and gave him a kiss. "You haven't seen me get really mad, Vic Voit."

He smiled back. "I hope I never do."

Frank LeGrau said, "We'd better get moving."

As Nathaniel Langford walked into Wilbur Sanders' Virginia City tent, Sanders and X Beidler stood. Sanders said, "Damn, I'm glad you got here, Nat."

"I left as soon as I got your message; what's going on?"

"We've got us a tiger by the tail."

Langford was peeling off his long canvas riding coat, his wool mackinaw, and his leather jacket as Sanders said, "X, go get Nat somc coffee—"

Langford, rubbing his cold hands together, cut in, "And something to chew on."

X Beidler said he'd be back in a few minutes and left his two friends alone.

Wilbur Sanders was doing well with his law practice, drawing up agreements between miners and sales of claims, and dealing with the other matters that came up among people trying to give birth to a community. He had even drawn three wills and started the paperwork on one divorce. Sanders was making his home in Bannack, but the sheer volume of business forced him to spend more and more time in Virginia City.

Nathaniel Langford had mixed emotions about Sanders having to be in Virginia City so much. Langford missed Sanders' company, but he was also determined that a Masonic Lodge have a solid beginning in the Gulch, and Sanders was seeing to that. The Virginia City Masonic Lodge was trying to find a location to build a second Lodge Hall. They needed it to handle the newer miners who were petitioning to transfer their memberships and requesting admission to the fraternity. As long as Sanders was helping to improve the status of Freemasonry, Langford was willing to accept the inconvenience of an interrupted friendship.

Sanders was not only a competent, forceful legal counsel, he also carried an innate ability to lead other men.

When the decision had been made the day before that there would be a murder trial of George Ives for the killing of Nicholas Tbalt, the leaders of the Miners' Court had come to Sanders, asking if he would serve as judge. Sanders refused: he felt his place was on the other side of the bar of justice. He said "But I'll be your man if you need someone to prosecute the lowlife!"

Sanders was named the court's prosecutor, and he immediately dispatched a friend to Bannack to get Nathaniel Langford.

The two men sat on a leather sofa while Sanders

related what was known of the murder. When he had run down the short list of known facts, he added, "We're going to have to slap this bunch of brigands." Gravely, he looked at his friend. "We're going to have to hang George Ives."

Langford digested the words. In a moment, he realized he was stunned, not at the suggestion that the Miners' Court could presume to impose capital punishment, but that the proposal seemed to be a logical step. The situation in the camps had proceeded so far that drastic action had become inevitable.

The shooting of Vic Voit came to Langford's mind. He related the story of the road agents, and their callous, cruel terrorism. "And it is interesting you're talking this way, Wil. I guess the same thoughts have been pushing their way into my mind with an increasing regularity."

Sanders rose and went to his desk, picked up a letter, and took it to Langford. The letter was from the office of the territorial governor. It was a series of innocuous platitudes about how the administration in Lewiston was going to take steps to assist the residents of the gold camps "as soon as it is humanly possible."

Sanders growled, "It's been the same thing time after time: nothing! We have a community threatened by a collection of murderers. We have to do something."

Despite the time and expense of a three-week round trip to Lewiston, Sanders had gone there in September, and Langford, in early November. Each had petitioned the territorial governor for some sort of law enforcement; both had met with polite, concerned acknowledgment, and promises were extended. The governor had been receptive to Sanders' petition for granting of a charter of incorporation for the camps, but of course, the main concern was that Confederate General Braxton Bragg had whipped the hell out of Union General Rosecrans at Chattanooga; the defeat might cause "some delays." When Langford was in Lewiston, he was received by the governor, "But, well . . . " General Sherman had whipped the hell out of General Bragg, who was hightailing it from Tennessee to Georgia. The success might cause "some delays." Sidney Edgerton, the former Ohio congressman, was still in Bannack, awaiting assignment of his judicial district in the territory. Equally concerned, Edgerton took to writing to colleagues still in the House of Representatives; pointed responses reminded him that the nation was in peril. Sanders had used his legal expertise to bring a semblance of authority to the Miners' Court. Resolutions were adopted by the membership, and new rules expanded their prerogative from only civil disputes into the area of criminal law. Still, the scope of power was limited to banishment.

Langford handed the letter back. "I think we have a sheriff who is a danger to this community."

"I don't trust Plummer. He is an enigma to me."

"Wil, I even accepted his offer of dinner for Thanksgiving. It was a lovely meal at his brother-in-law's cabin. Jim Vail had a turkey shipped in from Salt Lake City. Still, there was something that made me as uncomfortable as I have ever been with another human being. I try to work with him in Bannack; I try to see him as a good man. I can't put my finger on it, but I don't trust him, either."

Beidler came into the office carrying a small tray loaded with cups of coffee and a dish of honey buns.

The next few minutes were spent allowing Langford to get something into his empty stomach. As he wiped the sticky honey off his fingers, Beidler said, "They got Dan Byam to sit as judge."

Sanders said, "That's good. Dan's a fair man."

Langford asked, "But is he the man we need?"

Beidler said, "Don't worry, Nat. If he doesn't do what's right, then there are some of us who'll do the right thing."

Langford nodded. "It's time this camp began to stand up against this evil."

CHAPTER 23

(Saturday, December 19, 1863)

Henry Plummer sat at his small desk in the space he called his office. He was spinning a silver dollar on the polished surface of the desk and watching to see which side of the coin ended faceup; he had spun the dollar probably fifty times in an effort to distract himself from the dark thoughts that kept poking into his brain like sticks pushing into a fire and causing dangerous sparks.

Three times in the previous twenty-four hours, Plummer had actually risen from his desk, picked up the carpetbag by the door, and started to leave.

The carpetbag contained a few items of clothing, some small gifts he had received from Electa, and five leather sacks containing five pounds of gold dust. There was also a small wooden cheese box in which he had packed the seven pieces of jewelry that Electa had left behind when she left back in September. He hoped that she had left them as an oversight, or as an indication that she was intending to return; he prayed that she had not left them as a sign that she did not want anything he had given her.

Each time he started to leave, it was to find Electa; each time he hesitated because he was not sure she would welcome him back into her life. But Electa was not the overriding concern in his mind that morning; other, more pressing matters were urging him to leave Bannack.

When George Ives had been arrested and taken to Virginia City, the Innocents there had immediately sent word to Plummer; they had hoped to see him rescue Ives. But Plummer had read the mood of Bannack and its sister city over the past few weeks, and he knew that time was running out for the Innocents. The reason he had invited Nathaniel Langford for Thanksgiving dinner at the Vails' was to get a feel for what the people were thinking, and the message from Langford was clear: the people were fed up.

Plummer had lost any feeling of loyalty to George Ives. Ives had been becoming more and more brazen over the past month. He seemed to think he was invulnerable to any force of law and order; he was actually mocking any efforts to control the road agents. On the other side, Plummer had only contempt for the people in the camps who wanted to clean up the thieves; Plummer saw that the mass of individuals in the camps were there to grab some gold from the ground and head out. But Ives' attitude was too flagrant. Cyrus Skinner and Henry Plummer had designed an operation that had had some finesse. Plummer wanted to have people robbed with some style; he did not approve of cruel, profitless shootings like Nicholas Tbalt's.

But he could not decide what to do with his own life. The night before he had spent two hours talking with Skinner and had resolved nothing. Skinner was not going to "be stampeded by a bunch of old women like Nat Langford." Plummer had argued that they should leave Bannack "until things get a bit less hectic."

Skinner had argued back that they had over a hundred dependable men with guns: "If Langford wants a shoot-out, we can give it to him."

Plummer knew the notion was bordering on lunacy; the territorial government might not have much force, because of troops being needed to fight the Civil War, but there were enough lawmen in Lewiston to enforce the law. "We're lucky that Sanders hasn't convinced the governor to send some help."

The meeting with Skinner had ended with nothing.

Now, there was one thing certain in Plummer's mind: he would not show his face in Virginia City; not until the trial was over.

CHAPTER 24

(Monday, December 21, 1863)

The trial began, and Virginia City was electric with tension. The ruffians in the crowd made no effort to be unobtrusive; there were loud, vocal threats to the well-meaning men who sat on the jury. Wilbur Sanders came under nearly constant abuse, but he turned out to be the best possible choice for a prosecutor, and did not flinch when accosted by the mob. Sanders waded through hours of perjured testimony offered by Ives' friends and was able to show them as liars before the jury. There were legal arguments that had no foundation in law; there were implied threats right from the witness stand. But when the jury returned, they announced George Ives guilty.

Turmoil followed. Few heard Wilbur Sanders stand and demand of the court: "We feel the only sentence possible, Your Honor, is death by hanging."

The word spread quickly through the crowd; none of Ives' cohorts thought that such a sentence was possible, because no one had testified to actually seeing Ives do the shooting of Tbalt. But Judge Dan Byam had spent time before the trial with Nat Langford and Wil Sanders, and they had all agreed to a swift hanging if a guilty verdict was rendered.

Judge Byam ruled: "George Ives is to be taken from this court and hung by the neck until dead."

There had been other preliminary plans by Langford and Sanders. X Beidler had five armed men with him when he moved through the crowd to collect the prisoner. Justice was going to be swift.

Throughout the trial, Ives had seemed to be confident that some force—presumably Henry Plummer—would come to his rescue. But on hearing the verdict and the sentence, Ives' attitude changed. He wanted to talk to the judge, he wanted to talk to the sheriff, he even wanted to talk to Wilbur Sanders. "I need some time," he pleaded.

X Beidler glared down at the convicted murderer sitting at the defense table and snarled, "How much time did you give that kid before you shot him?"

Ives was taken by the execution squad to a tree where a rope already hung over a stout branch. Ives' hands were tied and he was put up on a three-foot-tall packing crate. The noose was set in place around his neck. He pleaded: "Wait!"

Beidler motioned for his men to wait a moment. He asked Ives, "What do you have to say?"

In a steady voice, Ives said, "It was Alec Carter who did the shooting."

Beidler waited a second before he said, "Why'd you keep your mouth shut for so long, Ives?"

"I was afraid . . . afraid they'd kill me."

Beidler snapped: "Who?"

"The Innocents," Ives whispered.

Beidler paused for a moment, wondering what Ives meant. The moment slipped away quickly; Beidler figured this was just another ploy. He ordered, "Tighten him up."

Ives begged, "Wait. Please. Wait!"

Beidler nodded to the man standing beside the packing crate; the man kicked the crate out from under Ives' feet.

That night the cold set in firmly. Light snow was beginning to fall.

Most of the Virginia City miners made for their bunks as soon as they had finished their evening meal; others passed time quietly with friends. There was no joy in having ended George Ives' life; the camp's paramount emotion was hope that the example set would finally halt the banditry in the community.

Even Skinner's Alder Creek Saloon was muted. The brotherhood of violence no longer found it funny to joke and quip about someone being dead; one of their own had paid a price. They had been allowed to cut Ives down after he had swung in the cold air for three hours; his body was out in back of the saloon under a tarpaulin and would be buried in the morning.

Many voiced anger at Skinner for not being there, and there was open criticism of Henry Plummer for not showing his face to save Ives. If the Innocents could not depend on their leaders, then it might be best to pull out and go find something else to do in some other place.

Two of the Innocents came into the saloon, bragging about how they had met Wilbur Sanders on the street, and how they had warned him that his life was not worth much now.

There was some halfhearted talk among the Innocents about getting even with Sanders, the judge, and the jury. But when the two men explained that they had not harmed Sanders because he had been walking with three armed friends, the conversation drifted away from revenge and began focusing on survival.

The main thing the Innocents wanted, and desperately needed, was the presence of Henry Plummer.

Plummer did not show up.

CHAPTER 25

(Tuesday, December 22, 1863)

The sky was mostly clear in the morning, although a few puffy clouds warned that snows might begin falling. Down by the creek the moisture that seemed to be steaming up from the water was painting bushes and trees with a hoarfrost that made the landscape a peaceful, gentle scene.

The tensions were in the people.

Wilbur Sanders had called a meeting in his tent office. Eighteen men were there.

Nat Langford had spent the night on a bench in Sanders' office, X Beidler had slept in his own bed, and Wil Sanders had slept on the cot he used for a bed in Virginia City. All of them had kept rifles or revolvers close at hand.

The conversation at the meeting was predictable: what was going to happen next?

X Beidler was pressed for sending a delegation to Lewiston to demand authority to form proper law enforcement.

Sanders agreed. He reminded them that he had always been in favor of trying to get a U.S. marshal appointed, a man who could effectively deal with the outlaws.

Beidler had brought to the meeting a cattle drover named James Williams. Williams had been in and out of Bannack and Virginia City for over a year, but had kept pretty much to himself. The day before, however, he had volunteered to help Beidler carry out the execution of George Ives without interference from Ives' friends. Beidler had brought Williams along now because, after the execution, Beidler and Williams had spent an hour over coffee, and Williams had expressed his own opinion of what should be done.

Williams was now asked to give his views. He told the group, "I think we've got to go after this whole bunch of scoundrels. They have intimidated our community for too long." He looked around, waiting for objections; none came. He continued, "I served on that jury when we tried Charley Moore and Charley Reeves for killing Frenchy Cazette and the Indians over in Bannack. There were two things that came out of that trial. First, the killers got off scot-free. Second, their friends came around and bothered the hell out of anyone who served on that jury. I had a run-in with a bunch of them the day after I served."

Nat Langford said, "I never heard about that."

"I never told anyone. Three of them came up and started to hassle me and I fired a few shots that drove them off. What happened to me don't matter; I can take care of myself. But there were a bunch of good, hard-working men who served on that jury yesterday, and that bunch of Ives' cutthroat friends could end up hurting men who were just doing their duty."

"What are you suggesting?" Langford asked.

"I'm suggesting we clean them out, Mister Langford. I think this talk of getting help from Lewiston, a proper marshal, is just fine. But in the meantime somebody could end up dead."

There was silence in the room; each man had to digest what had just been said.

Nat Langford broke the quiet. "What exactly are you suggesting, Mister Williams?"

"I'm talking about what's been successful in other places like this: a vigilance committee."

Sanders cut in, "That's a severe remedy, Mister Williams."

"We got a severe illness, Mister Sanders."

Each man in the room weighed the measure. All of them knew of vigilance committees, or committees for safety, or, more commonly, vigilantes. The idea of vigilantes was probably as old as the beginning of civilization, but the actuality had emerged only recently in the United States, and it was mainly identified with the gold camps of the West. Each man in the room had come from a place where law and order were established institutions; none of them relished the idea of assuming powers reserved to organized government. But over a hundred people had been murdered, wealth had been stolen, and the ugly face of anarchy was in full view.

Sanders said, "We'd be taking the law into our own hands, gentlemen."

X Beidler said, "There ain't no law here now, Wil. The only thing these outlaws understand is strong action. Did you see the way they backed off when we hung their buddy?"

Sanders said, "But they weren't scared enough to avoid threatening me last night."

Williams came back in, "That's just my point. We've let ourselves get into a position where there are a bunch of killers out there murdering honest miners and stealing our money. If we don't do something, we might as well just pack out and leave the whole place to the outlaws."

Sanders raised his hand. "I think that Mister Williams is quite right in his position, but I don't know if we have the men to do the job."

"I'll find the men," Beidler said.

Williams added, "That'd be no problem."

"Men we could trust?" Langford demanded.

"I don't know who we can trust," Williams said. "The road agents seem to know everything that goes on around here."

Beidler started to speak, but Langford raised his hand in a polite request for the floor. He asked James Williams: "Do you travel east, Mister Williams?"

Williams looked confused. He replied, "I travel anyplace I can make a living, Mister Langford."

Langford looked at Sanders, then at Beidler; they knew that Williams was not a Freemason. Langford said, "The rest of us here in this room are in the Masonic Lodge, Mister Williams. If you are looking for a group of men you can trust, a group of men who will be able to keep a secret, you are in their midst."

Williams said, "I don't know anything about Masons; all I know is that I want to get this mess solved, and we have to do it quick."

Sanders said, "If we take on a venture like this, we've got to have some strict guidelines, gentlemen. I won't be a party to going off half-cocked."

Williams said, "I've heard that vigilantes in other places take an oath. I'll take an oath."

Langford asked Sanders, "Could you draw us up some sort of legal document?"

"I don't know if it will be legal, but I can put on paper a statement that would show our good intentions."

Langford stood. "I think we should go forward with this, gentlemen. There is, as Mister Williams has stated, a real problem, a dangerous problem. I think it is time we clean house."

By late that day, Wilbur Sanders, working with Nathaniel Langford and James Williams, had drawn up the document that would endow a patina of legality in the absence of adequate law in their jurisdiction:

> We, the undersigned, uniting ourselves in a party for the laudable purpose of arresting thieves and murderers and recovering stolen propperty [sic], do pledge ourselves upon our sacred honor, each to all others, and solemnly swear that we will reveal no secrets, violate no laws of right and never desert eachother [sic] or our standard of justice. So help us God,
> As witness our hand and seal this 23rd day of December A.D. 1863

The signers could hardly have realized what they created, or the dramatic consequences of their simple declaration. They could not have known the scope and size of the Innocents. How could they have anticipated what would be discovered? Their efforts made history in Montana and in the West.

CHAPTER 26

(Wednesday, December 23, 1863)
to
Sunday, January 10, 1864)

The first squad of vigilantes rode out of Virginia City by midafternoon of the twenty-third, captained by James Williams. Their objective was to capture Alec Carter, who had been named in George Ives' confession. There was no tangible evidence against Carter, other than the words of Ives and Carter's association with other disreputables in the area. But the newly formed vigilance committee knew it had to start somewhere, and it seemed critical that they at least interrogate Carter regarding Ives' charges.

Each of the twenty men in the squad provided his own horse and food. They rode late and started early in the bitter cold that had taken a grip over the mountains. But Carter eluded them; he had been warned by his fellow Innocents.

Williams' squad visited all of the known hangouts of the road agents, but the trail had grown as cold as the winter nights. It was obvious to the searchers that word had spread, but the squad agreed to continue.

On Christmas Day they came on Red Yeager, a known associate of Carter. What the vigilantes did not know was that it had been Yeager who had slipped out of Virginia City and warned Carter to flee; in Yeager's words, "Get up and dust."

With Yeager in custody, the search finally led back to the Dempsey ranch, where they found only George Brown in residence. Brown had been the manager for George Ives, and had perjured himself in testimony on behalf of Ives at the trial. Brown was taken into custody.

The squad was tired and disappointed at their failure to find Carter. On January 4, Williams left half of the squad at the ranch and headed back to Virginia City to pick up supplies and confer with the other members of the committee.

At the ranch, after the evening meal, the squad members who had remained were taking turns catching up on some sleep. Brown and Yeager were in isolation, in different rooms in the main house. Leonard Seebold, who had been left in charge, was not able to close his eyes. He was frustrated by the lack of success; he was convinced that there was an organized group of road agents operating, because how else could they have all vanished so quickly? Seebold took a lantern and walked into the room in which Red Yeager was sleeping, tied strongly. He studied the sleeping man. Yeager was red-haired, with a ruddy complexion, and looked as young as his twenty-one years. To Seebold the sleeper looked free of any guilt, almost angelic, but he knew better. He crossed the small room and prodded Yeager. Yeager woke up, startled and confused. Seebold asked, "Boy, you have any idea what's ahead of you?"

Yeager blinked, then licked his dry lips. In a disarmingly mild voice he said, "You've come to hang mc, ain't that right?"

Seebold did not reply.

"I guess I knew it all along; I've had it coming for a long time."

Seebold put the lantern on the small table beside the bed and then sat on the bunk beside Yeager. He said, "Red, why don't you tell me about it?"

Neither threats nor physical abuse could have extracted what came next. Red Yeager, convinced he was about to die at the end of a rope, decided to cleanse his soul.

For ten minutes he recounted crimes he had known about or in which he had taken part. Names began to come out; all were names that had been discussed by the vigilance committee before they had left Virginia City. Seebold stopped Yeager from talking more, untied him, then led him into the dark main room of the building. There was a fire going in the wood stove and the stove door was open. Flickers of orange and yellow light painted the room with dancing images; Yeager went right to the stove and began warming his hands.

Seebold went and woke four other members of the squad, and they collected around the stove. Yeager looked nervous but said, "I'm glad to get this over with, you know that?"

Seebold waited until he was sure the other men were awake enough to understand. Then he said, "Red has some things to tell us, men. I'd like somebody to make a written record."

Thomas Baume, a man who had come west with his friend Nicholas Tbalt, offered to do the writing. Joseph Hinkley filled cups with the coffee that was left over from supper; the group gathered around a table near the stove.

Seebold ordered, "Okay, Red, start over, right from the beginning."

Forty minutes later, the whole scheme had been set out for the vigilantes. Yeager told about the password: Innocents. He explained about tying the sailor's knot in their kerchiefs, and he told them that "Clubfoot" George Lane in Virginia City would tie a brightly colored rag to the tailgate of any stagecoach carrying a shipment of gold to Bannack. Yeager confirmed George Ives' declaration that Alec Carter had done the actual shooting of Nicholas Tbalt, but he also said that Ives was the leader and stood there laughing as Tbalt was on his knees praying for his life.

It was Joseph Hinkley who asked the question that had not been asked. "Who thought of all of this? Who was your leader?"

"Sheriff Plummer."

There was a long, shocked silence. Many had little respect for Henry Plummer, but to find that the man charged with enforcing the law, the man trusted with information about gold shipments, to find that Henry Plummer was the chief of the Innocents—all of that was hard to accept.

Seebold ordered two of the men to take Yeager back to his room, then went and woke the rest of the squad. He gathered all of them and reviewed what they had learned. After ten minutes of discussion, they decided to confront George Brown with the information.

When Brown was brought into the main room, he walked immediately behind the bar, picked up a bottle of whiskey and a glass, and sat confidently at the table. He offered the bottle around, then poured himself a long drink. He smiled and said, "Well, boys, what's going on now?"

Ten minutes later his smile had disappeared and his glass of whiskey sat still full. At various moments while hearing what the squad had learned, Brown had snarled, "Red is a bastard."

Seebold had not mentioned Plummer or Cyrus Skinner during the session with Brown. It was left to Hinkley, again, to ask the final question: "Who was your leader?"

Brown remained silent.

Seebold pressed. "You're going to hang for this. You know that, George?"

Brown said, "You ain't gonna be hanging me. Believe that."

Hinkley, in a soft, quiet voice said, "Henry Plummer will not protect you; Red told us about the sheriff."

Brown erupted from his seat, yelling and cursing. Coffee cups and his glass of whiskey spilled; three men were needed to get Brown back down in the chair. With the liquids glistening on the table, Seebold said, "We're going to hang Plummer, too. You know that?"

Brown calmed down quickly. He said, "So, you got Henry, and that's too bad. But let me tell you about that little shit, Red Yeager."

Brown rattled off a litany of crimes for a quarter of an hour. Most of his information was only what they had heard from Yeager, but a few new names were added to the list. When Brown was through, Thomas Baume's notes included the names of twenty-three Innocents.

Seebold convened a meeting of the vigilance committee right there at the Dempsey ranch and a proper vote was taken: Yeager and Brown were found guilty of capital crimes.

A stout cottonwood tree just outside the front door of the ranch house was selected as the gallows. At eleven-thirty on that night, Red Yeager and George Brown were hung.

During the twelve days that James Williams had been out with his squad in the bitter cold, Nathaniel Langford and Wilbur Sanders had not been idle.

On Boxing Day, Langford had called selected Masons to a meeting in his Bannack home. By that time, Sanders had used his legal skills to draw up a proper set of bylaws, investing considerable effort in creating a fair, strict foundation for the committee, making sure that it functioned only for the well-being of the community.

As an example, one stricture read: "The captain will first take steps to arrest the criminal and then report the same with proof to the chief, who will thereupon call a meeting of the executive committee. The judgment of such committee shall be final. The only punishment that shall be inflicted is death."

The men meeting in Langford's house listened to the reading of the bylaws and voted to form the Bannack Vigilance Committee. They were sworn to secrecy, and then they set out to collect evidence about wrongdoers.

After the meeting, Langford asked Sanders to go with him to see Vic Voit. Both Langford and Sanders had come to like the young man and had been concerned when Vic told them he was pulling out of Bannack.

They found Vic in Frank LeGrau's blacksmith shop, packing up a sack of tools that LeGrau had given him.

Frank and Renee LeGrau had come to Bannack with Vic and Cora to make a smooth transition from Cora's competent operation of the café to the questionable talents of Lucinda Simons. The LeGraus' concerns could have been forgotten, because Lucy had changed. Cora was thrilled: Lucy seemed to have become again the woman whom Cora had first known. The change in her had come about because Clay Barrow had vanished from Bannack. Vic and Frank did not understand the disappearance, but Lucinda did; Clay Barrow had gotten word that it would be dangerous for him to stay in Bannack, because the men of Virginia City were getting serious about ridding the district of criminals, and Clay Barrow had been living too closely with Cyrus Skinner and the Innocents. Just a couple of days out from under the wicked influence of Barrow, and Lucy was her old self once again.

Cora was in the café going over business details with Renee and Lucinda. Vic wished she were there in the smithy to hear the nice things Langford and Sanders were saying.

"I won't try to stop you, Vic," Langford was saying. "You know what's best for you and your wife and the blessing you are about to receive. But we would be pleased if you would think about staying; this town could use more men like you."

Vic looked around the blacksmith's shop, trying to avoid gazing directly at the two older men who had become his friends. They had given him work, they had accepted him as a man, and they were doing everything they could to make Bannack a worthwhile place to live. But he had to face a reality that he had come to respect. "I'd think about it, but Cora is dead set against having our baby here; she wants us to head out."

Sanders smiled. "It's a wise man who knows where to seek advice." He reached into his inside coat pocket and pulled out a letter. He handed it to Vic, who opened it and read:

(Letter dated 26 December, 1863)
Voit/Harris Family Archives
Bannack Lodge AF&AM

Greetings Brother,
This will introduce with pleasure Brother Vic Voit as a member in good standing in our Lodge as of the above date.

We would appreciate it if you would accept Brother Voit in the spirit of true fraternity and friendship.

/S/ Wilbur Fisk Sanders
(Master)
/S/ Nathaniel Pitt Langford
(Secretary)

Vic actually blushed after he had read the letter. These men of substance had really treated him as an equal, as a brother. He stumbled through a thank you. To avoid looking too humbled, he quipped, "Maybe I'll just send Cora home, and then she can come back after the baby's born."

From the doorway in back of Vic, Cora said softly, "I don't think the gentlemen would like to see you with a black eye and a broken nose, Vic Voit."

Vic cringed. Langford and Sanders both laughed. They had seen her come into the doorway, and they knew she was grinning. Vic turned, hoping Cora did not have something to throw. Then he saw her grin, and he laughed with relief.

Cora came to his side. "We're going, and that's that."

"I was only kidding."

Sanders offered, "Missus Voit, we will miss both of you, but we know you are doing what is best."

Cora looked at Sanders, then at Langford, and said, "I wish Vic could stay and help you out."

Langford was not sure he had heard properly. Then he realized that Cora knew the plans for the vigilance committee. Softly he asked, "Can I ask how you know?"

Vic, confused, asked, "Know what?"

Cora said, "I know because I run a café in a town that is full of people who cannot keep their mouths shut."

"Know what?" Vic repeated.

Sanders said, "Some of us have gotten together to do something about the road agents. We were hoping you'd stay and give us a hand."

Cora cut Vic off before he could begin. She stated, "Mister Sanders, I believe in what you are going to do. Just about everyone in the camp is grateful that *somebody* is *finally* going to be doing something, but Vic is in no condition to help out on that sort of a thing. He'll be limping around for weeks with that shot in his leg."

Langford nodded. "Cora, it is best you get where you can have your baby in peace. We'll try and make this place livable and maybe, after a time, you and Vic will be coming back."

Cora said, "You clean up this camp and make sure men like my Vic don't get shot up, and you'll have all sorts of people wanting to live here. That's the truth."

Sanders said, "We'd better be going and let you two finish your business. We will miss you."

Langford offered his hand to Vic. "You get in touch with the local Lodge, wherever you go, Vic. Promise me that."

As the two men turned to leave, Sanders paused and asked, "Missus Voit, do you think Missus Simons would have any idea about where Clay Barrow might be?"

Cora said, "If I knew, I'd tell you where that no-good is, but I don't. And I'm sure Lucy doesn't know. She's well rid of him, and you are welcome to him and his kind. Good luck."

When the men were gone, Vic turned to Cora and said, "Now, what the hell was all that about?"

Cora, with an impish grin, said, "You don't want to know, my darling. But, if you're a good boy, I'll tell you all about it on the ride to Lewiston."

"Someday you're going to press me too hard, Cora Voit."

She scooted away from him and said, "We've got packing to do, so let's get at it. And, for your information, I'll tell you when I've pressed you too hard, Vic Voit."

CHAPTER 27

(Sunday, January 10, 1864)

On the night of January 9 four men rode through ten-below-zero weather to carry the grim news to Bannack that the job facing the vigilantes was going to be broader, more involved, than anyone had anticipated.

The men who had initially signed up in Virginia City had presumed their task would be to find, and hang, Alec Carter. They had assumed that the hanging of Carter would be sufficient warning to the lawless: get out or suffer the rope. But with the extensive list provided by Red Yeager and George Brown, the goal of vigilance had grown enormously: twenty-three men were listed as criminals.

A greater motivation than justice urged John Lott and his three companions through the bitter cold. While the vigilantes of Virginia City were protected by their own numbers and surrounded by thousands of prospectors who were in sympathy with any move to rid their community of criminals, Nat Langford and Wil Sanders were nearly alone and virtually defenseless in Bannack, which was now known to be the fountainhead of the Innocents. Langford and Sanders had only a few men signed up, and they were also in a haven for murderers protected by Sheriff Henry Plummer.

Lott and his companions arrived at the home of Wilbur Sanders just as January 10 was getting used to its first hour. Nat Langford was summoned immediately.

By the time Langford arrived, the fire had been stoked and the travelers had been refreshed. The news that had been brought could be measured by the stunned silence that settled in the Sanders' parlor; the room was still for a long, poignant minute.

In a serious voice, Langford said, "This is more than we bargained for."

Sanders' face was grim. "I received another letter from the territorial governor yesterday, in which he restated his previous platitudes and weak promises. We will be getting no help from Lewiston; I want you to know that."

Lott, who had given long hours of thought to the matter before signing up with the Virginia City committee, said, "We do know. But we also know there is a job to be done. Jim Williams has ridden out with one squad, Bill Palmer is taking another, and they will do what is needed."

Wilbur Sanders said, "We will do what is needed here. We are willing to face the obligation."

Lott said, "The four of us have been ordered by our committee to stay and help."

Langford rose, the look on his face solemn. "We will need your help. We thank you."

The men shook hands all around with the promise that they would meet in the morning.

Langford stepped out of Sanders' front door, and Sanders joined him on the porch. Inside, the visitors from Virginia City began finding places on the floor where they could collect a few hours of sleep.

Langford looked across the street at the home of James Vail, just a hundred feet away. The Vails had come to

Bannack from Sun River just two weeks after Electa Plummer had left her husband. Martha Vail had been shocked at her sister's unseemly departure; Martha's letters to Electa had been unanswered. Jim Vail had prospered, helped with investments and guided into ventures by Plummer. Plummer had availed himself of their friendship and hospitality. He had refused to continue living in the cabin he had built for Electa and had moved into Goodrich's Hotel. He was a frequent dinner guest, and sometimes stayed overnight in the Vail cabin.

"I wonder if he is sleeping there tonight?" Langford said, rhetorically.

Sanders said gruffly, "I don't know how that damned man can sleep with the lives of a hundred souls on his conscience."

"You put it well the other day, Wil. Plummer is an enigma. There are times when I am so angry at the man that I actually wish him ill; at other times he is completely charming, and I question my judgment."

Sanders, with a sarcastic tone, countered, "There is some mention in the Good Book about Lucifer having transformed himself into 'an angel of light.'"

Langford nodded. "Corinthians, two two."

"Plummer is evil enough."

"Unfortunately, I am afraid we are going to have to pass judgment on that."

Sanders said, "Nat, we will do what is right."

At that moment, Henry Plummer sat alone by a cooling wood stove in the rear of Cyrus Skinner's Elk Horn Saloon.

Some of the Innocents who had fled from the Dempsey ranch and Virginia City had made their way back to Bannack over the past three days. Most of them had quickly made themselves scarce and sought refuge with friends elsewhere in the mountains.

Five hours earlier, Cy Skinner had left to save his own

hide. His leave-taking had been abrupt. He'd said, "You're a damned fool, Henry."

Plummer had snapped back, "You're a quitter, Cy."

"You don't stay in the game when the other guy has three kings showing. Henry, we've lost the game."

"We had a good run going for a while, Cy."

Skinner snarled, "We played out our string; it's time to fold."

The two men took a moment to finish off their cups of coffee.

Plummer said, "This is a new way people have, of hanging men without law or evidence."

"They have the guns and they have the rope, Henry. Don't act like a thirty-year-old whore. Quit when you're out of luck." Skinner stood, extended his hand, and said, "I'm riding out."

"Where you heading?"

"If you're staying here, then I ain't telling you where I'll be."

"I might ride out."

"When you do, there'll be those who know where I am."

Plummer grinned. "Maybe we could find another camp."

Skinner shook his head. "I think we've run out of camps to bilk, Henry. I'm gonna find myself someplace safe to hide."

Plummer remained seated but he gave a final firm squeeze to his friend's hand then let go. He reached for his cup, but it was empty. When he looked up, Cyrus Skinner had walked out the door.

Since he had heard about the Ives trial and hanging, then the news about Yeager and Brown, Plummer had been slipping rapidly into the grip of lethargy. He had not shaved, and he had barely eaten. He had roamed around Bannack, not really feeling the cold that drove through the thick jacket he wore.

He knew Skinner was right, but he could not bring

himself to cut and run. In the foggy doldrums that gripped his mind, he gave no thought to Electa. It was as if he had hoped too much for her return; now, he was alone.

He went and lifted the coffeepot off the wood stove. There was about half a cup left. He poured the drink and went back to the table.

He was still sitting there when the dawn broke on January 10.

Getting the members of the Bannack Vigilance Committee to recommit to their oath was no easy chore for Langford and Sanders. All of the Bannack group were members of the Masonic Lodge. All felt a strong obligation to their Brothers, and to the good of their community, but agreeing to catch Alec Carter and hanging him was one thing, searching for and stringing up twenty others was another. Even worse was the fact that they were going to have to take part in arresting and hanging the man who was duly elected sheriff of their camp: that was a wholly different challenge.

An afternoon meeting in Sanders' law office was no more successful than a morning meeting in Langford's home. A consensus kept flitting away like an elusive thought that would not stay firm in the mind.

Langford himself had begun to have second thoughts, especially about Henry Plummer. Perhaps Plummer had changed his ways, had stopped being around the undesirable element in Bannack. It was Sanders who pointed out that Plummer had been merely playacting the well-meaning sheriff so that he could get the information needed to plan the murders and robberies.

As the afternoon sun dipped below the rim of the mountain-tops and dusk fell over the camp, the members of the Bannack Vigilance Committee finally saw that they must follow through on their oath.

At just before seven o'clock, three parties moved through the darkness of Bannack.

The first squad was led by Harry King, one of the vigilantes from Virginia City, who took four men to arrest Buck Stinson at the Goodrich Hotel.

The second squad was led by William Roe, a Bannack businessman, and was charged with bringing in Ned Ray. Ray was found in Madam Hall's saloon and bawdy house.

The third squad was led by Wilbur Sanders, who, with three men, was to make the arrest of Henry Plummer.

Plummer had stayed alone in the Elk Horn long after the coffee had gone and the fire had died in the stove. He had gone to the Vail cabin, where Martha had given him supper; Jim Vail was in Virginia City. Plummer had told her he was not feeling well; he rested on the sofa.

Word had spread quickly around Bannack as to what was happening. Sanders' squad of four was followed by a large, silent crowd—reports range from forty-five to eighty.

There was some milling around in front of the Vail cabin for three quarters of an hour. The cause of the delay has never been clarified.

Finally, shortly after ten o'clock, Wilbur Sanders went to the cabin door and knocked. Martha Vail answered the door. Sanders asked to see Plummer. When she turned, Plummer was already on his feet, his coat on and hat in place. Martha had seen the crowd outside, and she was concerned. Plummer calmed her by saying he was just going to a meeting; he seemed resigned to his fate.

On the porch, Sanders said, "We have a warrant for you, Plummer."

"Wil, this ain't right, and you know it. We got laws to take care of what that bunch wants."

Sanders looked into the crowd; some of them were carrying lanterns, their faces flickering in the eerie lighting. Sanders shook his head, "It is not any *bunch*, Plummer. We have a proper warrant."

"Wil, that is pure bullshit!" Plummer glared. "And, Mister Lawyer, you know it."

Sanders stepped very close to Plummer. "I know the

law, Henry Plummer. I also know that you have done, or caused to be done, some of the most evil deeds that have ever come to my ears. I guarantee you this: evidence convicts the guilty, sir, and you have been convicted."

Sanders walked off the porch. The three men of his squad went to Plummer and, tentatively, began leading him away from the Vail cabin.

The procession moved across Grasshopper Creek, down Main Street, to the corner of Second, where they headed north, to a knoll a hundred yards out of town.

Reports vary on Plummer's behavior. Some say he behaved with dignity; some say he cowered. It is possible that the truth of Plummer's final few minutes will never be exactly established. Those who reported their views seem to have been less than objective.

There is no question of what happened on the knoll. There was no proper gallows; only a large log supported by two posts, which were ten feet tall. Three ropes had been flung over the beam.

Ned Ray was the first to go. No one had brought a crate or any other elevating platform, so Ray was hauled by the neck into the air. He was drunk, so it is possible there is truth to the report that Ned Ray's last words were: "Hold on! Dammit, you're choking me!"

The spectacle of the prisoner being yanked into the air revolted the vigilantes, and it was not repeated. Buck Stinson was lifted into the air by three men, the rope was tightened, and they let him drop.

Henry Plummer was the last. The Bannack vigilantes had been guarding Plummer during the two executions. When John Lott gave the signal for Plummer to be brought forward, his guards hesitated, as if they did not want to move. Lott sensed the problem and made a hand signal to his men from Virginia City. They grabbed Plummer, placed the rope around his neck, and saw to his execution.

The three bodies were left hanging through the night. Burials were made by friends the next morning.

EPILOGUE

Over the next three weeks, squads of vigilantes from Bannack and Virginia City roamed the mountains and valleys, searching and capturing the fugitive Innocents.

When the pursuers could not find their prey, they would leave a formal warrant nailed to a cabin door or fence post. Each warrant closed with the numbers 3–7–77, which was the code identification for the members of the two committees. The legend developed that the combination of numbers referred to the three Masons, including Nathaniel Langford, who held the first Masonic meeting at Mullan Pass, the seven men who came together to plan the funeral for William Bell, and the seventy-seven Masons at the funeral of Bell on Graveyard Hill in Bannack the first year of the gold camp. (Bell, in this legend, is considered the seventy-seventh Mason.) The story goes that the secret 3–7–77 greeting was used between thc Masons, because they did not want to use the password of their order in the running of the vigilantes. The greeting goes: "Are you a vigilante?" When the response was "three," the challenger would say "seven," which was answered with "seventy-seven."

Another legend goes that the numbers were advice that the person being warned had three hours, seven minutes, and seventy-seven seconds to get out of town; still another version identifies the numbers as the dimensions of a grave three feet wide, seven feet long, and seventy-seven inches deep.

No matter what the truth was, the result was effective.

Most of the major cohorts of Henry Plummer were brought to task for their crimes. Over that three weeks, the names of Zachary, Cooper, Graves, and Hunter were ticked off the list compiled by William Palmer on the basis of the confessions of Red Yeager and George Brown. Alec Carter, who was confirmed as the man who had shot Nicholas Tbalt, was caught and hung on the twenty-fourth of January. On that same night, in a place called the Hell Gate—in what is now the city of Missoula, Montana—Cyrus Skinner was caught and paid the price for his life of crime.

Of the others:

William Fairweather, who was in on the first discovery of gold in Alder Gulch, ended up broke, the town drunk of Virginia City. He died young of his drinking.

Electa Bryan Plummer lived as a widow for ten years before she remarried and began raising her family in Iowa. She is buried in Wakonda, South Dakota.

Electa's sister and brother-in-law, Martha and James Vail, lived for several years in Bannack, then gave up the frontier to return to farming in Ohio.

Dr. John Glick eventually moved to the Montana state capital in Helena, where he established a large and respected practice and raised his family.

Hank Crawford arrived back in Virginia City in the summer of 1864, reopened his butcher shop, and eventually held public office in the town.

X Beidler became somewhat of a local celebrity for his

part in the operations of the vigilance committee and worked diverse government jobs in Virginia City until his death.

James Williams, the only non-Masonic member of the vigilance committee, slipped into a quiet obscurity, refusing ever to discuss his role or what had happened in those winters of 1863–1865. He lived out his life in Montana.

Nathaniel Pitt Langford continued in business in the territory and became president of the Missouri River Steamboat Navigation Company. In 1872, through political connections, he became the first superintendent of Yellowstone National Park. He is well remembered for his book *Vigilante Days and Ways*, which was his acaccount of what happened during his time in Bannack.

Wilbur Fisk Sanders continued living in Virginia City. He practiced law, and represented an association of miners before congressional hearings in 1865 in Washington, D.C. He moved to the state capital in Helena in 1889, the same year he was appointed to the U.S. Senate. He was a founder of the Montana Historical Society, was president of the board of trustees of Montana Wesleyan University, and became Grand Master of the Grand Lodge of Ancient Free and Accepted Masons in Montana in 1868.

Sidney Edgerton served as a federal judge for the territory of Montana, and was appointed the first territorial governor by President Lincoln, in 1864.

Frank and Renee LeGrau expanded their business holdings in Virginia City; at one time she was operating three cafés. There is no ready record of what happened to the Dick Sapps or the Stinson family. Old Brod existed, but his later life remains a mystery to me.

Cora and Vic Voit are fictional characters, but, from my writing experience with them, it is fairly easy to conjecture that they went to Pasco, Washington, and began a splendid family. Lucinda Simons and Clay Barrows, also fictional, slipped into obscurity; she, probably to a good life with some worthy man; he eventually felt the tightening of a rope around his neck.

The place called Bannack survived all of the abuse man could bestow on it, but finally, after nearly a hundred years of life, collapsed as a place for families to live. It is now a ghost town, preserved by the state of Montana as a state park.

Virginia City now flourishes as a restored town of the Old West, and it is a major summer tourist attraction. Worth visiting.

As for the other prospectors: there are still hundreds, probably thousands, of Montanans who scratch around in the dirt of the mountains and the banks of creeks, looking for that magnificent yellow stuff called gold. And there are still Montanans who hike up into the Magruder Corridor of the Bitterroot National Forest, giving a good, hard look for Magruder's sacks of dust and nuggets.

The other vigilantes drifted into the fabric of the history of the Montana frontier. The killings did not stop completely—there would continue to be infrequent murders and robberies. But the organized, directed, controlled aspect of the road agents faded from the scene with the hanging of Henry Plummer.